The Manhattan Gambit

The Manhattan Gambit

Benjamin J. Stein

DOUBLEDAY & CO., INC.
GARDEN CITY, NEW YORK
1983

Library of Congress Cataloging in Publication Data
Stein, Benjamin, 1944-
    The Manhattan gambit.
    I. Title.
PS3569.T36M3   1983   813'.54
ISBN: 0-385-17225-7
Library of Congress Catalog Card Number 81-43637

For Martha and Sid Davman

The Manhattan Gambit

Prologue: March 20, 1943,
Cambria, United Kingdom

Some damn hotshot major from Psyop, Psychological Opera-
tions, was at the briefing. Somebody Heinrich or something.
At the end he said a few words, sounding suspiciously like Fa-
ther Kenner, the base chaplain. The loony tunes at Psyop
thought of themselves as missionaries anyway, so the compari-
son made a lot of sense. This guy Heinrich (or whatever his
name was) started out with what Powers had come to expect,
some damn thing by some obscure Chinese philosopher be-
fore the birth of Christ who'd invented psychological warfare
or something. Then, winding abruptly into it with a logic that
Powers didn't quite follow, Heinrich stared at Powers and
Loughlin just as if he expected an answer: "If Satan should
come down among us, how would we recognize him? By his
hooves? How? By his fiery eyes? Is that how? By his horns?"
Then Heinrich actually shook his head as if he were answer-
ing himself. Christ, what a fucking ham. "I tell you he is
among us even now, waging his efforts." Powers just sat there
in his wooden chair and looked out the window at the coun-
tryside beyond the base. He had never dreamed any place
could be so green.

"What did Clausewitz say?" Heinrich continued. *"That war is just politics by other means? Or that politics is just war by other means? Same damn thing. And Kurtz talked about the horror. The horror,"* the major said, emphasizing the last syllable.

"Gentlemen," Heinrich said, his brow red and furrowed, *"we are in the presence of the horror right now, and if we forget it, we shall all be engulfed."* Then Heinrich glared at everyone and left the room.

Powers exhaled slowly. It was all so perfectly, exactly Psyop. Clausewitz he had heard of, vague rumors in flight school, but who the hell was this guy Kurtz? The godforsaken crazies they were getting for Psyop these days all thought they were God.

Out on the field, in a light drizzle that made the grass by the runway look greener, they were taxiing it out. Powers never got over how much it looked like a bird, a big goddamn hawk, painted gray-black, which was supposed to make it harder to see, even for the Krauts with their Zeiss telescopes and shit. It was just a B-17, but lighter and faster and higher-flying than any other airplanes in Europe, as far as anyone at Eighth knew. Clutching their briefs and their helmets, zipped up in their leather jackets, pulling on their pressurized geminis as they waddled across the asphalt flightline, Powers and his reconnaissance officer, Loughlin, talked about just how the Army thought that Psyop was any better than a good shot of Bourbon. Or a woman . . . one of those English girls at the canteen with their rotten teeth and their great asses.

Today's mission was Mystic Tango. It had a nice ring to Powers. Like it might mean something to somebody. All four engines had already been started up, so Powers and Loughlin just climbed into the belly of the gray-black bird.

Powers tugged his helmet on, slapped the hydraulic locks on the camera mounts, checked his fuel, flipped the crypto to *"operate,"* waited for the green cipher light to blink on, then pushed forward on the throttle. Seconds later, in a roar of Pratt & Whitney Stratoturbines, the bird lifted effortlessly into the Anglian sky, then with more throttle pierced the sky *vertically to the east and south, leaving the land behind and gliding higher and farther out over the North Sea, finally easing to an oblique gradient straight into the morning sky.*

They flew for fifty-five minutes before they entered Reich airspace, leveling out over the Pomeranian plain, overflying Wilhelmshaven and its U-boat pens, heading south over Oldenburg and the Rhine basin, cameras whirring smoothly, the automatic pilot taking Powers and Loughlin toward their destiny. After three hours, at thirty-one thousand feet, they were on the outskirts of Frankfurt am Main. Powers could see the smoke rising from factories and targets of the last night's Lancasters. Powers snapped on the forward reconnaissance gear, the Kodak Ektasharp lenses capable of scanning two thousand square miles each hour. Loughlin was bending over the cameras in the nose and Powers did not speak to him. At this point, with the automatic cameras shooting and the automatic pilot flying, Powers had little to do except think about getting back to Cambria.

He monitored the flight control mechanism, then the hydraulics, then the fuel supply, and watched the landscape slide by in a westerly direction as the gray-black bird flew toward Strasbourg, through blue sky over a dense forest. Powers had seen it all ten times, yet suddenly he stared. Across the forest, east of Strasbourg, where there had been only pine and poplars two weeks before, was an immense brown scar, like the roadbed of a highway, and then a cluster of buildings. Even from thirty-two thousand feet, Powers could see that in two weeks, something very much like a small factory and even a town had been created out of nothing. Then it was gone under a cloudbank, lost in the whims of the stratosphere, devoid of life at this altitude, whirring along six miles above life. The Psyop major's voice abruptly came back to Powers. "Would we recognize him?" By noon, they had reached Freiburg.

It was 1223 hours when God abruptly reached down from the infinitude above, shook the gray-black bird for three seconds, then tossed Powers and Loughlin out of the airspace above Mulhouse on the Swiss-French border. "Jesus H. Christ!" Powers screamed. His first thought was ack-ack, incredible at this altitude, and he craned his neck, looking for the puffs of smoke. Maybe Messerschmitts, diving out of the perihelion. . . . Nothing.

The fuel gauges shuddered toward zero. The annunciator lights on the cockpit dash showed rupture in the fuel supply tubes. A white vapor trail of gasoline hung spewn out behind them in a thin, straight trail, while other fuel poured into the nose tanks, lowering their angle of descent. "Loughlin!" Powers screamed, struggling with the hydraulics, hammering at them—anything to bring the nose up. He could hear Loughlin's head banging against the camera housings in the nose compartment as the plane pitched south, dead toward the Aargau range of the Swiss Alps. At twenty-five thousand feet, Powers gaped, frozen, at the controls. The earth had rushed up and become real again outside the cockpit, ice-topped peaks individuating as Powers held his breath—and then, inexplicably, the hydraulics were back. There was still no power in any of the engines. Agonizingly, Powers pulled the plane almost level on a glide, heading for a nameless blue-white plateau there in front of a huge, nameless granite mountain. Even with the engines dead, Powers managed to land butt-first across a tumbled waste of ice and snow, shearing a few meager trees in his path in an explosion of ice and snow, and then everything was fantastically quiet.

Powers sat there dazed for a minute and then moved. He ripped off his communications mask, then he struggled out of his gemini. He crawled forward to Loughlin. The RSO's mask was off. His mouth and eyes were open, and his face was tipped at an angle of astonishment at what eternity held in store. He was dead. Powers shivered, cold beyond what he had ever conceived of as cold. "The first thing I have to do," Powers said aloud to himself, "the first thing I have to do, uh, is, uh, destroy the R-systems under the nose. Then the crypto, then the, uh . . ." He shook his head to clear it. Blood came out of his nose and mouth. He slid open the bolt on the nose hatch and flopped out onto the snow. His red blood made a vivid contrast with the snow. It was cold.

Hypothermia, Powers knew from flight school, makes a man act strangely. Powers tore off his chest pack as if it were constricting his breathing. He scrabbled at his helmet and threw its weight away. He sobbed and sucked at the icy atmosphere. He wallowed to his feet finally, slapping at the crumpled fuselage to warm himself, trying to clamber back into the cockpit, finally sprawling on his back against the nacelle of the starboard outboard Stratoturbine. It was very cold.

There had to be people in these mountains somewhere, Powers thought. Someone must have seen him go down. Skiers or somebody. Little Swiss girls in full skirts with chocolate. Dogs, big St. Bernards with kegs of brandy around their necks. He ought to at least try to destroy the crypto, which was still broadcasting for all he knew. The cameras didn't mean shit. The Krauts probably had better ones anyway. A sudden gust blew snow across his face.

Dig a snow cave, he thought. That's what I gotta do. Get into a hole in the snow and wait it out.

The snow was as hard as carbon steel. Powers scrabbled at it for a few seconds and then gave up. His fingers had no feeling.

From a Fahrenheit of 98.6, you can let your temperature drop a degree or two and it doesn't really matter. It's like running a fever. You recover. When you get down to 96, your compensatory reflexes take over. You start to shiver uncontrollably. Your muscles contract to generate heat. When you hit 93, the cold begins to affect your brain. You can't concentrate. Your fingers fumble. You imagine you are doing what you imagine. When the shivering stops, it means the brain has given up hope, and it doesn't matter anymore.

Powers never stopped hoping. He imagined his fingers were warm. They were digging a hole in the snow, a burrow that widened out under the shelter of the plane until the walls were packed and smoothed like plaster and across the ceiling was a string of lightbulbs blazing, first white, then yellow, then all colors like a Christmas tree and, yes, there was a fire *and the Psyop major was asking, "How would we recognize him?" Then Powers' body stopped shivering, even in the warmth of the fire in Powers' imagination, and it didn't matter anymore because Powers was dead.*

Part I

April 20, 1943,
Monterey, California

The sun came over the Monterey offshoot of the Gabilan Mountains at almost 5:57 A.M. It threw a dazzling pink cover over the mountains and slopes of the central California coast, washing out hills and ravines with its fairy-tale unlikelihood. After about ten minutes, the pink became yellowish and gold, changing the fantasy landscape into a mirage of mountains and ocean made of moving molten ore. Almost immediately, all color disappeared from the light, leaving the sky its usual perfect azure, the mountains sere and brown, and the ocean an endlessly deep blue-gray, dotted with thousands of diving brown pelicans.

At the Monterey Police Station on Forest Street, a drunk sat on a wooden bench, handcuffed to a steel radiator. He closed his eyes and sang "Don't Fence Me In," while a desk sergeant with bloodshot eyes wrote out a warrant for public intoxication. Above the city, at the Presidio, two Army reservists sat at a World War I 70 millimeter artillery piece trained out to sea against the unexpected arrival of a Japanese submarine. One of the reservists, who sold Kelvinator refrigerators on most days, scratched his bald head and studied last week's *Time* magazine. There was an interesting article about how a scientist at the University of Wisconsin had decided that milk was nothing but a "bacterial soup," probably dangerous to adults. The reservist shook his head. That professor would not have his job for long. Not in Wisconsin.

Farther along the bay, at Fisherman's Wharf, a knot of gnarled Portuguese men sat on stools and worked furiously to make last-minute repairs in their fishing nets. As they worked, wearing berets and smoking cigarettes down to the butt, a man with one leg, also on a stool, read to them from *O Jornal da Lisboa*. The issue was dated March 15, 1943—more than a month before—but the fishermen liked to hear news from home, fresh or old.

A few miles inland, at the Pi Phi House of Monterey Peninsula College, a sophomore named Ellen Sweetwater sat in front of a small yellow vanity and stroked her hair two hundred times with a brush her mother had given her for her birthday two days before. While she brushed (to make certain that her hair would be lustrous, just like Carole Lombard's used to be), she had her Emerson radio turned down soft so that she would not wake her roommate, Janie Dieudonne, who was a light sleeper and had that date with a really handsome guy from Carmel that night. Janie did not want any circles under her eyes when she walked into the Del Monte Lodge. On the little white Emerson (a modern wonder, made with only seven tubes), Kay Kyser played "Stompin' at the Savoy" swing-style. Ellen looked carefully at her nose. It was just a little too short. She was sure that Randy, the guy who sat behind her in European History, really liked her. But she was just as sure that he wouldn't like her for long because her nose was really far too short. And probably Randy would be drafted soon anyway, and then there really wouldn't be anybody at all to date at MPC. That didn't seem very fair. But her father told her, very confidentially, that Roosevelt was a Communist anyway, as far as the ranchers in Fresno were concerned, so no one should expect him to be fair. The news came on KPEN, "the Voice of the Peninsula." An announcer was positively *droning* on about a coal strike or something back East, and really, who cared? Ellen hadn't ever even *seen* a piece of coal. She turned off the radio and went on brushing.

Almost next door to Monterey Peninsula College, Jim Burns stood at the first tee of the Del Monte Golf Course and studied the fairway. It was a long drive just to get past the water hazard at the first crook of the dog leg. A hundred and seventy-five yards easy. Burns wiped his hands on his blue cotton windbreaker and put on his dark glasses. He had better use his One Wood. It was almost brand-new—bought in January of 1942, just before J. C. Higgins had stopped making golf clubs for the duration. Needed the steel and the wood for other things. Burns was damned smart to have gotten them when he did. He was also damned smart to have lined up this game with Colonel Andrews. Andrews was a shrewd old clam who had just moved out to the Monterey area from Cleveland. He had made his money in scrap steel. Now he was retired, and everybody around the club said that he had plenty of money to invest. Burns had not been a stockbroker with Merrill Lynch, Pierce, Fenner, and Beane for twenty-seven years for nothing. First you got to know a man socially. Then you gave him a few tidbits about stock or bond tips that had turned out exceptionally well. Then you let him come to you.

This morning, Andrews looked happy and receptive. Any man who could get up at six for a round of golf and look that well rested had to have plenty in the bank. Burns would hit him with the story of how he shorted Radio ten days before the Crash back in '29. That should open his eyes.

Andrews nodded at Burns and bowed slightly. That meant Burns should tee off first. Burns gave him a twenty-four-karat Ipana smile and pulled at his cap. He addressed the ball on its little red wooden tee. He squinted—just like he saw Sammy Snead do before he teed off. Then he took a smooth backswing and hit the ball one hundred and eighty yards. He smiled at Colonel Andrews. "Just a lucky day, I guess," he said. "I've been pretty lucky in a lot of ways."

Andrews clapped him on the back and smiled, wrinkling the lines around his eyes. "That's what I need," he said. "A lucky man."

Maybe I'll tell him about the time I predicted the Dow would go over 200 by December of 1943, Burns thought, a prediction now certain to come true.

Six miles up the coast, the fog had completely burned off by six-thirty in the morning. The soldiers of Company C, training division, had already gone through their riflery practice and were now getting instruction in how to disassemble the M-1 rifle. In the open air, on a bluff about fifty feet above the ocean, Sergeant Clement Gifford glared at the draftees and held up an M-1 rifle. "This here is your M-1 rifle," he said in a Missouri drawl. "Take care of it and it will take care of you. First, the charging lever. You men will take the weapon and hold it so that your left hand is grasping the charging lever, as I am now doing."

Most of the men looked around in total confusion. Half of them held the M-1 so that its barrel was pointed at their nuts. "Jesus H. Christ," Gifford shouted. "Any one of you assholes not holding the M-1 properly within the next thirty seconds will hit the ground and give me one hundred pushups. Now watch me and do it right."

The recruits stared hard at Gifford. A few of them actually grasped the semi-automatic rifle with the right hand and the charging lever with the other, almost as Gifford had told them. In a moment, the others were grunting and sweating, doing their pushups. As they did, Gifford lit into them again. "The Japs won't give you a second chance, you asswipes," he said. "Do it right or you get sent home in a box."

Jesus, Gifford thought. I might as well be teaching coons as these farm boys from Oregon.

About half a mile inland from where Gifford was struggling with his riflemen, behind three barbed-wire fences about ten feet apart from each other, a group of officers emerged from their mess hall in khaki fatigues with long-billed fatigue caps shielding their eyes from the sun, which was now dazzlingly bright, bearing down from the east. The officers were in a good mood. For one thing, the night before, they had staged a little play. It was a rendition of a Venetian opera, with the group's own orchestra playing Venetian love songs by Rossini while some of the more talented officers sang along. Piwonka, a particularly good tenor, had actually moved several of the more sentimental officers with his rendition of a non-Venetian love song, "Ride Ragliacci." The evening had really been a great success. The Army Services Command representative had been most impressed. He had slapped Piwonka on the back and told him that he had a great future in recordings. That made Trattner laugh out loud. "I think Piwonka has different plans," he said jovially.

For another thing, breakfast on this morning in April had been especially good. For weeks, breakfast had been a monotonous routine of Corn Flakes, white bread, marmalade, coffee with milk, and some kind of sugared roll. But now, after some stiff demands by Trattner, the kitchen was making three strips of bacon for every officer's breakfast as well. That was more like it.

And most important of all, today was a holiday. Not simply any holiday either, but *the* holiday on the officers' calendar. It was a day that had to touch the heart of every man in the compound. The night before, the officers had consulted with the camp commander, General Whitlock, explaining just how important this holiday was and insisting on their right to observe it properly. "I need hardly tell you that if the celebration is not allowed, the authorities in the appropriate places will hear about it."

General Whitlock was a good man. He hardly needed any persuasion at all. Even Trattner said that after the war was won, Whitlock would be a good friend to have, the kind of man who could understand what was right in this world. So Whitlock had smiled, turned up his palms, and said, "Go ahead, boys. Have fun."

As the sun rose higher and higher, the officers returned to their cottages to clean up for the ceremony. Schlegel, technically the highest-ranking, was annoyed to see that the bougainvillea he had requested for his front yard had still not been planted. What was more, there was absolutely no sign of the gardener. This was definitely grounds for complaint. Many of the other officers had rosebushes and even pets. If

Schlegel, the highest-ranking of all, could not have a miserable bougainvillea plant, what was going on? Where were the
rights of rank?

Schlegel washed his face and made certain there was not
even a speck of dirt on his uniform. If there was, the valet was
going to catch hell for it. In this California sun, a uniform had
to be spotless or it looked like dirty linen. Of course, the sun
was not so pitiless as in Libya, Schlegel thought, but still, hot
enough. Schlegel inspected his blouse carefully. Trattner
would notice if it was not immaculate. Trattner noticed everything.

By seven in the morning, the officers had assembled at a
round, grassy area in the middle of the compound. It had a
commanding view of the shimmering Pacific, where a bank of
fog was still visible twenty miles offshore. The officers stood in
rows, by ranks, and faced Trattner. By virtue of his record of
incredible resourcefulness and bravery, he had been desig-
nated to lead this ceremony. Trattner virtually shone with
pride at the honor. His clean blonde hair was combed back
across his head. His perfect features and gleaming white teeth
stood out as a monument, a living monument, to the holiday.
His blue eyes sparked with thought and concentration. He
had never thought that at the age of thirty-two he might be
leading men who had seen distinguished service in *not only*
this war but the last war, as they celebrated this most festive
of days. Trattner was a serious man, though. He realized that
he had earned the honor. He was not going to act nervous
about it like a schoolboy. After all, his actions at Abu Massif
had saved three divisions. He deserved to lead men. Still, it
was humbling to face these officers, even if some of them, like
Schlegel, were definitely getting soft. Trattner would have to
deal with that on another day.

Trattner cleared his throat, clicked his heels together, and
raised his right arm stiffly in front of him. As he did so, a
young orderly quickly ran up the battle flag of the Third
Reich. In its stark black-and-white majesty, the iron cross with
the swastika on its right, the German nation with the National
Socialist beacon leading the way, was run up the flagpole. It

flapped crisply in an offshore Monterey Bay breeze. The officers all snapped to attention and raised their right hands stiffly in front of them.

In a deep, slow-cadenced voice, Obersturmbannführer SS, Totenkopfverbände Division, Joachim Trattner led the officers in unison.

"Ich schwöre dir, Adolf Hitler, als Führer und Kanzler des deutschen Reiches . . . I swear to thee, Adolf Hitler, as Führer and chancellor of the German Reich loyalty and bravery. I vow to thee and to the superiors whom thou shalt appoint obedience unto death, so help me God."

The men's voices boomed out proudly across the compound. Two American guards, a corporal and a sergeant, cradled their carbines and listened attentively. The corporal, Toby Moffatt, knew a little German, so he could make out the SS catechism. Trattner asked the questions. The officers answered as a group.

Trattner bellowed, "Why do we believe in the Führer?"

The officers' faces reddened with the enthusiasm of their answer. "Because we believe in God, we believe in Germany which He created in His world and in the Führer, Adolf Hitler, whom He has sent us." The shouting rang out over the hillside and came back like waves on the beach below.

Moffatt shook his head at the officers' ardor.

Trattner demanded, "Whom must we primarily serve?"

The officers, some of whom were still sunburned from months and years in North Africa, answered, "Our people and our Führer, Adolf Hitler."

Really, Moffatt thought, these guys are pretty amazing. After getting captured, transported eight thousand miles, living behind barbed wire, they still have what it takes to make a good soldier. If our officers had been that dedicated, we'd have won the war by now.

In a ringing, commanding voice, Trattner intoned, "Why do you obey?"

The officers, all Waffen SS, all captured after six days of fighting without sleep, roared their answer. "From inner conviction, from belief in Germany, in the Führer, in the movement, and in the SS, and from loyalty."

Toby Moffatt and his sergeant, Eddie Ratner, watched fascinated as a small detachment of valets and orderlies of the officers marched up at a perfect cadence, playing trumpets and drums, to stand behind the officers. The officers lowered their arms as Trattner lowered his. Several other American guards watched from different parts of the fence. A jeep came shivering up to the compound. General Whitlock, all two hundred and ten pounds of him in his five foot eight frame, bounced out of the jeep and strode toward the gate like walking Jell-O. Moffatt and Ratner saluted smartly. Then they unlocked the main gate and admitted Whitlock. He marched up to Trattner and snapped off a crisp salute. Trattner greeted him with a stiff-armed "Heil Hitler."

"Sorry I'm late," Whitlock huffed.

"Quite all right," Trattner said, clicking his heels in deference to Whitlock's higher rank. "May we continue?"

"Of course." Whitlock beamed. "Be my guest." He and Trattner exchanged salutes once again.

The general withdrew to the sidelines as the small band continued to play. Two valets appeared in their khaki Afrika Korps uniforms, carrying a large, rectangular object. The object had a black curtain over it. The valets set the object down on a rickety table next to Trattner, clicked their heels, and withdrew.

Trattner took one step toward the object and shouted at his fellow Death's Head SS officers as if he could levitate them out of prison with his voice. "Today is the most sacred day of the German people's calendar—the birthday of our beloved Führer." With that, he drew aside the black cloth. A magnificent oil painting of Adolf Hitler in full field marshal's uniform stared out at the officers. Moffatt noticed that many of them had the beginnings of tears in their eyes. But not that sonofabitch Trattner. He looked like a hungry wolf. A waiting, menacing hungry wolf.

Trattner cleared his throat again. *"Das ist der Geburtstag des Führers,"* he said, his voice quivering with excitement.

The Führer's birthday. "We have Oberführer Schlegel himself to thank for this magnificent portrait of our leader. And our thanks to General Whitlock for providing the canvas and the oils for this effort," he added in English.

Whitlock grinned and threw off a casual salute. Trattner returned it with a stiff "Heil Hitler" and a tight sneer. Then Trattner added, *"Für den Geburtstag des Führers, Sieg Heil!"*

The officers cried out "Sieg Heil" as if they expected their shouts to reach San Francisco—maybe even Berlin.

"Sieg," Trattner shouted.

"Heil," the officers responded.

"Sieg," Trattner boomed.

"Heil," the officers answered.

"Sieg."

"Heil."

For two minutes, the cry and the answer rang out over the Kriegsgefangenenlager Fort Ord, Monterey, California. Then Trattner raised his hands for quiet. "Again, thanks to General Whitlock, we will later tonight have cake and champagne. But for now, let us sing for this great day, and may it come again for all our lives in final victory." Trattner stared defiantly at Whitlock, but Whitlock understood no German. He did not think it was necessary to guard Germans. He had the guns.

The small band struck up a lively melody and the Sturmbannführer sang clearly, *"Die Fahne hoch, die Reihen dicht geschlossen . . ."* "The flag high, the ranks close together . . ." The entire corps joined in. Now Moffatt could see that some of the officers had tears running down their faces. Damn! Moffatt thought. I bet our boys don't cry like this when Roosevelt's birthday comes around. These Krauts have got something. I don't know what it is, but it's something. Again, Trattner was dry-eyed.

The officers finished *"Die Fahne Hoch,"* with General Whitlock tapping his feet in cadence. Then the band began another tune, again with Oberst Trattner taking the lead. The guy not only fought against our Shermans with grenades,

Moffatt thought. He can also lead his men in a prison camp. A helluva tough guy, Moffatt thought.

"*Unsere Fahne flattert uns voran,*" the German officers sang. "*In die Zukunft ziehen wir, Mann für Mann . . .*" "Our flag flying before us, into the future we march, man after man . . ."

As he sang, Trattner tried to gauge when to stop. After all, there was a certain point after which the enthusiasm of even homesick SS men would wear off. He had to find that precise moment, much as nature found the precise moment for making love and then the precise moment to stop.

After the rendition of the "*Unsere Fahne,*" Trattner made himself at attention and then stared straight ahead. "This year the Führer's birthday finds us in a strange land, although in the care of a kindly man." He nodded minutely at General Whitlock. Although Whitlock did not understand a word of German, he smiled back. "Next year, we shall be in the Führer's active service again on his birthday, destroying the enemies of the Aryan race." He paused. "Heil Hitler." He threw his arm into the air.

"Heil Hitler," the entourage responded.

By God, Moffatt thought, I feel tempted to join in. In his whole life, from his boyhood in Baltimore to his time in the Chrysler plant in Hamtramck to his Army service, he had never felt the excitement he felt when he saw these men of Germany.

Later, Whitlock served California champagne and cake from the Fort Ord bakery for the men of the Death's Head Division, Waffen SS, who found themselves in his custody. If he had been asked, he would have said he did it because he wanted German P.O.W. camp commanders to treat Americans just as kindly. If he told the truth, he would have added that these men had a forbidding air about them. He preferred greatly to humor them rather than to cross them. A camp where you bent the rules a little was a well-run camp. That was what counted in General Whitlock's Army. No complaints to the Red Cross, no sit-down strikes—just quiet, harmonious days. After all, the Army had a war to fight. Guarding

P.O.W.s was pretty small potatoes compared with the fighting in Tunisia or New Guinea. He did not want to use up valuable manpower when he could keep order by passing out a few bottles of cheap champagne. That was only good judgment, wasn't it? Whitlock even offered a toast to Oberführer Schlegel, drunk with California Inglenook champagne. In return, Oberst Trattner told Whitlock that some day he, Trattner, would return the toast with champagne from the Reich.

"What kind's that?" Whitlock asked in bleary puzzlement.

"Dom Perignon," Trattner said dryly.

After a steak dinner, in the gathering California coast evening, Trattner and Oberführer Schlegel walked in a small garden of pines and hedges that the prisoners' valets had made when they should have been working on Schlegel's garden.

"News from Europe?" Schlegel asked. He played with a Boy Scout pocketknife as he walked. Its edge glinted with sharpness in the twilight.

"Just the lies of the American newspapers," Trattner answered. He studied Schlegel's worried face, then the knife. He shivered involuntarily, then brought himself under control.

"Of course, they are lies," the older officer said. "But what do they say? We may get some clue from their inventions."

"Possibly," Trattner said. "But I prefer to keep an open mind." His eyes were hooded, careful. He avoided looking at the knife.

"Of course," Schlegel said. "But you are a physicist, or were before the Eastern campaign. You know that it is rarely possible to be totally precise. What do the American newspapers say?"

Trattner looked out at the pink haze settling over the ocean. "They say we are finished in Africa, that the Bolsheviks are on the attack throughout Russia and have thrown our forces back on every front."

"Lies!" Schlegel hissed. He folded the pocketknife and put it away.

"They say that Berlin is being bombed around the clock and that the Ruhr is in ruins," Trattner said.

Schlegel laughed. "Yankee pipe dreams," he said. "Now that is really preposterous. Berlin being bombed night and day! Hilarious." He laughed. It was a forced laugh.

Trattner looked at Schlegel sideways. The Oberführer's face was highlighted by the setting sun against the grassy slopes of the Monterey highlands. Trattner thought the Oberführer was getting a little overweight. His face was beginning to sag. If you take some men away from the rigors of battle for a couple of months and let them live a soft life, they get soft. Others, like von Bernath and Krank, joined Trattner every morning for vigorous calisthenics and weight lifting. Of course, the Oberführer had done fantastic work under von Hoth in the Donets Basin in Russia, but that was a long time ago. Sadly, people sometimes changed for the worse. More than once, the thought had crossed Trattner's mind that the Americans meted out such generous treatment to the captured officers of the Waffen SS exactly to destroy their fighting spirit, to undermine their pride and their ferocity. Alas, if that was the plan, it often worked perfectly.

But that would take a great deal of calculation. The Americans were an intelligent and resourceful people, but not calculating. They were soft on themselves as well as everyone else. In addition, they were frightened of what would face captured Americans. The whole setup of little cottages, a pushover camp commander, the perfect climate, meals that a Krupp would envy in today's Germany—these were not cunning ploys. It was the Americans' simple nature.

Still, the generous treatment was making the former warriors into hausfraus. Just yesterday Thost had made a joke about how long he hoped the war would last. It was not funny to Joachim Trattner. The war would end with final victory. Period.

Trattner snapped himself back into the train of thought that he had been sharing with the Oberführer, who definitely looked flabby about the chin. "Of course, all these American newspapers tell nothing but lies," Trattner said. "Our lines in the East were impregnable." He waited carefully for the Oberführer's response.

"Exactly," Schlegel said. "How I wish I were still there, fighting, instead of enduring this interminable separation from the fatherland. I hope my wife and Hans know I am well."

"I'm certain they do," Trattner said. He stroked his lean cheek and thought, This is exactly the problem. Since when does an SS man think that he is "well" when he is in captivity, not fighting for Germany? But one does not contradict one's Oberführer. Certainly not at this stage. "I feel certain that soon the Americans will sue for peace and we will be returned to fight on the Eastern Front, against our real enemies."

"That battle may already be won," Schlegel said. His voice was unnaturally high and thin. Trattner picked up the strain immediately.

"In that case, we will have other duties," Trattner said. "Other dangers and sacrifices."

Schlegel nodded, but was obviously distracted. He was probably thinking about his fat wife and his small schloss in Westphalia. It does not do to dwell on comforts when there is still so much hardship ahead, Trattner thought. But again, one does not berate one's Oberführer in the Waffen SS until one has the rest of the war behind one, and a rope waiting for one's Oberführer.

"I think," Trattner said quietly, so as not to disturb Schlegel, "that our days of struggle for the Führer are just beginning."

"Let us hope so," Schlegel said mechanically. Again, Trattner picked up the flat intonation immediately.

Yes, Trattner thought, you do not care any longer. But I still am committed. Still committed to the cause which took me out of a miserable, dusty laboratory and put me in a uniform and gave me a sense of manhood. You, Oberführer Schlegel, may be content to vegetate here. But I see opportunity where you see captivity. There will be work for us to do. In the meantime, we will stay fit and ready. And loyal to the man who made men of us all. The greater his need, the greater my loyalty. But, God in heaven, to have to be around men who forget the Führer! It was a trial.

Out at sea, the sun burnt the sky a magnificent gray and orange for a hundred miles past the stucco-and-brick buildings of the fort. It was a fitting end—overwhelming and evocative—for the birthday of the Führer, Trattner thought, and perhaps a fitting beginning for a great adventure the Norse gods would send his way.

Trattner was an experienced thirty-two and most of his experience had come from war.

April 21, 1943,
Los Angeles, California

The colored boy sprinted past a diner on Flower Street,
dodged into an alley, and disappeared behind three sailors,
who had been on the town all night by the looks of them. He
was wearing black high-top sneakers, which sure as hell gave
him a big advantage over middle-aged men, who had to wear
black oxfords. As John Quinn turned the corner by the diner,
he saw the woman's beige pocketbook lying opened and
empty on the ground. Detective Quinn did not stop to pick up
the bag. His partner, Rizzuti, was nowhere in sight. He was
probably still chomping on that meatball sandwich back at
Fourth and Flower.

John Quinn used his big Irish hands to gently but firmly
push the staggering sailors out of the way. They shouldn't be
out in daylight anyway, he thought to himself. "Get that
coon," one of them said to him and patted him on the back as
he disappeared past the trash cans of the diner.

"I will," Quinn puffed. There was a wooden fence about
five feet high behind the eatery. It had rubber scuff marks on
it. John Quinn threw all of his one hundred and eighty
pounds up on the horizontal board of the fence, then grabbed
the top. Goddamnit! He could feel a splinter go deep into his

left palm. He placed his weight on the hands and vaulted over. Thank you, Fairfax High track team, he thought, as he bolted along the alley toward Alameda.

Something caught his eye. Another sailor. With a Mexican girl in a long yellow skirt. A skirt that was lifted up by the sailor's hand. The sailor's head was burrowed in among all that thick, curly Mexican hair. He didn't feel the Mexican girl going through his wallet as he stroked her thighs.

Quinn did not even slow down. What consenting sailors and Mexican whores did in back alleys at eleven in the morning was none of his business. Let Downtown Vice take care of it. Quinn skidded out onto Alameda Boulevard into a crowd of clubwomen waiting for a trolley car on Alameda. He scattered their shopping bags all over the sidewalk to a chorus of small screams. One of the women, a determined, hawklike type, pointed west on Alameda. "He went that way, Officer," she said.

Quinn appreciated that the women did not even need to know whom he was chasing. If they saw a colored boy in black sneakers zooming along Alameda in broad daylight with an overweight Irishman right behind, they knew which was the cop and which was the mugger. He threw a salute to the woman and raced down Alameda past Seventh. The kid was right there, actually slowing down for the usual crowd lining up outside The Pantry for some bacon and eggs. Smart kid. The people who hung out at The Pantry would chase a colored kid down the street just for the heck of it. He didn't have to be a purse snatcher, which Raymond Washington was. He just had to be a coon. If he slowed down, maybe nobody would notice. Fat, fucking chance!

Quinn had it doped out just perfectly. As the spade tried to look inconspicuous—just another spook here in de white folks' part of town, doan pay no mind—two burly men in coveralls from the uniform factories down at Twelfth and Grand looked up and left the line. They ran after the colored kid, huffing and puffing, their shoulders looking like giant clods of meat that were just aching for a chance to pound some sense into a wayward boogie. The kid took off like a jackrabbit.

By the time the kid was at Eighth and Alameda, Quinn was past the two sweating citizen vigilantes. "We're right behind you, copper," one of them said, looking like a cartoon of an overweight Bugs Bunny fleeing a carrot patch. Quinn could smell the beer on their breath. If they caught up with that kid before he did, somebody was going to be in serious trouble.

The kid, good old Raymond, took a sudden right into an alley, skittering on his heels as he rounded the bend. By then, Quinn was right behind him, panting like a madman. Jesus, John Gregory Quinn thought, by all the saints in heaven, I am too goddamned old for this kind of shit. What if the kid has a razor and it's a blind alley?

As Quinn caught his balance around the turn, he realized that in his thirty-seventh year, he must be developing a psychic facility. Raymond stood there, sweat glistening on his face, breathing hard. In his right hand he held a straight razor. Behind him was a solid brick wall, two stories high.

Blessed be Captain Parker and his spring-loaded holsters. Quinn used the two-handed draw into his waist-pocket holster. In an instant, he came out with a snub-nosed .38. "Okay," he said softly, while his breath came out in gulps for air, "okay, Raymond. Let's go."

Raymond slashed at him with the razor. Quinn jumped back, taking his six feet two inches out of the breeze that the shiny blade made as it sliced through the air. "I be goin' nowhere," Raymond said. "You be gettin' out of my way, is what you be doin'."

Quinn pulled back the hammer on his snub-nosed Smith & Wesson. "Don't be like that, Raymond," he said. "It's no big thing. You put that away and we'll forget you ever had it out." Quinn could feel his heart racing, partly from fear, partly from running almost a mile on a hot April day.

Raymond swiped at Quinn again, but it was not a serious, killing swipe. It was more of a going-through-the-motions swipe, so that Raymond could tell everyone back at 101st Street how he had nearly cut this white cop's throat for him before the cop pulled a "muthuh-fucking tommy gun."

Quinn ducked out of the way again. "C'mon, Raymond.

Drop it. If you don't, and if Rizzuti finds us, he'll shoot you just for having those big, pearly teeth."

Raymond looked like he was thinking about it seriously. His big black pupils got smaller. The whites of his eyes got bigger. "How much time I get?" he asked arrogantly.

"I don't know, Raymond," Quinn panted. "How much time did you get last time?"

"Three months," Raymond said sulkily. Now he had let his razor fall to his side.

"Well, it'll probably be the same this time," Quinn said. "I don't know. Maybe they'll let you sign up to be a mess boy or something instead."

"Doan wanna be no mess boy," Raymond said.

At just that moment, the two men in coveralls rounded the corner into the alley. They saw Raymond's razor. One of them shouted. "Look out. The nigger's got a razor," he said.

Raymond looked apprehensive about it. He raised his razor again.

"It's okay," Quinn said without taking his eyes from Raymond, "he's just coming in real quiet with me right now. He doesn't want no trouble from two tough guys like you."

"They doan look so tough," Raymond said, letting his razor fall to his side again.

"They're packin' heat," Quinn whispered loudly. Raymond gave him a knowing look and let the razor fall to the pavement.

"I be ready to go in now," he said.

Quinn slapped the cuffs on him. As they walked by the two burly men, Quinn winked at them. "Thanks for the help, boys," he said.

"They're all workin' for the Japs anyway," one of the men said. He had a tattoo of a cross with rays coming from it on his forearm. "Shoulda put them in those camps along with the Nips."

"Goddamn right," the other man said.

"I'll take it up with Eleanor Roosevelt," Quinn said.

Rizzuti had the squad car right out on Alameda waiting for

them. "How come you didn't come to the party?" Quinn asked.

Rizzuti's breath smelled of garlic. He had a day's growth of beard on his oily face. There was waxed paper from the hero sandwich on the seat of the black-and-white as Quinn shoved Raymond into the back. "I figured I better stay out here in case I had to chase the spade," Rizzuti said. "Cover you in case he got behind you."

"Thanks," Quinn said, staring straight ahead.

Later that night, Quinn sat in the backyard of his house on Plymouth Street, a little Spanish job that Joan had really liked to work on, before she left with that lawyer from Encinitas. It only had two bedrooms, but it had room to add on another two if they ever started a family. "It would really be easy," Joan had said. "We could do it ourselves."

"I hate working around the house," John Quinn had said. "You must be thinking of some other guy."

As a matter of fact, she was thinking of some other guy. Or maybe a couple of other guys. It was always a little hard to tell with Joan. She was a busy person. It could've been that drummer who sounded just like Buddy Rich, ". . . only better, more sexy." Or it could've been that contractor from Ventura, the one with the Cadillac convertible, who thought that Joan really deserved to have a little place out in the country, and he'd just like to show her a few possible homesites.

But it was not either of those guys. It was a nice young man, U.S.C. boy, from a good family, father at the Jonathan Club and everything, who just happened to see Joan's legs when she was trying on some nylon stockings at Bullock's-Wilshire. He just happened to want to take her to the Windsor for lunch, and she just happened to go. That was the day after the Japs took Corregidor, as John Quinn recalled. Now, there was a Mexican divorce. ("You can have the house in L.A.," Joan had said. "It always had mildew anyway." As if they had some houses somewhere else that didn't have mildew.) And there was a new Mrs. Willard Willison, whose husband was some kind of big cheese at Lockheed, at the age of thirty-one. Which made him three years younger than Joan, which was lucky for him, because he was going to need every advantage he had.

On a police detective's pay, gone from home about half the nights tracking down some loco pachuco who had just knifed his girlfriend fifty-three times, and not quite in touch with what the glamorous people of Southern California were thinking or wearing, John Quinn could never really keep up with his wife. To tell the truth, for about the last year, he hadn't even tried. The house on Plymouth, just above Sixth, not far from Paramount, was where she hung her garter belt. That was all.

It had been almost a year now since she was gone for good. To tell the truth, John Quinn didn't miss her that much. He missed her about half a pint's worth of Bourbon on most nights and about two fifths' worth on Saturday and Sunday.

He had Marilyn, the little brunette from the payroll office over in City Hall, and she kept him company a lot of nights. She'd show up in her little Studebaker. It would be out in front, attracting the notice of the busybody neighbors, the Allens, until about six in the morning. Then Marilyn would go home and change so that no one in payroll would know that she wasn't really quite as good a Catholic as some of the other girls.

Marilyn was good company. She always looked nice. She didn't talk a lot. She had these really wild blue eyes, and a really nice slim set of hips. Marilyn always had a joke or two that he had heard a few years before, jokes about Harry Hopkins and General MacArthur and Captain Parker.

For example, she heard that the Three Stooges were going to sue Roosevelt, Hopkins, and Ickes for plagiarism.

That kind of joke would really go over bigger down at the Del Mar Republican Women's Club, or wherever Joan was hanging around these days. John Quinn had heard it in 1938 and hadn't really thought it was that funny then. He remembered that Joan had laughed like hell when a guy from Security Bank told them the joke at a party. She hadn't laughed six months earlier when he told it. Willard Willison, Jr., *really* was going to need all his connections and all his youth and all his money. Because some day he was going to take her to a party at the California Club, and some guy who just happened to have inherited five thousand acres of oil land outside Santa Barbara would meet her, and then it would be good-bye Willard.

Anyway, Marilyn wasn't really the answer to John Quinn's problems. She was a great girl, but she wasn't going to make him feel that his life hadn't been thrown away. Joan hadn't either, of course. Maybe Joan knew that. Maybe that had something to do with why she looked for other men.

Not that John Quinn was ashamed of his life. For a kid from Bunker Hill who had gotten a permit to take the bus to Fairfax High School because he could run like a bunny rabbit and had never gotten beyond the second year at U.S.C., John Quinn hadn't done that badly. From patrolman to detective in less than ten years. Not too bad, really.

His father hadn't even had a steady job during most of the Depression. His two brothers, Seamus and Pat, worked on the docks at San Pedro when they could. For a long time, John Quinn had been the only member of the family bringing home a regular paycheck. Of course, now his father was back at the Hughes plant in Inglewood, making close to a hundred and twenty a week with overtime, and his mother was taking something on at Bendix. The two brothers were both in the Merchant Marine. But that was now; a few years ago, they were goddamned happy if John came over with a few bags of groceries from the Safeway on Sixth Street.

But as John Quinn sat on a glider in the backyard of his house that was almost, but not quite, in Hancock Park, he could hear a voice inside himself saying that he was throwing away the only life he ever had chasing the Raymonds of this world down blind alleys. He wasn't even supposed to be doing that. He was Downtown Homicide, not frigging purse snatching. He should've just let the kid go. What could it have mattered? What was in the purse anyway? Twenty dollars? And he was almost going to get his throat cut for twenty dollars that the woman probably got by blowing her boss's son anyway?

"I don't see the problem," Joan used to say. "Just quit being a cop and do something else and stop complaining." That's what she would say on those occasions when she came home from an afternoon of "grocery shopping," smelling of cigars, Old Spice, and hotel laundry.

"The problem is a little more complicated than that," John would say, but by then Joan would be putting on a black silk slip for "a bridge game with the girls."

Why should I even feel this way? John Quinn asked himself as he sat in his backyard and listened to a news wrap-up about interminable fighting in New Guinea, and about an American rout at somewhere called the Kasserine Pass in Tunisia. Maybe it was from running all those afternoons, all by myself, with just my thoughts, running around the 440-yard track twenty times, sometimes more. You get to thinking about yourself a lot, John Quinn realized. You get to thinking that you're the center of the universe.

If the Army had just taken John Quinn, that would have solved the whole problem. But the Army had found a spot on John Quinn's lung, and even if it wasn't growing or anything, that was the end of John Quinn's thoughts of glory in the South Pacific or in Germany or somewhere.

So now he was just a draft-dodging cop in a little backyard in Los Angeles, without a wife, with neighbors who were looking out the window at him right now, monitoring how much he drank, resting after chasing purse-snatching jigaboos, while a World War raged around him.

"Something'll come up," Marilyn always said. "If you're thinking about it this much, it's your destiny that something will happen to you. Something bigger than getting shot by a wetback who's killed his wife. It's got to happen."

But where the hell was it? Maybe, John thought, I should try again to enlist. He wondered how he could fake his medical records while on the radio a congressman from South L.A. complained about how many German prisoners of war were being shipped all the way from Atlantic Coast ports to detention centers—P.O.W. camps—in California. "It is not fair that Californians, who suffer the greatest risk of Japanese invasion, should also have to shoulder the burden of guarding and feeding thousands of hardened Nazi prisoners."

Quinn laughed to himself. "Hardened Nazi prisoners." He had been down to the camp at Fort Beale, near San Diego, while he was looking for a missing Colt revolver. A friend from Wilshire Robbery was working down there as a guard. Most of those prisoners were so happy to be out of the war, getting some sun, getting decent food, that they wouldn't leave camp if you paid them.

At least, thought Quinn, I'm not a prisoner anywhere. He might still be able to accomplish something. Once you were a prisoner, your hopes to do anything lasting were pretty much gone. But John Quinn was still free.

April 25, 1943,
Berlin

The Reichsführer was furious. In his first-floor office in the Reich Chancery, he paced back and forth on a Kirman rug of delicate blues and reds. Occasionally his eyes flicked up from his sallow face to glance at the portrait of the Führer sitting atop a white charger, dressed in medieval armor. Then his eyes darted back to the two men who sat at his conference table. Outside the office, in the courtyard of the Chancery Building, the Reichsführer could see his four SS guards pacing back and forth, holding their Schmeissers in front of them. They were every inch Germans. Tall, lean, and muscled. Their faces held no trace of any emotion but watchful devotion to the Reichsführer. But the two men in his office were different. They were almost insolent!

Heinrich Himmler sat down behind his massive desk—crafted from the hardiest oaks of the Schwarzwald, the Black Forest. He toyed with his Schutzstaffel dagger, presented to him by the Führer personally. He slid it out of its black leather case and ran his thumb across the blade. Sharp. As sharp as an SS man's fervor to serve the Führer. Far different from these two "intellectuals" who sat across from him almost carelessly.

"I want to put this to you carefully, so there is not the slightest chance that you might misunderstand," the Reichsführer said. He removed his wire-rimmed glasses and played with the sides. "You are telling me that neither the Reich Research Council nor the Wehrmacht Ordnance Department believes that it can be done?"

Professor Werner Heisenberg answered first. He was a tall, cadaverous man with his shirt collar sticking out of his suit jacket. He had already won every award there was in physics. He did not look particularly in awe of the Reichsführer. His brown eyes looked weary. "Please, Herr Reichsführer," Professor Heisenberg said, "we do not say that it is impossible. Not at all. According to theoretical physics, even pure Aryan physics, it is possible to have a particle above 93, since 93 is a beta emitter and therefore unstable. . . ."

The Reichsführer slammed his hand down on the desk. It made a deadly thumping noise. He jumped to his feet and glared at the world-famous physicist. "No more of your cursed scientific jargon," he said. "Just tell me straight out. Can you do it?"

Heisenberg did not appear to be frightened by Himmler. He was accustomed to working with far more powerful forces. "It is theoretically possible, Herr Reichsführer. But I believe it would take us at least twenty years before we had enough material to even have a significant test."

Himmler snatched up a riding crop from his desk. He began to hit it against the top of his boots. "And you, Herr Doktor Diebner? You concur?" the Reichsführer demanded.

Diebner, a short, bald man in a leather jacket, like an Alpine villager, nodded sadly. "The Reich Research Council believes that it is a myth of Jew physics that the mass can go critical at all without using more electrical energy than there is in the entire world to sustain the reaction." He averted his eyes from the Reichsführer as he finished.

"More jargon," the Reichsführer hissed. The Reichsführer walked in front of Dr. Diebner and tapped him on the shoulder with his crop—lightly. "Once there was a Jew engineer at the Messerschmitt plant in Thuringia. We picked him up and asked him why he should be allowed to continue to work and live at home with his family. The Jew engineer talked to me about Jew aerodynamics and Jew vectors until I had to hit him. He went to work at Belsen, quarrying rock. I think he's dead now," the Reichsführer said. "I hate jargon."

"He was a Jew," Diebner said, with a slight quaver in his voice. "I have been a party man since 1937. I am telling you the facts."

"I *think* he was a Jew," Himmler said. "He might simply have used too much jargon. I cannot recall exactly right now."

Diebner turned pale. A line of sweat appeared just below his nose on his upper lip. "My Reichsführer," he said softly, "I will try to be clearer."

"Good, good," the Reichsführer said. "I only want to know one simple thing. Just one. Can it be made? Is it possible?" He moved around to his desk and sat in the sturdy chair.

Heisenberg looked at him and sighed. "It is theoretically possible," he said. "We can get the heavy water from Norway and the uranium from Joachimsthal in the Sudetenland. The materials are no problem. But to produce enough enriched uranium or a 94-weight beta-positive element requires either twenty years of meticulous work, or a thermal diffusion breakthrough which is inconceivable to me at this moment."

Diebner chimed in instantly. "In a word, Reichsführer," he said, "I believe it cannot be done before 1965, and by then our forces will have been victorious everywhere anyway."

The Reichsführer began to play with his dagger again. "If there were any way to break through in making the material, if there were a whole new level of understanding about the subject beyond what you have, could you then imagine that it would be possible?"

Heisenberg stood up to his full six feet. His face flushed a beet red. "Herr Reichsführer," he said solemnly, "I believe that you have incorrectly gauged the seriousness with which the entire body of German physicists has approached this matter. Aryan physics as a whole stands up and says that it is a myth of Jew physics that the pile can go critical."

Diebner took a cue of courage from him and said shakily,

"My Reichsführer, the mass cannot go critical or my name is Cohen."

"You are certain that the works in Hechingen have no one who disagrees, who believes the mass can go critical *soon?*" Himmler demanded, hitting his palm with the flat of the dagger blade.

"I swear it, on my loyalty to the Führer," Diebner said, "and as for Hechingen, of course that is no more than . . ."

Heinrich Himmler stared levelly into Dr. Diebner's eyes as he cut him off. "You are willing to stake your life that the mass cannot go critical?"

"The entire Reich Research Council agrees that it cannot happen without twenty years of unremitting effort," Diebner said. But he paled at the seriousness of the Reichsführer's proposed wager.

Himmler slapped his crop against the desk. How he would have loved to send the two arrogant physicists away to Dachau that very moment. He knew their type. Academics. Men who had never had to work with their hands. Men who lived in paneled libraries of country homes while he had been mucking out chicken coops. Diebner and Heisenberg did not fool him for one instant. They were the kind whom the entire revolution of National Socialism was directed *against*. He would love to see them pleading for their lives while the SS men strung up the piano wire.

But apparently, for the moment, that was not to be. In fact, he was going to need those two fools more than ever. When the Reich was in danger, he, Heinrich Himmler, would sacrifice his personal preference to see the two men treated as they deserved.

Ten minutes later, after Diebner and Heisenberg had left, Himmler walked into the adjoining office of his aide, von Trenck. The tall Swabian stood up and clicked his heels together as Himmler walked in. "I want to see the report from the Front again," Himmler said to the sandy-haired SS Oberst. "The most up-to-date you have."

Oberst von Trenck spread out an enormous map of western Russia and started to move around miniature swastikas and hammer-and-sickles. "The news is not, uhhh, uhhh, as encouraging as it should be, Herr Reichsführer," von Trenck said. "Temporary setbacks."

"Of course," Himmler said. "What about the Caucasus?"

Oberst von Trenck coughed discreetly. "Our phased move westward is proceeding in good order," von Trenck said. "There is heavy fighting at Krassin and our Eighth Army is giving a fine account of itself."

"In other words, we are retreating rapidly but not getting cut off," the Reichsführer said.

"As you say," von Trenck agreed.

"In Stalingrad? Any hope?"

"Reichsführer, the Reichsmarschall has guaranteed to keep our forces supplied from the air until von Paulus can break out of the pocket," von Trenck said. "Other than that, the situation is static. The Sixth Army Group awaits relief and then a further move into Russia."

Sweat had broken out on von Trenck's face as well. Questioning by the Reichsführer often had that effect.

"What of Manstein?" Himmler asked.

"There the news is more encouraging," von Trenck said. He exhaled loudly. Outside, the sound of air-raid sirens was beginning. That meant the American bombers were still fifteen minutes away. Plenty of time for more bad news.

"Manstein has pulled his forces out of the Rostov, Kharkov, and Rzhev-Vyazma salients, consolidated them, and is making a major offensive against Kharkov, the hub of the entire Soviet operation in the Donets Basin. He is gaining about five kilometers per day," von Trenck said.

"Is that true?" Himmler said. "I need the truth. Not Goebbels' fairy tales."

"It is absolutely true, Herr Reichsführer," von Trenck said. "Our information is from our own SS Abwehr, not Goebbels, and not the Wehrmacht."

"How strong are our reserves in the Kharkov counteroffensive?" Himmler asked. "Enough to withstand the Russians when they come back at us with ten times the forces we have?"

"My Reichsführer," von Trenck said, "we are always numerically inferior to the Russian hordes. We count on the superior zeal of the German soldier fighting for his fatherland and his Führer to win the day."

"Just as I thought," Himmler said softly. "Manstein may be able to make a few kilometers per day, but he cannot hold the ground for long."

Von Trenck did not contradict Heinrich Himmler. For one thing, Himmler was correct. For another, he did not particularly care to join his colleagues in the Waffen SS fighting in the Kursk salient. Casualties there were about 10 percent per day from the Russians, and double that from the cold.

No, one did not question the judgment of the Reichsführer.

"Speer's production figures?" Himmler demanded peremptorily. "Do you have them?"

"*Jawohl,*" von Trenck said. He flourished a thick folder with innumerable flimsy sheets of paper bearing columns and rows on tank production, artillery piece production, aircraft production, small-arms production, blanket production, V-weapon production.

Himmler studied the papers carefully. He was pleased to see that all categories showed improvement. The Allies might be bombing Germany day and night, but the German manufacturing machine was still producing the tools of war at a prodigious rate. What the Allied planners did not know was that every time they bombed a theater into oblivion, that released twenty ushers, thirty set builders, and fifty actors and actresses to go to work at Heinkel or Krupp. Every time they blew up a block of flats, that released one hundred maidservants to go to work at Thyssen, A.G.

Unfortunately, the process could hardly continue forever. At some point, every dayworker, every usher, every cook—not to mention every Russian laborer, every able-bodied Jew, every Romanian or Italian peasant who could be dragooned into becoming a cog in the war machine—would have been thrown into the gap. And then the well would have run dry.

Far worse, from what the Reichsführer knew, Allied war production was rising more than five times as fast as German war production. The Americans were soon going to reach a production rate of fifty thousand fighter aircraft per year. New tanks came off the Chrysler works alone faster than the entire Panzer output in Germany. Russian war production had stabilized, from its low point in 1942, and now was climbing astronomically.

And more than that, there were seemingly an infinite number of Russians. No matter how fast the Wehrmacht killed them, there were always new waves upon waves, overwhelming the armies of the Reich. From some bottomless pit, the Slavic hordes poured over the Teutonic defenders of Aryan values. The German nation was already bled white. Sixteen-year-olds were about to be conscripted. And the Russians kept coming, more and more and more of them.

"My Reichsführer," von Trenck said, to the accompaniment of a high-pitched wail from outside, interrupting Himmler's perusal of the statistics, "the air-raid warnings. Perhaps we should continue the meeting in the lower area."

Himmler actually smiled. Von Trenck was too fearful to say "bomb shelter" even as the sirens were becoming terrifyingly loud. "The lower area" indeed! Where was Goering's air force, the mighty Luftwaffe, now? Where were his vain boasts about how Berlin could never be bombed? Hundreds of Allied Liberators and Lancasters were pounding the Reich every day—including Berlin. And the Reichsmarschall was in his forest redoubt at Karinhall shooting his veins full of heroin and playing with young boys who should have been at war defending the Reich.

He, Heinrich Himmler, Reichsführer SS, had to cower in a bomb shelter because Goering was too busy studying his "*objets d'art*" and filling himself with venison and sherbet. It was really too much to bear.

Now, with the reports from Stockholm and the astounding news from Chicago, U.S.A., the picture had become disgracefully chaotic. And, of course, who else could the Führer turn to for salvation than his own Reichsführer? Who, of all the toadies around the Führer, actually delivered on his promises? Goebbels might make up tall tales for the masses. Jodl and Keitel might conceive vain fantasies about holding areas, kessels, and impregnable defensive lines, but they were all nonsense the next day when the Bolshevik hordes poured through. Goering was a bad joke, a dope addict, a fool. Heydrich, who delivered, was dead, a victim of the British assassins, and a thousand Lidices would not bring back a man of his ability. That had really been a cowardly blow. But then, no sense crying over spilt milk.

The guards in the hallway clicked to a smart attention as the Reichsführer left his office suite and headed down the hallway to the shelter. Fine men, those guards. Their faces gleamed with animal courage, almost superhuman fearlessness. Their Schmeissers seemed to be less powerful than their wills. That was as it should be.

Himmler walked down a marble stairway to his personal shelter. The Führer was building a far more capacious structure farther east by about fifty yards, and soon it would be ready to house the most important leaders of the Reich for all crucial wartime functions. It would have map rooms, meeting rooms, situation rooms, a dining room—and then would not life be grand? The most glorious leader in all history and his servitors living underground like moles.

Before the SS guard detail closed the thick, high-carbon steel door to the shelter, Himmler could hear the thud of the first bombs falling and the first rapid, staccato bursts of antiaircraft artillery fire. Himmler shook his head with rage. In his cramped shelter office, he opened the envelope that he had in his tunic. He read it again. The translation from English was quite rough, but Himmler had no trouble understanding the gist. And those fools Heisenberg and Diebner had said it could not be done. Sleights of hand of Jew physics, they had told him. It would take twenty years, they told him.

Shameful! The Führer was served by idiots and incompetents *and perhaps worse*. The source in America was completely trustworthy, of course, and that meant that Heisenberg and Diebner were completely wrong. They had spent millions of scarce Reichsmarks on cyclotrons and enriching reactors, and they were completely off the track. Of course, the money spent at Hechingen had its uses if you looked at it the right way.

And then there were the reports from Geneva, about that arrogant busybody Dulles, that self-righteous maniac. Really, to think that he, Heinrich Himmler, had to deal with the likes of Allen Dulles. But then, these were desperate times. Imagine, someone as gullible as Dulles entrusted with any responsibility at all.

Even through ten feet of reinforced concrete *below* the foundations of the Reich Chancery, Himmler could feel the vibrations from the American four-ton blockbusters that rained upon Berlin. His map of the Eastern Front wobbled slightly. He could feel the desk shaking.

At times like this, Himmler was ready to give up hope in everyone but the Führer. If a "genius" like Heisenberg was so totally out of touch with what was possible in physics, what hope was there except in the vision of the Führer?

Or in the vision and execution of his most trusted lieutenant, the Reichsführer SS? And in stratagems and deception? But they must look real. *Always.*

Negotiations were absolutely stalled in Stockholm. Totally on dead center. The Russians knew the battlefield statistics as well as anyone did. They might hate the British and loathe the Americans, but that did not keep them from knowing when the tide was turning.

Of course, back in December, when the scales in Stalingrad looked to be almost even, there was great good cheer among the Russian team in Stockholm. The Russians frankly told the Germans their situation. In Marshal Stalin's opinion, the Americans and the British were far too cowardly to ever do more than dip their toes into the *Festung* in Sicily or the boot tip of Italy. There would never be a really meaningful Western Front. In that case, since the two major land powers had fought themselves to a standstill in the Caucasus, in the Ukraine, in the Baltic Region, why not make peace and to hell with Churchill and the Jew-lover Roosevelt?

That was before the wily Stalin had thrown two hundred fresh divisions into Ordzkonikidze, hurled seventy-five winterized divisions into the counteroffensive at Stalingrad, cut off von Paulus, and gained one hundred miles in the Caucasus in one week. The Russians had drawn these forces out of thin air, as far as the Wehrmacht was concerned. OKW thought the Red Army was capable of a delaying action and no more. But that was an error. Conceivably, Himmler thought, it was a mortal error.

Now, the Russian envoys in Stockholm hardly agreed to schedule meetings. They knew that the tide had turned against Germany. The meetings would never start again, unless there was a miracle on the German side. Himmler felt the vibrating thuds of the bombs bursting. For the time being, von Manstein's assault against the Kharkov communications center would make the Russians reassess the situation on the battlefield. After all, if the Russians could be made to believe that the Germans were still capable of launching a major assault, they would be willing to talk more seriously about a well-deserved separate peace.

Von Trenck came into the cramped office and clicked his heels. "The Führer requests your company at a staff meeting in fifteen minutes," the Swabian said. He bowed slightly, as if the weight of the Führer's command were forcing him down, like snow on a birch tree. He looked expectantly at Himmler, as if there were any possibility of a negative response.

"Of course," the Reichsführer said. "Of course. I will be there. As always."

Not like that gross Goering, who made himself unavailable even in the Führer's direst need. Really, if the day should come, if there were any possibility at all, Goering should be held accountable to the nation for his crimes. There had been rumors of Jewish blood, far back in the past, and perhaps . . .

A large rumbling shook the Reichsführer out of his thoughts about the Reichsmarschall. One must face facts, Himmler thought. He looked at a small map of western Russia. If the Manstein offensive worked, that bought a month or two. In that time, a great deal could happen. A very great deal. The Russians could be convinced that it was in their interest to sign a separate peace. The secret—even from Goebbels, even from Bormann—negotiations at the Majestic in Stockholm could go on. They could bear fruit.

But the Russians had to believe that the Germans still had some valuable cards to play. Manstein would not be enough. Even with the best Waffen SS division, the Leibstandarte Führer unit that had taken Kiev in two days, Manstein could not hold Kharkov for long. And after that, after that—the barrel was empty!

That was the tragic truth. Guderian had confided as much to him at a meeting at Rastenburg two weeks before. "We can fight a delaying action, maybe for a year, perhaps eighteen months at most, but after that . . ." and then Guderian, the inventor of Panzer warfare, threw up his hands.

The two men—who bore a remarkable physical resemblance —had meandered through the aspen trees, and then Guderian spoke again. "We had hoped for a quick death blow. But when we did not take Moscow and Stalingrad, it was hopeless. The only way out now is to negotiate a settlement."

Of course, Guderian was not such a fool as to say that to the Führer. The Panzer leader was taking a risk talking to Himmler. But Himmler knew that Guderian was right. Once the hope of victory was lost, it was better to avoid defeat than to fight to the last Aryan against an ocean of Slavic *Untermenschen*. What did it matter to history if twenty million Russians died? But how could one account before history for losing a single drop of Aryan blood? And then the other possibility, too horrible to contemplate, which Himmler would have to contemplate anyway if efforts in Stockholm or on the battlefield got nowhere. Best not even think of that right now.

And so, Himmler thought, as the slender von Trenck gathered papers from Himmler's desk in preparation for the meeting. And so, a separate peace. Exactly. But what was in it for the Russians? Why would they not try for the whole ball of wax? Why should there not be a Soviet Europe if Germany had run out of momentum?

That was where Heisenberg and Diebner came in. Cruelly, that was where Himmler's entire plan had gone off the track. If the German scientific establishment were even close to doing what the Americans had done eight weeks before under Stagg Field in Chicago, with every crazed, rapacious Jew in the world cheering the Jew physicists on, then there would be hope. If the Aryan research community had even a glimmer of an idea of how to make the mass go critical, the Russians would go critical themselves. A chain reaction would set in, and the Bolsheviks would be eager to make peace. No need for further flirtations in Geneva. That was Hechingen. But was Hechingen enough or even close to enough?

Von Trenck coughed discreetly. An irritating habit, the Reichsführer SS thought. Perhaps von Trenck had gone soft. Perhaps he needed a few months in the Vyazma salient to toughen him up. "Five minutes until the meeting, Herr Reichsführer," von Trenck said. Then he resumed classifying and categorizing his endless, infernal documents.

Somehow, German science had to be brought up to the breakthrough that the Jew Americans had reached. By some damned Jew trick, the pile at the University of Chicago had been made self-sustaining. Now the Americans had not only all the Jew money, all the industries, all the oil, and endless supplies of every kind of raw material. They would also have the triumph of physics that Germany needed and deserved. They would have the trump card—as the *verdammt* British said. The Germans had to match that feat.

Himmler glanced at his Omega watch. Time to meet the Führer. He felt the vibration of more bombs. But now they were few and far between. The cowardly Americans would simply make one pass over the city and then flee, like the dogs they were.

Himmler waited as von Trenck swung open the heavy steel doors of his private bunker. He brushed an imaginary speck of dust from his *feldgrau* tunic and took his briefcase from von Trenck's gloved hand. As the Reichsführer thought of the Jews and their trump card, an idea began to form in his mind. The Jews and their magic. Well, we can use magic, too, he mused. He thought for another minute, and then he smiled. Then, Reichsführer Heinrich Himmler sighed. Of course, he thought to himself, I will have to do it myself. No one else will be able to help. That's the way it always is. Whenever anything important comes along, I always have to do it myself. Not that I mind, he told himself. Even the Führer will not be able to help this time, but never mind.

The only problem was that there was so much for the Reichsführer to do, and no one to share his burdens. Of course, Heinrich Himmler would not complain. That was not in his nature. Still, if he had to do it all, it was a weighty burden. Heinrich Himmler sighed again. It was a tantalizing prospect. And wouldn't Dulles be surprised! Magic indeed.

Himmler squared his shoulders and went into the Führer's meeting.

April 30, 1943,
Washington, D.C.

Alice Burton looked out the window at the Washington Monument. These old Navy buildings are drafty, dusty, and cold, she thought, but they have good views. She crossed her thin legs under her Garfinckel's wool skirt and thought about the snow. It makes the monument look like one of those toys they sell at Union Station, she thought. A miniature monument in a globe, with swirling snowflakes of rubber or something that fell through a watery solution and then fell upside down again, like snow falling out of the earth into the sky. A child's fantasy, like the kind her mother, Mildred, once read to her in the little house in Columbus, Ohio. But the snow outside Sam Murphy's office was real. A freak spring snowstorm. The man who owned that office (if "owned" was the right word for a government office) was real. At that moment, Sam Murphy stared out of his criminally handsome, fifty-year-old face, the one with the perfect blue eyes and the thin lips, stared out of his movie actor's face at her. He had a real question.

He held a flimsy piece of paper in the air, crinkled it with both hands, and said, "Well?"

"I don't know," she said, and looked out the window again. The snow still did not look real. Snow never looked genuine.

It always had a dreamscape quality to Alice Burton, as if it had been made up to mask a darker reality that would emerge as the snow vanished.

The life of Alice Burton had taken on a dreamlike quality in the last few years, she thought. If I had to say whether my life is real or a dream, I would definitely put an X in the "dream" column. Starting six years before, the fantasy had begun to take shape. A young, skinny girl who barely graduated from Northwestern University read an article in the Chicago *Tribune* about an antitrust case involving a huge electric power company—American Electric Power. She was puzzled about why it should be wrong to get so big as a company that you could provide really efficient, cheap power. She decided that she would take a course at the University of Chicago to understand what was happening in that bizarre field. By day, she worked at Marshall Field. By night, she studied with Jacob Viner about economics.

Three years later, she emerged from the University of Chicago Law School as the dazzling young genius of the intersections of law and economics. She was editor of the law review. She was first in her class. She barely had time to iron her clothes from answering the letters begging her to teach at a dozen different law schools, from Yale to the University of Maryland.

She was still a skinny girl with glasses, but she had blossomed into an extremely attractive skinny girl with glasses. She tinted her brown, mousy hair into a shining, cascading dark auburn. She rolled and curled it, and she wore high heels.

She was a popular figure, sauntering along the sidewalk of the Hyde Park campus, trailing admirers and young professors who wanted a date—and the answer to a complex question about horizontal mergers in the field of corporations. She declined most offers of horizontal mergers that came to her after nights at the movies or at dinner. She would bat her enormous brown eyes, smile self-deprecatingly, and put off her suitors with a cagey lifting of her graceful eyebrows. The lift might have said, "Not tonight, but . . ."

That was the first part of the fantasy, Alice reflected, as she looked back at Sam Murphy and his goddamned piece of paper. The second was that she was there with Sam Murphy at all.

Alice Burton graduated in the Class of 1938, U.C. Law School. Apparently, she would be able to teach at any law school in the country. But that was not what she had in mind. She wanted to crash an elite fraternity that was resistant to her type—Jewish women—and had been resisting for fifty years. Alice Burton had it firmly set in her mind that she would work at the most prestigious, most White Shoe Wall Street Law Firm (all capitals in her mind) that could be found in Manhattan.

To her shock, it was a walkover. She sent her résumé to the one firm where she thought she would be turned down flat. She also sent her latest law review article on why the Sherman Antitrust Act was *per se* unconstitutional. Two days later she had a telegram in her mailbox from Donovan, Leisure, Newton & Irvine offering her a job.

Three incredible years in New York City, in a small apartment at the corner of 66th and Central Park West, at the office talking with the presidents and chief counsels of Ford, du Pont, and Bethlehem Steel. Three incredible years at Carnegie Hall, out at the Hamptons, at La Côte Basque, occasionally under the care of Henri Soulé at Le Pavillon. Three incredible years with young millionaire clients, with artists she met at poetry readings at the YMHA, with other young lawyers burning with the same fire of ambition that smoked in her veins.

The work was the most exciting part. Of the entire crew of thirty associates, Samuel J. Murphy had picked her, on the basis of one conversation, to work as his closest aide. For Alice Burton, who had seen Murphy's name on appellate briefs for the most crucial, intellectually taxing antitrust cases before the Supreme Court, working hand in glove with him was like a sandlot player suddenly becoming shortstop for the Yankees. Murphy had been called "the Wyatt Earp of Antitrust" by a Yale Law School professor, Thomas Emerson. That was after Murphy had blasted the Attorney General of the United States right out of the Supreme Court by pointing out that the Attorney General had cited an obscure British case upside down. "One shot, one kill" was what the boys at the Links Club said about Sam Murphy.

Murphy belonged to the set of tennis- and polo-playing, fox-hunting, coupon-clipping, estate-living, horse-breeding Irish millionaires of New York. Unlike his brothers, who had all gone into the strenuous field of yachting, Murphy had taken up the law. But an air of languorous relaxation still hung about him even as he disemboweled his opponents by sheer hard work and rigorous thought.

When Franklin Roosevelt decided that the time was right to bring "Wild Bill" Donovan down to Washington to set up a surreptitious COI group to combat Axis propaganda and to prepare for U.S. entry into the war, "Wild Bill" could not possibly move to D.C. without his most feared litigator—Sam Murphy. Sam Murphy had to leave the world of the Flanigans, the Snows, the McDonnells, and the Fords to toil by the Potomac. But he took Alice Burton with him. "Bill," he told Donovan, "I can't pee one drop without that girl."

To Alice Burton, he simply said, "Pack your bags."

By the time Alice arrived, the COI had become the Office of Strategic Services. The fun was even greater in Washington. Parties every Saturday night. A little apartment in Georgetown, and a tiny 1936 Plymouth coupe—with her own parking space in a lot along Constitution Avenue. Young officers. Young government hotshots. Young spies. All a little heavy on talk and light on action, but that was Washington in spades.

True, Alice had to look at nine apartments before she could find one that would take Jews. The one she finally was allowed to have was above a DGS grocery store at the corner of 29th and P. The other tenant was a colored woman who had lived there since the days of Teddy Roosevelt. That did not matter. What mattered was that Alice Burton, of Columbus, Ohio, was doing important work with exciting people.

Alice Burton's mind drifted as she watched Sam Murphy

light a cigarette. He took a package of Philip Morris from his vest pocket. He shook one out and put it in his mouth with one smooth move. With his free hand, he whipped a gold Dunhill lighter from his desk drawer, flipped open the top, and sent a flame shooting toward the cigarette. He drew in a cloud of smoke and then exhaled a bluish-gray mist. "Well, Alice," he said, "you're supposed to be the smart one, the one who knows poetry and everything. What the hell does it mean?"

"I'm sorry, Sam," Alice Burton said. "I've been daydreaming because of the snow. I keep thinking that I should get a day off from school."

Murphy smiled. He blew out more smoke. He put his Peal loafers up on the desk. The soles were spotless. How does he do it? How can people keep the soles of their shoes spotless? I eat a salad at Harvey's and I have to get my suit dry-cleaned, Alice thought.

"British COE says the message was intended for shortwave transmission to the United States. Possibly Canada. Now who were they sending it to? And what is this stuff about *Tarnkappe*? What the hell is that? Who's this Siegfried guy?" Murphy asked. He was playing his innocent, rather dumb country boy routine. "You want some coffee?" he asked. No rationing here for the spear carriers of the republic.

"Thanks, Sam," Alice Burton said. "That would be great."

Sam Murphy pressed a button. A moment later, a stout, middle-aged woman with light-brown hair and smiling eyes came in, smoothing her skirt as she stood in front of Sam Murphy. "Two coffees, Joyce," Murphy said. "Thanks a lot."

Joyce did not say a word. Instead, she brushed her brown wool skirt and walked out. She did not look at Alice Burton. Sam Murphy had been almost curt to her. But he ordered her about with an air of such perfect command that he offended no one. His tone said that she was there to serve and he was there to be served. Period. Another mystery, like the mystery of the clean soles of Murphy's shoes. Where do you learn to command?

"I would make a guess," Alice Burton said.

"And I would be glad to hear it," Murphy said.

"I would bet it's addressed to Bundists or to Stalin, and I'll tell you why."

Murphy nodded encouragingly. As he did, Joyce brought in the coffee on a U.S. Navy serving tray, with two chipped china cups. She smiled at Sam Murphy, ignored Alice Burton, and walked out. Murphy did not thank her.

"Whoever is sending the message—and I guess we have to believe the British if they say it came from someone in the Himmler network—whoever did that took a risk that we would discover the message and try to figure it out. After all, Siegfried is a well-known guy. Just using his name might tell us something. On the other hand, it might be intended to tell less than it tells, if you know what I mean," Alice Burton said.

"No, I don't know what you mean," Murphy said.

"All right," Alice Burton said, folding and unfolding her legs under her black wool skirt. "The message says, 'Prepare Siegfried's sunken *Tarnkappe* for his return across the water.' Now what does that mean?"

Murphy sipped his coffee silently and listened.

"In the *Nibelungenlied*, Siegfried was a hero with magical powers of strength and an invulnerable skin. He got them from magical lizards. And he also had a magical cape that made him invisible. He got it from a dwarf named Alberich. He helped his step-brother win a woman named Brunhild, and then he was trapped by another step-brother and killed. And then, the cape was thrown into the Rhine. If anyone found it, he would become invisible, too," Alice Burton said. Thank God for freshman Humanities at Northwestern.

Murphy frowned. "So the way you see it, old girl, the Germans are sending someone invisible over here."

"Exactly," Alice Burton said. "Someone strong, someone who can maybe come back from the dead." She paused and looked at the snow. The darker reality underneath, she thought. "Or else, someone who can raise the dead."

"Who's dead?" Murphy asked. He answered himself. "Das Dritte Reich."

"Exactly," Alice Burton said again. She was accustomed to

being exact. That was what took people from Columbus, Ohio, to Wall Street law firms. If the exactitude concealed her continuous amazement at her station in life, so much the better.

"They're sending someone over here, and they want a helper here in the States to make him invisible," Murphy said. "Why?"

"Before we get to that, look at the other alternative," Alice Burton said coolly. "Maybe they're not doing anything. Maybe the whole point of the message is intended for people farther east. Maybe the Siegfried they refer to is supposed to be someone negotiating with us for a separate peace. Somebody so secret that he's invisible." Alice Burton sighed. "They may just be trying to make the Russians think we're close to a separate peace with them. That would make the Russians eager to make their separate peace a little earlier. Speed things up in Stockholm."

"I can't believe the Russians would fall for that," Murphy said evenly. "They wouldn't sign a separate peace."

"They wouldn't?" Alice Burton asked with surprise. "We've been making them crazy with Bill's maniacs out there in Switzerland negotiating with every Nazi that comes along for a separate peace. I wouldn't blame the Russians for anything they did, and I'm no Commie. They do all the dying and then we come along and nose around for a separate peace. What're they supposed to do?"

"Are you questioning Wild Bill's judgment?" Murphy asked. He did not ask it in an accusing or condescending manner. Murphy knew enough about Alice Burton to know that her judgment might very possibly be superior to Bill Donovan's, even though she was from a people with different customs and ideas from his and Bill's.

"In that one respect—no other, mind you," said Alice Burton as a small smile played across her lips, "—I certainly do question his judgment. It's supposed to be unconditional surrender, and we're negotiating with every errand boy Allen Dulles can lure to his house in Zurich or Geneva or wherever it is? What are the Russians supposed to think? They know we keep promising them a second front and they know we haven't delivered. That's what they know. It would be perfectly natural for the Germans to use this kind of radio message to encourage the Russian team in Stockholm," Alice Burton said. "The Germans are dying for a separate peace with Stalin. The Führer would give him Eva Braun for a month's armistice."

Sam Murphy twirled his gold Dunhill lighter in his hand. "I can see your point. It probably was a Pandora's Box we might just as well have left unopened. But you know Bill."

"Exactly," Alice Burton said. But how dumb can you get, she thought. "I know Bill is an amazingly smart guy, but we both know that he runs off half-cocked all the time. We both know that he makes a lot of mistakes because he doesn't think to tell the right hand what the left hand is up to. He could be getting us into really deep problems with his secret peace overtures that Stalin knows about before we do. It's a damned risky game and I don't see the point in it."

"I just have to ask," Murphy said as he puffed out another vast cloud of smoke, "if this Siegfried fellow is coming here, what the hell is he supposed to do? What could one guy possibly do to actually make much of a difference with the way the war's going? The Germans are getting their ass kicked on every goddamn front." He smiled. "I won't comment on your analysis of Bill. I have to play golf with him every Sunday."

"Siegfried could be more than one person," Alice Burton said. "Or he could have helpers already here."

"The Amerikadeutsche Bund," Sam Murphy said. "Is he going to lead them in some kind of rebellion? Is that crazy?"

"Yes," Alice Burton answered matter-of-factly. "Damn," she said aloud. She had spilled coffee on her skirt. It was amazing that black coffee stained black skirts, but there it was. She was always staining her clothes. She should own stock in a dry-cleaning company. That's what her father had told her. "But, yes," she said as she stared at her skirt. "That's crazy. The Bund never was more than a handful. And now it has no one. Fritz Kuhn is in jail and doesn't even get any mail. We once looked into that."

"Then what on earth could one man, or maybe a few, do that could make that much difference when the Germans are getting creamed everywhere?" Sam Murphy asked with the air of a man for whom the answer would be amusing, no matter what.

Alice Burton thought for fully two minutes before she answered. "He doesn't have to do anything," she said. "If the right people believe he can do something, it's just the same. It's all advertising, Sam," she said. "But what's the product?"

Sam Murphy smiled at her. "Jesus," he said. "You're smart." He stubbed out his cigarette in his gray metal ashtray. "I want you to go over every possibility about how this guy could get here, how he could be invisible, how he could even *look* like he was going to change the course of the war, and get me a report by tomorrow C.O.B." He got up from his chair. "Now I'm late for bridge with Senator Tydings at the Metropolitan Club. I'll see you tomorrow."

After Sam left, Alice Burton stared out at the snow. It was dark, but she could see the snow falling in the car headlights along 17th Street, moving toward the Tidal Basin. Soon it would turn to rain. She would have to cancel her date tonight with the hotshot economist from the Office of Price Administration. Tall fellow. Kenneth something. It didn't matter. She was sick of dates at that moment. They were so insubstantial compared with the work she did. Washington men were so insubstantial period, come to think of it. All manipulation. No strength. She would just as soon eat her chicken salad alone.

The snow. That had strength. It covered everything. But underneath, she knew, there was a darker reality.

That night, as she lay in bed, watching the snow still falling on the P Street Bridge over Rock Creek Park, she thought again of the snow and of Siegfried's invisible cape. The darker reality underneath, she thought. It was there, and all she had to do was find it. She could do it. Sam was counting on her. She just had to will her hands to stop shaking when she drank coffee and then she could do it.

May 1, 1943,
Santa Cruz, California

Beautiful, Maxine Lewis thought. Beautiful. The sunlight glittering off the ocean. The ocean broken and refracting into millions of different pieces. An endless shattered mirror of light and shade, bobbing up and down out to sea for hundreds of miles. She looked out the window of her 1936 Plymouth sedan and smiled. From Highway 1, the Pacific Coast Highway, she could see across the acres of the Bakshian ranch where artichokes grew to the very cliffs of the Pacific shore. A green carpet unrolled to the blue and silver water. Superb, she thought. This land is superb beyond what anyone in any other land could possibly dream of.

In the car, next to her, a thin man wearing a wool business suit perspired. In the back seat, his girl, a pill if there ever was one, kept looking at herself in a compact mirror. The bitch was also spilling some of her goddamned cheap powder on the upholstery. She was really a peach. Dyed-blonde hair. Light-blue eyes, the kind without any character at all, real Okie eyes, the wrinkles already starting around her eyes and her lips. Pretty soon they'd be all over her neck and her forehead, too.

And what taste! In this eighty-degree weather, the woman

wore foxtails. It was embarrassing even to be seen with them.

At least the man was well-dressed. Brown herringbone. Decent wing-tip shoes, even if they were a little scuffed. A decent necktie. It might even have been a Countess Mara. That was class. Gold rims on his spectacles. Definitely a cut or two above his girl. If that floozie even was his girlfriend.

Still, if they were the ones who had been sent, then who was she to question? Maxine Lewis always obeyed orders, but she didn't really trust the floozie. That woman in the back seat simply did not look like she had the discipline to do anything serious, anything daring. Of course, her duties might be in the sexual line. It was just possible that she might have some skill there. Maxine Lewis preferred not to think about such things. Maxine was a pretty girl, and there were not many women of thirty-five who were as firm on top as she was. Sometimes she stood in front of her mirror—shades drawn, of course—and just studied them before she went to sleep. That little apartment on River Street did not have much in the way of luxuries, but it did have a full-length mirror on the back of the closet door in the bedroom. She liked to just flick her breasts with her finger a few times. They didn't even quiver. Didn't even move at all. It was a cinch that the slut in the back seat couldn't make the same boast, even if she was some kind of sexual operator.

Only her first husband had ever known what those breasts felt like, but then he hadn't appreciated them. He hadn't appreciated a goddamned thing, as a matter of fact, unless it ran on four feet at a track. Too frigging bad for him. She kicked him the hell out *real* quick. If you can't shape up around Maxine Lewis, you ship the hell out.

If you can't keep your job at the County Water Department, then the hell with you, Charlie. If you can't keep from coming home at three in the morning plastered out of your mind on Four Roses, then you can find another bed to put your slippers under. And if you can't be man enough to tell your wife straight out that you've lost your whole salary for three weeks in a row betting on ponies that can barely walk, you can just take a hike.

Not that Maxine missed him one bit. When he wasn't bombed on cheap wine or gin or whatever weak-minded people drank to let them forget their weakness, he reeked of meat. It had gotten so bad that Maxine had had to open the windows when he was asleep to keep the smell of carrion from overwhelming her while she was trying to sleep. She felt as if she were choking on the fumes of slaughtered cattle, and in the stench of dead animals she could sense the cries and shrieks of sad-eyed cattle being murdered and mutilated in wretched, unspeakable slaughterhouses. All of that came to her through the breath of her now mercifully departed husband after he had stuffed himself with the flesh of those innocent animals. It had gotten so that she could smell the odor of dead animals and their agony in his clothes and even in his hair.

Maxine had been a vegetarian since high school, of course. If one truly respected life and nature, one did not kill nature's creatures, including animals. Moreover, if one respected one's own body, one did not fill it with dead tissue to weigh it down and choke it with the blood of blameless animals. Maxine had noticed even as a child that when she ate meat, she felt lethargic and edgy. Once, at the Soquel Country Inn, she had glanced at a plate of corned-beef hash and realized that just days before, that had been a living creature, into whom God had breathed life, just as He had breathed it into Maxine. Maxine had to run to the Ladies Room (tastefully called "Fillies") and thrown up into a "Kohler of Kohler" toilet. That was when Maxine was thirteen, about the same time she had started to develop as a woman. It was the last time Maxine had ever eaten meat, at least knowingly. Meat might have gotten into a bowl of soup by accident at a restaurant, but Maxine would never intentionally eat a fellow animal.

She did eat chicken and fish. Chickens, as she told her husband, were born to die anyway, so that was all right. Fish, as far as Maxine could tell, had no souls. She also ate a great deal of fine San Lorenzo Valley cabbage and lettuce and plenty of good, hearty Santa Cruz County spinach and mushrooms.

And, to judge by what Dr. Vogler over at the Dominican Hospital said, Maxine was in better shape for it. A lot of women had started to sag terribly by the time they were in their early thirties in a lot of bad places. Maxine was still girlish and hard as she had been since she was thirteen. Her lowlife husband looked like he was fifty by the time he was thirty-five. She still looked like the high school majorette she had been. In addition, she had the pride of knowing that she had not killed poor innocent animals just to feed her face, as most people did.

Of course, being a vegetarian and not being afraid to let people know how she felt about their thoughtless eating of animals added to the isolation Maxine Lewis felt in a small, ignorant town like Santa Cruz. She did not want to tell people in Santa Cruz that the greatest Leader of them all did not eat animals. They would get the wrong idea. She preferred to eat a small meal of vegetables and cottage cheese by herself while reading the *Chronicle* than to be with a lot of boasting, sweaty fools who fouled the air with their smell of the *abattoir* (a word she had learned from Adelle Davis). She would far rather be right and alone than a butcher and a murderess in a crowd.

So for the last four years, Maxine Lewis had just herself to admire that no matter how many years older she got, her breasts seemed to stay just as firm and great as they had always been.

Of course, she had other consolations. Such as working for the continuing survival of the Aryan race. The others might fall by the wayside. Fritz Kuhn might be a thief and a liar, even a psychopath. The whole bunch of them at the Bund might have been simply in it for the money. Maxine Lewis was not in it for the money. Maxine Lewis was not in it for glory. She was in it so that the race might not perish. Some nights when she looked at herself in the mirror, naked from toe to head, she knew that she, *she personally*, was what the struggle was all about. Perfectly proportioned, with slim ankles, a round derriere, slender inner thighs, a flat stomach, those breasts, her thin face with its deep-blue eyes—not wishy-washy Okie blue—and that blonde hair—natural, not from a bottle. She was what the struggle was for. For her and hundreds of millions like her.

So that they might not be swamped by baboons like the ones who came down from San Jose to walk along on the Santa Cruz boardwalk, making leering remarks to white girls. So that they might not be smashed against the anvil of Bolshevism by muttering Jews, always smelling of garlic and drooling at the thought of how much money they would make off this latest war in which the Aryans did the fighting and the Jews stayed home and counted their shekels.

Maxine Lewis might work, just to keep a roof over her head, selling real estate in Santa Cruz County. She might even be damned good at her job—which she was (she could count thirty-one hundred dollars in commissions in 1942, and that wasn't hay). But her real heart and soul were reserved for the duties that would come her way one day. She knew they would come. The duties that would tell her and the whole world that the beautiful things of this world—the Pacific Ocean seen from the bluffs of Santa Cruz—would be the birthright of the only people who knew how to take care of the world. Pure Aryans.

Maxine Lewis' thoughts were interrupted. "I want you to turn off at Bonny Doon Road," the man with the wool suit said. "Go down a couple of miles and then pull off somewhere quiet."

"Of course," Maxine Lewis said. "It will take only a few minutes."

She was happy they were turning off. They would now head up into the glorious Santa Cruz Mountains, covered with lordly redwoods and firs. This truly was a blessed country. Not only the shimmering ocean, not only the green fields of artichokes and the sheer cliffs, but also the mountains and the trees. Trees that were centuries old when man first arrived on the continent. When the *red man* first appeared on the continent. And now, the logging companies, the paper companies, the construction companies, the quarries—they were all cutting down the trees at a frightening rate. For ticky-tacky homes. For factories. For war production. For endless bureau-cratic forms. For all the worthless reasons of the trashy Ameri-can society, the mongrel American society, these magnificent trees were being sawed down by the thousands.

And they could never be replaced! Never. They were the heritage of the Aryan people of America. But they were being cut down to wage the war of the British and their Jewish masters and to fill the voracious maw of profit. *Profit!* How could anyone possibly even think of trees like these redwoods in terms of profit or loss? Only a subhuman could do it.

Adolf Hitler knew about conserving the natural beauty of a blessed land. He had been the first in the world to issue com-prehensive guides for preserving the trees, the forests, the lakes and rivers of the Reich. He would do the same here. The Führer knew what mattered, what endured. The trees and mountains and seashores had to be preserved for Aryan gener-ations yet unborn. *They* were the nation, not some agglomera-tion of politicians and chiselers in Washington and New York. The land was the nation.

If it took a lifetime of solitude to save the nation, a lifetime without the usual frivolity of her friends and the girls in her real estate office, well, that was what it took. The land and the sea and the trees were well worth it. Anyway, Maxine Lewis did not like the kind of men who were in Santa Cruz nowa-days. Roughneck Mexicans from Monterey. Dopey Okies from Fort Ord. Empty-headed grease monkeys from the aircraft plants in Sunnyvale.

She could remember the men of her childhood. They were the first- and second-generation descendants of the pioneers. They hadn't just stuck out their thumb and gotten from New-ark to California, or slept on a troop train while the maj-esty of the prairies went by out a closed window. The men she knew from her childhood in Santa Cruz had walked across the nation next to their wagons. They were men of determi-nation. Hardened men, but men with respect for the land. They did not take from it what they could not give back. They were strong family men, like her father. They dedicated their lives to their young and to the next generation of

America—not to squeezing out a few more bucks or getting a WPA leaf-raking job to avoid doing an honest day's work.

"You may pull over here," the sweating man in the wool suit said.

They were on a completely shaded dirt road off toward the cement quarry. Huge redwoods, spared by time, arched over the road, making it cool and dim even in the middle of the afternoon.

Without speaking, the man in the wool suit got out of the car. He slapped at his trousers in a vain effort to restore the crease. Then he pulled a large mop of a handkerchief out of his breast pocket and wiped his brow. Maxine Lewis stifled her distaste. That was all right for a farmer, but once a man put on a business suit, you might expect a little better from him, quite frankly. Certainly her father had never done that when he was manager of the A&P down in Watsonville.

Maxine Lewis got out of the car. She slammed the door with a decorous thunk. Then she walked along the road to where the man in the wool suit stood. Amazingly, the man took a cigarette from his pocket and lit it with a match that he struck off his thumbnail.

"Excuse me," she said as she tried to restrain herself. "These woods are mighty dry. I don't think it's safe to smoke here."

The man stared at her. "Safe?" he asked.

"You could start a fire," she said.

The man stared at her for a few more seconds and then smiled. He threw the cigarette to the ground, covered it with his huge wing-tip shoe, and smothered it. Then Maxine Lewis covered it with dirt and pine needles. "That was good thinking," the man said. "Why call attention to ourselves? That was very good thinking."

Maxine Lewis looked back to the car. The woman with the fox wrap was still studying her face in the compact.

"Thank you," she said.

The man cleared his throat. "You're a good-looking woman," he said. "I hope you don't mind my saying that.

Trixie said that the moment we walked into your office. She said you were a fine-looking woman."

"Thank you," Maxine Lewis said. She supposed Trixie was the slut in the back seat.

"Tell me," he said, "and I hope I won't offend you by even asking this, but just how committed are you? I mean to our side? To the Reich? To making America a country for Aryans again? I know you have passed on your messages at the Paraguayan Consulate, and that was an intelligent way to move. Certainly an intelligent way to move. But just how far are you willing to go?"

"I am willing to do whatever it takes to win," she said. "At first I had trouble explaining that to myself, but not anymore. If this country's government won't stand up to the Jews and the Russians, then this government isn't America. Not for me." She gulped and said, "What is it? What do you want me to do?"

"Tell me," the man said. "Do you know how the war is going? I mean how it is really going?"

"I hear the same lies as everyone else who listens to Roosevelt and his Jewboys," she said. "Sometimes I can get Radio Berlin on my shortwave. But I have a hard time following the names of all the places in Russia."

"I don't blame you," the man said with a trace of a smile in his brown eyes. "It gets very confusing for me, too, and my family is actually from there. Volga German, yes indeed, before we came to the U.S.A. From the Volga to Fresno. A long way."

Maxine Lewis didn't know what the hell the Volga was, but she nodded and smiled. It was probably somewhere in Europe. Maybe in France.

"The fact is that the war is now balanced on the edge of a knife. That is the truth. Just in the last week, General Manstein has retaken Kharkov. That is a titanic victory. No one thought that the Red Army could be rolled back, but they were. Kharkov was a great, great victory," the man said.

"Thank God," Maxine Lewis said. "The reports from the

Russian Front had been so discouraging. I had begun to fear . . ."

"No need to say it," the man said. "We all felt the same."

Maxine Lewis could see a woodchuck dashing along through the trees behind the man in the wool suit.

"In a way," the man in the wool suit said, "retaking Kharkov was insurance. The hub of the whole Donets Basin. Insurance for the rest of the Führer's moves into the Caucasus. That's really just what it was. Insurance. Same line I'm in. It's a good line of work."

"I'm sure it is," Maxine Lewis said. "I know the man in our office who handles property lines."

The man in the wool suit waved a hand deprecatingly. "Property is nothing," he said. "I sell life. That's the kind of policy people have to have. It doesn't matter whether there's a depression on or anything. People have got to have life insurance. They'll go without dinner, but they won't go without life insurance. They may pay in quarters and dimes, but they've got to have it."

"I guess so," Maxine Lewis said. She looked above the man's head. She could see a hawk wheeling about lazily in the blue sky. Where would the hawks go when Crown Zellerbach had cut down the trees? Did the fat board of directors ever think of that?

"I can tell you that it's kept me going all through this whole mess. Put bread on the table. Even given me room for a few luxuries," the man said, inclining his head slightly toward the woman in the car.

"Excuse me?" Maxine Lewis asked.

"Insurance. Whole-life," the man in the wool suit said. "I stay the hell away from term. If a man comes in and wants term, I tell him to go to Sears, Roebuck. I don't deal with term. Not enough profit in it."

"What does any of this have to do with our duty as Aryans?" Maxine Lewis asked. If there was one thing she hated, it was a line of bullshit from a man she didn't care that much for anyway.

The man in the wool suit smiled. "You're quite right. We

can talk about this some other time. Quite right." He cleared his throat as if he were about to say something important. Then he said something important. "There have been people watching you, Maxine. Important people. You haven't known it. That's because they're the kind of people who know how to work without being observed. Some of them used to be FBI agents before they realized which side they were on."

Maxine Lewis tensed. FBI agents working for the Reich? That gave her hope. She had always liked the FBI.

"Those people reported back good things about you. They said you were buttoned-down on the outside and the inside. Good-looking, but kept out of trouble, if you know what I mean."

"I know just what you mean," Maxine Lewis replied primly. She really didn't care too much for this man's line of innuendo.

"Of course, no one's a saint. We know that. They know that in Berlin, too. A woman's got to be a woman," the man said.

Maxine Lewis started to feel a little edgy. "What is the point, if you don't mind?" she asked.

The man looked embarrassed, as if he had just been caught trying to sneak a look inside her blouse, which, of course, he had been trying to do all day. She didn't wear a bra. What the hell? She didn't sag. If people were rude enough to stare, that was their problem. "The point?" Maxine Lewis asked again.

"The point is that the people in Paraguay passed the word to the people in Berlin, and the Reichsführer personally chose you for an assignment that can change the entire war. Himmler personally," the man in the wool suit said, staring evenly at his fingernails.

Maxine Lewis felt a jolt of electricity go right through her. It was like making love when her husband was sober, only far more exciting. Himmler personally!

A memory stirred within her. It must have been twenty-five years before, at least. She and her father and the minister of the Presbyterian church, a fine, white-haired figure of a man named Knowland, had been walking along Pacific Avenue in Santa Cruz. It was one of those days when the sun shines so beautifully that you know God is in a good mood. Just as the three strollers had crossed a street, a wagon—maybe it was a milk wagon—came careening along the sidewalk. The driver was obviously drunk, and his two gray horses were out of control. The wagon bore down on her. She was terrified. Her father and the minister, Dr. Knowland, snatched at her, but the wagon and horses veered, and for a horrible moment the horses looked as if they would ride down all three.

Then, as if by magic, out of a completely blue sky, there came a clap of faraway thunder. The horses were so startled that they stopped dead in their tracks. Snorting and drooling, they stopped on a dime, so close that Maxine could smell their breath. So close that Maxine could see the veins in their eyes.

That had been real scary. Dr. Knowland had insisted that all three "give thanks" right then and there, at that very moment. After a moment of silent prayer, the minister had hugged Maxine. In front of all the passersby and the shoppers and the drunk man in the milk wagon, Dr. Knowland said, "This child has been spared to do something great. The Lord moves to protect His own."

And now, Himmler himself had said the same thing. Out of all his busy hours and days, Himmler had taken the time to select little Maxine Lewis from Santa Cruz for something important. Maxine Lewis could feel her chest rising with pride and excitement. No, really more like anticipation. But she had to appear restrained. If she had been chosen for her restraint, why, obviously it was important not to go flying off the handle.

She cleared her throat. "I am honored," she said.

"And so you should be," the man in the wool suit said, rubbing his hands together like an overjoyed maître d' at a fake fancy French restaurant, like those ones in San Francisco. Those ones where her husband had taken her right the hell out after taking a look at the price tag. Three dollars for a minute steak! A dollar for a chef's salad!

"What is the assignment?" Maxine Lewis asked. She tried to sound as calm as possible, as if she were given an assignment that could change history every day. She also noticed that the man in the wool suit was staring at her white cotton blouse. He was trying to see if her nipples were standing out because she was so excited. He was crude when you got right down to it, but if he was the appointed messenger of Fate, well, so be it. "What am I supposed to do?" she asked.

The man in the wool suit smiled. "Frankly, I have no idea," he said. "None at all."

"What do you mean?" Maxine Lewis asked sharply.

"I mean that it is so important that I am not allowed to say, and I am Gauleiter for all of northern California, Miss Lewis, so it is pretty goddamned secret," the man said in a voice whose sudden severity shocked Maxine Lewis. It was as if he had just cracked a whip in her face. Now, for the first time, she saw the authority of the man! Obviously, he deserved whatever trust Berlin put in him. But the man in the wool suit did not keep the tone for long. That was the personality of command. First, awesome strength, then friendly camaraderie.

He put his arm around her shoulders. "The time will come, and soon, when your destiny is made clear to you. But for now, there is something important you must do. Something very important, so that we will know we can count on you for whatever lies ahead."

"Gauleiter," she said, standing stiffly, "anything." She meant it. Even if it meant something sexual, she would do it. The man had a tone of supreme importance, and she must yield to it to create her destiny.

"You will do anything for the Reich? For an Aryan, free America?"

"You have my word as an Aryan," she said. She was willing to do anything. Right there. Right then. In the woods, if necessary.

"You see that woman who came with me?" the man in the wool suit asked.

"Of course," Maxine Lewis said.

"She has become dangerous. She has come to snoop. She began as just a diversion for me. A man needs such diversions," he said in a perfectly straightforward way, without any embarrassment whatsoever. "But now, she has become dangerous. She wants to know this and then she wants to know that. She has become demanding. Extra ration coupons. Silk stockings. Gasoline points." He leaned forward confidentially. "Information."

Now there were two hawks circling majestically in the sky. They searched for food, for prey. They were natural creatures of prey. By God's law, they were to eat those who were weak. The weak, the small existed as food for them, and no more. Maxine Lewis could feel that she too was of that proud breed who were, by nature's design, above the mass, destined to prey on the weak.

"You are willing to be tested as to your strength of character? Your determination?" The man in the wool suit asked the questions calmly, as if there were no possibility of a negative response.

Maxine Lewis looked over at the woman once again. The bitch had her hair in peekaboo braids just like Veronica Lake in *Life* magazine that week. What vanity!

"Of course," Maxine Lewis said. "My honor is at stake and I will make certain that the Reichsführer is not disappointed in his choice."

"Good, good," the man in the wool suit said, once again rubbing his hands together. "That girl has no family, none at all. No one will miss her."

Maxine Lewis wondered if that was what people said about her.

"I have to kill that woman. Do you understand? She may well be working for the FBI. Or perhaps the OGPU. You understand?"

Maxine Lewis felt a wave of nausea. Nevertheless, she nodded her head.

"You must help me. You must help me get her across to the cliff at Bonny Doon. Will you do that?"

Maxine Lewis fought her nausea. She nodded again.

"Good," the man in the wool suit said. "I will leave it to you to get her to the cliff. I will do the rest. You won't have to touch her."

Maxine Lewis nodded again and wordlessly got back into the car. She slid into the driver's seat. The man in the wool suit sat in the passenger seat. Maxine Lewis glanced over her shoulder at Trixie. Now the cow was filing her nails with an emery board. They were supposed to be unavailable for the duration. Maxine Lewis had no doubt how Trixie had gotten her emery board.

"Trixie," Maxine Lewis said as the car got back on the road, "I love your face powder. Is that Coty?"

"Coty?" Trixie asked sarcastically. "No, dear, this is Chanel. From I. Magnin. In San Francisco." She did not look up.

The bitch deserved what she was getting.

"Do you mind if I try some on, Trixie? Just a little touch on my cheek? I get up to San Francisco sometimes. It's really becoming on you. Maybe it'll do something for me," Maxine Lewis said.

"Well, I only have a little," Trixie said in a slow whine.

"Maybe I could just see how it looks on you in the sunlight," Maxine Lewis said. "I can't really get the effect when you're inside the car."

"I guess that would be all right," Trixie said, adjusting her foxtails and taking out her compact mirror again. "I used to be a model once, you know. At a store in Bakersfield."

"I would have just bet that, you know," Maxine Lewis said. "I was just saying that you looked like a model."

Now Maxine Lewis' Plymouth was pulled over onto the spit of land next to the road at Bonny Doon Point. Maxine Lewis killed the engine. She could hear the waves crashing one hundred feet below—crashing against rocks, not sand.

"Would you mind?" Maxine Lewis asked as sweetly as she could. She could feel a twitch in her left leg. Two immense fruit trucks barreled by. One of the drivers beeped when he got a load of Maxine's chest. That made her feel more confident. "I'd just like to see your face in this light. This is the best light for my skin, usually. Natural sunlight."

"Well, I really don't think you're gonna be able to get this powder anyway," Trixie said. "They don't exactly sell it to everyone who walks in the door, if you know what I mean."

No, you slut, I don't know what you mean, Maxine Lewis thought to herself as Trixie awkwardly got out of the back seat. Her skirt rode up. Maxine Lewis was happy to see that her legs began to get pretty damned heavy above the knee. Trixie walked over to the side of the car, about two yards from the edge. She held up her chin as if she were waiting for Yousuf Karsh to snap the shutter. Behind her, the man in the wool suit emerged from the car.

"I can't quite see," Maxine Lewis said. "Would you stand so that I'm near the edge, just so you don't have any danger of falling over. So many girls are afraid of heights these days," she added.

"I'm not afraid of heights, honey," Trixie said. "I've been up to a lot of high places. Even been on an airplane between Fresno and L.A." As if to prove her courage, Trixie backed up even closer to the edge. Maxine followed her. She could see the waves smashing against the gray-black rocks. It made an odd contrast, the relentless power of the waves pounding below, the whining sound of the Okie in her fancy makeup up above. The man in the wool suit walked over.

"What shade do they call that, Trixie?" Maxine Lewis asked. "I think it's about the most perfect I've ever seen."

Trixie smiled for the first time. "You know," she said. "I'm not sure. I'll have to go back to the car and look at the compact in my bag."

Trixie took one step and ran into the man in the wool suit. "No, you don't," he said. Without another word, he punched her in the face, putting all of his weight behind the jab. The surprise thrust caught her in mid-step, as she was turning back toward the car. The blow lifted Trixie off her feet and made her fall on all fours right on the edge of the cliff. She scrambled to get up and stared suddenly up at Maxine Lewis. "What the . . ." she said, as the man in the wool suit bent over as if to pick her up. Instead, he gave her a huge shove, with every ounce of strength he could muster. With a breathless gasp, Trixie went over the edge. Except that she held on with her long-nailed hands to a thick clump of mondo grass on the cliff.

"For Christ's sake," she gasped. "What are you . . ." The man in the wool suit ground down on Trixie's hands with his leather heels. Trixie let go long enough for him to kick her viciously in the face as she slipped and then cascaded and then fell like a hunk of lead, a wildly flailing hunk of lead, onto the rocks below. She hit one rock, bounced onto another, and then slid into the white foam. For a moment, her blonde hair bobbed in the water; then it disappeared.

Maxine Lewis ran back to the car, wiped off her shoes with a handkerchief, and looked at the man in the wool suit. He had not spoken. "Do you want her pocketbook?" Maxine Lewis asked. She was out of breath. Blood pounded in her ears. She felt dizzy, excited. A bird of prey.

The man shrugged. Maxine took the pocketbook and flung it off the cliff. It too floated for a moment and then sank. Maxine Lewis was sick over the cliff, then wiped her mouth on her handkerchief and got back into the car.

On the ride back into town, Maxine Lewis listened to music from KSAL, Monterey. Kay Kyser's band doing "Harbor Lights." She loved that. She started to hum along. She felt invulnerable.

"We were not wrong to trust you," the man in the wool suit said. He had a line of sweat on his upper lip.

Maxine Lewis did not say anything. Her mind felt clearer than it had for years. Maybe clearer than it ever had. She felt powerful. This had been a big day. The car did still smell of the woman's perfume, but then again, Maxine could get it washed.

When Maxine Lewis brought the man back to his car on Pacific Street, he told her that there would be more instructions, that she should be proud of what she had done, that she was in a position to change the whole future of mankind, and perhaps to save the Aryan race. He also stared at her boobs. "Heil Hitler," he said softly as he got out of the car. "Polish up your German," he also said. "You'll be needing it, I suspect." Then he said "Heil Hitler" again. Then he left.

Maxine Lewis could not help but notice that he said that to

her on the very same corner where Dr. Knowland had told her that God had saved her for something really important.

At home that night, there was nothing on the radio about a blonde, slutty-looking woman drowned, head bashed in, near Bonny Doon beach. Probably no one had found her. With that kind of woman, no one would miss her for a long time, Maxine guessed. Maxine ate heated-up pork-and-beans dinner and thought about people like Trixie. In a way, it was a shame. She was an Aryan, after all, and here no one cared one damn about whether she was alive or dead. Probably in her whole circle of friends, no one would give that much of a good goddamn if she was around.

Maxine did her dishes and listened to a news show about whether soft-coal operators would go on strike. Then she thought about Trixie again. Now that Maxine thought about it, she realized that she didn't give that much of a damn whether Trixie was alive or dead either. Trixie was just unlucky, that's all.

For someone like Maxine Lewis, who would play a pivotal role in history, people like Trixie didn't really matter much. Not like the trees and the mountains.

May 4, 1943,
Chicago, Illinois

Five men sat silently in a classroom at the Metallurgical Laboratory of the University of Chicago. Windows looked out on the Midway, which was flooded from heavy rains for the last week. Students hurried along the sidewalks, casting worried glances at the rising water, as if it might sweep them away before they could get to Psych class or Poli Sci. In groups of twos and threes, the students talked about whether they were prepared for their quizzes in Humanities or Contemporary Civilization. Under umbrellas and raincoats, the students looked serious but cheerful as they talked among themselves. Inside Classroom 201, no one spoke.

Occasionally, one of the men stared at a mass of startlingly long equations in sloppy chalk handwriting on the blackboards. Then a man might make a calculation on a sheet of paper, stare at it, and study it.

One of the men made no calculations. Instead, he read a book about physics. That man wore a colonel's uniform. He had a narrow, bullet-shaped head and a wide, almost fat stomach. He looked stern and determined. Leslie Groves had the air of a man teaching second-year military cadets at The Citadel to march properly. Instead, he was waiting for the answer to one of the most complex problems of physical science.

His assistant, a young physicist from a mid-Atlantic university, dressed in the uniform of a U.S. Army captain, wore
thick, wire-rimmed glasses. He swore silently to himself as he
studied the equations on the board. His thin lips pressed and
unpressed themselves regularly as he saw why the equations
indicated that one solution after another was impossible to
translate into real life.

Next to him, a heavyset man with a wide face, twinkling
eyes, and a defiant, curved nose sat in chalk-covered wool
tweeds, working with fevered concentration on his notebook.
Leo Szilard occasionally stroked his paunchy stomach with his
left hand while he frantically wrote equations with the right
hand. Szilard kept glancing over at the other men in the room
to see if any of them had a look of triumph. Frankly, Szilard
would be extremely disappointed if anyone in the room had
the solution to this problem before he did. In Hungary, Szilard simply knew—as a matter of certainty—that if there were
a difficult problem, only he, in the entire nation, could possibly have the correct answer. At least he would surely have it
first. But here, in this group, in this glittering Manhattan District Engineering Project, it was entirely possible that he
could be outshone. In fact, he had to admit, it was likely, considering who the two men were to his left.

If it were at all possible, Szilard would like very much to
make the breakthrough that would make him *even more* in-
delible in the history of particle physics. He kept telling his
brain that it had to do more, be more resourceful. There was a
way to diffuse the U-235 particle so that it came out evenly
enough for a fission reaction to take place almost instan-
taneously. The goddamned element was so unstable though.
It was like trying to throw a thousand eggs the length of a
soccer field and have them all end up poached and suitable to
be served at the Waldorf.

Next to Szilard, a man with deep-set, cadaverous eyes in a
youthful face—he was four years younger than Szilard, a fact
which drove Szilard crazy, since he had already won the
Nobel Prize five years before—a thin man with hair already

yielding to age, sat with his eyes closed and his hands pressed together. Enrico Fermi's face was placid, almost beatific, compared with Szilard's frenetic expression. In Fermi's mind, the problem was by no means insoluble. In Fermi's mind, the whole body of physical science was a series of trunks in his attic. There were a great many of them, but certainly not an infinite number. If Fermi patiently, in his mind, unlocked all the trunks and rummaged within, he would find the answer.

Frankly, though, he probably would not have to do so. Fermi was a realist. If he had to solve the problem, he would. It might take him a month or even several months, but he could do it. But he was almost certain that the man next to him already had the solution. Otherwise, why would Albert Einstein have put aside his notebook and picked up that day's Chicago *Tribune?* The Herr Doktor genius was carefully reading a story about the next year's prospects for the dairy industry. That could only mean that he had solved the problem and was now absent-mindedly going back to his daydreams about creating a unified field theory, without remembering to tell his colleagues what the solution was.

Not that Einstein liked to be called Herr Doktor or told that he was absent-minded. It was simply a habit that Fermi had gotten into from knowing Einstein years before in Berlin, when Einstein was still at the Kaiser Wilhelm Institute, visiting as and when he could spare the time from the University of Berlin. Then, everyone was referred to as Herr Doktor. Even Einstein accepted it. Fermi recalled meeting Lise Meitner and Otto Hahn at the Kaiser Wilhelm Institute years before, perhaps in 1930. By that time, scientists were only starting to understand how important Hahn's discovery had been. Hahn and Meitner, acting on an off-the-cuff suggestion from Einstein, had actually found that a uranium particle, bombarded with neutrons, broke apart with startlingly greater force than the force of the neutrons. Luckily for everyone, many German scientists called Hahn's discovery a "trick of Jew physics." Even now, Fermi had to laugh at that. If the Nazis had not been so idiotic as to dismiss Einstein and Hahn, not to mention Szilard and himself, as pawns of Jewish finance, the war would already be over. Germany would have won.

How Heisenberg and Planck and the others must have kicked themselves since then! Unfortunately for them—luckily for humanity—the man who could have put them well down the path that the Manhattan Project had traveled sat peacefully in a warm room at the University of Chicago, reading the business page of the Chicago *Tribune*.

Einstein looked comfortable in his baggy trousers and freshly ironed sweat shirt. A pipe drooped from his lips. His hair stood out in enviably huge white shocks, crowning an imposing forehead. His face looked like the face of a child who had seen some harsh things, but was still a child. Around the eyes, there was suffering, and also in the chin. But the eyes themselves were warm, engaging, almost like the eyes of a particularly intelligent and lovable large dog. Fermi had to love this man who understood the ways of the cosmos, had seen the evil of Naziism from his young manhood, and still could wear a look of such sweetness. What kind of a man wore sweat shirts and baggy trousers when Enrico Fermi wore his last, best hand-tailored suit? A very confident man, Fermi thought.

The sound of rain off to the north, over Lake Michigan, disturbed the men in the Gothic building, in Classroom 201, seated at little desks attached to chairs. Colonel Groves coughed and cleared his throat.

"The problem is that the people at du Pont who have to manufacture the tubes for the pumps that are coming from Kellex simply have to have some idea of which process we're going to use for large-scale production. Otherwise, we could wind up with almost nothing in the way of usable pumps," Groves said. He tried to sound commanding, which was difficult when one was dealing with three Nobel Prize winners over whom he had only moral authority—and he often wondered who had the moral authority over whom when he saw Einstein's dark, solemn eyes.

"I think we've narrowed the choices down to the spray gun matrix, on the one hand, and the porous, corrosible screen matrix, on the other. If you gentlemen would just give us your opinion on which of them yields the highest probability for success, the people at du Pont would be most appreciative," Groves said.

"I still don't see why you ever turned this over to the du Pont people," Fermi said with a heavy accent. "Just what did you expect a group of chemists to be able to do with state-of-the-art questions in particle physics? We were making such good progress right here."

"Before we go any further," Szilard said, "can you tell us what Allied Intelligence knows about German efforts in the field? I think we have a right to know."

"That's all classified on a strictly need-to-know basis," Groves said somberly.

"Which means you don't have any idea," Szilard said. "What if they've already solved this problem? It would be good to know."

Groves sighed. "First of all, Dr. Fermi, no one questions what you people do for the Manhattan District. But we are talking about an immense manufacturing effort. We are not talking about small experiments under Stagg Field. We needed the best manufacturer in a scientific field. That's du Pont." He turned to Szilard. "Frankly, Professor Szilard, we don't know as much as we'd like to know about the German effort in this area. But our British friends at tube alloys say their SIS would know if the Germans had made a break-through."

Szilard snorted contemptuously. "The way they knew that Hitler was about to attack Russia? The way they knew that Japan was about to bomb Pearl Harbor?"

Fermi put a soothing hand on Szilard's knee. "Obviously, the colonel does not know anything about what you're asking about. Why put him on the spot? That's not his job. It's not our job."

Einstein did not even pay attention. He was carefully studying the sports page of the *Tribune* now, paying the most careful attention to a minutely printed column of statistics about college basketball wins and losses. Fermi had not realized how nearsighted the old man had become.

Szilard still seethed. "I think that if the Germans already have mastered this particular technique, we would be sparing ourselves a great deal of trouble if we simply adopted their technique."

"As far as we know," Colonel Groves said mildly, "the Germans are not even close to solving this problem."

"In that case," Fermi said, hoping to change the subject, "I think we might get down to the business at hand. For my money, the porous screen technique is the most likely to succeed. It is by no means a certainty, but the spray gun technique assumes that we can keep the liquid uranium in a state of even viscosity, which is by no stretch of the imagination a certainty."

Szilard chimed in. "I couldn't agree more. The spray gun technique is a brilliant attempt, but it was devised when we knew much less about the metallurgy of the element. As a theoretical matter, it is difficult. As a practicality, it is impossible. Of course, the porous screen technique assumes an acid with uniform corrosive properties. I'm not certain we have such an acid."

There was a fanning motion from Dr. Einstein's seat. The white-haired professor opened his Chicago *Tribune* to the stock market page. He spread it out flat so that the entire Big Board was exposed. Then he laid the paper on the floor. "There it is," he said. "That's the technique. I have already worked out the equations."

The men in the room looked at each other in mock exasperation. It was humiliating, Fermi thought, to be a Nobel Prize winner in physics and still have a man so far ahead of you that you could not even figure out what the hell he was talking about.

"Printing," Einstein said. "If you want to see a perfect example of how to spread out a substance in hundreds of thousands of perfectly identical shapes, look at a newspaper page."

Fermi felt as if he had just been slapped in the face. But of course! The problem had already been solved by having a rotating disk from which material was spread upon a matrix already made of a metal hard enough to accept and retain the uniform shapes. It was so obvious! Even Szilard was laughing to himself.

Einstein continued, oblivious of the shock in the room. "If a newspaper can print a stock market table, we can print a half million dots of enriched uranium on a plate to begin the reaction," Einstein said.

Groves shook his head in wonderment. The assistant, the young man in a captain's uniform, laughed out loud. Why, the man was unbelievable. The man was able to see the relevance of totally different contexts to one another when even brilliant minds in his field were left behind, gasping in the dust of their intellectual aridity, compared with Einstein. The assistant thought that Einstein was surely worth the entire Red Army just by himself.

"Now that I have done this little service for you," Einstein said as he picked up the newspaper and neatly folded it back into shape, "perhaps one of you will come back to Princeton with me and work on something really difficult." He looked around the room to see if there were any takers. His gaze paused for a long moment on the young assistant, as if he could see something in the man that no one else in the room could see. His eyes looked particularly sad as they met the young man's eager blue eyes.

"Perhaps you, young man, would come back with me. I'm told you know a great deal about waves and particles. Would you like to know what force guides both gravity and electromagnetism? Or are you more interested in current events? Perhaps in politics?"

Then Einstein's gaze moved on to Szilard. "I know you won't help me, Leo. You don't believe it's possible," the old man said.

The man in the captain's uniform felt as if Einstein had looked at him with X-ray vision. The old genius looked as if he could see every thought that the young man had ever had. He could see clear down into the bottom of the Chesapeake Bay. But Einstein's eyes had been so kind! Almost imploring.

What a man! Truly, a man to change the course of history. The captain shook himself mentally. A conversation was going on around him.

"I do not say that a unitary field theory is impossible," Szilard said cheerily. "I have just seen every indication that it is possible for you to do anything you want to do. I have merely said that Riemann's work does not take us very far toward the goal."

"He had the theory correct all along," Einstein said. "He lacked the equations to prove it. Anyone can get those if he works at them long enough." He looked sad, as if he knew that he would not have enough years to work out the equations. "After all, who would ever have thought that it would be possible to make an equation to explain heat fields and magnetic fields as part of the same force? But it has happened."

Fermi looked hard at Einstein. To carry in his head the equations necessary for solving unitary field problems, to do logarithmic summations in his head—several at once—was beyond belief. But far beyond that, incomprehensibly beyond that mathematical ability—Einstein was the Emperor of Abstractions, as he had shown this afternoon. If he could be put in charge of the Manhattan District, he could push the whole thing along far faster than any fat colonel or automobile paint experts at du Pont. But, of course, gigantic wartime projects were not run by scientists. In America, the capitalists and the Army ran everything important. At least during wartime. What a tragedy. Einstein as the head of a project to make one atom bomb—just one, to show the world the undreamt-of force —he could get it done in months. But, of course, in America, that was just a daydream.

The meeting went on for another half hour while Einstein slowly, laboriously wrote out the equations proving that the printing method could distribute the enriched uranium perfectly. Colonel Groves had his assistant go out to the telephone to make certain that the transportation to take the old man back to Princeton would be ready. The assistant, even though he was just a kid, was awfully good at that kind of

thing. Arranging accommodations, travel, meals—even intellectual companionship—for the great thinkers of the country,
for the men who made the Manhattan District run.

Then, just at class break-time, the meeting came to an end.
The scientists straggled out into the hall as an introductory
physics class for liberal arts majors was letting out. Colonel
Groves and his assistant made no impression in their uniforms.
After all, even at the University of Chicago, there were a lot
of uniforms these days. But the undergraduates could not stop
staring at Einstein as he walked down the hallway next to
Szilard and Fermi. The three men talked about Herr Doktor
Pick, who was rumored to have been put into a concentration
camp near Dachau, even though he was probably the out-
standing geophysicist in Europe. He was said to now be quarrying rock, Szilard said heatedly.

"They would have done it to me," Einstein said matter-of-
factly.

"No," Szilard said. "They would have made a better use of
you."

"To them, I was just a *Spieler*, a magician," Einstein said.
"By now, I would be just an old man with a number tattooed
on my forearm," Einstein added.

He bundled himself up in his floppy trenchcoat and walked
out into the windy May afternoon. The young assistant to Colonel Groves held an umbrella for the professor, then opened
the door to a Lincoln limousine as Einstein stepped in. The
white-haired old man stared at the efficient captain and shook
his head. So practical, so careful, Einstein thought. Yes, he
told himself, by now I would be in a concentration camp—or
far worse.

The young man in a captain's uniform watched the limousine drive off. Then he rummaged in his pocket for change.
He would need quite a lot of it. He had to place a long-dis-
tance call about something quite new in the world of particle
physics.

May 9, 1943,
Fort Ord, California

Hauptsturmführer-SS Hans Thost stared at the floor. He sat on a chair in his fatigues, in a small pool of light shed by one naked lightbulb in the lavatory area of the mess hall of the officers' quarters at Kriegsgefangenenlager Fort Ord. It was past midnight. The windows had been covered up with blankets so that the American sentries would not have any idea that their German charges were up so late. It was forbidden for the prisoners to congregate after 2200 hours anyway, but that was hardly the problem. General Whitlock would normally wink at a party or a theatrical after 2200. He was an easygoing man. The blankets were up on the windows so that the sentries and General Whitlock would not know that a trial was going on in the mess hall. A capital trial for the life of Hauptsturmführer-SS Hans Thost, judged by a jury of his fellow SS officers, on the charge of talking defeatism, was taking place just one mile from where the Monterey County Square Dancing Association was holding its monthly hoedown.

In front of the accused man, Joachim Trattner paced angrily. Like the other men, Trattner was dressed in starched, immaculate khaki fatigues. Behind the accused and around

him, a horseshoe of officers sat in wooden seats. At their head
was the highest-ranking officer, Oberführer Schlegel. He
scratched his chin as he listened to the evidence against
Thost. Not exactly the sign of a decisive man, Trattner
thought. One certainly never saw the Führer scratching his
chin like a Westphalian peasant. Another piece of evidence
that the Oberführer was growing weak.

"This man, entrusted by the Führer himself with the defense of the Reich, pledged on his honor to serve the Führer
and the German people unto death," Trattner said in a strong
voice. "There may be those of the Wehrmacht or the Kriegs-
marine who think that oath is void after capture. Apparently
so does this swine in front of you."

Trattner paused to glare at Thost. In the small circle of
light, Thost looked particularly pitiful. He was a man of me-
dium height, with a pale, almost pasty face. He had serious
acne scars. His eyebrows had been singed as his Leopard
Panzer Kampfwagen was hit by mortar fire in Abu Agheila.
They had not grown back. This deficiency gave him a particularly unprotected look. It was a serious setback among a
group of men who judged themselves and others on their
fierce, unyielding appearance, especially for a man accused of
a capital offense. A man who looked vulnerable and wounded
could conceivably be different, unpredictable, a wanderer
from the true path. There was no telling.

"Why did this man loiter by the fence, talking to the guard,
the Jew Ratner? Why would he tell that Jew that he was happier here than he was in Africa? An SS man happier in a cage
than fighting on his feet? What kind of *Untermensch* is he?"
Trattner placed his face a few inches away from Thost's and
stared at him. To his credit, Thost kept his eyes dry. There
were no tears. Thost looked more resolute than Schlegel,
Trattner thought with disgust.

Trattner paused for a moment. Thost took this opportunity
to speak. "If we are ever to escape, it might be useful to have
a few of the guards think that we are demoralized," Thost
began. "That was the only thing I was thinking of. . . ."

Trattner's face became an icy mask of command. "Yesssss,"

he hissed. "That was what you were thinking of. You were actually trying to help us by telling a Jew guard that you were happy being a monkey in a cage. Do you actually think that an SS man needs the help of a Jew draft dodger?" His eyes were like frozen spear points.

"If we are going to escape . . ." Thost began.

Trattner cut him off again. "Since what date is the planning of escapes the responsibility of a Hauptsturmführer?" he demanded coolly. "Since when does an SS man make his own escape plans and carry them out with the aid of a Jew?" Trattner gestured at Oberführer Schlegel. "Don't we have an Oberführer here in our midst? Would an American Army captain make plans for a general? Even they, toy soldiers, coddled weaklings, know that rank commands even in captivity. Did you take a special oath to the Führer that you are released from your duty to your Oberführer?" The Oberführer stopped scratching his chin.

Thost hung his head and stared at the floor. "I meant nothing but to help if we should ever try to escape," he mumbled.

"*Kameraden,*" Trattner said in a low bark, "I have heard far more than a few incidents with the Jew guard Ratner. With my own ears, I have heard the Hauptsturmführer tell new men here that they were lucky to be here. I have heard him tell wounded men that they would receive better care here than they would in the Reich. I have seen letters he has written to his family telling them that they have nothing to fear if they are captured by the Americans. Captured! Nothing to fear! From a race of mongrels led by the Jew Roosevelt?" Trattner paused and glared in frigid contempt. "I dare to say that if the Führer could hear an SS man talk like this, even his mighty faith in Germany might be troubled."

Several of the SS men sucked in their breath in shock at the mere mention of such a concept. Oberführer Schlegel said nothing. To himself, he thought that he had shared many of the same feelings as Thost. He had even hinted at a few of them to Trattner. He was extremely glad that rank still had a few privileges. Just to make certain that the point was made, Schlegel wearily got to his feet.

"I cannot keep silent any longer," he said. "An SS Ober-führer must be firm but fair. But in conscience toward the other men in this camp, in conscience toward those who still have the great good fortune to continue fighting for the Reich, I must say this. This man Thost is an infection in our midst. He is a gangrenous lump. He was once a man. No longer. We would be doing him and everyone else in the camp a favor if we excised this cancer among us." Schlegel looked to Trattner for approval, a gesture which Trattner noticed with secret approval. Definitely a step in the right direction. Even Schlegel was beginning to sense who was in charge.

He bowed from the waist and smiled his appreciation at the Oberführer. Sometimes it was good to appear modest.

Jan Whelchel, an Untersturmführer who had distinguished himself many times in Libya and had been an exemplar of dignity in confinement, cleared his throat. He looked up with his craggy good Aryan features. His light-blue eyes glinted in the light from the lightbulb. He caught Trattner's gaze. "If we let this man continue pandering to the glee of the Jew guards, we might just as well admit that we are defeated. I, for one, would rather die. For me, life has no meaning without a victorious Reich. I served with the Hauptsturmführer. I can tell you that he was often a laggard. This is hardly the first example of his dereliction of duty to the Führer. I think his life has no further positive contribution to make to the fatherland."

Thost looked up frantically at the men in the semicircle. "I never was a laggard. I always was eager to serve. Always. I never lagged in my devotion to the Führer. I have lost most of my sight and been made to look like a freak because of my devotion to the Führer." He pleaded with his face.

Trattner laughed harshly, then answered in a surprisingly sincere tone. "The accusations from the Front. The uncontradicted evidence of defeatism here in camp. These cannot be ignored. If we let the claims of pity keep us from our hard duty, we would not be worthy of the women and children we are still defending in the Reich." He scanned the officers. "Is there any further discussion, *Kameraden?*"

No one spoke. Thost stared at the floor. He lifted his head and looked at the unpitying faces of the SS officers. For a moment he thought he saw fear in the dimly lit face of Oberführer Schlegel. He looked to Trattner for a sign of mercy. But he saw no pity, no relenting in Trattner's decisive features. Untersturmführer Whelchel wordlessly got up and took a length of rope from his tunic. He threw it over a beam above a mess table. Then he climbed up on the table and knotted it tightly. He made the other end into a hangman's noose.

Thost's eyes widened in terror. "I beg you, Oberführer," he said, "I have no devotion but to the Führer. I made a mistake, but let me live to fight again for the Führer."

The Oberführer said nothing. The officers stood and formed two parallel lines between Thost's stool and the table above which hung the rope.

"At least die like a man," Trattner said evenly. "As an SS man, I hope you will have that dignity. Do not give the Jews the satisfaction of hearing your whining."

Thost looked at Trattner and suddenly a light came into his eyes. "Heil Hitler," he spoke clearly, clicking his heels to attention and throwing forward his right arm in a stiff salute. "I am ashamed to have humiliated you. I beg the Führer's forgiveness."

His entire countenance became alert, disciplined. He had the traces of a smile on his lips. That, together with his missing eyebrows, gave him an unworldly look which gave even Trattner a chill. But, to motivate a man to be eager to die was no small power. The chill disappeared from Trattner's spine.

Thost strode, arm forward, to the table. With one nimble vault he mounted the table. He put the rope around his neck himself. Untersturmführer Whelchel tightened the knot. Then Thost shook Trattner's hand. Whelchel jumped off the table.

"I am proud that I might at least serve as an example," Thost said, "to harden the fighting spirit of the German people. If I have done that, I die happy."

Without another word, he kicked over the table and fell to a quick death. He twitched for about thirty seconds, then was still. A small ferret of a man, Obersturmführer von Dank, took from behind a partition a sign reading, "I broke my oath to the Führer and the German people." He attached it with a string to Thost's neck.

The assembled men faced Schlegel and gave the out-stretched-arm salute. Then they took the blankets down from the windows, extinguished the light, and drifted out into the camp.

Trattner walked with Schlegel to the Oberführer's quarters. The cloudiness of the early evening had faded. Now the sky was clear, black, filled with glittering stars. It reminded Trattner of the stars above the mountains in Kitzbühel, where he had skied before the war. That was where he had first met English-speaking people, first learned a little English, first made love to an English girl, a buxom thing from a London bank on vacation in the Austrian Alps. The stars seemed to live and breathe fire from the heavens here in California, just as in the mountains of Germany.

"I will say, Thost died like an SS man," Schlegel said heavily. "He may have been a defeatist, but he had some con-science."

"I agree," Trattner said. "Yet, even his conscience was dis-eased if he allowed defeatist thoughts to pass before a Jew guard. After all, his loyalty is not to us, but to the Führer."

Schlegel coughed nervously. "So very true," he said. "That is, of course, what I meant."

"Of course," Trattner agreed. He looked sideways at Schle-gel. The man had a huge double chin, which he had not had in Libya or Tunisia. He was indeed getting fat and lazy. Still, it was pointless to quarrel with one's Oberführer. Schlegel and Trattner had important work to do together, work to win the war for the Reich. Trattner did not know as yet what that work would be, but it would surely be important. Creating factions within the camp by bringing charges against a man who had been with the Führer in Munich by 1925 was cer-tainly no way to get vital deeds accomplished. No way at all. Not yet. Soon, but not yet.

"Good night, Oberführer," Trattner said, giving a salute to

the Führer. "This was a distasteful job, but one which had to be done."

"It is never distasteful to serve the Reich," Schlegel said.

"Of course," Trattner said. "Good night."

Trattner hurried back to his cabin. As he did, he could see two American guards drinking from bottles of beer just outside the fence. They did not see him. Amazing, he thought, that we are being beaten (he would admit it to himself) by people as incredibly undisciplined as this. Soldiers who drink beer while on duty should be hanged from the nearest tree as an example to the others. If the Americans did that, they might get some action out of their troops, instead of the shameful cowardice that had marked the first American moves in North Africa at Kasserine Pass. If the American Jew-lover Eisenhower had an ounce of steel in his backbone, he would have shot every commander in North Africa.

That was not being cruel. It was being merciful to the soldiers. Why should they be led by cowards and incompetents? You do not save your soldiers' lives by losing battles. You save the women and children of your home country by promoting winning generals and shooting losing generals. The Americans mistook coddling for kindness. There was a great difference. Of course, the Americans spared themselves a great deal of unnecessary ceremony and waste about worship of Franklin Delano Roosevelt. But then why should anyone worship a cripple? Especially a cripple who had sold out his people to the Jews and the British, the gravediggers of Europe.

Trattner turned the knob on his cottage door and walked inside. He tensed instantly. There was someone else in the room. His hand went to his boot for his homemade dagger. He assumed the infighting knife combat stance. Holding the knife brought a line of sweat to his brow. He would lunge the moment he saw the intruder. It could be some ally of Thost's.

"Trattner," said a whisper, "it is a friend, *ein Kamerad*. There is work for you."

Trattner did not alter his stance as a man emerged from the shadows near his lavatory. It was Whelchel. "I beg your pardon," he said, almost matter-of-factly. "But I need a few moments of your time."

"You could see me at breakfast," Trattner said. "I do not like to be surprised by an Untersturmführer at one in the morning. People die in such surprises." He slid the knife back into his boot with a twinge of disappointment.

"That the Reich may live," Whelchel said. "Listen, something is up. Piwonka got a message this morning. It was from Himmler himself. Through the usual channels in the Red Cross."

Trattner relaxed now. He sheathed his knife and took a step backward. "Yes?" he said.

"It was for you," Whelchel said. "They have something in mind for you."

"Escape?" Trattner asked in a rush.

Whelchel shrugged his shoulders. "The Reichsführer does not confide in Piwonka," he said tartly.

Both men were silent. They heard the sound of gravel underfoot a dozen yards away, near the fence, as a sentry passed by. Probably looking for somewhere to pee, Trattner thought.

"You will have a visitor next week," Whelchel said. "Your cousin. From Santa Cruz. A woman. She will tell you more."

"I shall be ready," Trattner said.

Whelchel gave him an almost coy look. He cocked his head. "I wish you were," he said. "No disrespect intended." Whelchel looked him up and down, then gave the "Heil Hitler" and walked out into the night air.

So, Trattner thought, not all the perverts were in Röhm's SA. Well, we shall soon see about him. In the meantime, Trattner would prepare himself for whatever the Reichsführer had in store. To think that Himmler, in the middle of everything, had thought to find a chore for Trattner. Even the captives were not forgotten by the SS.

Trattner dreamt that night that he was flying in a fighter plane, wheeling and diving, strafing columns of British soldiers, then rising back up into the sun. It was wonderful.

In the morning, Corporal Toby Moffatt reported to General

Whitlock that a body had been found hanging from a rafter in the officers' mess hall. The man had a sign hanging from his neck which said something in German. Moffatt did not read German. Neither did Whitlock.

"Shall I tell the adjutant to notify the Army Service Command in Washington?" Moffatt asked.

"Of course not," Whitlock answered. He rose slowly from his desk. "A clear case of suicide. No point in disturbing Washington. Best leave it to the German guy, Schlegel, to decide what would be best. I'll take my cues from them. After all, he's one of them."

Moffatt saluted and left. General Whitlock sat down. He put his feet up on his desk. Too bad about the prisoner. But people became depressed in confinement. They saw no reason to keep living. That was a pity, but hardly reason to turn the camp upside down. Why stir up all these ridiculous rumors about secret executions and kangaroo courts? Why make it hard on everyone in the camp because of one depressed man?

If you rolled with the punches, life in this man's army went smoothly. If you looked for trouble, trouble would find you. Besides, one thing was for sure, and that was that one Kraut more or less would not mean a thing in this war.

BERLIN

WILHELM CANARIS
ABWEHR

May 10, 1943
Memorandum To: Himmler, SS,
                          Reich Research Council
Subject: Tour d'Horizon, Fission Project
Most Secret

The war as of this moment is stalemated. It is entirely possible that we have reached the utmost limits of our ability to take and hold territory. From now on, unless the enemy shows unexpected fatigue, the tide will inexorably begin to turn against us.

Manstein has conclusively taken Kharkov. We are experiencing severe difficulties in supplying him, however. When the Russians launch their counterattack, as they will, the contest will be an extremely uneven one in terms of matériel. The Russian Front in other areas north of Kharkov is deteriorating, although the rate of deterioration has definitely slowed. This is not necessarily a good sign, since it tells us that the Russians are probably concentrating their forces in the Kharkov-Ukraine area to dislodge Manstein. If Manstein is forced to retreat, it is difficult to foretell where his lines could re-form.

In North Africa, the end has been reached. The Americans and British have taken Bizerte and Tunis. There are pockets of resistance along the coast, but they cannot be resupplied. You can expect complete surrender in Tunisia any day.

There is, as yet, no sign that the Americans and British are making any serious efforts to invade Europe. General Eisenhower is displaying his usual caution in making certain that the Russians have taken away as much German strength as possible before he commits his forces. We can and do expect American and British moves in Sicily or Sardinia, but these can only be considered peripheral to the main war fronts.

Enemy war production is growing at an alarming rate, but since you have received our memorandum of May 5 on that subject, I will omit further mention here.

In Stockholm, the Soviets have brought out new proposals since Manstein took Kharkov. They were genuinely surprised at our ability to take the offensive. They have been negotiating seriously. Their latest proposal is on your desk. My personal and respectful opinion is that it is a fair proposal and that we should not be alarmed by a demilitarized Poland.

In the United States, the leading scientists in the Manhattan District have made a major breakthrough in the thermal diffusion process. I am not capable of understanding it. Attached is a separate memorandum from us on the technical dimensions of the American solution. I respectfully suggest you forward it to Dr. Diebner for analysis. We believe that the United States is at most two years from having an actual working device utilizing the uranium fission principle. The possibilities of the device are so large as to be almost impossible to grasp. According to the memo which the Jew Einstein has circulated, one such device could destroy an entire port, together with the surrounding countryside.

I can scarcely emphasize enough the significance of this project in terms of the eventual outcome of the war. The Americans believe that they will be invincible with this weapon. I daresay they are correct. Any nation which possessed such a weapon would be in a commanding position.

I can scarcely describe to you the effects of such a weapon if used in a densely settled area such as the Ruhr or the Berlin metropolitan area.

May I know what plans you have for ensuring that the Reich has caught up with the progress of the United States on this critical matter? Also for assuring the safety of the Reich from the possibility of such a weapon being used against us?

We believe the Hechingen gambit may finally be about to bear fruit. There was an item on the Geneva-Washington, D.C., wire about the recovery of bodies from a mountaintop near Strasbourg. I will keep you advised.

I would be happy to consult with you on ways and means to expedite the flow of information from the United States to the Reich.

> Sincere best wishes and a
> cordial Heil Hitler,
> Canaris

R.F. ⚡⚡
Heinrich Himmler
NACHRICHTEN-UEBERMITTLUNG

May 11, 1943
Memorandum To: Canaris
Most Secret

Your memorandum of yesterday received and read
here. The key problem in terms of the fission project
is not your fine production of American data. The
data are, sadly, too advanced to be absorbed by the
available scientific pool in the Reich at the present.
Our Reich Research Council is simply so far behind
the American level of technical competence that we
are unable to replicate the American results even
with their methods. This is particularly confidential.

I agree completely with your conclusion about the
progress of the war and the Stockholm meetings. Of
course, faith in the Führer and Teutonic fighting fury
will bring us final victory without question. Still, I
am in the process of expediting that event by means
of a change in the pool of scientific manpower available to the Reich. I am also well aware of the imper-
ative necessity for assuring that a fission device is
never used against the Reich.

To aid me in these efforts, may I have at once a
further listing of your most capable operatives in
northern California and Los Angeles, California, beyond what you have already supplied, if any? May I
also ask that you come to the chancery this afternoon
at 1700 hours to discuss the final plans for the beginning of the Siegfried Break as well as the "fruit" of

Benjamin J. Stein

Hechingen? We may need to change some of the objectives for the operation.

> Best personal regards to Magda
> and a hearty Heil Hitler,
> Himmler

May 13, 1943,
Washington, D.C.

Alice Burton peered over the top of her menu. Ugh. This was absolutely and positively the last blind date she was ever going to accept. She did not care if this guy was the top economist in the Office of Price Administration. Leon something. He was a grotesque, fat fool, who could not stop boasting about how he really tucked it to this corporation and really ruined that board chairman's weekend.

"There's this guy at General Motors, this hotshot executive named Harlow Curtice," Leon said in his endlessly droning voice. "He comes to me and he's wearing these fancy clothes like he's really hot stuff, and he gives me this big handshake and all this hooey about how he's come down from New York just to meet me."

Alice Burton tried to distract herself by studying the menu at the Mayflower Grille Room with extra care. Actually, under OPA, the prices here were not bad at all. A prime rib cost four dollars. That was high, but it did come with a salad and a baked potato. The whitefish was only two seventy-five, and Alice Burton loved broiled whitefish. Also, she always felt less sleepy after she ate broiled fish. Very wholesome. Not greasy.

Her mother's warnings about greasy food were still in her mind.

"So this jerk, this Curtice guy, thinks he's gonna put a fast one over on me. He starts to tell me that GM has a few thousand refrigerators from 1938 that they discovered in a warehouse. Did we see anything wrong with charging the same price as the 1942 models since they were basically the same thing and everything and he was just checking as a formality, and trying to pull the wool over my eyes the whole time."

Leon looked at her expectantly. He was thirty-four years old and had pimples on his chin.

"Uh-huh," Alice Burton said. She could not believe that she had bought a new red cotton-and-linen suit for this dinner. The guy had gotten a tremendous buildup from her friend Arlene Gordon. Arlene was going to hear about this.

"So I say, 'Look, if you bring them out in 1943 and they're 1938 models, you charge the same price for them as if they were used models, five years old. Try that on for size.'" Leon rubbed his stomach and stuffed another roll into his mouth. "I really did say that. I said, 'Try that on for size.'"

"Great," Alice Burton said. "I'll bet you ruined his whole day."

"I sure tried," said Leon. There was a smudge of butter on his tie. It was not alone. "Have you decided what you want? There's a special tonight. If you get the rump steak, you get dessert with it. I think we all have an obligation not to be extravagant during the war, don't you?"

It never failed. A guy who was a loser in most respects was also a cheapskate. Always. This guy was a world-class loser and a world-class cheapskate to boot. Takes a girl to a fancy restaurant and tries to shame her into ordering cheap.

"Uh, I think I'll have the broiled whitefish," Alice Burton said. "I hope that's not *too* expensive."

Leon coughed excitedly as he searched for the item on the menu. He looked visibly relieved and smiled broadly. "Have whatever you want, Alice," he said. "I like for a girl to have a good time." He chortled and raised his eyebrows suggestively. A shudder ran down Alice's spine. Could this toad, this loathsome reptile, even contemplate that she would let him touch her? Maybe, to be fair, she should just walk out of the Mayflower right then and there. She could tell him she had a flu.

She began to clear her throat. That suggested to Leon that he should talk. "The key to getting the most war production out of the workers is for them to feel that they're being treated fairly. That's why our job at the OPA is so important. You can understand that, can't you?"

Alice looked across the dimly lit room. She could see J. Edgar Hoover eating his roast beef in one corner. Senator Bankhead was his dinner companion.

"No, Leon, I don't understand," Alice said. "Maybe you could explain it to me."

Leon looked confused. "Are you pulling my leg?" he asked. "You shouldn't do that. We're all pitching in on this thing together, you know."

Alice smiled and touched her eyes with her fingers, as if they might be watering. "Just a joke, Lou," she said.

"It's Leon," he said, looking wounded. "What's gotten into you? Things must be really keeping you hopping over at the OSS. I guess that's why you're upset."

Alice Burton fixed him with a withering stare. "Leon," she said, "you know that we cannot answer any questions, no matter how indirect, about our work. I'm really surprised at you for asking."

Leon looked hurt once again. "I'm sorry," he said.

At that moment, a man in a dark-blue suit appeared behind Alice. He was a handsome lawyer of about fifty, with blue eyes and a movie actor's profile. He had a confident grin on his face. His hair was straight, parted on the right. Sam Murphy touched Alice Burton on the shoulder and smiled.

"Hey, partner," he said, "I have some bad news for you."

Alice Burton looked at him as if he were the risen Christ appearing to Peter and she were Peter. Before she could speak, Sam extended his hand to Leon and shook it cheerfully. "Hi," he said with a wink. "Sam Murphy. I'm afraid I have to take this little genius away from you. She's my top brain and I have some very heavy-duty thinking for her to do."

Leon looked abashed. He could hardly believe that Sam Murphy was standing in front of him, grinning at him. *The* Sam Murphy. The Wyatt Earp of Antitrust. Leon started to stammer, but before he could think of something witty to say, Alice and Sam were at the door, waving a cheery good-bye. Tears started to come to Leon's eyes. Alice was cute and smart, but to miss a talk with Sam Murphy . . . Well, he could always tell the people back at the OPA that he had talked to Sam Murphy, but that he was sworn to secrecy. That would set a few tongues going at the tempo back on Independence Avenue. Leon Swertlow and Sam Murphy having a talk about war production (oops, don't repeat that part), in the Mayflower Grille Room. Plus, they hadn't ordered yet. He'd just nip out. Maybe pick up a burger at the Little Tavern. Maybe three or four of them. They were only five cents each. "Order 'em by the bag"—that was their motto.

In the Lincoln sedan rushing down Connecticut Avenue, Alice Burton was beside herself with glee. Delivered from Leon by the man with the immaculate-soled shoes! She clutched Sam's arm and laughed as they passed Farragut Square.

"Sam, you must have been a lifesaver when you were a boy," she said.

"I was. At Portsmouth Priory. In swimming classes. Nobody ever even gave me a chance to try to save a life," Sam said, exhaling a huge cloud of smoke from his Philip Morris, so much that the driver started to gasp for breath.

He smiled. "Listen," he said. "Very hot news. A new communication from the same wavelength where we got the one about Siegfried. Very hot stuff." His nails were immaculate, too, Alice noticed. Probably better kept than Betty Grable's toenails.

"Sam," she said, "I hate to remind you after you just saved my life, but I never figured out what the first message was all about. The nearest I got was that it was maybe aimed at some agent here in America, someone at the top of the heap, but I never got farther than that."

"Also that it was supposed to shake up the Russians who were listening," Sam added. The car was heading down 17th Street toward the OSS offices on Constitution Avenue.

"Not to mention the Soviet agents in the OSS," she said.

Sam Murphy laughed. "Of course," he said.

In Sam Murphy's office, Alice had a shot of Courvoisier, then studied the typescript of the intercept. It was extremely simple. "Lorelei has found Alberich's cape."

Alice held the paper bearing the message in one hand and the Courvoisier glass in the other. She sat down on the brown leather, government-issued couch against the window. In the moonlight, she could see the powerful shaft of the Washington Monument gleaming over the Ellipse. She studied Sam Murphy's walls. There were prints of ducks in a marsh, prints of ducks in flight, prints of dogs holding dead ducks in their mouths. It was almost a code among wealthy gentiles. They all had pictures of ducks and none of them had their college or law school diplomas. Ducks were everywhere, as if the gentiles liked them, rather than killed them.

Jews had duck at Chinese restaurants and had their diplomas up on their walls. Only people as secure in this world as well-heeled gentiles would dare to make a stupid bird the insignia of their election to leadership and wealth.

Alice looked at the message again. Sam Murphy was looking at her expectantly. He had his feet up on his desk again. Again, the soles were spotless. "Well?" he asked with a pleasant smile. He puffed out a huge cloud of bluish smoke. "Now you have two messages. Now tell me in twenty-five words whether we have anything to worry about."

"Lorelei is the Rhine goddess, the Rhine maiden. She represents the spirits of the river. If she is out floating around somewhere too, it means that the whole force and power of the river is emerging. Since the river is really, really important in German mythology, if the river goddess is meeting up with the great warrior god, we can expect that something big is happening." Alice sipped her Courvoisier. It burned in her cheeks, then made a pleasant warm glow in her chest.

"Or," she continued, "we could go back to square one. It could be that the Germans are trying to make the Russians think that something big is going on. It could be nothing." She sighed heavily. "It's a totally random situation, Sam, unless we have some idea of just what the hell kind of answer they're getting from here. If any."

Sam Murphy frowned and fiddled with his copper navigator's lamp. It rested on his desk next to a wooden "in" tray. It had no lightbulb in it. It had no candle in it. Alice had no idea how it worked. No matter. Its significance was entirely talismanic. Like the ducks. "You know I don't think it's attractive for a pretty young woman to curse," Sam said.

"I'm sorry," Alice said. She meant it. "I don't mean to offend you. I'm really sorry. It's just a little frustrating going around with blinders in the middle of a swamp on a moonless night."

"When I first met Brigid," Sam Murphy said, "her father told me that she would make a fine wife. He said to me, 'She can cast a good line, ride a good horse, shoot a fine pistol.' You know, I've never heard that woman curse. Never."

"I'm sorry," Alice repeated. Her palms were beginning to sweat. She did not like to be on Sam's bad side.

"No problem," Sam Murphy said. "But I think your troubles are about to be over," he added.

Don't tell me, Alice thought to herself. He's leaving Brigid and coming to live with me. She said nothing. Instead, she looked at Sam levelly.

"This evening, when this came in, we had something really rare happen. Really, really rare. The system worked," Sam Murphy said.

"How do you mean that?" Alice asked.

"Very amazing," Sam Murphy said. "Almost the moment this transmission stopped, there was an answering transcription in voice, coming on the same wavelength, picked up by a ham operator in Seattle."

Alice Burton shook her head.

"Now," Sam said, "the answering transcription said, in English, very simply, 'Received and acknowledged.' That was all. That was the whole response, and then the guy went right off the air."

Alice Burton thought for a moment and said, "I'm no expert in radios, but I don't think that takes us very far. How on earth will we ever find him?"

"That's just it. That's how the system worked like a charm tonight. The ham operator who picked up the signal was a part-time Civil Defense worker. He teaches at a high school in Seattle. Elocution. Speech. He remembers the way people talk. He can remember an accent or a nasal something for years. So he recognized this voice from years before," Sam Murphy said, as if he were explaining something to a parrot.

"How did we get onto all this?" Alice Burton asked.

"That's the most amazing part," Sam Murphy said. "This fellow calls Washington, at his own expense, and tells about what he heard. And he calls the headquarters of the Civil Defense, right up on Pennsylvania Avenue. There's nobody much on duty except some kid from Georgetown who's working there at night while he studies pre-med. So he gets this message and he calls up the duty officer here at the OSS and tells him the whole thing and leaves his number. What a break, hunh?" Sam Murphy said confidently.

"Absolutely," Alice Burton answered. "How did that happen?"

"Well, this is the best part," Murphy said. "That boy's father and I play golf together out at Burning Tree. So he said he wouldn't even dream of telling the FBI if it were something that might help us here. So there you are."

"The old school tie," Alice Burton said.

"Something like that," Sam Murphy said. "We hunt together, too. Anyway, now we have something. The ham operator in Seattle swears that this is a guy who's been talking on the radio with people in Berlin for years. He's been talking in both English and German. He's their pal. Has been for ten years."

"How could he have been so dumb as to use his voice?" Alice asked.

"First of all, he's not right in the head if he's one of them, I would say," Murphy said.

"So true," Alice agreed.

"Second, what are the chances that anyone's going to be able to hear him and recognize him? That was a one-in-a-million shot," Murphy said.

Alice Burton furrowed her brow.

"I know what you're thinking. It's such a coincidence that it's not a coincidence at all. Isn't that what you're thinking?" Sam Murphy asked.

Alice Burton stood up. She smoothed her red cotton-and-linen skirt. She walked over to the window and looked out. Then she sat down. "It's an extremely large coincidence," Alice Burton said. "What would you say if there was a murder in New York of one Texan by another Texan and it so happened that the only eyewitness was the killer's next-door neighbor back in Abilene?"

"I'd say that the FBI does not have one word on the ham operator in Seattle. The man is as clean as a hound's tooth. If he's one of them, he's covered his tracks awfully damn well."

"You know I don't hold with cussin'," Alice Burton said.

Sam slammed his feet down on the floor and smiled. "No, Alice, you can't explain everything away with tricks and convolutions and ploys. People make mistakes. Coincidences do happen. They made a big mistake."

"So who is this Nazi radio operator?" Alice asked.

"He's a man in Fresno, California," Sam Murphy said. "He's an insurance man. Record of pro-Nazi sympathies, but nothing overt."

"Sic the FBI on him," Alice said with a chuckle.

"Certainly not. Hoover shares nothing with us. We share nothing with Hoover. We're going to get to the bottom of this all by ourselves and rack up some very nice points for Wild Bill along the way," Sam Murphy said, lighting yet another cigarette with his Dunhill lighter.

Oh, Jesus, Alice thought. Here it comes.

"Alice," Sam Murphy said, "how would you like to see beautiful Fresno, California?"

"Sam," Alice Burton said, "I'd love to."

Sam smiled a coy smile. He opened his desk drawer. He took out a thick railroad ticket and a wad of twenty-dollar bills, and handed them to Alice. "Don't forget to write," he said. "Let me know how you're getting along."

"I'll send you a postcard of a palm tree," she said. But Sam had already picked up a file which Alice had seen on his immaculate desk. The file was entitled "Hechingen Photo Analysis."

May 14, 1943,
East Los Angeles

Detective John Gregory Quinn hit the door like the locomotive of the Twentieth Century Limited. It was a flimsy hollow-core door, the kind that greedy Armenian landlords liked to put into big mansions when they divided them into single-room-occupancy shooting galleries. The whole place reeked of beans and onions. When John Quinn first walked in the door, he felt like it was a job for Rizzuti. As usual, though, Rizzuti was behind him and not in front. "Just in case somebody sneaks up on you," Rizzuti said.

"Fuck you," Quinn said. Then he went into the door. What the hell. He had asked Reynaldo Cruz to surrender fifteen times. All that Reynaldo could bring himself to say was, "Screw djou, cop."

The door gave way with a tearing, wrenching sound. It gave way so easily, in fact, that Quinn tripped over it as he came tumbling into the room. He fell over and rolled on the floor so that he would at least be a moving target. Reynaldo Cruz pointed a .38 right at Quinn's brain and began to squeeze the trigger. Then Reynaldo's eyes rolled upward until they looked like egg whites. Reynaldo sighed and collapsed onto the floor in a pool of urine.

By the time Rizzuti appeared, cowering along the wall, Quinn had figured out the whole thing. It wasn't really that hard. Reynaldo, who had held up the Garden of Allah liquor store on Sixth Street an hour before, had put three slugs—hollow points—into the attendant of a gas station across the street who had tried to break up the crime. The attendant, one Pat Brown, had died on his way to Hollywood Presbyterian Medical Center. If Reynaldo were taken alive, with a felony murder rap on top of a robbery charge—and they would both stick—Reynaldo would be breathing sodium cyanide up at San Quentin pretty soon.

Reynaldo wasn't that dumb. So there he was, in his undershorts and undershirt, a plate of refried beans in front of him, a rosary across his knee, his .38 in his hand, and the syringe still in his arm. He was a smart little pachuco. Why waste all that time getting the shit beaten out of you down at the station, then spend a month or two getting scared on death row, when you can cook up, shoot up, and go up the stairway to heaven? It was really a pretty smart way out, when you came to think of it.

Reynaldo's head was back, his eyes were closed now, and there was a smile on his face. It was a grim smile, but a smile nevertheless. Not stupid at all, really. Quinn would take an overdose of horse over the gas chamber at Q any day of the week.

Quinn made a mental note of the room, just in case there was an inquest. There usually was no red tape when a beaner died of a drug overdose, but it was still good to make certain of what the place looked like. Not that there was much to see. A miserable, ratty, fake Oriental rug. A green-felt sofa that had long since lost its nap. A table with a pile of Spanish-language newspapers and an empty can of sardines. A toaster. Three unopened bottles of Stroh's beer. Four cellophane packets.

On a small table in front of the couch, a candle, a wad of cotton, an eyedropper, several books of matches, a curled paper clip—the paraphernalia of a trip to eternity by the scenic route.

On the wall behind Reynaldo was a print of "The Last Supper." It was not framed, but instead affixed by thumbtacks. There were grease stains on Judas' face.

"You think he's dead?" Rizzuti asked, pointing his revolver at the dead man.

"No. I think you ought to put a few slugs into him just in case he comes back, like Lazarus," Quinn said.

"Very funny. Very good at cracking wise, ain't you?" Rizzuti said.

"Let's call the morgue for this boy," Quinn answered. "He ain't gonna be needing any more zoot suits."

"He ain't gonna be needing this beer either," Rizzuti said, tucking it under his arm. "I'm thirsty."

Three hours later, Quinn pulled his black-and-white into the parking lot of City Hall. As he walked toward the locker room, he passed Marilyn. She pulled him into a corner and gave him a brush on the lips. She looked especially perky today in her corduroy suit. It was old, but Quinn didn't care. Her eyes looked like blue diamonds from somewhere in Antarctica.

"Listen," she said. "I've worked out something really good. You're gonna like this."

Quinn could smell her perfume. It was something by Revlon. It made him excited even in the damp, cool corridors of City Hall.

"What's that, Marilyn?" Quinn asked, popping a mint into his mouth, so that he would smell good, too. "What did you work out?"

"I worked out a trip for us both to Carmel. On the city," Marilyn said. She smiled a big smile. Her teeth were crooked but small and childlike. Joan had sharp, large teeth.

"How's that, Marilyn?" Quinn asked. It sounded like a great idea.

"There's this guy that Wilshire Vice picked up on a Mann Act charge. Some band leader or booking agent or something for colleges. He's charged with transporting some college girl from Utah to be a prostitute for some guys at the studios. So he was charged by a federal court in San Francisco because that was where he first brought her into the state," Marilyn said. "I heard the girls in the file room talking about it. So the next thing you know, I was sitting at lunch next to Shirley, the girl who arranges travel, and she says that they need somebody to bring this creep back here for some I.D.s."

"And we're gonna do it, right?" Quinn asked.

"Exactly," Marilyn said. "And the city picks up the tab. See, then we can stop in Carmel on the way up there. Have a night on the beach," she whispered urgently.

"When's all this supposed to happen?" Quinn asked.

"Next week. Friday," Marilyn said. "We get five cents a mile if you drive your car. If we just eat sandwiches, we can charge for meals at restaurants, too," she said. "We might even be able to come out ahead on this whole thing."

"In every way," Quinn said with a smile. He sneaked a look into the hallway, then, when the coast was clear, kissed Marilyn longingly on the lips. She was soft, melting into his arms. Not like Joan, who was like a steel beam, utterly hard and unbending to his touch.

"I'm ready to leave right now," Quinn said. "They gonna give us municipal gas coupons?"

"All we need," Marilyn said, holding his hand.

"What's the weather like in northern California this time of year?" Quinn asked. He could see Rizzuti strolling down the hall toward them. He let go of Marilyn's hand and winked at her.

"It's cold," she said, "but don't bring any pajamas."

Quinn squeezed her hand and said, "I'm ready," and then walked along the hall to talk to Rizzuti. It was no good for Marilyn for people to gossip about her. After all, she was just a kid. Some day she would meet someone who could really settle down with her and make her happy. She did not need a brooding harp, a man with enough discontent and frustration to sink a cruiser.

He would go with her to San Francisco, and they would have a great time. But really, Marilyn deserved someone a lot better, and that was the truth. When it happened, though, when Marilyn found the man who would treat her the way

she should be treated, John Gregory Quinn was going to be a
plenty sad cop. That was when he might ask Rizzuti for a
couple of those cellophane bags of smack that Rizzuti had
copped off the table in Reynaldo's room when Rizzuti thought
John Quinn was not looking. If it felt that good to Reynaldo,
it might feel good to him, too.

May 15, 1943,
Monterey, California

Otto. That was the man's name. Otto Seamans. It was a perfectly ordinary name. Maxine Lewis certainly did not understand why Otto had made such a big deal out of not telling her his name forever and ever. Really, who cared anyway? What did a name matter. "A rose for all its sweetness would smell just as sweet by another name." Or something like that. Poetry was never Maxine Lewis' strong point. Anyway, she knew what she meant. Still, maybe Himmler had told him not to tell her his name.

Maxine Lewis thought about all of this while Otto drove his new Studebaker along Del Monte Drive off Highway 1 toward Fort Ord. As usual, the sky was a dazzling, magnificent crystalline blue. As far as Maxine could see, the ocean broke and broke again and reflected the sunlight in a million billion places, making light and shadow across an endless plane of water. I love this country, Maxine Lewis thought. Beyond what anyone could imagine love, that is how much I love this country. Not the people or the things people made. But what God made.

On the car radio, a band played "Tiger Rag," and not very well at that. She preferred the Tommy Dorsey version. Then the news came on KPEN. Most of it was depressing war news about how many hundreds of tons of bombs had been dropped on the Reich by British and American bombers. A lot of the rest was about fighting in some island named Attu up near Alaska. Maxine did not have the slightest idea why anyone was fighting near Alaska. If it was the Germans, they would do a lot better to fight it out in Russia. Then there was some news on about heavy fighting between the British and the Japanese in Burma. Some place called Buthidaung. The announcer spelled it.

There were some commercials in which Clark Gable asked everyone to work even harder and buy even more war bonds. "To put nails in the coffins of the White Race," Otto said in a hiss as he heard the patriotic musical flourishes at the end of the commercial.

"I never buy them," Maxine said. "I tell people at the office that they're a bad investment. They only pay two-and-a-half percent interest."

"Very clever of you," Otto said. "That makes you sound like a Jew. Talking about interest and money."

"I hadn't thought of that. I just can't bear to think of my money going to buy bombs that will kill people in Germany," Maxine Lewis added. "I can't bear to think of the trees and the mountains being disfigured by bombing either."

"I understand completely," Otto said with a tight smile.

The announcer on KPEN then came on the air with society news from San Francisco. "Bitsy" Crocker and "Bootsy" Stanford and "Muffy" Hopkins were giving a big War Relief Ball on the roof of the Fairmont Hotel. Tickets were *the* prized item in this year's social calendar. They were two hundred and fifty dollars a couple, and people were killing themselves to get tickets.

"Can you believe this?" Maxine Lewis asked Otto. As she waited for an answer, she noticed that he was wearing a wool suit again. He was sweating like a pig, too. This time it was a brown wool suit with a houndstooth pattern. It was a nice suit, but Maxine could not for the life of her understand why anyone would wear wool in eighty-degree weather, even if there was a pleasant onshore breeze. Maxine herself wore a white cotton sunback dress. It was designed to show off her best features so that the guards would never dream she was anything but a dish. She wore no stockings between her feet and her high-heeled pumps. Let the soldiers get a load of that.

The announcer was going on about how "Tina" Gianini was so happy that Mrs. Roosevelt was coming out for a really substantial bond drive kickoff at the Lockheed plant in Sunnyvale, which would be followed by a white tie dinner dance at the Woodside Hunt Club.

"The Führer understands this," Maxine said. "The entire foundations of National Socialism are about a society in which people cannot rape the land, pillage it, destroy it, make it ugly, and then make great fortunes for themselves. That is what the National Socialist movement is about, for me. Free people, under one leader, respecting and loving the land."

"Good, Maxine. Very good," Otto Seamans said in a soothing voice. "Now, Maxine," he said, "do you understand just exactly what you are supposed to be doing when you get to Fort Ord? We've been over it several times, haven't we?"

Maxine Lewis smiled sarcastically. "I don't need to be talked to as if I were a child," she said. "I'm perfectly capable of remembering what you told me."

"I think it would be best if you spoke only in English while you are at the camp," Otto Seamans said. "That would arouse the least suspicion. They may snoop on you if you speak German."

"Otto," Maxine said, "I've told you ten times that I can barely speak German." She laughed cynically. "So that's not going to be a problem, is it?"

"If you're questioned, where do you know Trattner from? What is your relation?"

Maxine sighed. Really, this was getting to be the least little bit boring. But she would go along. "I am from Halle. I was born there, but we emigrated to America when I was still a baby. My father and Trattner's mother's sister's husband were brothers. They both died in World War I. I have only met

Trattner once, on a vacation in Austria in 1936. I had no idea he was a Nazi and I am heartsick about it." She added with a mock whimper, "And he seemed like such a *nice* boy."

Otto said, "Go on."

"I have been married and divorced once. My husband was a Jew." She paused. "Do I have to say that part?"

Otto exhaled loudly. "This cover story was made up at the Reich Chancery, Maxine," he said.

Maxine drummed her fingers against the car's dashboard. It really wasn't new after all. It was just shiny. Otto obviously took good care of it. "Okay," Maxine said. "My first husband was a Jew, but he was a gambler, so I left him. But I came to admire the Jewish people very much because of their energy and ambition," Maxine said sarcastically. Just saying the words made her sick.

"Good, good," Otto Seamans said.

"I am hoping that by visiting my cousin Joachim, I can help him to convince the other prisoners what a bad man Hitler is and how Germany is going to be ruined by the war." Maxine felt queasy just saying it. "Is that right?"

"Exactly," Otto said. "You are a good learner." He reached out to pat her on the leg. She slapped his hand sharply. He withdrew it without changing his expression.

"I learn my lines. You stay behind yours," she said.

"A comradely touch is not wrong," Otto Seamans said as the car swung up Eucalyptus Road toward the guard house at the entrance to Fort Ord. "But I will respect your wishes."

"I should goddamn well hope so," Maxine Lewis said. "By the way," she asked casually, "did you ever hear anything more about that business with Trixie? Anybody miss her?"

Otto slowed the car down and stared coolly into Maxine's face. "Who?" he asked. "I never heard of anyone named Trixie."

Maxine looked out her window at the ocean. The ocean knew Trixie. The ocean probably understood Trixie better than Otto or anybody else ever had. "Never mind," Maxine said. "Forget I even mentioned it."

"I really don't know what you're talking about," Otto said. But the sweat stood out clearly on his upper lip.

"I said, forget it," Maxine Lewis said. She felt cold, but the feeling passed. What a creep to have to work with. Jeeze, what an oddball.

Otto Seamans' Studebaker climbed up the long driveway to the post guard house. The white clapboard structure glistened in the morning sun. Two smartly dressed MPs saluted as Otto slowed down the Studebaker. One of the MPs, a handsome fellow with red hair, leaned down to the window and asked where they were going.

In a sorrowful voice, Otto Seamans told the guard that it was visiting day at the P.O.W. camp. He was bringing this young woman to see a distant cousin who was a P.O.W.

"He's a lucky guy," the MP said, getting a look at Maxine's boobs. "Those P.O.W.s have it pretty good."

"Yes, really better than they deserve," Otto Seamans said. "After what they're doing in Europe."

The MP squinted at Otto to see if he were Jewish. Might be. "Actually, once they're here, they're pretty good guys," the MP said. He hoped it might get a rise out of Otto, but Otto stared straight ahead.

"They're up at the playing field. Straight ahead and your second right. You can't miss it. They're playing the base team in soccer. You can probably hear the shouting right now," the MP said. He figured Otto was a Jew for sure and the idea of the Nazis whooping it up, playing soccer, would really get to him.

"Thank you very much," Otto said. He put the Studebaker into gear and headed up the hill. He drove past the red-brick Presidio of the old Fort Ord, past a line of wooden warehouses with metal roofs, past a post exchange, and then turned right down a slight incline.

As soon as he made the turn, both he and Maxine could hear wild shouting. It was so loud and there were so many people shouting that they could not make out what was being shouted, except for a great many catcalls and cheers. But once the Studebaker was parked and Otto and Maxine were at the edge of the field, they could hardly believe what they saw.

On a regulation soccer field, two teams in athletic costumes were frantically kicking a black-and-white ball around a field. The players charged into each other, punched and kicked at each other, dove into piles on the ground, all to chase a little ball. On the sidelines, on bleachers, hundreds, if not thousands, of soldiers and civilians watched the game intently. It was a hometown athletic event. The crowd, mostly dressed in casual sporting outfits, were eating hot dogs, drinking Coke, and laughing to beat the band.

"Where are the prisoners?" Maxine asked.

Otto did something rare. He laughed. He gestured at the players. "That team," he said. "Those are the Germans. Look how well they play."

Maxine stared in surprise. The P.O.W. team did indeed play fiercely, shouting and urging each other on. They looked as fit and tanned as any men Maxine Lewis had ever seen. In their soccer shorts, their leg muscles bulged as they caromed across the field, following the ball. Maxine Lewis marveled at the resilience of the German soldier, to keep so strong in confinement.

"And those are the Germans," he said, gesturing with his chin toward a group of men and women in the stands. They looked virtually indistinguishable from the other spectators, except for their khaki fatigues, their long-billed caps, and, upon closer examination, their swastikas on their breast pockets. In and among them were many young and middle-aged women. The prisoners usually sat up straight on the bleachers. Many of the women leaned against them, often putting their arms around them as well.

"Are those women prisoners?" Maxine asked.

Otto smiled. "Not at all, Maxine. They are American women from Monterey who are, ahem, friends—yes, good friends of the prisoners."

Maxine looked startled. "Are you kidding me? The Americans allow them to have women come to visit them?"

There was a loud scream from the German section of the

stands as a handsome, rugged-looking German with blonde hair and fine features kicked home a goal past a lunging American goalie.

"The Americans allow the Germans to pretty much come and go as they please. They place the soldiers under guard. But the officers, like the men here, they are allowed to simply sign their word that they will not try to escape. Then they can have passes for work in town," Otto said.

"For work in town?" Maxine asked. "They work in town?"

"Only in nonmenial tasks," Otto said. "After all, they are officers. They work at libraries, at banks, some work in stores." Otto Seamans smiled again. "They have Aryan good looks. They have charm. They are real men. So they have no trouble attracting friends."

Maxine was confused. This was obviously some kind of trick by the Americans to break the fighting spirit of the German prisoners, but it also had some spark of generosity about it. Well, there was an easy explanation. The people who felled the redwoods and the people who fought the wars were two entirely different groups. One group had no semblance of generosity whatsoever. The other were decent, normal Americans, many of them of Aryan descent. That explained it.

"And there, dear Maxine, is your cousin, Joachim Trattner. Look happy when I point him out," Otto Seamans said. He pointed at the man who had just kicked in a goal for the German side. "Surely you remember him?"

Maxine looked at him carefully. He was one handsome fellow. He reminded Maxine of a younger Tyrone Power, with blonde hair. Really perfect features.

There was a wild dash of men and soccer ball on the playing field. Trattner disappeared into a crush of men. When he emerged, he was kicking the soccer ball along, staying just inside the sideline. He stepped nimbly around two American players who sought to kick the ball away from him. Then, in an instant, he moved his foot from right to left across the ball and sent it flying into the goalie's net with a rush of cheers. Trattner threw up his hands and smiled. Then there was a loud whistle from a referee.

The German players gathered in a huddle. There were arms and legs going in all directions and then Trattner emerged on the shoulders of his teammates, smiling and shouting in German.

Maxine was impressed. Even among German heroes, Trattner stood out as a hero. The American players beamed and patted the German players on the back. There was obviously respect for this man even from enemy soldiers. Quite a guy, Maxine thought. I can see big things happening with this guy. Very big things.

Later, as Trattner and his teammates were leaving the field, a heavyset American in uniform, with stars on his shoulders, walked onto the field. He presented Trattner with a huge loving cup trophy and shook his hand. To Maxine's shock, Trattner responded by giving the arm's-length Heil Hitler salute. She gasped and opened her mouth. Maybe Trattner would be disciplined for the salute, she feared. But instead, General Whitlock simply returned the salute.

Otto Seamans said, "The Americans have learned to respect the German fighting man and his customs. They think they are de-Nazifying the prisoners, but it is the other way around. Our values are too strong for their weakness." He thrust out his chin and laughed harshly.

Maxine nodded. "I can understand that," she said.

After the game, there was a picnic given by the German prisoners for their guests. On a large, grassy field, surrounded by eucalyptus trees, there were a number of wooden picnic tables. The prisoners had decked out the tables in red-and-white tablecloths. A field kitchen staffed by German enlisted men dispensed sauerkraut and sausages. A small band of noncoms from the Wehrmacht played light German marching tunes and fast waltzes. The noise of the band wafted out over the field and across the base. American guards walked among the prisoners, slinging Thompson submachine guns.

At one corner of the field, there was a display of artwork and handicrafts made by German prisoners. There was an excellent oil portrait of Frederick the Great which had been painstakingly crafted by Oberführer Schlegel. Piwonka had a miniature Rhine castle, complete with Rhine maidens. There were innumerable model Messerschmitts and Stukas. General Whitlock had hesitantly requested that no portraits of Adolf Hitler be displayed and the Oberführer had agreed, since this was a mixed prisoner and American day.

Maxine Lewis and Trattner strolled by the edge of the field, as far as possible from any prying guards. Trattner still wore his playing outfit. Maxine Lewis was intrigued by the powerful musculature of his arms and back.

At a discreet distance behind the couple, Otto Seamans walked, head bowed, arms behind his back, hands resolutely clasped.

"Are you happy here, Joachim?" Maxine asked. It was a dumb question, but she was afraid that people were listening. Maybe reading lips with telescopes or something. "Are they treating you well?"

Trattner looked at her with his blue eyes blazing. "Are you mad?" he demanded. "Are you stark crazy? How can an SS man be happy behind prison fences?"

"I'm sorry," Maxine Lewis said hurriedly. She had no idea he would be such a grouch. But, wow, was he good-looking! A real Nordic god.

"They treat us generously here. I cannot deny that. I eat better than I did in Germany when I was a student," Trattner said. "I am sorry. I did not mean to leap down your throat." The Nordic god even managed a smile.

"I can understand the strain," Maxine Lewis said. "I often feel as if I'm a prisoner, too."

They changed direction and headed toward an unused water tank. When they got there, Trattner leaned against the tank and said, "Why would a beautiful woman like you think of herself as a prisoner?" He stared at her chest. America was a really bounteous land.

"Oh, I don't know," Maxine said. "People just see me and they think I'm one kind of woman and then they get this idea about me and really I'm a totally different kind of woman." She flushed.

"Of course," Trattner said. "I understand." In fact, he did

not understand at all. How many different kinds of women could there be, after all? There were little girls. There were women to bear children. Women to satisfy men. And there were mothers. What kind of woman could Maxine possibly be? But he did not want to start a quarrel with a woman with such fine breasts. He wanted the breasts and not an argument. The last woman he had slept with had been an Italian woman orderly with the Italian Twelfth Army in Libya. What a pig! She had thicker body hair than he did.

"Men think that I have no feelings," Maxine Lewis said. "I know that German men are different, but American men just think of me as a toy. Just something to play with."

"How insulting," Trattner said. "That would never be tolerated in the Reich." He looked at her seriously. She smiled and batted her eyes. Good God, he thought. All breasts and no brains.

Toby Moffatt, the American guard, ambled by Trattner and Maxine. He took a look at Maxine's bosom, looked at Trattner, and winked. Trattner did not make any response. Then Moffatt moved on. Jesus, he thought to himself, these Krauts really do have something. I don't know what the hell it is, but it's something. Otto Seamans watched him go.

"In the Reich," Trattner said, "we would treat a woman like you with the respect that a *deutsches Mädchen* deserves." With that, he leaned forward and kissed her hand.

Maxine Lewis felt a thrill. How gallant this man was. How understanding. And what a looker! She felt a warmth which she rarely felt. She wished she were back at her apartment on Water Street with this man. He had a substance to him that her husband—that louse—did not even approach.

General Whitlock came strolling up to Trattner and Maxine. He bowed politely to Maxine and patted Trattner on the back. "That was a fine game," he said. "Where'd you learn to play like that?"

Without hesitation, Trattner answered, "At SS training camp in Thuringia."

"And this lovely lady is your cousin, I understand," General Whitlock said.

"Yes, General. May I present my cousin, Miss Maxine Lewis. General Whitlock. Our very kind host."

General Whitlock bowed again and shook Maxine's hand. Maxine noticed that his hands were fat. Also sweaty. Still, she smiled. Best to lull him into false confidence. "You run an out-standing camp, General, if I may say so."

That pleased General Whitlock so much that he giggled with pleasure. "I try, Miss Lewis. I try to keep everyone happy until this little misunderstanding in Europe is over and done with."

Inwardly, Trattner bristled. "Misunderstanding"! That was the life-and-death struggle of the Aryan race. Nothing less. If General Whitlock did not understand that, he was a fool. Of course, Trattner already knew that General Whitlock was a fool. In fact . . .

Trattner cleared his throat deferentially. "General Whit-lock," he asked, "may I ask your permission to have my cousin Maxine accompany me to my quarters while I change my clothes? She is very shy. I would hate to leave her here with all these strangers. And I really must shower and change. I will remember your kindness if you allow this."

Whitlock hesitated for a moment. He wasn't running a whorehouse. But, what was the point of his acting as a guard-ian for a woman who was obviously no angel, even if she were a cherub. "I will make an exception for you, Obersturmbann-führer, because you were so helpful in answering the inquiries from Washington about the suicide of your comrade, Thost. But please keep it between us. I do not want to be deluged with requests of this kind. There may be other soldiers who have cousins."

Trattner clicked his feet together, making a dull smack, be-cause he was wearing athletic shoes, which Whitlock had al-lowed him to buy in Monterey. "I appreciate this," he said.

Maxine blushed.

Ten minutes later, Trattner's face was buried between Max-ine Lewis' perfect breasts as she lay on his bunk staring at a portrait of Adolf Hitler. Trattner, for his part, realized far bet-ter just what he had been missing. He had to get some of this regularly, without question. If he had to listen to her idiocy, that was a small price to pay. A very small price.

They lay on Trattner's bed for two hours, alternately smoking, talking, and making love. "I have never known a more beautiful woman than you," Trattner said, pressing his lips to her neck. Or a stupider one, he thought.

Maxine ran her fingers along Trattner's chest. She felt as if a new avenue of feeling in her emotional road network had been opened up this afternoon. Whole new vistas of mountains and redwoods, more richly misted than she had ever seen, more ringed with rainbows and hazy sunlight. It was like entering an enchanted forest above Carmel.

"Have you ever seen the redwoods in the hills above the ocean at Santa Cruz?" she asked him.

"*Niemals*," he said. "Never."

"They are lordly, magnificent, designed by God to be an inspiration to all mankind. They live for thousands of years. And people cut them down to put siding on tract houses. Can you really believe that?" She did not wait for an answer. "A man like you understands instinctively just exactly what I am talking about. Nature is beautiful, overflowing, kind to a responsive humanity." She curled against Trattner's leg. "I feel that you're like those redwoods." She laughed, embarrassed. "Not just, well, you know. But because you are strong. Because your strength is inspiring. Because you are kind to a woman who responds to you."

"Is a redwood tree actually red?" Trattner asked.

"As red as blood," Maxine said, staring so hard at him that her blue eyes looked hollow.

God, Trattner thought. An escapee from a sanitarium.

Trattner kissed Maxine Lewis again. They made love for a fourth time in the cottage. The sun was beginning to set outside while Maxine got dressed to rejoin Otto.

As she put on her panties, he pulled her to him to embrace her and feel her. "You are a very remarkable woman," he said. He could not think of anything else to say.

She whispered in his ear. "Whatever they have in mind for

us, I'm ready. I don't care what it is. I don't care how rough the road is. Just show me where it starts."

Trattner looked her in the eye. "What do you think it is?" he asked. Could any secret have been entrusted to this cow?

"Maybe to help you get back to Germany," she said in a hushed whisper. "That could be it."

Trattner looked like he might burst with excitement. "That could be," he said. "That would be paradise." Then he regained control of himself. "I'm being foolish," he said. "I will do what I am asked to do."

"That's all any of us can do," Maxine said.

Trattner brought Maxine back to Otto Seamans, who looked as if he might have a stroke right there in front of the models of Stukas and Messerschmitts. "Thank you, Cousin Otto, for bringing along Maxine. We have had so much to talk about."

Otto smiled thinly. "It was always my pleasure," he said. "I hope she talked you into at least thinking about just what Hitler and that crowd are doing to Germany, to the whole world. I know it's hard for you, but you might at least consider that you've been wrong."

As he spoke, a guard named Ratner listened intently. Otto had befriended him while Maxine was away. Now Otto made the relationship pay off. Ratner looked encouraged by what Otto said to his cousin. But Trattner was the perfect foil. Otto beamed inside as Trattner said, "I have my obligations to my Führer and to my fatherland. Nothing you can say can change that."

Ratner shrugged his shoulders. At least the guy in the wool suit had tried. Trattner was an impossible nut to crack anyway. That guy would still be saluting Hitler when Berlin was part of Russia.

Otto looked helplessly at Ratner. Both men exchanged resigned smiles at Trattner's intractability. Then Trattner kissed Maxine's hand and the party was over.

In the car, heading up the Pacific Coast Highway in the gathering evening, Otto seethed with rage. "I see that certain men may not give you a brotherly touch, while others may spend the afternoon alone in a cottage with you," he hissed.

"I am not at all certain that this is what the Reich has in mind for you. I am not certain that you were brought into this to be a concubine."

Maxine looked at his sweating, weaselly face. "How the hell do you know what I was doing? You some kind of peeping Tom? Some kind of pervert?"

Otto said, "I am only guessing. That is all. Just guessing. Do you have a guilty conscience?" His upper lip was now sweating profusely.

Maxine Lewis snickered and crossed her legs. She allowed her sundress to ride up to her knees. She noticed Otto staring at her. She rolled down the window to breathe the fresh ocean air. "I don't have a guilty conscience. I did not endanger a major project of the Führer and his minister, one Heinrich Himmler, by tricking an innocent follower of the Reich into helping me murder his little floozie. I think we had better get straight who's up and who's down, you little creep." She looked over at Otto. "Forget the cross-examinations. Forget the touching. Forget your dirty mind about me and Joachim. Just do your job and I'll do my job. Get it, Otto?"

Otto let his breath out slowly. "Anything you say," he told her after a minute of silence. Women are all alike, he thought. They get one little thing on you and they try to break your balls. Why couldn't the Reichsführer have hooked me up with a man? He set his jaw and drove on.

Back at his cottage at Kriegsgefangenenlager Fort Ord, Trattner's day was coming to a close. Trattner lay on his bunk reading *The Decline of the West.* He thought about what had happened that day. He did not know what god of good fortune had sent him Maxine Lewis. He knew that Berlin had arranged it. He also knew that he was more serenely ready to do the Führer's bidding than ever in his life. To reach into an enemy prison camp and give him a woman, a beautiful, voluptuous woman to satisfy his needs, even if she was completely stupid—that was power. If the Führer could do that, the Führer could do anything.

Trattner did not want to think excessively about Maxine as a person. She was an excitable, emotional woman of low intellect. He must be the strong, cool one in the situation. As a duo of emotionally wound-up, story-book lovers, their usefulness to the Führer would be nil. He was not a child at Heidelberg to be infatuated after one afternoon of love. It would be easy for him to lose his concentration to a fellow servitor of the Reich. Easy, but wrong. He must stay above emotion, devoted only to his duty, whatever that duty might be.

Yet he could still smell her perfume on his chest. He could still smell her on his thighs. She might be stupid, but when she was there, she was all there. Yes, it would be a struggle to stay committed only to his oath as an SS man, but he would win the struggle. To clear his mind, he began to think how long he should wait before drawing up defeatism charges against Oberführer Schlegel. He felt the knife in his boot. A tingling ran down his spine.

May 16, 1943,
Princeton, New Jersey

The old man at the desk looked around the room as if he were in a daze. He held a writing pad on his knee with one hand, then lifted his head to examine the hundreds of books, the foot-high stacks of papers, the walnut tray of letters from that day's mail. He rubbed his hand on his brown leather jacket. He stared down at his baggy slacks. He absently pulled the old necktie which he used as a belt tighter around his stomach. He put the pad on top of a stack of scientific journals. His eyes darted among the many pipes and the smoking tobacco on his desk. He found a pipe and stuffed it full of tobacco from a metal container that said Balkan Sobranie.

Then Albert Einstein turned to his visitor and smiled. The visitor, Miss Dale Graham, age twelve, from 116 Mercer Street, two doors down from Albert Einstein, smiled in return. She shifted in her well-upholstered seat and adjusted the hem of her white taffeta dress. Her blue eyes opened wide as she watched the flames shoot out of the bowl of Einstein's pipe while he held a large kitchen match to it and puffed in and out. She rubbed a freckle on her nose, then coughed discreetly. After all, the old man might have forgotten why she was there.

"I am thinking, dear child," Einstein said. "Why can't you make your calculations come out to give you the exact area of a circle? Why can't you make *pi* come out to be an even number?"

Dale Graham smiled happily. He had not forgotten. Miss Moore and all those other snotty people at Gouverneur Morris Junior High were sure gonna be surprised when she got Albert Einstein to tell just exactly what number you were supposed to come out with when you divided the area of a circle by the square of the radius. Miss Moore was just a mean old lady with bad breath. Dale Graham was darned if she was going to believe her when Miss Moore said that no one knew exactly why the relation of the circumference of a circle to its diameter was an endlessly repeating decimal. That might be all Miss Moore knew, but it surely was something her neighbor, Professor Albert Einstein, knew all about.

For as long as she could remember, Dale had heard about the smart man who lived in the white frame house at 112 Mercer Street. He was supposed to be famous all over the world. Everyone was afraid to talk to him. But that made no sense at all. Because just yesterday, Dale's dad said that everyone in the physics department said that Professor Einstein wasn't stuck up at all, but was just an ordinary, sort of dreamy man. Dale Graham bet that if Professor Einstein had a little girl, he would take her to see *Gone With the Wind*, which her dad said was no kind of movie for kids. Anyway, Dale Graham had gone up to the front door at 112 Mercer, rung the bell, and Professor Einstein had answered the door just as if he were expecting her.

Now he took a long pull on his pipe and laid down the pipe on the desk. It tilted to the left. A burning ember fell out onto the desk surface, but Einstein ignored it.

"Dale," he said, looking at her exactly as he looked at Leo Szilard, "a circle is an infinite number of points on a plane, all equidistant from a midpoint."

"Uh-huh," Dale Graham said. "That's why the radius is the same at every point."

Even Dale's mom, who was really a pill, told everyone that Dale was a smart little girl.

"Very well then," Einstein said. "The key word is *infinite*. If there are an infinite number of points, we can never say for certain how many points there are in the circle. That makes sense to you, doesn't it?"

"I think I understand," Dale said.

"An infinite number of points. Not like three cars in a row at a traffic light. An infinite number of points. Like an infinite number of cars. Yet there is only one midpoint in the center. Correct?" Professor Einstein smiled as he asked the question. His brown eyes were like the eyes of a particularly sensitive child. Even Dale Graham felt moved by the force of their longing, as if they were looking beyond the world as it was, for a far better world.

"I think I get it," Dale Graham said.

"If there are an infinite number of points," he said, "then the relation of the midpoint to the infinite number of points can only be an infinite number. Do you see? It is like the relation of one grain of sand to all the grains of sand on the beach. That number must be infinite in theory. That is why the decimal in *pi* keeps repeating indefinitely." He looked concerned about whether Dale followed him. He held out his hand and took her small hand. "Do you follow me?" he asked again.

Professor Einstein's gaze shifted. He stared out the window at the maple tree just beyond the wide sash aperture. His eyes misted over slightly, seemingly lost in a sad thought. His face relaxed, as if he were starting to fall asleep. The afternoon sun poured through the leaves of the tree and made dappled shadows on the paneled walls of Einstein's study. For a moment, Einstein could remember explaining other problems to other students at Berlin University, at the Kaiser Wilhelm Institute. He could remember walking with Professor Infeld or Professor Bloch or Professor Balch, or any number of other colleagues who were now being carried in cattle cars to Dachau and Auschwitz. There were long afternoons of talk about fields and forces and particles. The sunlight there passed through the linden trees onto the grassy lawns of the institute. The chats lasted for hours. It seemed to Einstein that time at the institute in Berlin was like the train he used to explain the theory of relativity. It went on and on until it finally became pure energy, lasting, indestructible, permanent.

After Einstein left Germany, the thugs had come to his office, written JEW TRAITOR on the walls, burned his papers, and turned his private laboratory into a lavatory. That was Nazi humor.

Einstein turned back to Dale Graham. His gaze sharpened. He smiled at her. "I wish I could explain it to you better," he said. "It has been a long time since I was a teacher." He looked at the innocent girl in her white taffeta dress and then deep into her childish blue eyes. There was no anger in them. Only trust and hope. The professor could remember other blue eyes, hot, blazing, angry, like the eyes of wolves. The eyes of young men in his classes at the university in his final semester in the spring of 1932. The eyes belonged to men who asked questions. "Is this Aryan physics, Professor Einstein, or Hebrew physics?" One of them actually was so benighted and ignorant as to ask that question.

"I have to go home now," the little girl in the taffeta dress said. "Mommy said that if I got home early, I could help her bake chocolate-chip cookies. She had to save up her coupons for two months to get enough."

"I wish I could have been more helpful," Einstein said mournfully. He stood up politely to show her out. He picked up his pipe and puffed on it again, but it had gone out.

As Dale Graham walked down the stairs, she tried desperately to remember what Einstein had said to her about the circle being infinite and that was why *pi* was infinite. If she could remember that and tell Miss Moore, she would get an A and then her father would just have to take her to see *Gone With the Wind*. Ha-ha on her mom anyway.

Just at the moment that Miss Dukas, Einstein's angular, cardigan-wearing secretary, let Dale Graham out the front door, a DeSoto pulled up in front of the house at 112 Mercer Street.

A man with a heavy topcoat despite the spring temperatures hopped out and opened the back door. A trim man with a short beard and a homburg and salt-and-pepper hair walked heavily up the steps. Miss Dukas hugged the man with the beard and kissed him on the cheek, after which she gave a sort of curtsy. The man's cheeks were unshaven. His eyes were bloodshot and fatigued.

"How is the Herr Professor?" Louis Cantrowitz, head of the Jewish National Fund, asked Miss Dukas.

"He is expecting you," Miss Dukas said.

In Einstein's living room, Louis Cantrowitz waited and paced. The room was large and dim. It was a little bit of Berlin taken away intact and placed in an American college town, Cantrowitz thought. There were the expressionist paintings. There was the violin stand. There was the pair of Russian icons and censers, blackened by smoke. There was the dark-green rug and the solid-oak coffee table.

Einstein padded in, wearing tennis shoes and smoking his pipe. He looked at Cantrowitz for a moment as if he could not remember who the philanthropist was. Louis Cantrowitz might be the owner of the largest chain of department stores in the mid-Atlantic states, but to Einstein a subatomic particle was more familiar, more easily recalled. He was still considering whether he had truly understood whether *pi* was infinite because of the infinite number of points around a midpoint or for some other, totally different reason. By God, he wished Professor Balch were here to discuss this problem with him. He understood the most complex things and even joked about them to explain them to his students, among whom was Albert Einstein, if the truth were known. Einstein should have pleaded more persuasively with Balch for him to leave Germany when there was still time. God in heaven, human life was so complex, so unpredictable. It made fields of gravity and magnetism appear elementary by comparison. His visitor brought him back to the present sharply.

"I have to beg you to do something," Cantrowitz said after a moment of greetings. "This time we have no doubt."

He sighed heavily and sat down on the ornate beige couch. He wiped his forehead. There were bands of sweat running across it.

"We spent the entire night talking with refugees from Poland," Cantrowitz said. "There is no longer any question about the camp at Ozwiecim, Auschwitz. It is an extermination camp. They are killing Jews by the hundreds of thousands."

Einstein sat forward in his chair. He looked as if he had been struck. "I cannot believe it. Even for Hitler, this is too incredible."

"There is no doubt of it, Professor," Cantrowitz said. "If there were even any question, I would spare you this. But there is no doubt."

Einstein buried his face in his hands. The hands were soft, smooth, large, like the hands of a manchild who did not understand how cruel life could be. The hands were deceptive. Einstein did understand, Cantrowitz knew. He understood everything.

"How can they even kill so many in such a small place?" Einstein asked.

Cantrowitz inhaled deeply. "They bring them there in railroad cars. They take them to huge gas chambers, as big as movie theaters, and tell them they are going to have showers. Then they gas them. Women, men, children—everyone. They strip them naked and take the fillings from their teeth. They melt down the gold into bars. They use the gold to buy high-carbon steel. They burn the bodies down to a powder. They use the powder for fertilizer."

Einstein rocked back and forth in his chair. "Dear God," he said. "Dear God."

"They are killing five thousand each day at that one place," Cantrowitz said. "Five thousand a day!"

"Oh God," Einstein said. He felt as if he were floating in midair with no moorings, no gravity, no substance, no anything to hold him in place.

"You must go to Roosevelt," Cantrowitz said firmly. "Only

you have the prestige to make him realize what is right and wrong."

"Five thousand a day," Einstein said. "For that many to be killed, they must be running an assembly line of death. A whole mass production of murder." Tears came to his eyes. He looked out the window. He could see three children playing tag in the afternoon warmth of America. Five thousand a day in Auschwitz. The children threw a red rubber ball to a white dog, who caught it and brought it back to the children in its mouth.

"If the Allies would only bomb the railheads into the town, the whole operation would be thrown off kilter. Maybe not stopped, but slowed down," Cantrowitz said, breathing heavily. "You must persuade the President to do it."

"It cannot take much persuading," Einstein said. "If the facts are laid before him, that is all it will take, surely. He is not a brilliant man, but he is a decent man."

Cantrowitz stood up and walked back and forth twice. "I would have said that myself, until very recently," he said. "But the fact is that Roosevelt has known about this for at least a year. Morgenthau has been asking him to help for more than two years. He has not ordered the Army to bomb the railways at all. He will not even allow Jewish representatives to meet him any longer on the issue."

"I find that hard to believe," Einstein said.

"I did, too," Cantrowitz said. "I assure you that it is true. Only if a man of your stature goes to the President can he possibly be convinced. That is the only way. If I go, if Bill Loeb goes, the Bilbos say that we are fighting the Jews' war. If you go, you go as a man of science. You go as a man above petty concerns. That is why it must be you. Only you can tell the President that if he does not do something, you will go over his head to the people and tell them that the worst crimes in history are happening right now, today, in Europe."

Einstein said nothing. Tears were rolling down his lined cheeks, running into his mustache, falling onto the carpet.

"You are a man above interest groups, above money, above

religion. You must speak to the President and tell him to do the right thing," Cantrowitz said.

Two hours later, after Cantrowitz had left, the professor still sat in his living room. He played a Mozart violin concerto. Yes, he thought as the intricate, serene rhythms washed over him. I will talk to Mr. Roosevelt immediately. I will tell him what is happening to the Jewish people, what is happening to human beings. He will surely listen. He must listen. I would never have dreamed of helping an inhumane man to make a device powerful enough to throw the Earth off its axis. I have done that for him, for America. Now, let him do this for my people. Let him save their lives and I will build that bomb.

BERLIN

WILHELM CANARIS
ABWEHR

May 17, 1943
Memorandum To: Reichsführer, SS,
　　　　　　　　Heinrich Himmler
Most Secret

Per your requests, developments in the most recent phase of the "Manhattan District" are summarized herein.

The U.S. has apparently decided to attempt two alternative approaches to constructing a fission device. They have had success with experiments with both uranium-235 and enriched plutonium, a derivative of enriched uranium. Although there are many technical hurdles to surmount before either method can be described as certain of achieving an explosion, the leader of the Manhattan District has authorized the construction of plants for producing explosive-grade uranium and explosive-grade plutonium at the earliest possible moment.

The uranium-producing facility will be located at a new town to be created by volunteer labor, paid at going wages, in central Tennessee, near a small village named Oak Ridge. This location was chosen because it has access to large amounts of hydroelectric power from the various dams erected along the Tennessee River.

The plutonium facility, also built on the free labor market, will be located in Hanford, Washington. The residents of both areas are being compulsorily evacuated from their homes to make way for the building and land each will require.

We estimate that scientific and production work at each facility will begin within two to three months at the shortest length of time and in six months at the longest. Each facility has been given the highest priority to draw materials and labor from the U.S. industrial apparatus.

As we reported earlier, the Manhattan District has chosen to use the Jew Einstein's process of printing the uranium particles to achieve uniform distribution. The factory now making the press is the same factory that is used to make the wrappers for a certain kind of chewing gum called, in the U.S., Chiclets.

One of the foremost problems of the process of separating the oxides of uranium has apparently been solved. The Chrysler Corporation, a large manufacturer of tanks and military vehicles, has developed a nickel-plating device for covering the steel drums which will be used to store the uranium hexafluoride until it is used. This is a serious sign. Our "experts" at the Reich Research Council had assured us that this problem was insoluble and that finding an alternative to nickel-plating would take the United States at least one year.

(This is only the latest episode of the utterly faulty and obsolete estimates of the Reich Research Council. I hope that the tenure of those who serve on the RRC is under examination.)

According to the latest information, a site is now being developed in the desert of New Mexico which will house those scientists who will assemble the various elements into an explosive device. This is the most ominous sign of all. The Jews Szilard and Einstein must be certain indeed that the Manhattan District is close to success if they are willing to endorse the building of an entirely new town in the New Mexico desert at great expense.

You have asked for an estimate on when the U.S. might be likely to have a fission device prepared, suitable for use as a mine or a bomb. I will not go to you with useless predictions. It is simply impossible for our staff to guess at the future rate of progress. We estimated two years some time ago. It is conceivable that the device could be ready by late 1944 or early 1945, given the seemingly tireless effort that has been put into the project.

As you know, this schedule is so far in advance of our own barely functioning efforts that it poses the gravest dangers, even should our Eastern Front be stabilized—as we fully expect after Manstein's heroic efforts in the Ukraine.

Our staff believes that the principal problem with the Reich effort in fission is not a shortage of materials or of power. Also, we can spare the laborers from other projects if we simply had something useful for them to work on. The main flaw in our Reich Research efforts has been the timidity and lack of innovation in the thinking of the scientists attached to the enterprise. If our scientists were as daring as the Manhattan District magicians, we would already have the fission device.

I hope and trust that you can remedy this problem
by some means. If we do not, we can anticipate the
severest consequences.

> Best wishes and a
> very warm Heil Hitler,
> Canaris

R. F. ⚡⚡
Heinrich Himmler
NACHRICHTEN-UEBERMITTLUNG

May 18, 1943
Memorandum To: Admiral Wilhelm Canaris,
Abwehr
Most Secret

Yours of yesterday instant received and appreciated here. I agree entirely with your conclusions. If
the Führer were not so generous of spirit, I would already have punished the weaklings on the Reich Research Council quite thoroughly for their lack of ini-
tiative under the most exigent conditions.

As I told you at Obersalzberg last Sunday, Siegfried will soon offer us the opportunity to drastically
improve our performance in the fission area. As we
further discussed, this should have marked impact
on the meetings in Stockholm. I can only hope that
you have prepared your people for Siegfried and
Lorelei.

Please tell your operatives that the Siegfried Break
is presently scheduled for not less than seventy-two
hours after midnight tonight. Its culmination should
take place within one week after that. Donitz' part is

crucial, of course. After that, all depends on time and tides. The deterioration of the Kharkov salient and the "recessed" talks in Stockholm lend particular urgency to the entire enterprise.

For protection and safety, please destroy all documents about the Siegfried Break when read.

Best regards and a cordial
Heil Hitler,
Himmler

May 18, 1943,
Washington, D.C.

"Missy," Franklin Delano Roosevelt said with a smile.

The President's secretary looked up from her light-green memo pad and stopped taking notes. Her slate-gray eyes fixed first on Albert Einstein, then moved over to that abominable Harry Hopkins, who was filling the Oval Office with his filthy cigarette smoke. His teeth were positively brown from the nicotine. A cigarette every now and again was fine. But to smoke incessantly, from morning until midnight, coughing and wheezing the whole time, that was absolutely ridiculous. Even suicidal. Missy LeHand turned away and looked at the President's magnificent, leonine head. "Yes, Mr. President?" she asked.

"I don't think we'll need notes of the rest of this meeting. For the record, you can simply say that we had an interesting exchange of views about scientific developments during the war so far."

F.D.R. placed a Philip Morris cigarette in his long Dunhill cigarette holder and stuck it in his mouth. Harry Hopkins lit it in a flash. The effort of lighting a match made Hopkins cough. The cough shook loose ashes from his cigarette. The ashes joined many other ashes on the lapel of his suit. Luckily, the suit was gray, with faint black checks.

F.D.R. inhaled from the cigarette, blew out the smoke, and grinned at Albert Einstein. "Will that be satisfactory, Professor?"

Einstein thought for a moment. He rubbed his smooth hands against the trousers of his loose-fitting tweed suit. He furrowed his brow. Then he said very softly, "You are the President."

F.D.R. shook with laughter. "That must have something to do with the theory of relativity," he said, "but I'm sure I don't know what it is. You are the scientist and the genius and the world-famous scholar. And, yes, I am the President." F.D.R. laughed again, as if he were making a joke. No one else in the Oval Office laughed. The President stopped laughing and blew a cloud of smoke toward the portrait of a sailing ship which hung over his fireplace.

"I think that what you have just brought up is so sensitive that I do not want the subject to be in anyone's memoirs, even mine," F.D.R. said. "Now, let me try to understand what you have been told."

Einstein's gaze at the President did not vary for an instant. "You know what is happening in Upper Silesia, do you not?" he asked.

F.D.R. shook his head. "Horrible," he said. "Absolutely horrible. If it's true."

"Mr. President," Einstein said. "I have been told this by a source who has never lied to me, never even exaggerated by one bit. He was told this dreadful story by an eyewitness." Einstein put his hands in his lap and looked past the President to the dahlias blooming in the garden past the French doors. "I am sorry to say, Mr. President, that I understand that you already knew about these inhuman acts."

F.D.R. put his hands on his desk, a desk that had been first brought to the White House by James Monroe. He said, "I may have heard . . . reports. But I certainly have never been told about . . . this . . . by anyone who was an eyewitness. I can promise you that. Although," he added, "it is not the place of the President of the United States to make apologies to a professor at Princeton, even Albert Einstein." F.D.R. blew a stream of smoke toward Harry Hopkins.

"Mr. President," Einstein said, "I understand perfectly what you are expressing. I do not come to you to call you to account. I am here to inform you that what you might have suspected is a certainty, and to urge you to stop it."

Harry Hopkins coughed loudly, shaking still more ash onto his trousers. "Just how could we prevent something that's happening in Poland?" he asked, wrinkling his brow above his pince-nez.

"Mr. President," Einstein said, "you have airplanes that can reach Poland from Britain. You can bomb the rail lines to the camp. You can bomb the camp itself and destroy the gas chambers."

"I'm not sure our planes can reach to Poland," F.D.R. said. He leaned out of his cane-backed chair and patted his small black scottie, Fala, who turned over on his back. Fala wanted F.D.R. to rub his stomach. "Harry," the President said, "our planes can't reach Poland, can they?"

Harry Hopkins shook his head. "No, sir, Mr. President," Hopkins said, wheezing after each word. "They can barely reach Berlin."

"I think we discussed this with General Bradley," F.D.R. said. "The idea of bombing civilians in concentration camps does not exactly appeal to me in the first place," F.D.R. said. "But since our planes can't reach there anyway, the problem is moot."

Einstein had always had a good ear for accents. He had noticed before that F.D.R. always sounded most calm, most offhand, most American upper-class nasal when he was lying. He was clearly lying now.

"Mr. President," Einstein said, "with the greatest possible respect, may I suggest that you may have been misinformed. American bombers are presently flying from Britain to Ploesti, Romania, and on to bases in Turkey. The total distance is longer than from Britain to Poland and back. I hope you will not be swayed by a clear error on the part of your aides."

Roosevelt laughed out loud. He leaned over and rubbed Fala's stomach again. "I guess that's why they call you a genius," he said. He took a Parker 51 pen from his desk. He unscrewed the cap and started to draw doodles on the pad on his maple "In" box.

The doodles were of crosses falling from a cloud, in a kind of stylized snowstorm.

"Professor Einstein," Hopkins said, "we will get right to the top brass with what you've told us. If there's any way at all we can hit those camps without harming civilians, you'll be the first to know about it."

"I don't care about being the first to know about it," Einstein said, looking angrily at Hopkins. "I am not doing this for my own prestige. I am not seeking headlines. I do this because my people, innocent people, are being killed by the thousands, maybe by the millions, by Hitler."

The French doors were open. A bee flew in and buzzed around Missy LeHand. She airily waved it away without taking her eyes from her beloved boss. F.D.R. looked at the bee and laughed again. "Probably sent over by Hoover," he said. "That's what they call a bug in the police business, I think."

Harry Hopkins laughed cheerfully. Even Missy LeHand let out a giggle. Albert Einstein figured that in the half hour he had been bantering with the President, about one hundred and eight Jews had probably been killed in Auschwitz alone.

"Mr. President, may I take it that you have committed to bombing the rail lines to the concentration camp at Auschwitz?" Einstein asked without removing his gaze from F.D.R.

"If we can find a way to do it without causing any civilian casualties," Harry Hopkins said hurriedly, as if his words could rush Albert Einstein out of the Oval Office, like a broom sweeping out dust from an office building corridor.

Einstein did not turn to look at Hopkins. He simply continued to stare at F.D.R. with his enormous brown eyes. "I would appreciate a reply from the President of the United States. It was to the President that I wrote about the fission device that may well win this war. I did not write to Harry Hopkins."

Outside, the sound of a siren could be heard. Probably an ambulance rushing down Pennsylvania Avenue toward Columbia Hospital for Women. In the garden outside the French doors, a robin redbreast stalked a piece of wood and a pipe cleaner. Material for a nest. Every creature needed a home, Einstein thought.

F.D.R. took his Philip Morris stub out of his cigarette holder. He rubbed it out in a crystal ashtray. The stub made an unpleasant squeaking sound. F.D.R. took another cigarette from a cigarette tray of blue porcelained steel with a Navy escutcheon. He inserted it into his holder. Harry Hopkins struck a match from a book of matches, then lit the President's cigarette. Roosevelt sucked in the smoke. Then he let it out in a long sigh.

"Professor Einstein," F.D.R. said, "what do the people at the camps care if a few of them are killed by bombs if the trains stop coming in? Correct?" F.D.R. shivered as he smiled. "That's what you were thinking, isn't it?"

"Precisely, Mr. President," Einstein said. He could see the fluffy clouds in the sky far out on the Virginia side of the Potomac River. They were like clouds from an illustrated version of Grimm's tales, thought the professor of physics. But real life is far stranger than any fable. Far more frightening than the meanest giant or the most ravenous witch.

"I'm not going to hide behind that. Thank you, Harry," F.D.R. said. He nodded at Hopkins. "But I do not need to hide behind that with a man who has some understanding of the world." F.D.R. took a deep inhalation of smoke. Then he looked at Einstein and smiled a more intimate, less political smile.

Roosevelt continued. "There are a lot of people who already think that I'm fighting the Jews' war. You don't hear them at the barbershops in Georgia or the Elks meetings in Scranton, Pennsylvania. But I hear them. I hear them loud and clear. They're saying, some of them, that the Germans aren't really such bad people. What're we doing sending our boys over to save a lot of Jews that we wouldn't want in our houses anyway?"

F.D.R. looked profoundly sad. "That may shock you," he said. "But people can't see that far. They see that there aren't any Germans invading Kansas, so they wonder what we're doing over there."

"Yes, Mr. President. They may not know about right and wrong," Einstein said, pressing his hands together. "But you do."

The President's expression changed. He picked up a model four-funnel destroyer from the days when he was Secretary of the Navy in World War I. He held it, turned it upside down, shook it to see if any parts would fall off. He put it back on his desk. Then he smiled an almost pitying smile.

"I know that it's right to win this war," Roosevelt said. "I know that to this day, there are plenty of people getting War Department telegrams in the middle of the night who will never forgive me even if it is right, who will curse me to their dying day. I know that."

Einstein said nothing.

"I know what a struggle I had to get the American people into this war. You think it was easy? You think I just waved a wand and made it happen?" Roosevelt demanded. "It was damned hard and I had to do it myself. I have to go upstairs every night and sleep, knowing that there are a goddamned lot of American boys without any legs because I decided that it was right for us to be in the war."

"The whole country knows you are a moral man," Albert Einstein said. "It is that same force which will make you bomb the railheads at Ozwiecim, I hope."

Harry Hopkins started a long, hacking cough. His face turned scarlet. He looked as if he might choke on his own breath right in the Oval Office. He grasped the white linen arms of his chair and coughed for over a minute. During that time, no one moved or spoke.

"I wonder if you realize," F.D.R. finally said, "just what would happen if we sent a few B-17s over to Auschwitz and one or two of them were shot down. Maybe a pilot bails out and is captured. And the Germans put it out over the wires that this man, a poor innocent farm boy from St. Paul, Minnesota, was shot down and his crewmates killed trying to save some Polish Jews from doing an honest day's labor at a work camp?"

"Why do you care about that if you know that it is right?" Albert Einstein asked. "If you know why you did it, if you are the leader of all free men everywhere, why do you care about what German propaganda says?"

F.D.R. scowled. His face flushed. "I do not work with inanimate objects," he said. "I do not work with particles who can't vote or talk back. This is a country. With people. With people who are not saints, who are just confused, sad people. They've been through a lot. A depression that lasted ten years. A war. Seeing their brothers come back in pine boxes. A lot of those people would scream pretty loud if they thought they were losing their husbands and their fathers to save the Jews."

"But the Jews are people, too," Einstein said. "How much have they been through?"

F.D.R. sat forward. He slammed his left hand down in a fist upon the Monroe desk. The model destroyer fell on its side. Hopkins began to cough again.

"I do not represent those Jews in Poland," Roosevelt said in an angry bark. "I am already sending American boys out to get killed to beat the people who are murdering those Jews. I am not going to run my whole war effort to save those Jews in Poland. The world just does not work like that. We are not a country of saints. We are good people, but we cannot save everyone in the world. If we try, we get the country split down the middle and we drop out of the war. Then see what happens to the Jews in Poland."

He stopped speaking. He took a breath of smoke. Then he let it out. Suddenly he looked like a different man to Einstein. He looked old, ashen, bowed down. He looked as if the logic of his words had defeated him. "I'm sorry, Professor," he said. "I try to do what is right within the limits of what is possible. That's all anyone can do." He smiled in a more friendly way. "At least, that's all I can do."

Einstein looked steadily at F.D.R. "I have done you a great service," he said. "I have helped to develop a device out of hell so that the United States could not fail to win this war. If for no other reason, will you please bomb those railheads for that reason?"

F.D.R. shook his head. "I think you are helping with the Manhattan District because you know that it is essential for the United States to win this war. What good would come of your stopping work on the project? Would you rather Germany got it first? Do you think if they get it that they will put all the Jews in Poland into apartments on Fifth Avenue?"

Harry Hopkins laughed, looked abashed, then coughed again. His whole thin frame shook mercilessly as he rocked in his chair and doubled up in pain.

"Perhaps later in the year," F.D.R. said. "When there is more action in other areas. Maybe then we could sneak in a raid on those camps. That might be possible. I'm not going to promise anything. But it's possible. In the meantime, the sooner you get that fission thing done, the sooner everyone will be safe."

He nodded barely perceptibly at Missy LeHand. She stood up and walked over to his wheelchair. F.D.R. smiled broadly as Einstein stood up out of respect. "I always enjoy visits with first-rate minds," Roosevelt said. "It gives me a chance to know what I'm missing." He tapped jovially on the side of his head, as if he were missing something up there. He shook hands with Professor Einstein as he went out. Then he was gone.

On the "Virginian" train back to Trenton, where he would transfer to Princeton, Einstein sat in his roomette. He watched the Maryland countryside coming to life in the spring sun. Near Aberdeen, he saw a large flock of quail flapping their wings, heading north. Just beyond the Elkton Railway Station, he saw an old black man driving a cart pulled by a shuffling, piebald horse. In the back of the cart was a pile of corn husks. The black man wore a straw hat.

The sky was azure, with the same fleecy clouds Einstein had seen from the Oval Office hanging over the lush countryside.

Einstein paid no attention to the noise of Miss Dukas plying her needlepoint—a pattern of the Liberty Bell. He left his dinner of Salisbury steak untouched on the Pennsylvania Railroad blue-and-white dish.

In the world of forces and particles, there is at least some order, some predictability, even if mankind has not discerned its principle. In the world of man, there is only confusion and weakness, he thought. And fear.

May 19, 1943,
Fresno, California

Alice Burton turned off the radio in her DeSoto Firedome. She hated to switch it off because it was playing one of her favorite songs: Louis Armstrong's version of "Shine." Something about curly hair, something about pearly teeth, or something like that. Alice Burton loved to sing along with "Shine." She felt an identification with it. The underdog sympathizing with the underdog. Nothing more complex than that.

She parked the Firedome carefully on the street, at an angle, in front of Farmers' Equity Insurance Agency, 198 Oak Street. The building was a two-story, brick-and-wood structure with two large plate-glass windows on either side of the door, with gold-leaf lettering in a hemisphere around a shield on each window saying the name of the agency. In a neat row in the left-hand corner of the windows was a row of insurance specialties handled by the Farmers' Equity Insurance Agency. "Whole Life." "Automobile and Farm Implement." "Factory Liability." "Annuities." Alice Burton noticed that the agency did not handle term insurance, which she believed was the most economical form of life insurance. Maybe she should open an agency in Fresno specializing in term insurance for farmers who were getting robbed by the Farmers' Equity Insurance Agency.

In the lower left-hand corner of the window, there was a small, gold-leaf legend saying "Otto Seamans, Prop."

In fact, when Alice Burton stepped off the blistering sidewalk, out of the punishing San Joaquin Valley sun, she found that Otto Seamans was the only person in the office. He sat at the back of the room, far behind a large green-topped counter, at a wooden desk, wearing a green celluloid eyeshade, studying a contract or some other finely printed document under a fluorescent lamp. The office was cooled by a slowly revolving ceiling fan. Still, it was hot and dry. Papers of every description—leases, sales contracts, options on policies, claims—lay on the counter, occasionally blown this way or that way by the fan.

Otto Seamans could be identified by the nameplate in front of his desk. He looked up at Alice Burton with a ferretlike face and squinted at her. It was unusual to see a face so strained and anxious in a farming community. Alice Burton had seen plenty of farming communities in the vicinity of Columbus, Ohio. The people there had open, brooding faces with bad skin. Otto Seamans had a closed, worried face with bad skin. He wore a heavy wool suit in the ninety-degree heat. Sweat poured from his brow and occasionally dripped onto the contract.

"May I help you?" he said.

"Yes, you can," Alice Burton said. She smiled at her most disarming. He did not return the smile.

Alice hoped she had not made a mistake. Sam Murphy told her that she should not attempt to corner Seamans or make contact with him by herself. He could be dangerous. After all, "if he's a Nazi, all the signs are that he's not exactly a solid citizen," as Sam put it. If it looked like Otto Seamans was the man sending the radio messages, call in the FBI. That was what Sam had told her. But Alice was going to try something else. She had a plan all her own, to trick Otto into telling a little bit more before he went into the slammer and clammed up, as they said in the James Cagney movies.

"How can I help you?" Otto Seamans asked. "Not a bereavement, I hope."

"Certainly not," Alice Burton said. "I have come to talk to you about someone who is very much alive and getting stronger every day." She idly flipped through a Fresno telephone book as she talked.

"Perhaps a policy on your husband or your father," Seamans said. "I'm afraid the man who writes those lines is not in today. In fact I'm the only one here today. But I could tell you a little bit and then you might know what questions to ask when Jim comes back." Otto Seamans got up out of his chair and walked, smiling, toward the front counter. "How old is the insured?"

"Immortal," Alice Burton said, still looking at the telephone book. "His name is Siegfried. I have some news about him. I thought you might be interested in hearing it."

Otto did not miss a step. He smiled more broadly, then walked through swinging, waist-high gates at the edge of the counter. He passed Alice Burton and lowered the shade of the front door. He slipped a sign in the window that said "Closed —Please Come Again." Then he gestured to Alice Burton to sit down. As he did, Alice could see that he was sweating even more heavily than before, especially on his upper lip.

Alice passed through the gates and sat down on a wooden swivel chair next to Seamans' desk. Otto cheerfully sat down at his green-covered accountant's chair and rummaged in his lower desk drawer for something. He bent down to sift among various papers, and then let out a small sigh, which meant he had found the looked-for object.

It was a Colt .38 Python. He brought it out, lifted it high into the air, and pointed it at Alice's head on the downswing. He smiled maliciously.

"I don't know any Siegfried. Who sent you here?" he asked in a rasping voice.

"The same people who sent you here," Alice said. She could feel her pulse racing. Sam Murphy had been right after all. What a fool she had been. How unbelievably stupid could a person be?

"I think you're a little Jew spy," Otto said. "That's what I think. You were sent to torment me just because you Jews can't leave well enough alone. That's what I think." His upper lip began to twitch rapidly.

"I think you might like to know what I have to tell you about Siegfried," Alice Burton said. She tried to sound cool, but her voice was shaking.

"I don't have any idea of your Jew tricks," Otto Seamans said. "But just to make sure you have a better idea of what kind of people you are dealing with, I think I will give you a little lesson. Just sit right there, if you don't mind."

Alice did not mind. In a moment, Otto had tied her hands behind her back with an extension cord. It was rough and painful on her wrists.

In a few minutes, Otto Seamans had hustled Alice Burton out the back door of his office, into a dirty, paper-strewn parking area. It gave onto the backyard of a small, white-stucco house. There was a cat hanging by its paws from a clothesline. When the cat saw Otto, it meowed, then ran away. There were two parking spaces. One was empty. The other had a gray Studebaker sedan, covered with dust. Otto Seamans forced Alice Burton into the back seat. "Lie down on the floor," he said. "There are a few papers back there, but you won't be too uncomfortable." There was an edge of mocking sarcasm in his voice. Alice would have been tempted to scream, had Otto not gagged her with a greasy necktie.

"I want to know where you got the idea to come to see me," Otto said as they drove out of town. Alice Burton could not see where they were going. She was face down, amidst a pile of standard riders to personal property floaters. But if she could have seen, she would have followed the path of the car out of town, past a few service stations, a bedraggled Flying A, a gritty 76, a grimy Gulf, past a few corrugated-tin warehouses, out to a two-lane highway which led through fields of waving wheat, irrigated by sprinklers casting jets of water high into the spring air. There was an occasional tractor coming the other way into town. The tractor drivers looked sunburned, elderly, wrinkled, determined. They did not wave to Otto. He did not wave to them.

"I wonder who you work for," Otto said. "Just grunt one of your Jew grunts if you want to say yes. Are you from the FBI?"

Alice Burton did not say anything. She was fumbling with her fingers to untie the extension cord. There was no chance of doing that. The cord was tight. The ends were out of reach of her fingers. She wondered if she could undo the cord with her feet. She tried. Out of the question. She was not Harry Houdini.

"From the FBI, yes?" Otto Seamans asked. "They probably are snooping around just because I did my best to keep the United States out of this war. Is that it? The FBI?"

"No," Alice Burton said thickly, through her gag. "No."

Alice Burton suddenly had a blindingly clear thought. It was along the lines of a saying her mother was fond of. "No smoke without fire," her mother used to say. If Otto Seamans was pulling guns, tying women up, throwing them face down into cars, there was something fairly serious going on. No, strike the qualifiers. Otto Seamans was doing something damned important. Not only that, but Otto Seamans, in his wool suit on a ninety-degree day, was planning to kill her.

The car sped up. Alice Burton could feel the acceleration.

"Are you from the War Department?" Otto Seamans asked. "Are they snooping around just because I fought against the draft?"

"No," Alice Burton tried to say. "I am a friend."

Otto Seamans laughed gutturally. "A friend," he said. "You are no friend. I have no friends who come around with their Jew noses asking questions. Are you from Sacramento? Who sent you? I will just let you go if you tell me why you are bothering a poor innocent man like me."

Alice Burton's heart raced. This man was going to shoot her and leave her in a wheat field if she did not do something. There was not much doubt of that. But what could she do? What weapon did she have against a man in a two-ton car with a gun?

Of course, of course. The answer shot back in Alice Burton's brain. The car was her weapon. If she could distract Otto Seamans, she might just get out of this alive. After all, he was in the front seat. She was in the back seat.

She could feel the car accelerating further. It went into a long curve. This was the time.

"I'm going to send you to talk to a friend of mine," Otto Seamans said. "Trixie. A lovely girl. She's like you. She's always asking questions. The two of you will have a lot to talk about." He giggled sickeningly.

In an instant, Alice Burton jackknifed her legs, raised herself into the space above the seat and could see over the front seat. Otto turned suddenly at the noise. His mouth opened in surprise at seeing Alice Burton behind him. The car swerved. He turned back around again to straighten it out.

In the moment that he turned back around, Alice Burton cocked her head back and then slammed it into the side of Otto's sweating face as hard as she could. He gasped in shock as his head smashed against the metal doorpost. Like a butting goat, Alice Burton smashed Seamans' head again while he was still groggy. This time, Seamans' eyes rolled upward in his head. He let go of the steering wheel. The car curved wildly, first left, then right, and then into a milk truck that was parked by a farmhouse next to the road. There was a jolting, overpowering collision. Alice was thrown back into the back seat, against the back of the front seat, down onto the floor, and against a door.

Otto Seamans was thrown through the windshield. He landed, with his neck broken, in a pile of shattered milk bottles. His blood mixed with the white pools of milk and ran into the San Joaquin Valley dust.

In the fog which swept over her, Alice Burton saw fragments of white-jacketed men and women bending over her, putting needles in her arms, lifting her onto a stretcher, putting Otto into an ambulance, clucking their tongues, talking among each other about whatever might have happened.

"I'll bet it had to do with insurance fraud," one woman's voice said.

"I've heard that Otto Seamans had back-street women. She doesn't look like the type, though. She looks wholesome enough," said another voice. "Too skinny for most men."

A man's voice poked its way through the haze that swam in Alice Burton's brain. "I'll bet it had something to do with that cousin of his," the voice said.

"What cousin?" asked the woman who thought Alice Burton was too skinny.

"The one who's a Nazi. The one who's a prisoner of war down in Fort Ord. My friend Trixie, the one who moved down to L.A. a while back, she told me Otto used to go visit him all the time," said the male voice.

An alarm went off in Alice Burton's head, a fire bell reverberating in the night air of her consciousness.

Part II

May 20, 1943,
Santa Cruz, California

When Marilyn awoke, she was in John Quinn's arms. She could see out the window of the Sea'n'Sand Motel to the beach at Santa Cruz. The sky was a magnificent, rich azure, with only a few fleecy clouds off to the south, above the amusement park. She felt peaceful, contented, as if a new life were beginning for her and John. This trip had really been a wonderful idea. The order had been perfect. They would pick up the prisoner in San Francisco and bring him back, and that was fine. John was so relaxed. He had visibly lost his tension as they drove out of Los Angeles, up the coast. The worry lines next to his eyes had disappeared by the time they reached Santa Barbara. By the time they had lunch in San Luis Obispo, he was smiling and humming along to "Little Red Wagon" on the radio. Count Basie was one of Marilyn's favorites, too. They both sang along when Frank Sinatra sang his throaty rendition of "Stormy Weather." John Quinn was a different man away from the muggers and the murderers and the pimps. He was cracking jokes about John L. Lewis and Captain Parker, oohing and aahing at the seals off Carmel. He even kissed her spontaneously while they watched the seagulls eat bread crumbs off Pebble Beach.

They had eaten an Italian dinner on the boardwalk at Santa Cruz and then made love until two in the morning. When John was happy, Marilyn was happy, too. She felt as if a life together, maybe with him in some other job, was just beyond the hills outside of Santa Cruz. The golden possibilities of the rest of her youth stretched before her. She did not know that she would be dead by noon.

She kissed John Quinn and brushed her lips against his neck. In his sleep, he reached down between her legs. She smiled and pressed herself against him.

A few blocks away, on River Street, Maxine Lewis called the real estate brokerage to tell them she thought she might be coming down with that influenza bug there had just been a story about in the Santa Cruz *Sentinel*. She did not want to take any chances, and besides, she was just planning to spend the day going over the rents from the Khachigian estate. So maybe she would just stay home and take it easy and see if she could beat that flu bug. "If I don't," she said, "I'm going to go down to my mom's place in Modesto and have her take care of me. It's damned hard taking care of yourself when you have the flu."

The other girls at the brokerage looked at each other. Maxine Lewis had definitely been acting strangely lately. She had not even gone with them to see the Santa Cruz High School performance of *The Pirates of Penzance* the night before. As Leah Steuer put it so succinctly, "It spells M-A-N to me."

In her apartment, Maxine read and reread the letter that had arrived in the morning mail. It had come in a large envelope that said "U.S. Government—No Postage Necessary." But then when Maxine opened the letter, she found that it had been sent to her by that creep Otto Seamans and not by the government at all. That was just his little way of being clever, Maxine guessed. Pretty simpleminded. Just like him.

Maxine read the letter as she listened to Lowell Thomas telling about an enormous "irresistible" counterattack by the Red Army under General Tomashevsky in the Kharkov salient. "It looks as if the Germans' lease on the hub of the

Ukraine is going to be month-by-month, if not day-by-day," Lowell Thomas said with just a hint of a chuckle in his voice. To hell with him, Maxine thought. She flipped off the Emerson and opened the folded stationery. As she put down the envelope, a smaller envelope fell out of it. In large block letters the envelope-within-an-envelope read "To be opened only by Obersturmbannführer Joachim Trattner." Maxine put that envelope into her pocketbook and looked back at her letter. It read:

Dear Maxine,
You are to destroy this letter the moment you have read it.

It is to be burned and the ashes flushed down the toilet.

On May 20, you must be at the corner of Laurel Street and Pacific Street in Santa Cruz at noon exactly. You should have your car with you, in good working order. You should have the gas tank filled with gasoline. You should also have two sets of men's business clothing from shoes to shirt to tie, etc. These should be in the sizes marked at the bottom of the page. Your "friend" Joachim Trattner and a man named Whelchel will meet you at that corner. You should take them to your house, allow them to change, and then give them the enclosed letter.

If they do not appear by twelve-thirty, you should leave the area and destroy the envelope for Herr Trattner by burning it and flushing the ashes down the toilet.

Whatever reservations you have about your assignment once you learn it from Oberst Trattner are unimportant. This assignment is paramount in the salvation of the Reich and the entire Aryan people.

God be with you in this magnificent epoch of your life.

Otto Seamans

Jesus Christ. Otto had sure cut it close. Maxine was out of the house and down at the J.C. Penney on Pacific Street in a flash. She had been friends with Donna Blakemore, the saleswoman in the men's department, for years. Maxine just said that she was getting the clothes for a client who was buying a little cottage down in Soquel and had asked her to do some shopping for him. "The market's so slow these days that I'd build him a roller coaster for that six percent commission," Maxine Lewis said. Donna just smiled and found the clothes. A plain blue serge ready-made for the size forty-two and a gray herringbone for the size thirty-six. They weren't stylish, but they would do.

The shirts and underwear and ties and socks and shoes only took a few minutes longer. It was amazing what Maxine Lewis could do when there was no one standing over her, judging her.

Maxine's heart was racing the entire time she was at J.C. Penney. As she neatly took the pins out of the shirts and the underwear and laid them on her bed, she felt a thrill. Out her window, the sky was a magnificent blue, with only a few clouds far off in the distance above the roller coaster. The sky was endless, limitless, filled to overflowing with possibilities of every kind. This might be the day that Maxine Lewis and Joachim Trattner began a new life together. After all, if the masterminds in Berlin had sent her into town to buy clothes for two men, they must have planned that she would be found out right away and implicated in whatever was going on. That meant she would surely (oh, no doubt about it!) be spirited out of Santa Cruz and maybe all the way to the Reich with Joachim, who was the only man she ever wanted to be with.

As she thought about the possibilities of a united life under the Führer, Maxine realized she had not yet burned her letter from Otto. She held the document over the toilet, lit it with a Diamond kitchen match, then let the burning black paper fall into the toilet. She flushed the paper away.

Then she walked back into her living room, looked out the window at the clouds, and smiled to herself. Yes, indeed, she thought. A sure sign that something good is about to happen.

Over on Main Street, John Quinn and Marilyn sat in a booth eating a late breakfast. They were in Ferrell's Donut House and John Quinn swore that Ferrell's had the best donuts he had ever had in all his life. The eggs-over-easy and the crisp bacon were still to come. There were tall glasses of freshly squeezed orange juice on the tabletop. It was almost eleven. John and Marilyn were the only people still eating. The lunch crowd wouldn't start coming in until eleven-thirty.

John Quinn wore brown lightweight wool trousers and a Hawaiian print shirt open at the neck. "You look like Arthur Godfrey," Marilyn said. "You look as cute as a button."

Marilyn wore baggy red-checked slacks and a blouse of light blue, almost mauve. She was not wearing any stockings between her feet and her open-toed, high-heeled sandals. She had let her light-brown hair fall over her shoulders. Her blue eyes were sparkling and well-rested. She looked, John Quinn thought, like a happy woman.

"You know," Marilyn said, munching on a honey-dipped donut, "some day we should come up here and really spend some time. This is a really cute town. I wish we had time to go on the boardwalk. You think we could? Maybe before we leave town?"

"Why not?" John Quinn answered. "We don't have to be in San Francisco for another day. It's only a few hours up there. We can just laze around today."

Marilyn smiled and John kept talking. "You know, when I'm in a place like this, I just have to keep asking myself, What the hell am I knocking my brains out for, struggling like a dog, getting cut and maybe shot, just so that I can maybe make thirty years and then get a pension I can't live on anyway?"

"I bet people here just live a really quiet life," Marilyn said. "They probably don't get ulcers and die young and things."

John Quinn nodded and pressed his lips together. "Not only that," he said. "It's a long way away from Joan. I wouldn't have to keep running into people who tell me how she's got a new Packard or has martinis every day at the Riviera Country Club. I'm sick of that."

"I can type really well, John," Marilyn said. "I could probably get some little job here. Maybe we could still see each other if you moved up here." Marilyn's eyes were moist.

John Quinn picked up a copy of *Time* that a previous customer had left lying on the table. There was a picture of Omar Bradley on the cover with the caption "The Soldier's General." Bradley looked kind.

"I just wonder," Quinn said, "how I'm ever gonna be able to hold my head up high ever again when I haven't fought in this war. Everyone is going overseas or doing something here or just doing something. If I was up here, I'd be doing even less than I'm doing in L.A. A man's gotta do something, or else he feels like a bum," Quinn said.

Marilyn looked into her napkin. Then she picked up the magazine and turned it over. An advertisement for Lucky Strikes showed a cowboy lighting up as he sat on a brown-and-white stallion.

"You can't be in the Army because there's a spot on your lung," Marilyn said softly. "No one on this whole earth thinks you're a shirker. There's not a man on the force who thinks you're anything but a cop who's less afraid than they are. You think people are talking behind your back, saying that you're a coward? That's wrong. I'm sorry, but that's wrong. You're in a lot more danger every day than the guys at training camps like Fort Ord." She reached across the table, past the empty light-blue china dish which had held three donuts. She covered his large hand with her small hands. "You're a brave man," she said. "Everyone knows it but you."

John Quinn actually raised himself from his seat and kissed Marilyn across the table. The counterman giggled as he walked over with their eggs and bacon. "Must be nice," he said cheerfully. He had a wide face with a gray beard.

They ate in silence for a moment. Then John Quinn spoke again. "You know," he said, "it's been so long since I had a woman around who treated me like I was something different than what the cat dragged in, I guess it's just hard for me to handle it. That's all. It means a lot to me to have you say it, though, Marilyn. It really does."

He forked a mixture of egg and toast into his mouth and chewed for a moment. Through the plate-glass window of Ferrell's Donut House, he could see clouds rolling into town from the ocean. "I've felt most of my life like I was a bum," Quinn said. "Like I was a bum who had just lucked into being on the track team and then lucked into a couple of years in college, then lucked onto the force. And everything I got, I always felt like I was still a bum, and I should be in an alley somewhere unloading trucks and that's what I'd wind up doing if I didn't really watch myself."

"You're not seeing things plain," Marilyn said, covering his hand with hers again. "You've done everything because you've got good stuff inside you. That's the one and only reason. You've got what it takes to rate in this world."

"With you," John Quinn said softly, "which is more important than I ever thought it would be."

Marilyn looked at John mischievously. "You never thought it would be?" she asked, raising her sparse eyebrows. "You thought I was just this little trick from the records department who kept the other side of the bed warm after Joan left? Just a little shack job from Boyle Heights?" She smiled as she asked, but her eyes were shining with emotion.

John Quinn sighed heavily. "I make a tremendous number of mistakes," he said. "Tremendous. I can't keep track of all of them. I guess telling you what I just said was a mistake." He smiled. "I just think that I never realized how important you would be to me. It never occurred to me until today that we might be able to be together for a long time and be really happy."

"That's nice of you," Marilyn said, mixing sarcasm and emotion. "I've known it for a long time." Tears formed in the corners of her eyes. She tried to blink them away.

"You might be right about the force and L.A. and everything else, too," Quinn said. "I could see living here. Maybe working on the local force. Maybe working in industrial jobs, guarding shipments and things. That could work out. I don't know. Maybe if I got away from a place where there're so many crazy people, I wouldn't feel so lonely and so crazy."

Marilyn looked down into her bacon, as if it might hold a clue to why John felt so different today, why he might be shedding his skin and letting her approach so close to him. "L.A.'s a big city filled with people who came there because they were lonely where they were," Marilyn said. "They all get together and they think they won't be lonely. But a person who's lonely in Baltimore is gonna be just as lonely in L.A. A person who's lonely when it's snowing outside is gonna be just as lonely when the sun is pouring down and it's seventy-seven degrees."

John looked at Marilyn and smiled. He turned his palm upright and squeezed her hands. "Let's finish up here," he said. "I'd like to take a stroll through the main shopping street. Pacific Street, that's what the maid called it. That'll be a little treat. Going strolling down a street where you aren't scared that your wallet's gonna get lifted if you relax for a minute." He ate a large piece of crisp bacon. "And it'll be nice walking somewhere I can hold your hand and nobody'll start whispering to Old Parker that he's got a maniac on his hands." He swallowed a mouthful of coffee. "And not only that," he added, "but you're a damned smart kid. You ought to spend more time talking and less time with those corny jokes that the girls in the file room tell you. You're a smart kid."

Marilyn felt a tingling in her cheeks. "I think this is the best vacation I've ever had," Marilyn said. As she ate and drank, she looked at John, who was chewing his egg and studying *Time* magazine. He really and truly sees me for the first time, she said to herself. He sees more in me than I ever saw in myself. That's what being in love means. Someone appreciates you more than you even value yourself. Someone sees depths in you that you didn't even know were there.

She wished that they never had to get to San Francisco, that they could stay in Santa Cruz forever.

John read two stories about the war in North Africa. As he read, he thought that he could feel the worry, the self-doubt rolling off his spine, like clods of dirt coming off under a strong jet of water. Yes, he thought to himself, I could be happy in Santa Cruz. I could just live a quiet life and forget that there are people like Joan who leave working men for the sons of bankers and oil millionaires. He was eager for a good, brisk walk along Pacific Street.

In the Army staff car racing up the Pacific Coast Highway, Eddie Ratner, Sergeant, Top Kick, U.S. Army, cradled a Thompson submachine gun in his lap. He sat in the passenger front seat of the Ford sedan while Corporal Toby Moffatt drove, his eyes occasionally straying from the asphalt highway to the glistening ocean to his left.

Once they were past the Moss Landing Power Plant, the scenery between Monterey and Santa Cruz was rolling hills, usually uncultivated, a few cabins off the road, and the ocean, broken into a million pieces by the cloudy haze of the day. Up ahead, toward Santa Cruz, Sergeant Ratner could see clouds rolling in. By the afternoon, perhaps sooner, there would be rain. The highway would be slick. Moffatt was not what Ratner called a great driver. He had this bad habit of daydreaming. It was easy to imagine the car going into a skid and running into one of those drainage ditches off the shoulder of Highway 1. Then, there would be a real test. Then, how would General Whitlock's fair-haired little Nazi P.O.W.s, Whelchel and Trattner, respond? Would they give their efficient German first aid to the wounded Americans in the front seat? Or would they just laugh and run the hell off for a weekend in town with one of their girlfriends?

Whelchel wore a mocking look in his well-starched Afrika Korps uniform in the back seat. He perpetually wore a mocking look in his light-blue eyes, as if they were laughing at a fate that had eluded Ratner's notice. His friend Joachim Trattner looked more pensive. Trattner was the taller man. His legs were drawn up in front of him in the back seat. His uniform was not so perfectly displayed as Whelchel's. He looked like he might have some redeeming qualities. His eyes were darker, more thoughtful. Maybe he was almost human. Probably not, though. He would probably just as soon shoot Ratner as look at him.

"Sergeant," Whelchel asked Ratner in a singsong, but almost unaccented English, "may I speak to you?"

"I guess so," Ratner said.

"Do you know the store where we are to go to find our costumes? For the play? For *Hamlet*?" Whelchel asked.

"You mean, have I ever been there?" Ratner asked. "No, I've never been there. I have the address. Somewhere on Pacific Street. I have a map. It's right near Laurel Street. We'll find it. We still have plenty of time."

"I meant, perhaps a relative of yours owned it," Whelchel said. "I thought that might be a possibility. It is probably a very profitable little business, yes?" Whelchel smiled sarcastically.

"I have no idea," Ratner said. God, he wished he had been sent somewhere else instead of to this damned Kriegsgefangenenlager Fort Ord. Somewhere he could shoot Germans and not baby-sit them and put up with their crap. If it hadn't been for his backsassing that sergeant at Camp Polk three years ago, none of this would have happened. But then, it wasn't right for that hillbilly to call him Cohen all the time. That kind of thing made him mad. Now, here was Whelchel giving him a lot of lip. Ratner wished he could stove in Whelchel's mouth with the butt of the tommy gun. That might teach him something. But then Ratner would get into more trouble with General Whitlock than Whelchel would.

"Yes, yes, very profitable, these little shops," Whelchel said. "We had them in Saxony as well. A little man with his little cap, and he was taking two thousand marks a month out of the little shop. He had a cousin who had another little shop and they all went to synagogue together and met other people, doctors and lawyers and speculators and they all did very well indeed. There was one of them who owned a scrap metal factory. Making steel. He did the best of all. During the inflation of '23, he paid off all his debts and came out of it richer than ever. Your people are very good at making money, Sergeant Ratner," Whelchel said in a mocking way.

"I think that will be all for you," Ratner said. The nerve of these Nazis! They needled you even when you were holding a tommy gun on them.

"Yes, they all got quite rich while everyone else was starving," Whelchel said. "Of course, none of them had served in the army during the Great War. They were well behind the lines, making money from our wives and children while we were at war. Selling our children into whorehouses. I think you people have a real nose for making money," Whelchel said. "I have to hand it to you."

"Shut your mouth, mister, right this minute," Ratner said. "You'll be on bread and water if you don't just shut up right now." He fingered the safety of his Thompson nervously. This might be a setup, some kind of trick to get him off balance so they could escape. Just get him provoked, get him to lose his head, and they could be off and running.

"Yes, indeed," Whelchel said without pausing for even a moment. "You people know how to make good money from a war. Of course, Germany is a small country compared with the United States of America. Here you have real opportunities to make dollars while the gentiles are off getting blown up by our Panzers in North Africa. I have to hand it to you for getting this country into the war. No one was ever going to bother you. The Americans were quite safe. You managed to fool this whole continent of stupid gentiles into sending their sons off to die so that your stocks would go up. Brilliant!"

Whelchel then gave the kind of laugh which is meant to convey admiration and a touch of envy and belittlement at the same time.

"Shut up, goddamn you," Ratner said. "If you don't shut up, we're turning around right now." He brought the barrel of the tommy gun above the front seat so that Whelchel could see it. Whelchel stopped talking, but he kept laughing.

Moffatt laughed, too. Jesus Christ, Ratner thought, what if Moffatt's in on this, too? What if it's three against one? What if they're planning to kill me before we even get to Santa Cruz?

"I mean it. One more word out of you and we're going back to camp. And you're going on report," Ratner said. Moffatt stopped laughing. Whelchel giggled to himself, but did not speak.

In a moment, they were cruising silently over the highway toward Santa Cruz. Ratner could rest easier. They probably were not planning to drive the car off the road and murder him right then and there after all. Thank God for that. Really, a man was completely alone, totally by himself, even in this man's army. You have to take care of yourself in this world, and that's for sure. That's what Ratner's mom had always said. And she was almost always right.

A few minutes later, there was a small black-and-white sign announcing that the Ocean Street exit for the Downtown Business District was one mile away. Moffatt guided the staff car off the ramp and into the midst of a number of auto repair shops, body shops, donut shops, and hamburger stands. "Where to, Sarge?" Moffatt asked in a slightly mocking tone of voice. Goddamnit. Everyone was out to drive him crazy today, and that was the truth. But Ratner would not let them.

"The store's supposed to be at the corner of Pacific Street and Laurel Street," Ratner said, studying a map. "Go down here four streets, then turn right for four blocks and we should be right there."

Now, Joachim Trattner thought, is the moment. In the entire world, only I—and the fool Whelchel—have been selected to do something so important that the entire resources of the Reich are devoted to taking me away from Kriegsgefangenenlager Fort Ord and putting me somewhere I can be helpful. Whelchel is just the messenger. He got the instructions which take us this far from inside a model of a Heinkel 111 that Otto Seamans had delivered to him. He is a good messenger, but a messenger nonetheless. No more than that, surely.

As the car crawled through the lunch-hour traffic of Santa Cruz, Trattner could see an immense wooden roller coaster in the western distance. He knew what it was because he had seen movies of America in Germany before the war. Oh, God, to think that in America—safe, secure, fat America—there were still roller coasters and children riding them. Screaming and yelling with glee. Carefree. Not worried that a bomb from a B-17 or a Lancaster could fall from ten thousand feet and blow their mother and father into such small pieces that no one could ever find them.

If only Germany could be like America. Safe, peaceful, a place where little children could play and feel no fear. But that thought did not relax Trattner. Instead, it hardened his resolve. For that to happen, the Reich would have to win the war. To win the war, Trattner would have to do something. He did not know what. But he liked the idea that he was going to be doing it with Maxine Lewis. She was his idea of a dream woman. In fact, he had often dreamt of her since their meeting. In the dream she was always alluring, seductive, beckoning. The perfect adornment for a strong man, even if she was of subnormal intellect.

The staff car pulled up in front of a "poker club" at the corner of Pacific and Laurel. The poker club was on the northwest corner. On the southwest corner was a Chevrolet dealership, with three or four dusty used cars and a row of forlorn yellow, blue, and red pennants. On the northeast corner was a parking lot and a small hamburger stand. Really no more than a shack. It had a counter and a counterman dispensing hamburgers and hot dogs. On the southeast corner was a hardware store—"Sweet's Implement Company." In front of it was a gray 1936 Plymouth sedan. Its motor was running. In the driver's seat sat a pretty woman with her hair pulled back into a bun. She had a severe look, as if a man might be in trouble if he stayed out all night playing cards and then came home drunk and broke. Maxine Lewis had all four doors of her car unlocked. She could see Trattner in the back of the staff car as it pulled up.

"With your permission," Trattner said in a firm voice, "the store is on the second floor. It is our usual lunchtime. Might we go to the hamburger stand for lunch? We have money from the canteen redemption program."

Ratner looked over at the hamburger stand. A sign said "Blakemore's Eats." At the counter sat a man in his thirties with a slight paunch. To Ratner, he looked like a cop. He was with a much younger woman with these really wild blue eyes that Ratner could see from thirty feet away. She and the man were smiling and laughing, as if an angel had appeared and told them they might live forever.

Trattner actually did something which he thought he would never do. He smiled at the Jew Sergeant Ratner. This was highly unorthodox, but in the service of the Reich, deception was often necessary. Even stooping to friendship with a Jew might be justified.

Eddie Ratner decided that Trattner might be a good influence on that little sonofabitch Whelchel. "Since you have some idea of proper behavior," Ratner said, "you're welcome to go and get whatever you want. The corporal and I will be right behind you, though. Corporal, give me your sidearm."

Ostentatiously, Moffatt handed a large Colt .45 automatic to Ratner. He looked slightly apologetically in the direction of Whelchel. But Whelchel did not notice. He was looking all around the intersection. He was looking especially at Maxine Lewis, wondering why the Reichsführer had ever entrusted a woman, especially a thoroughgoing slut, with the responsibility for an operation of this magnitude.

Ratner slipped the Colt .45 into the waistband of his khaki fatigues and opened his door. He gestured with his chin to Moffatt, who got out of his side of the car. Ratner flipped on the safety catch of the Thompson, then laid it carefully on the floor of the staff car. Then Ratner nodded to Trattner and Whelchel. They each opened their doors and slowly got out of the car.

"After we have won the war," Trattner said good-naturedly, "we will have to start serving hamburgers in the Reich. They simply smell too good to be ignored. They are better than bratwurst."

Moffatt smiled at the remark. Ratner kept on his guard. Trattner was now behaving entirely too well. Either he was scared about getting put on report—and that was a dim possibility, considering General Whitlock—or he was up to something. Ratner kept his hand on the handle of the Colt.

At the counter, Trattner pounded with his palm on the tabletop and announced, "Two hamburgers with everything," in a jovial voice with only a hint of an accent.

"I'll have a hot dog with mustard," Ratner said.

"Make mine a cheeseburger," Moffatt said.

Maxine Lewis studied them from across the street. She kept her motor running in every way. She could feel her heart pounding. She started to take her pulse, but then she was never able to find it. Today was no exception.

At the counter, John Quinn wondered who his fellow lunchers were. Maybe Swedish resistance fighters getting trained at a nearby base. Maybe Fort Ord. Or maybe just American farm boys from Minnesota or somewhere who still had an accent. Anyway, they were awfully fit and healthy-looking specimens. Mentally, Quinn compared his paunch with their slimness.

Marilyn noticed that John looked uneasy around the men in their uniforms. She also noticed that the two men who had ordered hamburgers with everything were wearing German uniforms. She may have been just a little dumb file clerk, but she could recognize an Afrika Korps uniform from the newsreels. That was a snap. She gestured to John to put his face close to hers. "Those two guys are prisoners of war," she said. "Look at their uniforms."

As soon as Marilyn pointed it out, John realized it was true.

The taller of the two prisoners of war looked into Quinn's eyes just as Quinn met his stare. To Quinn, the eyes of Joachim Trattner were frightening, almost unfathomable eyes. They were the first Nazi eyes he had ever looked into. What crazy, crazy people they must have been to bomb Rotterdam, to think they could take on the whole world and win. To shout and scream like that at those insane rallies in Nuremburg. Here was one eating a hamburger (with everything on it) right in the middle of an American town. His eyes were devoid of any kind of doubt or worry. They were like the eyes of slightly psycho murderers that John had sometimes seen. But more self-contained. Less wandering. Less frantic. For that reason, the eyes were possibly even more dangerous than the eyes of the crazy men who hacked up their children with a kitchen knife, then waited for the police to come. This one would not wait for the police to come. He would not wait at all. He would go out and do it again and not get caught.

The other one, the smaller P.O.W., just looked like a surly, maybe homo punk. His eyes darted everywhere. Looked like he would kill for the thrill of it.

To Joachim Trattner, Quinn looked like a weary old weimaraner dog. His eyes had lost some of their sharpness and their edge, but they still belonged to a hunter. Even across the gulf of time, culture, and space, Trattner recognized a hunter.

"Eat that in a hurry," Ratner said when the wrinkled old counterman served the P.O.W.s' hamburgers. "We haven't even started looking for the costumes."

Quinn thought he must have misheard. "Costumes." What on earth could that mean? Costumes?

A light rain began to fall at just that moment. There was a roof extending about five feet over the counter at Blakemore's. The two P.O.W.s, Ratner, Moffatt, John Quinn, and Marilyn all huddled together under it. Quinn felt uncomfortable. So did Marilyn. "I think we ought to go. We can go back to the motel," John Quinn said with a wink. "It'll be dry there."

"Not for long," Marilyn whispered, brushing his ear with her lips.

"Excuse me," Trattner then said quite clearly to the counterman. "Do you have any more catsup?" The counterman pointed at a tall bottle of Heinz catsup on the edge of the counter near Quinn. "Excuse me," Trattner said, reaching for the bottle. Quinn moved out of the way. As he did, he glanced at his watch. It was one minute before noon.

Trattner picked up the bottle of catsup. He lifted it high into the air, swung it backward and stared for a split second at Eddie Ratner, who was looking off toward the roller coaster. With one horrifyingly fast sweep, Trattner smashed the bottle against the American's skull. Ratner turned, his eyes blank, his scalp bleeding, and grasped the counter to steady himself. With one continuous motion, Trattner drew his knife from his boot, raised it to his chest, then drew it across Ratner's throat. Blood spurted onto the counter. As Ratner gurgled and fell, Trattner grabbed the Colt .45 from his waistband. He hit

Ratner hard on the head as Ratner fell, although Ratner may well have already been dead.

"No one moves," Trattner said. "Hands up!" He pointed the pistol at Moffatt and Quinn. For a long moment, he looked at Quinn, as if debating whether to shoot him. Then he said, "No one moves until we are gone. We will be watching."

Corporal Moffatt simply stared with his light-blue Okie eyes.

Trattner and Whelchel backed toward Maxine Lewis' car. They were almost at the street when Whelchel suddenly ran toward the staff car. He yanked open the front seat and pulled out the Thompson submachine gun. With a savage grin on his face, the kind Quinn had seen before, Whelchel pulled back the charging lever and snapped off the safety.

In an instant, John Quinn hit the sidewalk, pulling Marilyn down with him. But not fast enough. The noontime whistle was battered by the sound of the Thompson blasting at the customers of Blakemore's. Bullets tore the little counter to pieces, made the face of the counterman into a bloody pulp before he died, came near to cutting Corporal Toby Moffatt in two, stitching right across his waist, blowing him into surprised eternity. A blast aimed precisely for Quinn missed its mark. The bullets went just under Quinn and smashed Marilyn's rib cage to little pieces, pulverized her left lung, and punched a hole in her heart, killing her instantly. Quinn's face was covered with her blood. When he looked up, Whelchel was throwing down the tommy gun and running toward a 1936 gray Plymouth sedan while a surprised-looking Trattner clambered into the passenger side of the car.

Quinn was still a cop. He reached into his belt for his belly gun, the little surprise he kept with him for whatever might come up. It was a Browning .32 Interceptor with a two-inch barrel. Quinn had it out, sighted, and the hammer back before Whelchel reached the car. He shot three times, through a veil of light-pink blood which had seeped into his eyes. The shots boomed in his ears, made them ring and burn. Whelchel turned around, looked stunned, then grasped his back and fell down. He died before he hit the ground.

"For Christ's sake," Trattner shouted at Maxine Lewis, who was gaping at the blood and flesh all over the sidewalk and street. "*Nix wie raus hier. Sofort.*" Maxine just stared at him. "Let's get out of here. Right now," he translated, pushing her to make her go.

She let out the clutch. The car shot forward onto Pacific Street, just in front of an REA truck. Its wheels burned rubber into the concrete pavement. It turned onto Elm after a block, and disappeared.

At Blakemore's Eats, a crowd had started to gather. Men in coveralls, women in rollers and scarves, stared at the wrecked counter, the burning burgers still on the grill, the dead counterman and soldiers, and the big Irish guy who was holding a dead girl with blood pouring out of her chest and the wildest blue eyes you ever saw. The Irish guy was crying like a baby. He still had his gun in his hand.

May 21, 1943,
Santa Cruz, California

The Santa Cruz County Sheriff's Station was a small white-stucco rectangle on River Street. It had a sloping tile roof. A forest of radio aerials sprouted from the orange terra cotta. Inside the double oak doors was a waiting room with copies of *Hunter's World* and *Guns and Ammo*. A wit had also put a copy of the *Police Gazette* on a battered metal ashtray stand that stood next to three straight-backed chairs. The lead story was called "Love Slave for the FBI—My True Story."

Then there was a high desk, almost like a magistrate's bench. At it, a sheriff's deputy spoke into a telephone with a separate earpiece. The sheriff's deputy was a handsome, square-shouldered man with a rugged face and a mop of curly brown hair struggling to be orderly. He was fighting to keep his composure. Deputy Brown had already spoken to at least twenty reporters that morning. That was just counting the ones over the telephone. A unit from Mutual News had already been in to interview him for the radio. Robert Trout, who happened to be in San Francisco, had come down with a team in a Chrysler station wagon. Trout had asked Deputy Brown for all the details of the daring shootout and getaway of a German prisoner of war, who had apparently kidnapped a local woman and fled.

"All I can say is that it's under investigation and we will find the killer soon," Deputy Brown said calmly, preening as if he were in front of a movie camera.

Trout had then turned away and spoken into the microphone in solemn, basso profundo tones, "This sleepy California coastal town is already in shock over the brutal murders of at least four innocent people by desperate Nazi prisoners of war. There are more than fifty thousand German prisoners of war in this country. And the question that Americans are asking tonight is a basic one: Is there to be guerrilla war on the home front? Is anyone safe anywhere?"

Then Trout shook Deputy Brown's hand and walked back to the car. "Where can a man get a decent steak in this burg?" Trout's microphone man asked Brown. Brown recommended his cousin Tommy's place right off the boardwalk.

Then there had been the FBI agents. Four of the most sinister-looking men Deputy Brown had ever seen. They simply flashed their identifications, then rushed into the office of Chief Bates. They looked as if they could whip out a tommy gun and pick the eyes out of a snake at two hundred yards. No funny business. Just get the job done. Chief Bates's office was right behind the deputy's desk. When people raised their voices, Deputy Brown could hear every word. The FBI agents never raised their voices. Not once. They stayed for a half hour, getting all the details. Then they left, staring straight ahead.

The reporters from the San Francisco *Chronicle* had been the worst of the day. A tough girl with no stockings and a man smoking cigarettes right down to the butt made a helluva scene when Deputy Brown told them that Chief Bates was not seeing reporters. He, Brown, could give them a statement. "And who the hell are you?" the woman reporter had asked. "We ain't used to talking to errand boys. We like to talk to the boss. Let the people from the *Examiner* talk to you."

Deputy Brown had wanted to throw the bitch right out onto River Street, where she might get hit by a truck. Instead, he thought of the example of the FBI agents and kept his composure. Eventually, it all worked out pretty well, because they took his picture and he saw in a later edition of the *Chronicle* that he was right there on page one, with a caption that said "'Situation serious but under control,' says Santa Cruz deputy."

Chief Bates (who liked to be called "Chief" even though he was technically a sheriff, because he liked to compare himself with the big-city chiefs in terms of quick wits and fast movement) would be a little jealous, but he had only himself to blame for not coming out of his office.

The guys from Fort Ord had really been pitiful. The cameras from Movietone News caught them coming in the door, and you just knew that they were going to be the fall guys for this fiasco. That General Whitlock had a hangdog look about him. He was just going through the motions in terms of acting like he was going to help catch the prisoner Trattner. He talked for two minutes to Chief Bates, then he stood in front of the movie newsreel cameras and said, "We take the strictest precautions against any escapes or any danger to nearby citizens. Occasionally a mad dog like this man Trattner can slip through our tightest security. But you can be sure that the Army will take care of this. Our search teams are already spreading over this town like a net and we will get our man."

It sounded silly even when Whitlock said it. Here was this fat guy, who looked like he ate awfully well and drank even better, telling how he was going to catch someone in these wild Santa Cruz Mountains. It was pretty damned ridiculous. Even people in great shape could hardly maneuver in those mountains. That Whitlock fellow was going to be in deep shit and that was for sure. He was going to wind up in the stockade.

Then these last two who came in together—what an odd couple. Deputy Brown thought he could tell a lot about a man —woman, too—by looking at him. He wouldn't have picked these two to have anything to do with each other. The guy was a big Irish guy. Real strong looking. Maybe a high school athlete. Probably a cop, now. That would make a lot of sense. He was the guy who was with that little Marilyn girl who bought it from the Nazi who got killed. Matter of fact, he was the guy who shot the Nazi. Whelchel. The Irish guy was mighty fast. Good eye, too, to get off three shots right after his girlfriend had been shot, two of them right on the money. Definitely a guy to be afraid of, even though he had this real hurt look in his eyes. A guy that Deputy Brown would not like to cross in an alley or on a back road.

The broad was something different. Real sensitive-looking. Thin little mouse. Glasses and everything. Real mousy-looking brown hair. Like a lady professor or maybe a woman lawyer. He had seen one or two of them in Santa Cruz County Court. Nasty bitches. But this one looked like she was smart, but maybe not so mean. Kind of cute, almost, in a mousy sort of way. Bandages all over her legs. Big bruise on her forehead —God, her whole face looked like it was in pain. But the more he thought about it, he had to admit that she was kind of cute. Brown had heard that those brainy girls went all the way. Sounded good to him.

The two of them arrived at the Sheriff's Station at the same time. They both said they had to see Chief Bates right away. The girl flashed a telegram from the White House from some assistant to Franklin Delano Rosenvelt himself. The guy said that he had to see Chief Bates because "the bastards killed my girl and damn near killed me, and I don't give two cents' worth of a damn if that thing's a telegram from Saint Peter. I have to find out where that Nazi S.O.B. is holed up so I can go and kill him."

The girl had turned white. "That's exactly why I have to find him first. He's got to answer a few questions," she said. "This is a national security matter."

"Screw national security," the Irish guy, John Quinn, said. "I'll let him answer your questions after I've shot him in the kneecaps."

Now both of them were in with Chief Bates and there were definitely some raised voices this time.

In Chief Bates's office, a rectangular room with waist-high pine paneling and lime-green plaster walls, a calendar, a large portrait of the state attorney general, Goodwin Knight, and a cowboy belt with two real, working six-shooters hanging from a nail, Alice Burton and John Quinn sat with Chief Bates. They stared angrily at each other while Chief Bates puffed on a huge Havana cigar. Bates, a florid, slow-talking man in a tan uniform and hand-stitched cowboy boots, looked from one to the other and smiled languidly.

Sunlight poured in through a mullioned window with bars on the outside. It lay on the linoleum floor for an instant, then melted into the warm, smoky air.

"There's not a goddamned thing either one of you can do right now," Bates said, "because we don't have any idea at all of where they are. They might be in Canada by now, or they might be still up in the mountains, or they might have taken a fishing boat out from Monterey and met a Jap submarine. So you two can yell all you want, but it doesn't make a dime's worth of difference. We don't know where they are."

"Of course," Alice said soothingly. "It's just that when you do find them, we have reason to believe that an important matter of national defense is involved. We don't want people like Mr. Quinn running all over the place with bloody murder in their eyes. I know he must feel terrible, but this takes precedence. Other people might die if we can't get some information out of this Trattner."

"I told you, lady, we don't know where the hell he is," Bates said. "You're fighting about something that just ain't there."

"I think it would help find him if you told us more about this Maxine Lewis, Chief," Quinn said familiarly. He was trying to keep a lid on his feelings. He had been wound up like a bowstring since Marilyn got shot. If he did what he felt like doing, he would just go down to Fort Ord and shoot every Nazi in the place. He felt as if a hungry, sleepless beast had been unleashed inside his chest. If he could not tame it or somehow get it under control, he would start shooting. He might never stop. So now he had to act like he was really taking it like a man and staying calm, cool, and collected.

"This Maxine Lewis, Chief. Apparently she knew the P.O.W. Maybe it wasn't a kidnapping after all?" hinted

Quinn. "She have a cabin up in the woods or anything? Maybe a place on the beach? Maybe a close friend with a place up in the mountains? You know how criminals are, Chief. They tend to work from habit. They're usually too scared to try anything new. But you know all that, Chief. Cops know that kind of thing," he added, with a sidelong glance at Alice Burton.

Alice Burton sighed. "I understand how you feel, Mr. Quinn," she said.

"You do?" Quinn barked. "You had the woman you love shot in front of your face by a Nazi maniac?"

Dammit, Quinn told himself. He had to keep himself buttoned down a little better than that. If he looked too crazy, he'd be back in L.A. on psycho leave, and that would be the end of his chances for catching Trattner and blowing his brains out.

"Look," Alice Burton said, "I can't understand exactly how you feel, of course. But I know you must be going crazy with grief. I know you must feel incredibly angry. I don't blame you. No one blames you at all."

"That's very nice of you," Quinn said. "Very generous." That was more of the ticket. A little sarcasm. Let people know that he was zipped up enough to still make a wisecrack. Maybe a little bitter, but not totally insane. The only problem was that John Quinn at this minute, and for the last twenty-four hours, felt completely insane, crazy with loss and anger.

"What I'm trying to say is that I know you must feel as if you're losing your mind, but there are national security needs that come before any one of us. That's all," Alice Burton said with a genuine smile.

In her mind, Alice Burton felt distressed, even frantic. For all she knew, they would never find Trattner. That idiot Whitlock had no ideas. Chief Bates had no ideas. She had no ideas. The only man who had an idea was John Quinn, the big Irish cop who felt so angry that Alice Burton could feel it radiating in waves outward from him across Chief Bates's office. Quinn had a simple idea, which was that if he didn't get back at that Nazi, he would explode. He hadn't said it, but

Alice Burton could feel it as clearly as she felt heat when she touched a hot radiator. Quinn was right, of course. He had the monopoly on real emotion in that room. The human being who felt the strongest emotion was usually the one who would do what was right, Alice Burton believed.

"I'm not asking for much," Quinn said. "I'm not asking that you tie up Trattner and let me shoot him in one leg at a time and turn him into warm Jell-O. I'm just asking you to let me join in with your search people. That's all. I won't do anything crazy. You can pick up the phone and call Captain Parker in L.A. He'll tell you I'm not rash."

"I'll tell you what," Chief Bates said, slamming his feet down on the linoleum floor. "I'll just make you a deal. You two go out and find the sonofabitch, and then you two just decide between yourselves what the hell to do with him. You're talking to me as if I had him locked up in the cooler. I don't. I don't have one damned thought about where he is. There are roadblocks everywhere. So if you can do better than the roadblocks and the FBI, and if you can find him, just leave me out of it. Just do it yourselves."

Quinn had to struggle to manage a smile. He had worked with these small-town police chiefs, or sheriffs, or state highway patrol, or whatever they were, many times before. You had to play it very cagey. You couldn't act crazy or angry, as if your whole life had just been snatched away from you on a street corner in some no-name little town.

"I think that's a good idea," Alice Burton suddenly blurted out. "I think that Lieutenant Quinn and I might be able to help a little in finding him."

"What the hell makes you think that?" Quinn demanded.

"Because we may be able to piece together a few things about him from the War Department and maybe from the folks back in Washington. Might make it a little easier to track him down," Alice Burton said. "What do you say, Lieutenant? You want to help out with me? Maybe a few of my friends from Washington?"

Quinn scuffed his black shoes along the floor. This little bitch was really a pistol. Here she was, three thousand miles from home, in a town where she'd never been before, with two cops who obviously couldn't have cared less if she dropped dead. As a matter of fact, she had apparently come near to getting killed the same day that Marilyn got shot—yesterday. Now here she was, cool as you please, sitting back in her chair, telling the sheriff of the county that she was going to find a guy who was probably halfway across Utah by now, or else in some Jap submarine.

The kid had spirit. No doubt about it. It wasn't her fault that Marilyn was dead. And who knew, maybe that OSS or whatever back in Washington really did have some dope on where Trattner might go. She sure looked a lot smarter than any if these hillbillies here in Santa Cruz.

"I don't know what you're talking about, specifically," Quinn said. He looked keenly into Alice Burton's brown eyes. "What do you really think we could do? The goddamned FBI is out manning roadblocks."

"I think that sometimes two people who are really motivated, who have some good ideas about what they're looking for, can do a better job than a bunch of people who are just doing it because it's their job. That's all."

Chief Bates pointedly looked at his watch. "Look," he said, "I don't mind. I need all the help I can get. Why don't you two just go out and have some lunch and try to figure out how you can help. How's that sound?"

He rose, opened his door, and smiled at the two visitors. "I know you'll really contribute a lot," he said.

John Quinn stole another sideways glance at Alice Burton. The girl really had some bruises. "You feel like eating?" he asked.

Ten minutes later, Quinn and Alice Burton sat across from each other at a table covered with a red-and-white checked tablecloth in Dominic's, an Italian restaurant where the waiter was Deputy Brown's brother.

"I'm just curious to know," Alice Burton asked, "how come a guy who can shoot like you isn't in the Army?"

Quinn felt a wave of anger break over his brain. He grasped the salt shaker and squeezed it. He stared at a map of

Calabria on the wall above a simulated fireplace. He took a sip of his red wine ("Chilled or room temperature?" the waiter had asked) and looked at the only other diners, a pair of elderly women in shapeless dresses and slippers.

"Because I'm a draft dodger," Quinn said. "Because I'm afraid of getting shot." He looked angrily at Alice Burton. What a fucked-up question.

"I know that's not right," Alice Burton said. "I already got your record at the L.A.P.D. read to me. I have a pretty good idea of what kind of a man you are. You have asthma? Something wrong with your stomach? Don't give me that whining about being a coward. It doesn't fit and you know it." She looked at a spot on the wall just above his shoulder while she spoke. Then she looked straight into his face. "Let's not play games. I'm here to find this Trattner guy. So are you. Don't fight me. Fight him."

Quinn opened his mouth in shock. He studied Alice Burton's brown linen Garfinckel's suit, as if that might tell him just exactly why this woman had been able to make him feel as if there might be some life after Marilyn. He almost smiled. He said, "I have a spot on my lung. That's why. I've tried to enlist three times."

"I thought it was something like that," Alice Burton said, smiling confidentially. "Listen, I'm not selling you a bill of goods. If you can help me to track this guy down, you'll get a medal. From F.D.R.'s own fingers."

"How important can this guy be?" Quinn asked, his mood broken—improved. "I mean how much damage can one guy do? Even one very bad guy."

"Listen," Alice Burton said as she spooned steaming minestrone into her mouth, "it isn't just this guy. There's something going on. We don't know what it is, but we think that it's directed from Berlin, and we know they've put a lot of thought into it. A lot of effort, too. It's complicated, but it's very damned scary."

"How do you know that?" Quinn asked. He did not complain about her cursing, although he was tempted.

Alice Burton let out a long sigh. "All right," she said. "I'm probably gonna lose my job for this, but I'm gonna tell you some things you should probably know if we're gonna be in this together."

For half an hour, over spaghetti with garlic sauce (one of the only unrationed items, as the waiter explained cheerfully), the woman from the OSS told the man from L.A. Downtown Homicide about a certain mention of Siegfried; about certain hints in the air of negotiations in Stockholm ("I always knew the Commies would try to pull something," said Quinn); about Nazis running around Switzerland; about just how many P.O.W.s were in the U.S.; and about a legend about an invisible hero, a cape, a Rhine maiden, and a magic dwarf . . . and then she gave a few meaningful looks.

When Alice Burton was finished, she placed her knife and fork neatly on the plate of spaghetti, played with them for a moment, and said, "If we don't catch this guy, there could be big trouble."

Quinn shook his head in amazement. "I didn't have any idea that our people were so hep about what the Nazis were up to. I thought we were always getting caught off guard."

"We were," Alice Burton said. "But we were almost there. If I had gotten to Otto Seamans a day earlier, we would have been all set. The thing is," she said, "we don't even know what this guy's supposed to do. If we don't get to him in time this go-round, a lot of people might die."

"Some people have already died," Quinn said softly.

"Exactly," Alice Burton said. "That's why you're the man to make sure nobody else does. If anyone can stop Trattner, you can. I don't know how, but you can do it. And I'm going to help."

Outside Dominic's, across Front Street, children began to line up to ride the roller coaster on the Santa Cruz boardwalk.

May 22, 1943,
Ely, Nevada

The sun broke in the east above an endless expanse of desert. Joachim Trattner pushed aside the curtains at the Ely Desert Lodge room and stared across the parking lot at the pink and purple shadows lengthening and then shortening on the desert. There were no other guests at the Ely Desert Lodge, so there were no sounds to disturb the majesty of the morning.

Trattner glanced behind his shoulder. Maxine was still sleeping soundly. A light-green comforter and a dark-blue blanket were pulled over her so that only the top of her head showed. A mop of her blonde hair tumbled out onto the comforter. In the corner of the room, a space heater wheezed continually in its futile effort to keep the room warm. Maxine moaned in her sleep occasionally. Trattner ignored her.

If Trattner had not been the kind of man he was, he might have been tempted to stay in that room in the Ely Desert Lodge with Maxine Lewis until the war was over. He would not mind looking out at the sunrise every morning without the fear that a Hawker Hurricane might suddenly appear from Ras Bubasa and scatter 50 caliber slugs all over the desert. He thought again of how lucky the Americans were—how incredibly lucky—that they had not known a foreign invader, had not

known war on their continent for eighty years. Lucky, rich
. . . and ignorant.

But there was little enough time for that kind of thinking.
Trattner went into the shower. He ran the water scalding hot
—amazing, to get scalding-hot water in the middle of the desert, at five-thirty in the morning. The Americans really were
the finest mechanics in the world. In the emptiness of the
great American desert, he stood in a shower surrounded by
ceramic tiles such as a Thyssen would envy in today's Germany. He let the water sear into his pores. This was the first
hot shower he had ever had in his life. In Germany, one took
baths. In England one used cologne. In the Libyan desert,
one was fortunate not to have one's eyes eaten out by flies. At
Kriegsgefangenenlager Fort Ord, the water was warm but
never really hot. Taking a hundred showers in lukewarm
water at Fort Ord had readied Trattner for a blindingly hot
shower.

Trattner dried himself, then studied the map on a small
maple desk thoughtfully equipped with color postcards of the
desert and a caption which read "Ely, Nevada—Gateway to
the Golden West." Imagine the wastefulness of these Americans. To throw money away on color postcards when there
were maps and war documents to be made.

Abruptly, Maxine was up and by his side. She stroked his
neck and then kissed his ear. "No time for that now," he said.
But he let his left arm run up under her robe to her thigh. It
was warm, glowing with heat. Trattner reached farther up. In
a moment, he and Maxine were back in bed. When they
finished, Maxine lay on her back. Trattner stared at the pine-
beamed ceiling. By God, it would not be so bad to be here in
this room with Maxine Lewis for the duration! If not for his
oath as an SS man, of course. And, of course, one could easily
tire of a sow like Maxine Lewis.

And anything else would be a betrayal of all his oaths and
his solemn promises to Führer and fatherland. Besides, he was
ready for the moment of glory that he knew was his due.
Maxine fell back asleep. Trattner slid out of bed, walked
across the cold floor to the desk, and studied the map again.

His instructions—as relayed in an envelope given to him by Maxine—were completely explicit. He was to take random routes, never staying on one road for more than a day, but making certain to get across the country in less than ten days. The envelope had a neatly folded packet of gasoline ration coupons in addition to the instructions. It also had five hundred dollars in twenties. Then it had the bombshell, the instruction on where he was to go, what he was to do. Trattner had hardly believed his eyes when he read (in Maxine's speeding car) the seriousness of his errand. Then he realized, in a crescendo of understanding, just what his adventure, his duty, must mean. After all, he had been a physicist!

On him, on the shoulders of Joachim Trattner, fell the responsibility to literally save the Reich! Himself!

If Joachim Trattner could carry out his orders, the Reich would have an entirely new chance at winning the war. Trattner would not admit it to a living soul, but he knew in his own heart and mind that the situation of the Reich was desperate. In the filling station in Carson City, where Maxine had stopped for gasoline, there were old copies of *Time* magazine. There was also a new copy. Trattner had taken it with him to read.

Even if one allowed for the lies of the American Jew press, the war news was grim. Germany was being bombed night and day. The cover of *Time* had borne a picture of a British swine of a bomber commander named Harris. He gleefully told about bombing German civilians, killing young German mothers and their babies. Even Berlin was being bombed regularly now. Ten thousand tons of bombs each day! Falling on the cities of Germany. Even if the estimate were twice too high, a lot of people were dying.

On the Eastern Front, the Russians were pounding Manstein so hard that he would surely have to retreat. Even German communiqués as quoted in *Time* said that the Reich was forced to adopt "flexible lines of defense." Trattner knew what that meant: retreat.

The Russians and the British were becoming as thick as Jew thieves. Small wonder, since the strings were pulled from on high by the same clique of Jew financiers. Now that vermin, Stalin, pretended to abolish the Comintern. That was in return for the British signing a twenty-year pact of friendship and fun and games. Abolish the Comintern! Who would ever fall for that trick? The same gang would be trying under a different name to wipe free white men off the map, no matter what they called themselves.

It was really too much to bear. But now, if Trattner could do what he had to do, the tables would be turned. If Trattner did not succeed, he, Trattner, would be dead anyway. So might the Reich be. An icy determination settled upon Trattner's mind. He would not fail.

"Come back to bed for just a little minute," Maxine whined sweetly. Trattner turned to see her arching her back and making seductive faces at him. She was a temptress, like a Rhine River goddess. Maxine was no maiden, however.

"Let's get something to eat," Trattner said. "We'll have plenty of time for that later."

"Ohh, you're such a mean man," Maxine said in her little-girl voice. Trattner was powerfully tempted once again. But his Teutonic duty lay across the desert, not in bed with Maxine Lewis. That was perfectly clear. Well, almost perfectly clear. He shook his head. "Let's go," he said stonily.

Soon Maxine and Trattner sat in the Ely Desert Lodge Coffee Shop, eating eggs and toast. Trattner had carefully avoided eating bacon or ham. Maxine watched approvingly. Again, he felt the same sense of wonder. In the middle of a total war, five hundred miles or more from a major city, there were fresh eggs and whole-wheat toast. There were large cups of real coffee, and a small glass of orange juice, a delicacy which he had enjoyed only twice before in his life.

Maxine and Trattner were the only customers in the coffee shop. It was a small room with a plate-glass window and venetian blinds warding off the morning sun. The booths had vinyl slipcovers and varnished wooden tables. A chrome border ran around the wooden tops of the tables. On the wall were relics of the desert—desiccated cow skulls, the skins of rattlesnakes, worm-eaten wagon wheels, rusted and bent rifles.

The food was served on porcelain plates colored a light blue.

The waiter was also the cook. He disappeared behind a counter, then behind a wall with a long window. He cooked for a few minutes. Then he brought out bacon, toast, and more coffee. "No charge," he said. "We'll just throw it away unless somebody eats it."

Trattner had to struggle to control his amazement. The abundance was overwhelming. Maxine pushed the plate of bacon away. She fixed the counterman with a stern look and said, "We don't eat meat. You ought to think about it yourself."

The counterman cocked his head. He screwed up his watery eyes. "Come again?" he asked.

Trattner looked at the man icily and said, "We love animals. We don't eat them."

"Jehovah's Witness?" the counterman asked. "We have a few of them right here in town."

"We just don't eat things with feelings," Maxine said stonily. The counterman watched as Maxine patted Trattner's hand. He shook his head and retreated into the kitchen to read something. Then he reappeared. "You read about those Nazi guys shooting up people right in California. Right here in the U.S.A.?" He poured two glasses of iced water. "Nazis. Right here in America. Pretty hard to swallow."

"I don't believe anything I read in the newspapers anymore," Maxine Lewis said cheerfully. She smiled and sat up straight. She wore a tight-fitting shirtwaist dress of blue cotton. The counterman stared at her breasts and swallowed. He was obviously struggling to concentrate.

"We had a call from the highway patrol last night," he said. "They're looking for that Nazi guy everywhere. Even in Nevada. But I don't think he's gonna be that easy to find. After all, he ain't exactly gonna be wearing a swastika around his neck, is he?" the counterman, who had a day's stubble on his chin, asked. The counterman had a tattoo of an anchor on his right forearm. Inside it was the word "Mother."

"Not unless he's crazy," Maxine said.

"I guess we're supposed to look out for anybody who acts strange," the counterman said.

"Like people who love animals?" Trattner asked. His eyes bored into the counterman, who began to wipe the counter in rapid, circular motions.

"They say he kidnapped some dame from California. Maybe he's killed her by now," the counterman said. "I wouldn't be surprised."

"Probably has. That's my guess," Maxine Lewis said. "If the story's true at all. It might just be some G.I. went crazy and started shooting. It's been known to happen."

"Yeah, that could be," the counterman said, leering at Maxine's bosom. "Anything's possible."

The counterman slowly glanced sideways at Trattner. "You home on leave, pal? You look like you've seen some time in the service."

Trattner lifted his head from his food. He gave a withering look to the counterman. His blue eyes seemed to freeze the counterman where he stood, with his greasy T-shirt and his hand holding an old glass tray. "I try not to talk too much about what I have had to do," he said. "Loose lips sink ships."

The counterman looked terrified for a moment. Then a smile crossed his lips. His Lucky Strike butt almost fell out of his mouth. "I get it," he said. "Underground work inside certain countries," he added. "You don't have to say another word."

Trattner thought that for a counterman the fellow looked unusually intelligent. "I hope you can keep a secret," Trattner said.

"I sure can," the counterman said. "I'm a deputy sheriff, you know. I don't do too much on account of I broke my hip a while back, but I can sure keep a secret."

"Norwegian underground," Trattner said. "Of course, I'm from Minnesota, but my family's back in Norway. I sometimes see them, if you know what I mean."

The counterman raised the sparse eyebrows above his brown eyes knowingly. Almost too knowingly, Trattner thought.

"Listen," Trattner asked, "do you have any gasoline out there?" He jerked his thumb backward to point at a gasoline pump in front of the "registration desk area" of the Ely Desert Lodge. "We've got to get going before it gets too hot."

"Sure," the counterman said. "I do that, too. You got coupons?"

"The government makes certain I have everything I need," Trattner said with a confidential lowering of his voice.

"You pull it up right to the pump," the counterman said. "But take it easy. That Ford convertible's mine. I don't want to get any scratches on it. It's a 1940. I'm watching it for a big rancher in these parts who's fighting in North Africa. Tunisia or somewhere."

As Trattner paid the bill, the counterman smiled disarmingly and asked, "Whereabouts you headed now?"

"Can you keep another secret?" Trattner asked. His eyes were hooded, lazily taking the counterman into his confidence.

The counterman nodded. "Damned right."

"Now we are going to Los Angeles," he said. "I will have to drop off my friend in Pasadena."

"Too bad," said the counterman.

"You're not kidding," Trattner said. He made the smallest beginnings of a smile.

Trattner whispered to Maxine Lewis to pack everything and be out by the gasoline pump in "five minutes—no longer."

Then Trattner told the counterman to help him guide his bulky Plymouth so that he would not even come close to touching "your beautiful convertible."

Trattner and the counterman stepped out into the dazzling desert sun. The air was dry and almost cool, despite the light of the sun. Inside Maxine's car, though, the air was warm and still. Trattner slid behind the driver's seat. He started the engine and headed slowly for the gasoline pump across the parking lot. He smiled at the counterman as a huge truck rumbled by on Route 50. The counterman pointed this way and that, as if he were a pilot docking a huge freighter. In a few seconds, Trattner had the car at the gas pump. The counterman unlimbered the gasoline hose and began to fill the Plymouth's tank.

"You really have that convertible?" Trattner asked. "To use? I wonder what it's worth." Trattner felt a tingling up his spine and in his fingertips. Now was surely the moment.

"Nowadays?" the counterman asked. He fished in his pocket and took out two keys. "Nowadays these keys is worth a couple a thousand bucks, easy. When the girls see a car like this, well, I don't have to tell you."

Trattner got out of the car. He peered curiously at the price posted for the gasoline. Fifteen and nine-tenths per gallon. Flying A regular. He stood behind the counterman and watched him pump the gasoline. He whistled "Home on the Range," a tune he had learned from Corporal Toby Moffatt. He reached into his pocket for a long kitchen knife he had picked up in the Ely Desert Lodge while the counterman was not looking. The tingling in his fingers grew. A mask of cruelty locked his features in place.

With one deft movement, he grasped the counterman's face and covered up the man's mouth. As the counterman struggled, Trattner stabbed the man in his back just above the bottom of his rib cage. The counterman tensed and stood up straight, tried furiously to get out away from the knife, then collapsed on the asphalt.

The gasoline was still flowing into the Plymouth. Trattner picked up the counterman's body. He dragged it across a few feet of black, oily ground and stuffed it into the trunk of the Plymouth.

At that moment, Maxine Lewis appeared from the room with two small suitcases. She saw Trattner wrestling with the body. He gestured toward the convertible with his face. Maxine understood. She ran to the Ford. With a swift step and a whipping motion, she threw the bags into the back seat. Trattner slammed the trunk, hefted the car keys in his hand, then drove the Plymouth to a remote corner of the parking lot. Several trucks had driven by, but no one thought to stop and look more closely.

Trattner parked the Plymouth, locked all the doors and

windows, and removed the license plates. Then he ran to the Ford. It was already running. Maxine thought of everything.

Maxine drove them along Route 50 in silence for fifteen minutes. In the white, unfiltered early-morning light, they hurtled past sagebrush and scrub oak. On both sides of the road, they could see hawks wheeling in the blue sky, scanning the desert floor for prey. Maxine remembered that she had seen hawks in the sky above Santa Cruz on the day she met Otto Seamans. God, that was a long time ago now. She wondered what Otto Seamans was doing. Probably had another slutty little girlfriend somewhere. That would be Maxine's guess.

There were occasional billboards for hotels and natural thermal springs. There were jackrabbits which darted out from behind rocks and ran parallel with the Ford convertible for a few yards, then dashed back into the desert. Coyotes, like long, lean, emaciated dogs, stood by the side of the road as if they had never seen an automobile before. They stared and then meandered off to search for desert mice.

In the sky, an azure-perfect blueness shone, like a radiant sapphire inside which Maxine Lewis and her beloved were gliding noiselessly. This was what it was like to be in love, to feel she was doing something important. To Maxine Lewis, it was all there, every hope, every dream, every longing, right there on the spot on this earth where she and Joachim Trattner traveled together.

There had been other moments in life, but for Maxine, every instant with Trattner, on a mission of life-or-death importance to the future of man, was what she had been prepared for since her miraculous escape from the runaway horses on Pacific Avenue more than twenty-five years before. Compressed into her time with Joachim was all the meaning of life. She loved that phrase. She had read it in a book.

That might be silly, Maxine knew. It would really mark her as a sap in front of the other girls at the real estate agency. But she didn't care. Her life with Trattner might end with both of them stretched out on a cement block at a morgue, the way she had seen her cousin Jimmy after the accident with the silo ladder in Watsonville. But for now—which is the only time that counts—everything was right there in that car, in that desert, at that moment.

Maxine passed a gasoline tanker truck with a gaudy Sunoco diamond in black, blue, and red. The driver took a look out his window at Maxine's legs—her skirt had been blown back to her thighs by the wind—and leaned on his horn. Maxine mashed down the accelerator. The Ford shot still farther ahead.

"Not so fast," Trattner said sternly. "If they think to stop us, we could be in serious trouble." His features were starting to relax now. The mask was gone. Only a slight tingling remained.

"There's no one here to stop us," Maxine said. "They don't bother to stop a car in the desert. If you crash, they just scrape you off the highway." She reached over and stroked Trattner's knee. There were a few bloodstains on it. They were sticky to the touch. "But I won't let us crash," she said. "We have great things to do."

"How do you know?" Trattner asked sharply. He had not shown the letter to Maxine before burning it.

"I know because you're the kind of man who only does great things," Maxine said. Jeez, what a grouch.

"You are a sorceress," Trattner said cheerfully. "You know what to say to a man." He scanned her breasts and asked, "But seriously now. Really. Do you know what we are supposed to do? Did anyone tell you our mission?"

"Just that it was real important," Maxine said. "That creep Otto Seamans told me that."

" 'Creep'?" Trattner asked. "What does that mean?"

Maxine scrunched up her back as if she had a chill or as if someone had run a fingernail against a blackboard. "It just means the kind of person you wouldn't ever want to touch you. It would make your flesh creep. You know, crawl."

"Did he ever touch you?" Trattner demanded as they passed a billboard advertising a shop down the road which sold "Real Indian Scalps."

"He tried," Maxine answered with a toss of her head. "I wouldn't let him near me."

"I would not respect you if you had," Trattner said. "What we have is not to be shared." *Gott in Himmel,* the things he had to say to this whore!

Trattner rubbed his jaw thoughtfully. "I still cannot understand that fool Whelchel. What could have gone through his mind?"

"People can be real funny when they get a gun in their hands," Maxine Lewis said. "I've seen a lot of movies. Punks just go crazy when they get a little power."

"I think you are right," Trattner said. "But what a fool. We could have gotten away with only a few M.P.s looking for us if he had not been so hot-headed. This is serious business."

Maxine clucked sympathetically. Off to the left, she could see the dim outline of mesas. According to the map, they would soon be traveling through some of the most beautiful countryside in the western United States. Huge ravines and buttes formed by glacial movement many years before. Long before Maxine was born. Millions of years ago. Still there.

"He was always a rash man. I remember once when we had a shipment of new Schmeissers in Libya. We were not certain how far the shells would travel. He lined up four Arab men, tied them up, and took shots at one from a hundred meters, then one from two hundred meters, then one from three hundred meters, then one from four hundred meters. Just to test if the Schmeissers could kill at that distance."

Maxine was horrified. She was happy that Whelchel was not there.

"It was all so unnecessary," Trattner said. "If he had to test them, he could have just put one man at four hundred yards. That would have solved everything. I did not like killing those Arabs. An Arab is not like a Jew. The Jew has been mongrelized, contaminated from living in Eastern Europe. The Arab is a free, purebred product of the desert, like a fox or a goat."

Maxine admired this quality in Trattner. The man was not simply brute strength. He had some discernment, an ability to see that the world was complex and that moral values had their place. Why kill four men when one is sufficient?

"You see this desert, Joachim?" Maxine Lewis asked. "This is the product of millions of years of glaciers moving across here. It took millions of years. You know how long that is?" Aloud he said nothing. He had more serious matters to think about. Physics. The future of the Aryan race.

"These layers of sand are all different colors if you look at them closely. Some of those buttes up ahead . . . That's what they're called. Buttes. They rise straight up for five hundred feet. Maybe more. That takes millions of years, too."

Trattner nodded again. What the hell was she getting at?

"But the Jews are putting in factories and hotels and ruining all this beauty," Maxine Lewis said. "The Führer understands that. That's why it's so important that we succeed at whatever we're doing. To save the deserts and mountains and the trees. You see what I mean?"

"Of course," Trattner said soothingly. But really, what on earth was she talking about? What could she possibly mean by talking about the desert getting filled up with factories and hotels? He had not seen a building of any kind for thirty miles at least. What on earth did she mean by saying that she was fighting for the trees and the mountains? How could you fight for a mountain? The mountain would be there no matter what you did.

Not that Trattner could spare much time to think about the entire subject. If he were to get his work done, to accomplish his mission *zu Befehl des Führers,* he would have plenty to do besides worrying about this woman's mania.

"That man at the lodge," Trattner said. "He was too curious. I had not planned to kill him. But the way he spoke to me. That made me suspicious. I had to wonder just what he would do when we left. I regretted having to kill him, but it was necessary."

Maxine took her hand from Trattner's knee and squeezed his hand. "I understand," she said. "I understand perfectly. Sometimes you have to do things you don't like."

Trattner had not said that he did not *like* killing the counterman. But he did not make an issue over the difference in meaning. What was the point in discussing the manly hunting spirit with a woman and an American vegetarian woman at that? God, to get away from her crazed, prying eyes and have a decent steak! She was good for satisfying his *sexual* needs but not for much else. He merely squeezed her hand and smiled at her.

Still, there was something about her. Just holding her hand, he was starting to get excited. She could sense it somehow. She brushed his fly with her hand. Then she started to unzip his fly. He did not stop her.

These American women, he thought as they flew along the road. They will do anything.

May 24, 1943,
Ely, Nevada

Damn, damn, damn, Alice Burton said to herself. If only this guy had just taken a look at the license plate and then run for his life, called the state troopers or the FBI in Reno or just kept his mouth shut. She looked at the body of the counter-man with his dead blue eyes, the stubble on his chin, and the look of surprise still lingering around his mouth. He had a tattoo that said "Mother."

The body rested on a marble catafalque in the County Memorial Hospital coroner's office. The doctors had told Alice that the counterman, one John Riley by name, had died of traumatic injury to the kidneys and severing of the left main subaortic artery. He had really died of curiosity, Alice Burton suspected.

"It was damned lucky that he thought to write down the license number in the register and then write it again on the pad in the kitchen," John Quinn said. He stared at the body as if it might sit up and apologize for having gotten itself killed just when it might have given some really good clues about where the hell Trattner was.

Quinn rubbed his chin. "The way I figure it," he said, "the poor slob figured out that he had something pretty hot going on. So he maybe started asking a few questions or something."

"And Trattner killed him. What the hell does Trattner have to lose, after all?" Alice Burton asked. She wrapped her camel-colored cardigan closer around her chest. It was cold in the mortuary room.

"So the owner comes along and sees there's no counterman and he thinks the guy's drunk again. Then he sees blood coming out of the trunk of this strange car. Then the police go over the license numbers in the guest book. Not bad police work from these small-town cops, I'd say," Quinn said. He wore his usual blue suit that he wore when he was on a case. It was shiny in the seat and in the knees, but it was his business suit, his lucky suit. He was usually able to find somebody when he was wearing that suit. Thirty bucks at the May Company. It better last a good long time.

"I don't think we need to see any more of this," Quinn added. "Let's go back to the motel."

In the car, a blue Buick which the Ely sheriff had put at their disposal after a few calls from the White House and from some bigshot named Donovan in Washington, Alice Burton stared at the nighttime sky. There were more stars above Nevada than she would have ever thought possible. It was like being a million miles out in space to see all those stars. There were a hundred times as many stars as Alice Burton would ever have believed existed.

"It's just a damned shame that it took the owner so long to tell the police that he thought the FBI should know, too. And it's a damned shame that the FBI took twenty-four hours to tell your people in Washington," Quinn said.

"That's politics," she said, staring at the Big Dipper and the Little Dipper. She had not known there were two of them until tonight. "I think your big break is that we've found out a lot more about the woman than we knew before. That woman at the department store really was smart to come forward and tell us about Maxine buying those men's clothes the day of the killings. It takes guts to do that when you've known a woman all her life." Alice Burton thought that it would take guts to have bought the clothes, too, but she did not say that.

"So Maxine was in on it from the beginning and now someone at her real estate office says she remembers Otto Seamans coming in and taking her for a ride," Quinn said. "It all adds up. Pretty soon someone'll appear and say that Maxine had this plan for blowing up the George Washington Bridge."

"I doubt it," Alice said. "I doubt it very much. They make mistakes and they get careless, but not that careless."

"You don't know the criminal mind," Quinn said. "It likes to leave little messages, little clues. It likes to tease. That's what they call psychology," he added.

Alice Burton looked out the window at a lighted billboard that advertised Camel cigarettes. A man in a sailor's suit was holding a Camel and smiling as if God had told him he would live forever. He was alone on that billboard in the middle of the Nevada desert. Alice Burton, who had read *Civilization and Its Discontents,* did not comment on the criminal mind.

"I can't get over the sperm residue on the sheets," Alice Burton said. "I guess they're in this a little thicker than we thought."

Quinn flushed in the darkened Buick to hear her talk like someone from Wilshire Vice. Maybe that was what they did at those fancy colleges, but he didn't like it. Decent women were not supposed to talk like cops.

Alice continued as if she were talking to Sam Murphy and not to a prudish Irish cop. "I feel as if Maxine must be a relative of someone important. That's the only possible reason why she would have gotten hooked up with this whole operation. If she's the conduit, then maybe the plan is that she takes Trattner somewhere to meet somebody important."

Quinn looked at the gas stations and the "help wanted" billboards for the tin mine in Ely. Then he thought about how Marilyn, who was a hundred times sexier than this intellectual broad Alice Burton, would never ever have talked the way Alice Burton talked. It was a cover-up, Quinn figured. If Alice Burton was a real sex bomb, like little Marilyn had turned out to be, she would never have to use that kind of trashy talk. It was like the most chicken-shit guys on the L.A.P.D. talking the most about shooting people. Still, Alice Burton was one smart, confident cookie, and Quinn would not criticize her.

"But who could it be?" Alice Burton asked. She rubbed her hands against the skirt of her brown suit. "I just can't think what they have to gain by getting one guy out of one prisoner of war camp. Especially shooting up all those people." She paused and gulped. God, she made a fool of herself sometimes. She really was an idiot to talk like this in front of Quinn.

"I'm sorry," Alice Burton said. She reached across the seat and touched Quinn's arm. "I'm really sorry. That was pretty dumb of me. It was really stupid."

Quinn shrugged. "It's all right," he said. "It's all right. She didn't know what hit her." His voice trailed off into the desert night. It mingled with the cry of a coyote.

"Yes, but you knew," Alice Burton said. "I'm really sorry."

"It's a funny thing," Quinn said. "Well, not really funny, I guess, but really sad for Marilyn. I had this wife and she left me. She left me for a rich guy whose father has a lot of oil money and I'm just a dumb cop. So she left me, and I used to sit around in my backyard drinking whiskey and beer and I'd be thinking about how much I missed my wife. And meanwhile, Marilyn would come over, and she was really a strict Catholic, and she'd tell me jokes and cheer me up. And she'd stay with me sometimes." Quinn felt a wave of longing coming over him as he spoke to Alice Burton. "So Marilyn's coming over," Quinn said, "and she's really doing everything she can to make me feel better. And I'm just moping around and thinking here's this little kid and I can take her or leave her. The main thing is," Quinn continued, "I'm thinking about Joan, who treated me like I was dirt, and the whole time, here's this little Marilyn, who is just breaking her neck trying to make me happy. And I'm worrying about why I couldn't get into the Army and why Rizzuti might get promoted ahead of me—he's my partner—and I'm worrying about what the neighbors think when Marilyn comes over and spends the night.

"And the whole time, I have something really precious, something really beautiful right in my hands and I treat her like she was invisible or something. I don't know. I guess I'm just a dumb harp."

"We never realize what we have until we lose it," Alice said slowly. Immediately, she felt ashamed of the cliché. There was obviously a lot more to this man than she had thought. She could not remember Sam Murphy or that Kenneth guy from the OPA ever opening up and talking like this. Maybe it was the emptiness of the Nevada sky at night. Maybe it was just that she was a stranger. Maybe it was that the woman he loved had been shot and he was feeling lonely. Come to think of it, his story made her feel alone as well. What on earth was she, a nice little woman lawyer, doing out there in the middle of nowhere looking for a crazy Nazi killer? Of course, Sam had men looking at all the sympathizers that the OSS had run to ground. The FBI had men at every train station. Alice's mission with Quinn was just one of a hundred, maybe a thousand sorties to cover the area. Still, what was she doing wandering around the desert looking for something she would never find? She should be back in a library, reading things and analyzing them.

"When I used to run track at Fairfax High," Quinn said, "I had a lot of time to think. I'd think about how crazy the world was mostly. How all these bad things happened in the world and there wasn't a thing you could do about them. Your dad loses his job. Your mother stays up all night crying and darning socks. Your brother drinks too much. Your best friend gets run over by a trolley car. Your cousin Mike dies of flu.

"I'd think those things and then I'd keep running," Quinn said. "I figured that as long as I was running, those bad things weren't ever gonna catch up with me. As long as I was running, I was like a kid on a bicycle. As long as it's going fast and moving in a straight line, you know it's not gonna turn over and you're not gonna scrape your knee. But if it does turn over, sometimes you don't want to get back on."

"I understand that," Alice Burton said. What else was she doing if not trying to stay on the bicycle herself? She studied and she thought and she worked her way up, and in a way, that was like staying on a bicycle, too. As long as she kept working, kept moving forward, she never had to ask herself where she was going, or why she was working in a classy office in Washington while her cousins in Romania were getting put in cattle cars. If she started thinking about that, she might find that her knees were getting pretty cut up.

Quinn stopped at a stoplight in Ely. On one corner was an all-night diner. On the other was an agricultural implements store. It was closed. There were no other cars on the street. No one was in the diner. The light went from red to green and Quinn went ahead in the borrowed Buick. He fiddled with the radio. For a moment, he could hear Frank Sinatra singing something about blue Hawaii, but then the signal faded. There was nothing but static elsewhere on the dial. Even clear-channel stations could not reach all the way to Ely, Nevada.

"I'm a cop now. I'm not a dreamer. I'm a cop," Quinn said. "I stopped running a long time ago. But I'm still on that bicycle. Only now it's not a bicycle anymore. It's like a room that I keep locked with thirty padlocks on the door. I hide in that room. The world is total madness outside my room. Pachucos kill each other over a beer. Husbands carve their wives up into a thousand pieces and try to flush them down the toilet. Sailors get so drunk they fall off merry-go-rounds at Santa Monica pier. Bus drivers go berserk because their wives leave them and they run their buses into people's houses.

"Japs kill a million people in Nanking. The Germans blow up every house in Rotterdam. The Russians kill their own people. It's just complete craziness out there. And I'm in my little apartment up in my head trying to keep everything nice and neat and orderly and meanwhile there's a lot of Frankensteins outside pounding on the door. That's why I'm a cop. To try to keep that door closed, to keep that bicycle upright, to keep running," Quinn said.

"I understand," Alice Burton said. What else could she say? God, she had been wrong about this guy. He was a strange cop. This was a guy who could feel things. Most of all, this was a guy who was obviously suffering terribly. If she had ever seen a man who was feeling more loss, she could not think when. Pure loss poured from him like water out of a broken main.

"So I try to live my life so that there's all this madness out-side and inside everything's just perfect, just going along smooth as you please. And then I decide maybe I'll just take one little chance because here's Marilyn and she's so safe, so comforting, so orderly. And then—bingo!—she's gone, and that door I had kept barred is broken down and a lot of crazy peo-ple come running in with straight razors."

Quinn stopped in front of the motel. There was a county sheriff's deputy waiting for him at the "registration area." Quinn pulled the Buick into about the spot where the owner had last seen the Ford convertible parked.

"I don't know why I told you this. You probably think I'm drunk," Quinn said with a self-deprecating smile.

"I'm glad you did," Alice Burton said, touching his arm in the cold air outside the car.

"I think I told you so you'd know that even though nobody else thinks we can do it, and maybe you don't even think we can do it, we're going to find that German sonofabitch, and after you've asked him your questions, then we're going to kill him."

Alice Burton gulped as she followed Quinn and the deputy into the motel office. Another deputy sat in a vinyl chair with tubular steel arms. The room was lit by bright fluorescent lights. A thousand flies batted against the window and the screen door in the quiet night. Alice could hear crickets chir-ruping in an overwhelming chorus. There was a cup of coffee for her, wrapped in a handkerchief so she would not burn her fingers.

"It's her handwriting on the registration sheet," the deputy said. He was just a kid, with pimples and thick glasses and unruly hair coming down out of his hat. "They already re-ported back from Santa Cruz. They got the sample this morn-ing. She's calling herself Lorelei Calhoun. Can you beat that?" the deputy asked. "What the hell kind of name is that? Lor-elei?"

"It's the name of a Rhine River goddess," Alice Burton said tonelessly as her heart raced. "From Germany." Outside, a coyote howled in the starry night.

May 25, 1943,
Chevy Chase, Maryland

Outside the oak-paneled dining room of the Chevy Chase
Club, there was a swimming pool. It was not in use yet, because the Chevy Chase Club had been opening its pool on
Memorial Day weekend for thirty-one years and saw no reason to change the practice. Besides, there had been that freak
snowstorm only a week or two ago, and who knew what
might happen between now and the end of the month. However, just to be sure that the pool would be ready for the children of Washington's best families as well as their parents,
some of the club's colored help were scouring the bottom of
the pool on their hands and knees at this very moment. The
men worked in black trousers and white shirts with leather
bow ties in eighty-degree weather. They scrubbed away at
the blue bottom of the pool with large horsehair brushes,
which they occasionally dipped in a sudsy pail. Sam Murphy
could see sweat pouring off the men's faces and running into
the soapy mess on the bottom of the pool.

Inside the dining room, on the cooler side of the French
doors that led to the pool area, only five tables of the dining
room were in use. Four of them were occupied by middle-
aged or elderly ladies in floppy hats and flowered dresses. Al-

most all of them wore lorgnettes and did not smoke. They all stared at Sam Murphy's table constantly. One of them even dropped a chunk of aspic on the black-and-white tiled floor because she was staring so hard. Even the black waiters, in their leather bow ties and black jackets, stared at Murphy's table. The man who had taken their order had actually been shaking, like a caricature of a black man in a bad movie.

"Is there anywhere you go where you're not recognized?" Sam Murphy asked.

Murphy's luncheon guest plunged his fork into his boiled whitefish and said, "I never really noticed, Mr. Murphy. I don't care whether I'm recognized or not. My job is to serve the President and catch Nazi saboteurs. It isn't to get my picture in a fan magazine."

Murphy noticed that John Edgar Hoover said the words with a practiced irritation that spoke of careful preparation and endless repetition, among other things.

The man who sat next to Hoover, a thin, serious-looking man in a suit that might have come from J.C. Penney, looked curiously at Murphy as if thinking whether or not Murphy, properly deboned and boiled, might make a good meal for the director. "We're not looking for headlines," Clark Wilson said. "We're looking for enemies of the republic."

Wilson also ate boiled fish. He had a bulge under his right shoulder. Hoover, on the other hand, was clearly not "packing heat," as they said in the "Gangbusters" show on radio. His suit also had a look of quality. Probably from Woodward & Lothrop, Murphy thought. The stuff was unpretentious, but it was made all right. Murphy could tell a lot about a man by the kind of clothes he wore. He could tell that J. Edgar Hoover, for instance, did not need to make any statement at all by the way he dressed. The man was strong enough in a Woodward & Lothrop suit for anything that might be needed.

Sam Murphy picked up half of his club sandwich—he had made a joke about ordering it at the Chevy Chase Club and Hoover had smiled but Wilson had not changed expression— and took a bite. It was good. The Chevy Chase Club food was pretty horrible, but at least they could get this right.

"You know, when I was a boy, my father used to drive us by the gates of this place," Hoover said. "Of course, we could never in a million years have afforded to join. But I could see the people inside in their carriages. —Yes, there were still some people in carriages then. They looked like they were enjoying themselves," Hoover added, as if "enjoying themselves" were a synonym for "abusing themselves." Hoover took a small swallow of Coca-Cola and added, "Of course, they were from a different class. Not civil servants like me and my father."

"You aren't missing a whole hell of a lot," Murphy said. "It's a pretty dull place."

"No, when I was a lad, we didn't have any private clubs for swimming. I swam at the public pool on Blair Road, just the same as everybody else," Hoover said. "I think maybe that's where I actually learned to swim." He looked at his colleague and friend and said, "It doesn't hurt a boy to swim in a public pool, does it, Clark? You don't learn to swim any worse, do you?"

Clark Wilson set down his Coca-Cola and said, "No, Mr. Director, not at all."

Jesus, Murphy thought, this is going to be murder.

"Of course, the American way is that some people are just naturally going to be richer than other people. I think that's the way the world naturally turns out if you leave it alone. The Communists want everyone to be equal, except for the people in the Communist Party. They're PCs," Hoover said. "Everybody else goes to Siberia."

"PCs?" Murphy asked, trying to smile.

"Privileged characters," the director said.

"I see," Murphy said.

"Now, listen," Hoover said, carefully folding his napkin and putting it on the table in front of him. "I think we ought to talk about this Trattner fella."

"Yes, sir," Murphy said.

Hoover smiled and even laughed. "I notice the way people always say 'sir' to me when they're trying to put something over on me. You ever notice that, Clark?" the director asked.

Wilson, who was carefully folding his napkin, said, "I've noticed that."

Two of the women in the dining room were walking out slowly, looking behind them the whole time, trying to decide whether to come over to Hoover. Hoover turned to them and smiled. The women looked as if they might pass out right on the black-and-white tiled floor. They put their hands to their hearts and fluttered out of the room.

"I think you boys have gotten yourselves into a helluva mess," Hoover said. "I don't normally like to curse, but I have to say that I don't see a way on this earth that you're going to be able to get that boy before he does something terrible."

"Well, that's why I'm having lunch with you," Murphy said, smiling his best hail-fellow-well-met smile. "I've got to admit it when we need help. We need help."

"They need help," Hoover said. "That's very interesting that they need help now."

"Very interesting," Wilson said.

"We were a little cautious about getting together after the business with the Portuguese Embassy, and you've got to understand that," Murphy said. "So we made a mistake and we thought we could do it by ourselves. You can understand that, can't you?" Murphy spoke to the director as he would have spoken to a Supreme Court justice, only more respectfully.

"This Trattner boy is out shooting up half of California, and putting people in trunks with their stomachs cut out, and now you need our help," Hoover said.

"After the business at the embassy, you can understand, I'm sure," Murphy said. "That was a bad moment."

Hoover noticed that Murphy was taking out a cigarette. It looked like a Philip Morris. Hoover frowned and Murphy put the package of cigarettes back into his pocket. "That business at the embassy. Now, let's see. That was when you were trying to break into the embassy of a country with whom we are not at war and place faked secret documents in a file that was supposedly going back to Berlin. Is that what you're talking about?" Hoover asked.

Murphy shot back, "Yes, and that was when your agents actually arrested two of our men in the alley behind the embassy."

"And I believe that the President thought about the matter and told your Mr. Donovan that if he ever did that kind of thing again, it would be back to Wall Street. Correct?" Hoover asked. He nodded at Wilson.

"I believe that's correct, Mr. Director," Wilson said.

"I believe that the President said that breaking into embassies of neutral countries was just about the stupidest bunch of bullshit he had ever heard of, if I am not mistaken," Hoover said. "I believe he asked your Mr. Donovan what kind of idiots he had working for him."

"Colonel Donovan and the President are on perfectly good terms now," Murphy said with a sigh. "If you want to check on what the President thinks of Bill Donovan, I'll give you the number at the White House."

Hoover leaned forward as if to share a confidence. "I don't give a damn about your Colonel Donovan," Hoover said. "I'll be here working with whoever's President when you and Donovan are back on Park Avenue."

"Well put, Mr. Director," Wilson said.

"Now, Mr. Murphy, I wonder if they have any peaches here for dessert. I like peaches," Hoover said.

"I'll be glad to ask," Murphy said with a smile. *You prissy, fat asshole,* he added under his breath.

The waiter came and then returned in a minute with a bowl filled with sliced canned peaches. The waiter, a black man with bloodshot eyes and gray hair, like a child's version of Ol' Black Joe, asked if that would be satisfactory.

"You bet it will," J. Edgar Hoover said. "You bet it will."

The black waiter bowed from the waist and walked away with an exaggerated shuffle. The Director of the Federal Bureau of Investigation looked after him admiringly. "A man who knows who he is these days is a rare man. A fine man, I'd say. A colored man who isn't ashamed to work for a living is worth his weight in gold."

Without asking, Clark Wilson began to eat peaches out of

Hoover's bowl. He looked defiantly at Murphy, as if daring him to make something of it.

"A colored man who understands how the country works is a very wonderful kind of man to have around," Hoover said. "You agree with that?" He stared at Murphy.

"I'm sure," Murphy said. Jesus, he thought, not only are the stories all true, but they don't go half far enough.

"You want me to help you find this Nazi guy who's running around loose, right?" Hoover said. "Is that why a civil servant gets taken to lunch at the Chevy Chase Club?"

"We need your help," Murphy said. "The lunch is just my pleasure."

As he chewed on a peach, Hoover said, "Forget it."

"I beg your pardon?" Murphy said.

"'Forget it' is what the director said," Wilson hissed.

"I can't believe you mean it," Murphy said.

"Oh, I mean it," Hoover said. "Now, I don't think you're carrying any little microphones, are you?" Hoover almost smiled. "Because if you were, all kinds of little things about you when you were in that eating club at Princeton, when you were dating that little Italian girl from Camden, the one who took a trip up to Montreal, might get around to people who think your ass is made of gold."

Murphy set his jaw and stared back at Hoover. "I'm not carrying a microphone, you sonofabitch," he said.

"That's good," Hoover said. "Now, I'll tell you why I'm not going to lift one finger to really help you. First, I don't like being frozen out of something at the beginning because the President and some other people wear the same school tie. We public school boys don't like that too much." He scowled at Murphy. From out of the kitchen, Murphy could hear a fine Count Basie rendition of "Mood Indigo." It added to the surrealistic tone of the lunch. He wished he did have a microphone and a hidden wire recorder. "You wanted us to stay out so that you could take all your Ivy Leaguers and your Commies and outsmart us. Go right ahead. More power to you if you can. We'll show the flag, but we won't do a thing."

"This is a matter of some national concern," Murphy said

angrily. "This isn't one of your bureaucratic wars." He took out a Philip Morris and lit it with his heavy Dunhill lighter, avoiding the director's glare.

Hoover looked at Murphy with what might almost have been pity. "You people really don't know anything about Washington, do you? You never did and I guess you never will. My bureaucratic wars," Hoover said. "That's funny, isn't it, Clark? Really funny."

"Extremely funny," Clark Wilson said, eating another peach slice.

"Look, my friend," Hoover said. "Bureaucratic wars are no small thing. I got a bureau big enough to protect the country from Nazi saboteurs out of bureaucratic wars." He ate a peach slice. "These are mighty good," he said.

"I'm glad you like them," Murphy answered drily.

"I'm not going to ruin that damned fine bureau and have people laughing at us because you people screwed up this investigation. There's no way you're going to find that Nazi now. There may not even be any way we can find that Nazi ever. He seems to be pretty resourceful. I'll bet he's in Mexico now. So when people are wondering how the government fouled everything up so bad as to let a Nazi go running around loose in America killing people, I'd like to have them blame you and your friends with their fancy ties. There's no reason to blame us. We weren't even called until it was too late. It was your play and you fumbled. That just makes things easier for me after the war," Hoover said.

At that moment, a dowager in a floral dress walked shyly to Hoover's side of the table. She did a semi-curtsy, then cleared her throat. Hoover, on cue, stood up and took the lady's hand. "You probably don't remember me," she said. "I'm Sara Aspinwall. We met at Colonel Lee's house."

"Of course I remember you," Hoover said. "You were with Mrs. Burton Wheeler. My dear friend Senator Wheeler's wife. How are you, Mrs. Aspinwall?" He smiled at her, showing even white teeth. He introduced her to Murphy and Wilson. She batted her eyelashes at all three and then cleared her throat again.

"Yes, Mrs. Aspinwall?" Hoover asked, still smiling.

"Mr. Hoover," Mrs. Aspinwall said, "I want to help catch spies."

"That's grand, Mrs. Aspinwall," Hoover said. "Just grand. I'm sure you would."

"But what I wonder is this. My husband, Major Aspinwall, and I are both getting on in years. We don't get out much except for some golf and bridge, of course," Mrs. Aspinwall continued.

"I understand," Hoover said.

"What can people like us, people who live on our dividends, do to catch Nazi spies?" Mrs. Aspinwall asked. "Is there anything at all?"

Hoover stretched out his arm and let it fall lightly on Mrs. Aspinwall's ample shoulder. "Of course there is," he said. "Keep your eyes open all the time," he said. "Notice anything out of the ordinary. The Nazi spy depends on Americans' trusting, careless nature. If a strange man is on your block when he's not working for anyone. If someone unusual comes to your door asking for directions to Fort Meade. Notice those things. Then report them to your local FBI. Do you understand? Trust them to the FBI. If you see a Nazi saboteur, Mrs. Aspinwall, don't try to capture him yourself. Leave that to us. We're professionals at it."

"Thank you, Mr. Hoover," the woman said. "I want to do my part, even if we are just living on dividends."

The woman walked away and out of the room.

Hoover sat down, along with Murphy and Wilson. "People trust us," Hoover said. "There's a reason."

"I know," Murphy said. "I don't think you understand that this man, this Trattner, is dangerous. He could be part of something a lot bigger. Something even bigger than protecting the FBI."

Hoover flushed red and spoke in a rush. "I don't think you and your Mr. Donovan understand that you're dangerous," he said. "You amateur college boys in your fancy suits pretending you know anything about catching saboteurs. That's dangerous, not Trattner. He's just one man. He may do one big thing and then that'll be the end of him. If I let you college boys hurt the reputation of the FBI by dragging us into your mess, that would be dangerous."

Murphy summoned the waiter in his black leather bow tie and ordered coffee. Hoover and Wilson each ordered another Coca-Cola. "I don't believe in coffee," Hoover said. "It makes me irritable."

Even Wilson laughed at that.

"Let me just suggest to you that there are things going on in other places. In Europe, maybe, that have to do with how important it is that Trattner be caught. You understand?" Murphy asked. "It may well be more than blowing up a train track."

Hoover smiled maliciously. He glanced over at Wilson, who was thoughtfully eating a cracker while watching the black men work on the swimming pool bottom. "That's grand, isn't it, Clark?"

"He still doesn't understand how life works," Wilson said without looking away from the window.

"No, he doesn't," Hoover said. "I wish I had time to teach him, but then this is just one luncheon out of a busy day."

"I'm talking about important plans in Europe," Murphy said. "Very important to the outcome of the war." He felt more and more as if he were in a fantasy of trying to climb up a sheet of ice. The ice was smooth, and there was absolutely no way to gain any traction at all.

"I know all about your college boys traipsing around Europe, pretending that they're Big Men on Campus," Hoover said. "You think we're dummies? I know that you're a damn sight more likely to make the war last longer than make it shorter. We don't want to get involved in that mess either. You let the whole thing get out of control, as I hear you have, let the Nazis think they can get a deal from you, and then see how angry they are when they find out you're playing with yourself. We don't want to be part of that mess either. You're in charge of this mess and we're going to let everyone know it."

Wilson glanced at his Hamilton watch. "I think we had bet-

ter get back, Mr. Director," he said. "We have a meeting with
the Secretary of the Treasury."

"Morgenthau," Hoover said. "A smart man. You have to say
this for the Jew. He works hard and he's not afraid to use his
head. Also, they always know a way to make a buck. I don't
hold it against them. Obviously, that's how you get to be a
member of a place like this, if you're not a Jew. Right, Mr.
Murphy?" Hoover laughed out loud. "They know how to
make the money, but you've got the best clubs, Mr. Murphy.
I'm sure that makes your day."

"I didn't come here to talk about clubs," Murphy said. "The
President is going to learn that you didn't help when we
needed you." It was Murphy's last card.

Hoover actually slapped his palm on the table and
guffawed. "Clark," he said, "now that's one for the books.
That really and truly is one we have got to remember. The
President is going to know about us if we don't help these college boys. Doesn't that scare you all to hell?"

Wilson looked straight at Murphy and said, "I'm shaking
like a leaf."

Hoover leaned forward, so close to Murphy's face that
Murphy could smell his breath. It smelled like peaches in
heavy syrup. "Now, listen, you punk," Hoover said. "You may
be a tin god to your friends on Wall Street. But to me you're
just another rich man who thinks he knows it all. Tell the
President any damn thing you want. I have enough on you
and Donovan and all your pretty boys to put you out there in
the sun cleaning up with the niggers." He drew back his face
a few inches. "Not to mention that while the President is
sending American boys to die in the desert for unconditional
victory, you have agents in Zurich promising Nazi bigwigs the
earth and the moon if they'll make a deal without F.D.R. even
knowing about it. So you just go and tell the President anything you feel like telling him."

"I think it's time to head back to Pennsylvania Avenue, Mr.
Director," Wilson said. "We don't want to keep anyone important waiting."

Hoover relaxed in his seat and smiled at Murphy. "I'm

sorry," he said. "I didn't mean to get carried away. That was wrong of me. I hope you'll accept my apology." Hoover looked as if he really meant it.

Murphy gritted his teeth. *You pompous fat shit,* he thought. *Or maybe he's really crazy.* "Of course. No harm done. We just happen to all be on the same side," Murphy said. "I hope you'll think about that."

"Yes, I will," Hoover said. "Of course, the investigation is completely in your hands. You understand that now, don't you?"

"Yes," Murphy said. The man really was not all there, Murphy thought. Or else more than all there.

"But I can give you a piece of advice. If you'd like to have it," Hoover said politely, as if the man who had just threatened Murphy were on another planet.

"Yes, indeed," Murphy said.

"You have that girl and that cop looking. And you've got people shadowing all the Bundists who aren't in jail yet. Forget about the people from the Bund. There's no one in Berlin stupid enough to have Trattner hook up with Bundists once he gets rolling. That would just slow him down and they know it. Plus, it gives you a ready-made way to find him. Forget the Bund."

Murphy had to admit that it made sense. Hoover might be a megalomaniac, but he was no fool.

"Trattner's an educated man. He's got an American gal with him. He doesn't need any half-baked Bundists to help him get across the country or wherever he's going. That's my opinion," Hoover said. "Of course, you might have your own opinions. But I'll tell you one more thing. Trust that cop who's working with the gal. Cops are better at figuring things out than anybody else. Plus, I read that the cop's gal got killed back in Santa Clara."

"Santa Cruz," Murphy corrected him.

"Right, Santa Cruz," Hoover said. "Trust the cop. He'll figure it out if anybody can. And, Sam, I don't think you need to ever worry about anyone knowing about that little Celestina from back in school. That's in a file I keep right in my office so that no one else will ever have the chance to see it and embarrass you."

"Thank you, Mr. Director," Murphy said. "Thank you very much."

On the way home, Murphy looked at the stately houses on Connecticut Avenue and thought that now he knew exactly how it felt to have his balls in a nutcracker. He hoped that no one from the OSS had been listening in on the conversation. Murphy also hoped that the next time he saw the Director of the Federal Bureau of Investigation would be at John Edgar Hoover's funeral.

Albert Einstein felt the warmth of the spring sun through his office windows in 323 Fine Hall. Through the mass of papers, *Journals of the Academy of Physical Science, Annals of the Society for the Natural Sciences,* treatises concerning the possibility of a unified field theory sent to him by researchers as far away as Johannesburg, through the dust on his bookshelves and his windowsills, a glorious May sun permeated Einstein's bulky, almost dingy cable-knit sweater and sent a pleasant feeling into his chest. Out his window, he could see a game of touch football. It looked to him as if one side was from the Cottage Club and the other was from the Cannon Club. The teams played recklessly, careless of broken arms or sprained wrists. The full strength of youth and beauty spread across the easy smiles of the players. For them, life was an eternal quest for happiness and success with no penalties for failure.

On a day like today, a young man at Princeton could feel that God had told him that life was heaven unto itself, and that this paradise would continue forever. Even an old man like Albert Einstein felt the caress of the sun and thought that the greatest of all luck was to be alive, neither more nor less.

Just to smell that damp, rich smell of the lawns at Princeton after a rain the night before, to see the emerald magnificence of the grass and the leaves in the warm sun, to feel that hope of renewal in the air and in oneself—that was well worth living for. Far more than that, the richness of life on a day like today was incomparably greater than any act, any accomplishment—even the discovery of the unified field—could possibly match.

Einstein, the old Jewish genius in his office at the Institute for Advanced Study, knew it. The kids on the lawn in their blue-and-orange sweaters and Brooks Brothers shirts knew it.

The Jewish prisoners marching into the gas chambers at Auschwitz did not know it. Einstein quickly calculated that perhaps one hundred and twenty of them had died at Auschwitz alone—God forbid! he had heard that there were other camps—just while the boys in the chino trousers kicked around the football below his window.

There was a grunt from the couch in his office. On the pitiful cracked red leather, Enrico Fermi sat reading papers Einstein had given to him. Leo Szilard read in silence. Fermi's cadaverous eyes seemed to glow with emotion as he read the documents. His neat suit, his neatly trimmed hair, his carefully knotted tie all were at odds with the colossal emotion playing across his eyes as he read Mr. Cantrowitz' report about the Nazi nightmare.

Even Szilard, who played at feeling cheerful no matter what the situation, had turned white. His hands were apparently sweating. He repeatedly wiped them first on his broad forehead and then on his checked suit. His breath came in short stabs.

"Can this be true?" Szilard asked, turning his ashen face to Einstein.

Professor Einstein nodded. "It is," he said. "It is probably much less than all that is going on."

"Surely the President will do something. Send in commandos. Bomb the camps. Something," Fermi said in his precise English, "which would be appropriate to the horror of the situation."

Einstein lit one of his meerschaum pipes—filled with a new mixture sent to him expressly by Robert Reynolds from Reynolds Tobacco—and puffed on it for a moment. He glanced out his dusty windows at the boys playing football. "The President will not do anything. He does not want the American people to think they are fighting the Jews' war."

"Yet if he knew the scope . . ." Szilard said. "Then surely he would do something." He was sweating at his temples now.

"The President knows far more of this than we do," Einstein said. "He will do nothing. He feels that if the American people lost even a single man to save the Jews, they would demand to be out of the war."

Einstein could still vividly remember his meeting of only a few days ago with the President. F.D.R.'s refusal to act had been so startling that it had divided that day from every earlier moment of Einstein's life.

"We should face the fact that we are acting in the Manhattan District for different people from the ones we thought we were," Einstein said. "That is the main thing I have learned."

He puffed moodily on his pipe. His immense, childlike brown eyes filled with moisture. Szilard thought that Einstein was going to cry. But Einstein did not. Instead, he turned and again looked out the window. He could see a tall blonde boy getting tagged by a shorter blonde boy and then a chorus of voices rang out "Safety." Einstein did not know what that meant. He did not really care, for that matter. It probably had something to do with football.

"Let's not go rushing off like madmen about this," Fermi said, wringing his hands. "Let's just think where we are. You have had one meeting with the President about this. He might have just had a fight with Senator Bilbo. He might have just gotten a brickbat from Senator Jenner. We do not know how he would respond if the three of us all came in and spoke to him. It might be entirely different."

"Don't be a fool," Szilard snapped. "The President does not even know who you and I are. He is like those boys outside playing football. They know one scientist and only one and that is Albert Einstein. If Einstein could not persuade the

President, surely you and I cannot add one particle to the weight."

Fermi snapped back his head as if he had been struck in the face. He flushed. He started to speak, stammered, and then said, "I think perhaps you and I carry at least some weight in this country because of our contributions to the Manhattan District. Remember, it was we who were mentioned in the professor's first letter to the President."

"None of us carries any weight with the President," Einstein said sharply. Both men stared at him. Einstein usually spoke in barely more than a whisper. If he ever spoke sharply, it was to tell the punchline of a joke or a remembrance. For him to speak up so sharply now, in the midst of a deadly serious discussion underlined how powerfully Einstein felt. "The President is concerned that he be allowed to prosecute this war as if it were a matter of life or death for the white, Christian American."

Szilard could not remember the dreamy, mild-mannered Einstein ever appearing so serious or so angry. It was as if a good angel had suddenly started to lash the other angels with a horsewhip.

"Every day, thousands of Jews are dying in these camps. Poles, Russians . . . gypsies, too. We are at war with the country that is killing these innocent people. Our President will take no steps to save the victims. That much is perfectly clear. We can surely agree on that, can't we?" Einstein asked.

There was an edge in his voice that Fermi found alarming. If a man of Einstein's genius, his capacity for seeing every facet of a problem, of staying unperturbed by the chaos around him, of living in the clouds—if a man of that ability were driven to desperation, something desperate was in the air.

"Yes," Fermi said. "Though I still believe we should have another meeting. The President should know that you do not stand alone in this matter."

"That is what I want to assure," Einstein said thoughtfully. His face was once again dreamy and relaxed. "Let me tell you something. During the Great War, I worked in a laboratory at

Berlin University building models of the nitrogen molecule. I did this for the Kaiser, so that we might take nitrogen from the air and use it to make phosphates for explosives. I did not want to do it, if you must know. I am a pacifist by nature. But I did it because I believed that there was something noble about Germany and what it stood for. Again, I did not want to do it. But Germany had been good to me and to my people, so I did a little experimental work.

"Now, time passed, and before a wink of the eye, young people were parading in Germany carrying signs saying 'Jude raus.' They were beating Jews to death in the streets. These were the people I had thought possessed a certain inherent nobility of spirit. The same people for whom I did experimental work during the Great War," Einstein continued.

"I understand," Szilard said. "That must be a burden to you even now."

Outside, there was a huge groan and cheer mixed together. Einstein could see that one of the players had scored a touchdown while the other team groaned and pretended to cry. That was what the American youth had to cry about, Einstein thought. Touchdowns.

Einstein whipped his head back around to face Szilard. "No," he said, "no, my friend, I do not regret that work. There are far better explosives made right now. The Germans can take all the phosphates they need from Macedonia in Yugoslavia. I have a far greater fear. If the Germans changed so horribly after the war, who can predict what men will do? Who can predict what even the most generous, most gentle, most peace-loving people will do?"

Fermi took Einstein's point immediately. "And this time, we will have made far more than artillery shells," he said softly, from between his thin lips.

"Precisely," Einstein said. "If we have made an atomic bomb for the gifted, law-abiding people, that is good. But who is to say that the same mean spirit which I saw in our President might not some day put down roots, might not some day flourish into a tree of evil? Who can promise that some day there might not be young people not playing touch football, but marching down Fifth Avenue shouting, 'Jude raus'?"

"And by then," Szilard said carefully, "the genie will be out of the bottle. There will be no returning it to its place."

All three men stared at the shabby Bokhara carpet on the floor of the office. In each of them, a similar thought roared: What have we done? Why were we so quick to unleash this force?

Why did we run to put the power of the gods in the hands of men?

Fermi ran his hand through his thinning hair and shook his head, much like a dog shaking off fleas. "It cannot possibly happen in America. Not possibly. There were always anti-Semites in Germany. This has always been a free country. It is not the same at all. We have nothing to reproach ourselves for."

Einstein looked at Fermi pityingly. "I wish what you say were true, Professor," he said. "That would be a pretty tale if it were so."

"And?" Fermi said. "Do you mean to deny it?"

"Professor," Einstein said, "if I had a son who was a student at this college, he could not join those boys playing on the lawn. He could not belong to their eating club. Not to any eating club at Princeton. And this is not because his father is such a fool as to pursue the theory of the unified field. It is because he would be a Jew. For that reason, he would not be allowed in the door."

Einstein shook his head in amazement at Fermi's innocence. "At this college, where they make so much of me, where they trot me out like a prize terrier whenever they want to impress a wealthy man, I could not own a house in the really best neighborhoods, even where the houses are owned by the university. I have to live only in the neighborhoods where Jews may live."

Color came into Einstein's face. He was obviously deeply moved by what he was saying.

"If I were a colored man or an Oriental, my children would be laughed at in school. In many states of this country, colored children cannot even go to the same schools as white children. That is not just a prejudice of a few parents. That is a law. In the Army of the United States of America, black soldiers cannot fight in the same units as white soldiers. That is the law and not the stupidity of simply one foolish sergeant," Einstein said. "We thought, or perhaps I thought, well, this is something which does not concern me. The Americans are blind, they are a little crazy where colored people are concerned. But they are a good people, and that will change and it will all change. At heart, they are the most generous people in the world."

Fermi looked at Einstein defiantly. "I believe they are," he said. "They are not perfect, but they are fine people. The best people there are."

The sun was beginning to set toward the west, off toward the library of Princeton University. The New Jersey sky became blue and gray with the dark tones of evening. The students who had been playing football abruptly stopped and started to pat each other on the back. They found a huge wicker basket loaded with ice and bottles of beer. One boy passed around a bottle opener while the other boys snapped off the tops of their bottles of Pabst beer, then drank.

A gleaming yellow Pontiac convertible was parked next to the playing field. A girl with blonde hair and a blue blazer turned on the radio in the car. There was a rush of static, then the car radio blared out a song with trombones in the background. The words were about a highball at nightfall, but the three wise men could not make out any more of the lyrics.

How perfect, Einstein thought. It is nightfall and the children are drinking their beer, and the words come out just as if the heavens were writing the song for them. In Europe, if those boys were Jews, they would be gasping for breath in a gas chamber while the Nazis laughed outside the doors. Einstein returned to the conversation.

"I agree with you," Einstein said. "The Americans are the finest people in the world. But even they are racists, even they can sleep easy while they torment people of another race.

If the Americans can do that now, is it not at least possible that some day they will change for the worse?"

Szilard threw in another thought which had apparently been weighing on him, to judge by his wrinkled brow. He held out his hand and pounded it into his knee. "It is not only that," he said. "If the Americans have it, then, pretty soon, everyone has it. The world is filled with spies and traitors. What if there are traitors within the Manhattan District right now? What if we are doing this work for the Soviet Union or for Germany? What if, even after this war, a new madman appears and by then the atomic fission equation is general knowledge? What then? What would the world be like with a maniac dictator with an atom bomb?"

Fermi looked at his brown leather shoes, then noticed that his socks were unmatched. One was a light brown with ribs. The other was a dark-brown lisle. "I think you are becoming unreasonable," he said, a powerful accusation when thrown by Enrico Fermi at Leo Szilard and Albert Einstein. "The only nation which can possibly build an atomic bomb is the United States. Only the United States has the industrial plant to build this bomb. It cannot be done in a garage laboratory. It must be done in a large, rich, advanced country. There is only one and that is the United States. For now, the United States is the most law-abiding, freest country in the world. I say again, we have nothing to reproach ourselves for."

"What about the photographs of Hechingen?" Szilard asked. "They are uncannily like what Oppenheimer has in mind for Los Alamos, and they are already built."

"We know that they may have buildings," Fermi said, "but so far they do not have a critical mass, even if the War Department is terrified."

"Very well," Einstein said. "That is today. But tomorrow we may be living in a totally different America. Tomorrow we may live in a world where—because of what we started—someone can make an atomic bomb in his garage." The gray sweater heaved as Einstein sighed deeply. "I make only this point, Professor. I thought I was building a bomb for people who would lift their little finger, at least, to save Jews. I was wrong. It has given me second thoughts. That is the only point I care to make. It gives me pause about what I should want to do next on the Manhattan District."

Szilard stood up and walked a few steps toward the window. The sky was a luminous dark blue, with a row of gray clouds, like a sandbar, running out toward the horizon, as if a ship might come along the sky and become beached in that blueness. The students were breaking up. Several got into the Pontiac convertible. Others lit pipes and strolled toward town, where they might find a drink of whiskey before they had dinner. In a few days, Szilard guessed, they would be leaving for the summer holidays. They would swim, play tennis, ride horses, perhaps work for their father's business, maybe even pitch in at a factory making gas masks. Golden days of youth, Szilard thought. It was a song which had been popular in Heidelberg when he had been a student there, long before this madness, one semester only, sandwiched into his time at Prague and Budapest. Golden days . . .

Szilard had a sinking feeling. "In a way," he said, "we have foreclosed, or at least mortgaged, the future of the world for the sake of shortening one war by a few days or a few months," Szilard said.

"Oh, you're being foolish," Fermi said. "Completely foolish. The world is not run by madmen. Even Hitler is not using poison gas," he said.

"Not against Aryans," Einstein shot back. "He uses it every day against Jews. That is just how mad this world is, and that is the world to which we are about to give this terrible secret. We are now giving to infants the means to end humanity. These bombs can be made larger and larger. They will be radioactive. God only knows what that will do to the human body."

There were a few moments of silence and then Einstein cleared his throat. "In a few days," he said, "Colonel Groves will come to us about the latest problem, whatever it is. It will probably be the question of the weight of the neutrino, whether it will be a beta emitter or collector. I can tell you that I am going to think very carefully indeed before I tell him my opinion on that question. I may have already done too much. I will certainly not go forward without a great deal of thought."

Fermi played his trump card. "And what will you do," he asked, "if the Germans get the atomic bomb first?"

Einstein pounded his fist on his desk so hard that a blizzard of dust arose into the still air of Fine Hall. "I cannot believe you would even ask that," Einstein stormed at his colleague. "Even if they had the physical plant at Hechingen and the workers and the enriched plutonium and the deuterium water, even if they had the ability to assemble all the ingredients while they are having ten thousand tons of bombs dropped on them each week, do you suppose that cretins like Diebner and Heisenberg could possibly solve the kinds of problems that the Manhattan District has solved? The whole concept of the Germans having gone out in advance of us in this area is fantastic. Only the War Department would even conceive of it."

Szilard turned to Fermi and smiled in a condescending way. "If you are afraid to stand up to Colonel Groves, do as your conscience dictates. For me, I think that Professor Einstein's comments have great merit. I am not at all certain that I can continue to work for an enterprise that is led by men who have no respect for human life, even if it is Jewish life, which is inferior in their eyes."

"I would not go that far," Einstein said. "But there are certainly grounds for us all to wonder if what we are doing is in the best interest of the human race."

Night had fallen while the men talked. Lights came on next to the front doors of the comfortable frame houses on the border of the campus. In the field where the students had been playing, a street light picked out a white varsity sweater someone had left behind. A gray dog walked up to it, sniffed it, caught the sweater in its mouth with one swoop, then walked on . . . a dog carrying a college letter sweater in the evening air of Princeton, New Jersey. The dog walked purposefully, as if it had an appointment.

Einstein got up and switched on an incandescent bulb, which lit up the room. When he returned to his seat, he could see the faces of his colleagues far more clearly. He saw tears coming down Enrico Fermi's cheeks. Einstein did an uncharacteristic thing. He walked to Fermi, stood over him, and held out his arms. Fermi rose. The two men embraced. Einstein could feel Fermi's tears falling on his shoulders through his bulky cable-knit sweater.

"We thought we were doing good," Fermi said. "I thought we were going to save so many lives, shorten the war." His shoulders shivered with agony. "I never set out to do anything but good, to enlarge science, to beat the fascists. In my whole life, I never set out to do anything wrong, never set out to hurt anyone."

"Who in this world ever does?" Einstein asked. "Certainly none of us."

Half an hour later, Einstein walked through the New Jersey spring night alone toward his house on Mercer Street. Miss Dukas would have had the cook make his dinner. He could use it. He preferred fish, and he knew that Miss Dukas had been able to buy some especially fresh fillet of Dover sole. He was looking forward to it a great deal. Sole was light, fell apart at the touch, never left him feeling stuffed or overfed. It was a good dish to have, then curl up in a chair from Mr. Cantrowitz ("This is a chair our factory in North Carolina had made especially for a great genius such as you, Professor Einstein. It would be an honor for me if you took it. Please. Sit. Feel the coils. Not stuffing. Hundreds of little coils and with steel rationing yet.") and consider the possibilities of a unified field.

Only tonight, Professor Einstein would not think about the unified field. He would think about what he should do or not do on the Manhattan District. He suddenly felt a sharp pain in his right foot. He glanced down. He noticed that he was not wearing shoes. He must have taken them off in his office and forgotten to put them back on. Then he had stepped on a thorn. He pulled the thorn out of his sock and his flesh. He felt better instantly. That was science.

As Einstein passed the Colonial Club, he could hear the men singing inside. He could only make out some of the words: "Troubadour, troubadour, sing troubadour," in a high baritone. The interior of the club was polished paneled maple. The boys looked well-fed and happy through the mullioned, white-painted windows. Some of them wore naval uniforms. Even they looked more as if they were in a theatrical than as if they were preparing for a genuine war, in which they might lose their limbs or their lives. Outside, Einstein thought, the whole world is outside to these Americans. Inside, everything is warm and cozy. Inside, there are steak and potatoes and ice cream. Outside, Jews are put into ovens and no one lifts a finger. Outside, a world prepares to receive a weapon which might one day throw the Earth off its axis. And still, inside, the boys play and sing about medieval troubadours.

Einstein ate his fillet of Dover sole, then went to bed early. Before he fell asleep, he saw a fantasy of Franklin Delano Roosevelt and Harry Hopkins inside the Colonial Club, laughing at him through the window, pointing at him and imitating his accent. In the waking fantasy, Albert Einstein held a rock in his hand. He was just preparing to throw it through the window when he fell asleep and dreamed instead of his life in Prague when he was a young man and thought long thoughts.

May 28, 1943.
Idabel, Oklahoma

Obersturmbannführer Joachim Trattner had never seen countryside like southeastern Oklahoma. It was utterly unforgiving, completely sparse and uncompromising, which should have given him warning. He and Maxine drove along State Highway 70 between Hugo and Idabel. He stared at the flat land, occasionally with a hint of a rise or a valley, always planted with corn or else in timber. The sky was blue, with only a few clouds, but was not a welcoming, happy blue. It was a light, flinty blue, as if in the sky itself there might not be room for the errant soul. The ground was red and unlovely where it had been scratched by the farmer's plow. An occasional stream was no more than a muddy running pond, often with old automobile wrecks in the water, trailing rusty stains for a long way down the line of sight.

By the side of the road, there were oleander bushes, with sharp, ugly branches menacing the driver and the passenger.

But the worst of all was the evidence of depraved human habitation. Every few miles was a shack or cabin. They were not picturesque or well crafted like the cabins they had passed in New Mexico or Texas. Instead, they were tumbledown clapboard disgraces, with peeling paint or none at all, windows covered over with dust, scraggly plantings in the front yard, and always, inevitably, some piece of decaying machinery. Occasionally it was a refrigerator, left lying on its side with a wide-open door. Other times it would be a washing machine, with its rollers at the top tilted askew, hinting at some kind of prayer for dirty clothes to wash as it once did before it was abandoned. But most often, it was an automobile. To Trattner, the southern American landscape looked as if a rain of 1926 Fords had fallen on it and had never stopped falling. Everywhere, in front of every dwelling, no matter how lowly, was one or more abandoned cars. They lay on their flattened tires or just on their wheel rims, with their doors open and their seats ripped and springs popping out into the air. Their windows were often shattered, as if the local children had made a habit of shooting at them with small-bore rifles.

Trattner felt as if he had seen ten thousand abandoned Fords on this trip. How many more must there be in the rest of America? He knew that he was traveling through a relatively poor part of the nation. From his studies of America while he was a guest at Kriegsgefangenenlager Fort Ord, he had learned that, by and large, the Far West and New England were the wealthiest parts of the United States. The southern and southeastern states had languished because of the lingering effects of the Civil War and year after year of poor crops caused by devastatingly dry weather. From this part of America came the "Okies," whose gaunt, beaten faces he had seen in newsreels in Heidelberg when he was still a young man, before he became an SS man of steel.

These were "poor" Americans, yet they simply threw away an automobile or a refrigerator when they were tired of it. They did not repair the thing, but simply left it in their front yard. Even with a war on, and with a great need for scrap metal, the United States was so rich that it could leave millions of tons of usable steel lying in front yards in the form of cast-off autos, refrigerators, and washing machines.

Maxine had tried to explain to him that Americans were not all as wasteful as these people in Oklahoma and Texas. "See," she told him, "if they were smart, they would keep repairing these things until they just couldn't run anymore. But they're real stupid, lazy people, so they don't even try to keep up the things they own. That doesn't mean they're rich. It means that they're so stupid that they're poor. In America," she added, "it takes some doing to be quite this poor."

But Trattner had a deeper view of things. If these southerners, mostly pure Aryans, as he knew from talking to Toby Moffatt, were so deluded as to throw away an automobile which could have been saved and made to run again, it must have been a result of manipulations by those on high in American society. In other words, as Trattner said to Maxine on Highway 70, "The Jew, Maxine. Always look to the Jew. Somehow the Jew is making money from this. He has tricked these innocent people into believing that they are better off wasting their money, throwing away these things that they could have kept."

Trattner and Maxine sped by a house which was covered only with canvas on one side—how cruelly cold it must be in winter—and saw a little white girl with a face like an angel, framed by pale blonde hair, playing in an abandoned car. To Trattner, the thought that the pure Aryans of this world were so oppressed by the international Jew simply added to the grim severity of the landscape. Perhaps Trattner's basic sensitivity to the feelings of the Aryan race was what made the landscape so barren in the first place. He might be able to feel the pain of these tormented people, just as the Führer could feel the anguish of the German people after the Great War. An SS man must be stern, but he must also feel for his fellow Aryans.

"Slow down, Maxine," Trattner commanded for the hundredth time since they had started their trip. Maxine was greatly enjoying the 1938 Packard they had stolen from a shuttered mortuary in Santa Fe, New Mexico. It was obviously used as the lead car in funeral processions. Now it was under the command of a woman with a "lead foot," as Maxine jokingly referred to herself. Maxine liked to keep it at seventy miles per hour even when they were going around curves or approaching towns. Trattner found that it disturbed his calm to contemplate getting smeared all over the asphalt because Maxine got a thrill out of driving fast. "This is not a pleasure trip," he constantly reminded her in frigid tones. "We are on a mission of great importance. If we failed because of your poor driving skills, it would be a world-historical catastrophe."

Trattner said that to Maxine just after they left Hugo, a town so featureless and weary-looking that it depressed Trattner just to think about it. It seemed to exist solely to show that the human spirit had been utterly crushed by the sinister combination of poor weather and the depredations of the international Jew.

Hugo had a drugstore, a barbecued spareribs restaurant, two gasoline stations, two agricultural warehouses, and raised wooden sidewalks. There were no people on the street except for two old white men leaning against a truck. Like many of the people Trattner had seen in the last two days, the two old men wore bib coveralls, a form of dress he had never seen before in his life. The blue-denim outfits reminded Trattner of gigantic aprons with leggings attached, almost like clown suits. Yet the men who wore them looked serious, even distressed.

The main street of Hugo was astonishingly wide, something Trattner had noticed in several other towns they had passed through. On either side of the street, the ubiquitous cars were parked at an angle against the raised wooden sidewalk. These were the cars waiting to be put in someone's front yard.

"It never ceases to amaze me," Trattner said as they slowed in obedience to his command, "that Americans can be so sanctimonious about our having problems with the Jew when you people have your own problems with the Negro. In Germany, we have a leader who has the foresight to face up to the question now while there is still a possibility of solving it."

"I see," Maxine said. She did not care as much for Trattner's conversation about race as she did for his conversations about how the Führer was going to make certain that in the Amerikanisches Reich, the trees and the wilderness would all be preserved forever. She liked it best when Trattner was in bed with her. Of course, she understood ex-

actly the difficulties which lay ahead if the Jewish problems
were not attacked in the United States and everywhere. But
she preferred to address the problem in terms of what it
meant to the precious landscape of this planet, rather than
what it meant in terms of money or something like machinery.

"In Germany, we already had Jews marrying our women,
driving our honest Aryan workmen out of their jobs, plotting
to ruin the society by mixing their Jew blood with our
women's white blood. Can you imagine how it felt—as a German—to walk down a street in Berlin and see a German
woman, sometimes a fine-looking one, like you, walking hand
in hand with a long-nosed, sniveling Jew?" Trattner shook his
head in rage at the thought. "The Jews who were staying
home making money from the war while our fathers were
dying of mustard gas in the trenches? Can you imagine what
that felt like to a man who is dedicated to the Aryan race?
Can you imagine how the Americans would feel if there were
Negro men, colored men, looking like grinning apes, walking
down Fifth Avenue clutching white girls?"

Imperceptibly, Maxine leaned on the accelerator. The Packard V-12 went smoothly forward, so quietly that Trattner
could not even feel it, did not even tell her to slow down. It
might have been pretty risky to get a car like this one, a car
that stood out like a Packard, but on the other hand, it sure
made for traveling in style and Maxine Lewis liked to travel
in style.

"I damn well hope that the American people would realize
that the struggle against the Jews is their struggle, too,"
Trattner said angrily. Frankly, he did not know exactly what
to say when Maxine started to jabber about the trees and the
mountains and the squirrels and the deer. What concern were
they of his? The Aryan people at this moment were fighting
for their lives. What did it matter if a few squirrels or deer
got killed? There were plenty more. And this vegetarian
madness. Was the entire nation insane? Trattner was beginning to think so.

Maxine drove by a small rectangular white stone church in
the middle of a field. "Full Gospel Day of Reckoning Taber-

nacle" said a sign in front of the church. "Donald Simpkins, Rev." Then there was a hand-lettered sign in front of the church announcing the next Sunday's sermon: "Would You Die for Christ As He Died For You?"

Trattner had seen more churches on this journey than he had ever dreamed existed. Sects and subsects and divisions within sects that went on forever. Pentecostal. Evangelical. Baptist. Methodist. Church of Christ. And within them, a hundred thousand wild names, usually connected with fear and dread, attached to each individual church. The Americans were like savage tribes, each with their own tribal totems. The gaunt faces and the terrifying church names made him fear the Americans if they were ever truly mobilized against Germany. He did not like to acknowledge fear, so he clamped down his teeth and stared at Maxine.

"What is your sect?" he asked Maxine in a hiss. He had never thought to ask before. He assumed she was Lutheran.

But Maxine did not answer the question. She was frozen down to her marrow by a sound she had prayed not to hear. From behind a billboard advertising "Red Man" chewing tobacco abruptly appeared a police motorcycle. It roared onto the blacktop—as Maxine Lewis could see in her rearview mirror—with its siren blaring and made a squealing sound as its tires caught the road. Maxine could see the state trooper—or whatever he was—gesturing at her to pull over while he gunned his machine.

"Sweet Jesus," she said, "hold on." She floored the accelerator. The Packard shot forward as if it had been hit from behind by a diesel locomotive. Trattner was actually snapped backward by the force of the acceleration.

"What the . . . ?" he asked before the siren told him all he needed to know. He turned around and saw the policeman gaining on them. The mixed sounds of the state trooper's siren and the roar of the state trooper's engine crowded into Trattner's head. His fingertips grew cool. "I told you, you stupid little whore," he spat out. "Get away from him or I'll kill you," he barked.

Maxine was stunned. She swerved sharply from the mental

shock of what Trattner was saying. Nevertheless, she kept her foot on the floor. The tires of the Packard screamed as the huge machine took a curve near a silo of red-painted corrugated tin. "Don't say that," she said. "You're hurting my feelings." She took her eyes off the road to look reproachfully at him. Then she returned her gaze to the road just in time to avoid colliding with an oncoming hay truck. "How can you talk like that to me?" she asked. "After all I've done for you? I've risked my life for you. I've thrown away everything that went before for you."

She stuck out her lower lip in a pronounced pout as the speedometer nudged 100.

"Are you mad?" Trattner demanded. "Don't whine to me. Just get us away from here." He really was with a maniac after all. A true-to-life genuine maniac. He had suspected it all along. But what a time to find out! On the *Autobahn* at a bloodcurdling speed. "Please," he suddenly said in a subdued voice, "I'm sorry. I spoke in haste. Please get us away from here."

Maxine looked like a simpering but pleased woman. She made a kissing sound, then focused more sharply on the road.

She did not like what she saw. In the rearview mirror there was now not only the motorcycle state trooper, but a state trooper's car. She could make out the chrome siren on top of the hood. The two sirens made a horrible, doomed sound.

For three miles along Highway 70, Maxine struggled to keep ahead of the patrol car and the motorcycle cop. But the powerful Harley-Davidson was more than a match even for a V-12 Packard sedan. By the time Maxine reached a road sign that read "Idabel—3 Miles," the motorcyclist was so close behind Maxine that she could see his face in the rearview mirror. It was a flushed, angry thin face. The man was gesturing furiously to Maxine to pull over.

Within a few moments, the trooper was alongside Maxine's window. He pointed at the nickel-plated revolver in its holster next to his hip. Then he pointed over to the side of the road. "Pull over, you asshole," he shouted at her.

Maxine plunged the pedal to the floor again and for a minute, she again outdistanced the state trooper. But when she looked in the rearview mirror this time, she saw that there were now two motorcycle troopers and two state trooper's cars in the wake of her Packard. They were all gaining quickly.

"*Grosser Gott*," Trattner mumbled to himself. The speedometer had edged above one hundred miles per hour. Maxine might be ready to continue to race, but he would rather take his chances talking than speeding along a one-lane blacktop where the churches were called after the Day of Reckoning. If it were necessary, he might be able to avoid the clutches of the Oklahoma state troopers. He had little chance of continuing with his mission if the Packard smashed into a live oak tree. He made a calculation and then a command.

"Pull over," Trattner said, biting off each word. "Pull over and act very sorry. Tell them I'm a mute."

Maxine looked disappointed that the chase was over. Nevertheless, she pulled over onto a sandy stretch of road shoulder next to a small sign which read "Burma-Shave."

She squeezed Trattner's hand and whispered to him, "We'll get out of this. You leave it to me." As she drew back her hand, she pulled back her skirt so that her thighs were revealed up to just below her garters. With another quick brush, she unbuttoned the top button of her blouse and shook her bosoms so that the nipples would brush against the fabric and become hard. Then she smiled as the state trooper sidled up to the car.

His face was livid. "Where the hell's the fire?" he demanded. "Just where the hell do you think you're going? We don't like this kind of thing too much in McCurtain County." His voice was considerably higher at the end of his tirade than at the beginning because by then he had taken a gander at her breasts and legs.

Maxine turned her head down demurely and said, "I'm really sorry, Officer. Sometimes I just like to see how fast this thing can go."

She turned to him and pursed her lips as if she were about to kiss someone.

"You were going at least ninety miles an hour and that's too damned fast," he said.

"That is fast," Maxine said. "I must have just lost control of myself. I just get so excited when I'm driving a big fast car. God, it must be great to have a motorcycle like yours." She batted her eyelashes at him.

Now the trooper was starting to blush. He was also craning his head in the damp Oklahoma sunshine to get a better look at her chest. "Is this your car?" he asked.

"As a matter of fact, it belongs to my cousin in New Mexico," she answered coyly. "He's really not exactly a cousin, but we're real close," she said.

"Is this man your cousin?" the motorcyclist said, pointing at Trattner.

"My, but you're a curious one, aren't you?" Maxine said with a smile, trying to sound like Vivien Leigh. "No, this is a friend of mine. He's a deaf-mute. He can do a lot of things, but he can't talk. Sometimes that's good, if you know what I mean."

The officer smiled and said, "If you say so, ma'am. Can I see your license and the registration for this car? I'm going to have to issue you a speeding ticket. It's gonna cost you twenty dollars or a night in jail."

"Twenty dollars!" Maxine said in mock horror. "I can't believe that. Twenty dollars. For just raising a little bit of hell here in this pretty part of Oklahoma. Can't it be ten?" She reached inside her blouse and scratched her chest just above her bosom. The officer stared and scratched his own chest. "I'm sorry, ma'am. It's got to be twenty dollars."

"Well, all right," she said, reaching into her pocketbook.

At that moment, two more troopers appeared next to the car. These were older, paunchier men. One of them had bright red hair under his cap. The other one was bald. Both of them had such thick southern accents that Maxine could barely make out what they said. But she could make out that they had their guns drawn. The guns were big, ugly pistols. In her rearview mirror, she could see that there were two more troopers standing behind the car. They held shotguns, leveled

at the car. Another trooper materialized from in front of the
car. He, too, held a gun. It was another pistol, pointed at
Trattner through the windshield.

"What's going on here?" Maxine asked. "Do I look that
dangerous?"

"Bobby, get away from that car," the redheaded trooper
shouted. "Get away."

The motorcyclist backed rapidly away from the car. He
drew his gun, too.

"I think these two look a helluva lot like those pictures of
the Nazi and his girlfriend," the bald man said. "I really think
we've got us a helluva big fish for a few little country boys
from McCurtain County."

The redheaded man walked closer to the car. He cocked
the hammer on his revolver, then said to Trattner, "What's
your name, boy?"

Trattner stared straight ahead and did not say a word. Inwardly he shivered. The fate of the Reich. Betrayed because
this fool of a woman insisted on driving too fast. It would be
funny if it were not so tragic. Trattner began to calculate
again.

There must be a way out of this, Trattner thought. Out of
the corner of his eye, Trattner saw the field next to the car. It
was a wide, furrowed field. The troopers were carrying shotguns. They might miss him if he could first get to the field.
The others carried pistols. Not accurate enough to hit a man
trained to escape sniper fire in the Benghazi Desert. But if he
were going to try, it had better be now, while the bald man
with the shotgun was not on top of him.

"Hey! You a Nazi, boy?" the bald man called out again.
"You some kind of Nazi running around killing people? We
ain't that wild about Nazis running around McCurtain
County." He edged closer to the car and cradled his shotgun
in his arms. "What's the matter, boy? No spreichen the English, boy?"

Trattner looked at the bald man with cool indifference.
Suddenly, he threw open the car door and hurled himself out
onto the ground. He rolled in the gravel of the shoulder for a

moment, then picked himself up and braced to take off into the field. Trattner, however, had no experience with how fast a fat man with a bald head in McCurtain County can move. The German felt a crashing blow on the side of his head. It was as if he had run into a stone wall. He wobbled for a moment, and then he fell down onto the gravel with his face on one side, out "cold as a mackerel" as the bald-headed man said when he felt around Trattner for any weapons.

The redheaded state trooper yanked open the door of the Packard on the driver's side. He reached in and grabbed Maxine Lewis with one hand while holding a shotgun on her with the other. He threw her to the ground with one powerful twist of his wrist.

"You rotten bastard," she said. "What're you doing? We didn't do anything."

The redheaded man stepped forward and put his booted foot on the gravel next to Maxine Lewis' face. "We don't like girls who run around with Nazis too much around here, honey," he said. "We sometimes have to kick 'em in the face if they talk too much, you hear?"

The bald-headed man appeared on the other side of Maxine and told her to roll over onto her stomach. As she did, another button popped open on her chenille blouse. One firm right bosom appeared in the Oklahoma sun. The troopers stared as if they had never seen a bosom before. But the bald-headed man, who was a Baptist, told her to cover herself up before she caught a cold. "We don't hold with brazen women here," he said, "and I think you're in enough trouble already."

The state troopers put the still unconscious Trattner in one car and a handcuffed Maxine into another. They headed for Idabel, now only two miles away. As they drove, the redheaded trooper kept staring at Maxine's chest. Every few seconds, she would say, "Now, you boys seem like nice boys, but I think you've made a big mistake. I don't know a thing except what I read in the papers about any Nazi. I was just taking my cousin's car for a ride and I found this poor deaf-mute guy and I took him for a ride. I didn't kidnap him or anything."

Then Maxine would wink at the redheaded trooper and twist her chest in his direction. Spittle was forming at the sides of his parched, dried face. His eyes, behind their thick glasses, were bulging.

The bald-headed man, the Baptist, listened to Maxine talk for a minute, then picked up a sheet of paper lying on the front seat. It was a wired photo of Maxine that had gone out to every state trooper and every police station which could be found by wire or special delivery. It had arrived in Idabel that morning. The bald-headed man pulled the car over and stopped it. He held up the paper in front of Maxine and let her stare at it.

"You understand now? You starting to catch on that we're not as dumb as we look?" he asked. "Now just shut up. You can talk to A. E. Warmack when we get to town. He always likes to look at a pretty girl."

An hour later Maxine Lewis was in a cell at one end of a narrow corridor in the McCurtain County Sheriff's Office. She sat on a cot which was bolted to the wall. Across the hall from her, Trattner was locked in a room which had only an iron door and no windows or bars. She could at least look through her bars into the corridor.

At the other end of the hall, Maxine could hear Sheriff Warmack shouting into a telephone. He was talking long distance to someone named Bill. Actually, Sheriff Warmack wasn't such a bad Joe. He had told her he wasn't going to touch her or molest her. He just thought if she had done something this crazy, she must have had her reasons. He just wanted her to know that he was her friend, and if she had any doubts or remorse about what she had done, she could tell him. Of course, Maxine had no doubts, but she liked A. E. Warmack's kindness. He was not at all like those horrible state trooper police guys, and that was just fine with her. He had a wrinkled, weather-beaten face with wispy eyebrows and a dapper, almost anachronistic mustache of silver and gray. His eyes were a deep blue, even deeper than Joachim's. He had put his hand on her shoulder and said, "Now, honey, that man you're with is a mighty bad man. I know sometimes a girl can fall for a mighty bad man, but I think this time you were lucky we found you before anyone else did. A lot of people would have shot first and asked questions later. But that's not the way I let people do things here in McCurtain County. I just want you to know that."

Maxine thanked him but said she had nothing to say. "I'm not the girl you're looking for," she said. She continued to say that until they found her California driver's license in her wallet. Then she began to cry. "It's all right," Sheriff Warmack said. "When you decide to talk, we'll be ready to listen. In the meantime, I'm not going to have any reporters or photographer fellows in here to embarrass you. You just take it easy and maybe you'll decide to tell us just where the Nazi boy was taking you. That's really all anyone wants to know. Then you can go home and forget about this," he said.

Maxine thanked him but said that she did not know what he was talking about. She said that between her tears. She was tempted to say she would rather just stay there and die with Joachim, but she restrained herself. Jeez, what a mess! Joachim would be really mad at her.

Now she heard Sheriff Warmack telling Bill that he would keep her real safe and warm and just wait for your people to get here. "Oh, she'll talk," Warmack said. "She's not a bad girl. She'll 'fess up."

It made Maxine proud that even in this situation a kind man like Sheriff Warmack knew that she was a nice girl.

May 29, 1943,
Idabel, Oklahoma

"Pure luck," said Alice Burton as she watched the Arkansas countryside fly by in the dark of the night. An almost new moon cast long silvery-blue shadows on the gently rolling ground, lit up tabernacle churches, put rusting car hulks into eerie relief, and barely allowed the Army staff driver from the Texarkana Arsenal to keep the Ford staff car on the road.

"More than luck," Quinn said. "Connections. It's always connections."

It was chilly in the back seat of the car. Alice Burton and John Quinn unthinkingly sat with their arms touching in the darkness lit only by the moon and the faint dashboard lights.

"I think the whole OSS is based on connections, really," Alice Burton said. "Everybody knows everybody—everybody worth knowing, that is. They know them from boarding school or the right college or the right club. If you ever wondered if there was a ruling class in America, just take a look at the people who work for the OSS. If you put them all together, they control half the big companies in America."

"I guess that's why I'm a cop in L.A.," Quinn said. "I don't even know what a big company looks like except when I drive by Southern California Edison."

In contravention of strict Army orders, the driver had the radio on KOAT in Hugo. Through the static, Quinn could make out a big band swing rendition of "Am I Blue." It was one of Quinn's favorite songs. He loved to hear it when it came on in the backyard of the house on Plymouth Street in Hollywood. He had a long extension cord.

"The world runs on who knows who," Alice Burton said. "That's the only reason to go to a fancy college. You don't learn any more than you would learn if you really read a few books carefully. But you make important friends."

"Or," Quinn said, "you can do it in the Army."

"Exactly," Alice Burton said. "Sheriff Warmack had been in the Rainbow Division with Wild Bill Donovan. That was back in 1918. They kept in touch. Sheriff Warmack knew that Donovan was really close to F.D.R."

"He knew that if he told Donovan he had a guy who was almost certainly Trattner, that if the guy was Trattner, F.D.R. would be given a little nudge to make sure that the next time they were building a highway or a dam in those parts, McCurtain County would get the first shot, and Sheriff Warmack would have a lot to say about where it went," Quinn said.

"And that way he maybe gets to be a judge, and that's where these good old boys like to wind up," Alice Burton said. "Especially if he could be a federal judge. That's three squares a day for life."

"So we got the call and we get one night with Trattner, just asking him a few questions, maybe tapping him on the shoulder to encourage him, maybe slapping him if he gets rude, and then Sheriff Warmack tells the FBI," Quinn said.

The car pulled off Route 71, then hurtled down Route 70 into the outskirts of Idabel. To Alice Burton, the scene was a scientific amalgam of all that was small-town America. There were the signs for the Rural Electric Co-operative, then billboards advertising for Farm Credit. Then there were a few gasoline stations, Mobil, Flying A, Esso, Amoco, offering gas to anyone who had coupons for 17.9 cents for ethyl, 15.9 for regular.

When the car reached the town itself, Alice's watch read exactly 3 A.M. She had been traveling now for eight hours, ever since she got the call while she was racking her brain at the Palmer House in Chicago, trying desperately to figure out where she would go if she were a fugitive Nazi in the United States of America. The subject had largely disappeared from the news, pushed out by the massive Russian counter-counteroffensive at Kursk and the final triumph of the American Marines at Kiska and Attu. There were also many pictures in the Chicago *Tribune* of Roosevelt, Churchill, and Molotov meeting at the Trident First International Conference in Washington. Colonel McCormick had forced himself to put a smiling picture of the Chief Executive on the front page of his newspaper, a first for Chicago.

Then came the call from Sam Murphy, a rushed trip through Chicago to Midway Airport where an entire DC-3 had been put at their disposal for the flight to Texarkana, and now the three-hour drive through the night to Idabel.

At 3 A.M., Idabel was as closed down as a town of living people can be. There were no lights at the Smythe General Store. Nor were there any lights at the Mabel and Sally's Coffee Shop. The marble front of the First Oklahoma Bank gleamed in the moonlight, but there were no lights there either. At the McCurtain Lumber Yard, there was a night watchman leaning on a wire fence, but he had no light, only the weak glow of his cigarette.

Then, half a mile down Main Street and a right turn to Southeast Avenue A, and the McCurtain County Sheriff's Office stood in its red brick solidity in the moonlight. There, lights were blazing. Two state trooper's cars were parked out front and one McCurtain County Sheriff's car (one of three). All the lights inside were on, so far as Quinn could tell. The effect, in a town as small and quiet as Idabel, was of a festive party hidden behind those windows.

The Army driver hopped out and opened the back door for Quinn and Alice Burton. They stepped out into a deafening chorus of cicadas and crickets. A virtual wall of cricket sounds in the Idabel night greeted visitors to a Nazi in a sheriff's jail.

"He's right here," Sheriff Warmack said. He wiped his brow with a comically large white handkerchief, then smiled from his eyes down to his even, white teeth. "You ought to thank these two boys," he added, gesturing at two state troopers lounging on a bench. One of them was paunchy and bald. The other one was paunchy and redheaded. The bald one was severe and serious-looking. Probably a Baptist, Quinn thought. The other one was far more relaxed-looking, although he too was sweating. No wonder the crickets were chirruping. It must still be eighty-five degrees, Quinn thought. And 95 percent humidity.

Quinn strode forward and shook hands with the two state troopers. "I'm a cop myself," he said. "I appreciate that kind of careful police work. I think you boys are probably in line for some kind of recognition."

"It was really Dale," the bald one said, gesturing at the redheaded one with his chin. "He got the idea that maybe they were the Nazis. I thought it was just some dumb woman driving her daddy's car too fast."

"I figured it was pretty damned strange," Dale said. "From behind, they looked as if they could be the ones. Both blonde. Both coming from the West. But I read about what they did in Nevada. I wasn't about to take no chances. Not me, boy."

"Then that Nazi guy tried to run, but I clonked him pretty good with the stock of my Winchester. I think he's gonna have that bump on the back of his head until this war's over."

Both state troopers laughed. Their stomachs heaved, reminding Quinn of the Christmas rhyme about St. Nick laughing like a bowlful of jelly.

"The war's over for him right now," Quinn said. "Thanks to you boys."

They both saluted him casually as if they were waving to him on the main street of Idabel and had known him all their lives. That's something for being a policeman, Quinn thought to himself, even if the pay is lousy. You're part of a fraternity, even if you're from L.A. and they're from Idabel, Oklahoma.

"That blonde woman's quite a looker," the redheaded man said, casting a furtive look toward Alice Burton. A lot better looking than this mousy one, he thought to himself. He had heard that Jewish girls were really fast, although he doubted that she could be anywhere near as fast as that Maxine Lewis. The redheaded man noticed that Alice Burton had walked toward the water cooler. He cupped his hands around his mouth and whispered to Quinn, "Great tits."

The bald-headed man heard him and shot him an angry look. No doubt about it, Quinn thought. A Baptist. Fire and brimstone up above and, like everyone else, the fire down below.

The whitewashed sheriff's office reverberated with the sound of crickets. Five-hundred-watt bulbs made the room as bright as an operating room. "I think I'd like to see Trattner now," Quinn said. "Are you ready, Alice?"

"I'm ready," Alice said. She squared her shoulders. She had never met a Nazi before, unless you counted Otto Seamans.

"I think I'll take a walk down the hall and see what Maxine is doing," the redheaded man said. His bald-headed friend shot him a dirty look, but he went on anyway.

"I think I'll come along and listen while you talk to the Kraut," Sheriff Warmack said. "I'd just like to be there in case you make history."

Warmack smiled broadly at Alice Burton and John Quinn, then went down the hall just ahead of them. Quinn thought that probably someone had warned Sheriff Warmack not to leave Quinn alone with the Nazi. Probably Alice Burton had told Sam Murphy that he was an angry, dangerous man when it came to Nazis who had killed his girlfriend. Still, Quinn felt certain that he would have his chance before the night was finished. If he couldn't kill Trattner, he could remind him of his sins, Quinn thought with mental glee.

Behind Warmack, Quinn, and Alice Burton walked the redheaded state trooper. He moseyed lazily along the corridor. There were no other prisoners besides Maxine Lewis and Joachim Trattner in the McCurtain County jail. All the likely candidates were now in the armed forces of their nation. The redheaded man felt as if he were in store for a little treat from that Maxine. You couldn't tell with those girls who liked

Krauts. They were a little like the girls who liked niggers. They might do anything. So the redheaded man thought.

When Alexander Warmack took a key ring from his belt and unlocked the door to Trattner's cell, Quinn felt light-headed. The door squeaked open. There, lying on a cot, was Joachim Trattner. He appeared to be asleep. His hair fell across his forehead. His chest rose and fell regularly. His eyes were closed. There was a bruise extending just beyond his hairline on his temple. He wore a cotton shirt and the pants of a wool suit. He wore brown lace-up shoes, which were now pointing straight up toward the cell ceiling.

The cell had only a cot, which was bolted to the wall, a lavatory toilet, a sink, and a pile of paper towels. The single one-hundred-watt bulb in the ceiling was enclosed in steel tubes so that Trattner could not break it into shards and use it as a weapon. The precaution actually predated Trattner's arrival by ten years, but Warmack thought of it as especially apt for a Nazi fanatic who might do anything.

"Look at sleeping beauty," Sheriff Warmack said. He kicked the underside of the bunk and Trattner stirred slightly. He groaned and tried to turn over in his sleep, but Quinn caught him around the neck with a powerful hand and squeezed. Trattner moaned again.

Then Trattner opened his eyes and surveyed the room. Two men and one little Jew girl, his eyes told him. In an instant, he wriggled out of Quinn's grasp and leapt out of his cot. His hands were handcuffed. Even so, he lifted them up, pulled them back, and made a vicious swipe at John Quinn's face. The Irishman ducked out of the way and caught only a glancing blow on his cheek. Then Trattner took a step back and kicked powerfully toward Quinn's stomach. This time Quinn had his wits about him. He waited for the downswing of Trattner's foot—which had missed his stomach—then caught the foot in his hand. He twisted it hard and sent Trattner wobbling off balance. While Trattner stood with one foot in the air like an arrested ballet dancer, Sheriff Warmack brought the butt of a Smith & Wesson Highway Patrolman down on Trattner's neck. The blow was not strong enough to

knock Trattner unconscious. But it stunned Trattner enough
so that Quinn could loose his grip on Trattner's foot. Then
Quinn let go a haymaker that sent Trattner reeling backward
toward the wall of the cell. While Trattner gasped for breath,
and while the bald-headed man and the deputies outside
started running down the hall toward the ruckus, Sheriff Warmack got out a blackjack. He laid it against the side of
Trattner's face with one smart move.

Trattner's eyes tried to focus. He stuck his arms out like a
sleepwalker. Then he made one more robotlike stab at the
fuzzy outline of Quinn. He stammered out, "Jew pig," and
then Quinn caught him in the side of the face with his right
fist. Trattner slumped to the hard floor of the cell. His legs
spread out under him. He groaned and passed into unconsciousness.

The redheaded man, the bald-headed man, and two of the
deputies appeared in the doorway of the cell. "Ambitious little feller, ain't he?" Warmack said, leisurely slapping his
blackjack against his hand.

"How come you didn't shoot him, Alex?" the bald-headed
trooper asked. "Ain't no way that boy's ever gonna be a pro-
ductive member of society, now is there? Might as well shoot
him. Get yourself in the papers."

"I didn't shoot him, you old fool, because I have to let this
man and this woman ask him a few questions," Warmack said.
Then he flushed—as he hadn't during the struggle—and said,
"I'm terribly sorry, ma'am," to Alice Burton.

One of the deputies went to fetch a bucket of water. The
sheriff took the bucket and threw the water on Trattner's
head. Trattner stirred. The deputy refilled the water bucket.
Trattner looked up out of his bloodshot eyes just in time to
see more water cascading down on him. He opened his eyes
and looked around the room. The sight of the barrel of a
12-gauge shotgun peering out at him from under a deputy's
armpit restrained him from heroic thoughts.

Quinn was still breathing hard. He leaned down and picked
up Trattner, dragged his still limp body along the floor, then
propped him up against the wall. Quinn knelt down next to

him and said in an urgent, low voice, "Now listen, you Kraut sonofabitch, we'd like to know a few things."

Trattner looked at him in disgust. He said nothing. He looked around the room at the hardened-looking men with guns. He still said nothing.

"We want to know where you were going in such a big hurry, my friend," Warmack said, towering above where Trattner lay.

Still, Trattner said nothing.

"You better tell us, boy," Quinn said. "You're a long way from Berlin. You ain't going yelling to the Red Cross or anybody else. You tell us what you're up to, or we're gonna attach your balls to that light socket."

Trattner still said nothing. This was typical Yankee Jew fighting, he thought to himself through the aches which radiated like drumbeats from his head and neck. Five of them with guns and clubs against one Nazi. Yet they are still afraid of me. And they should be!

"If you talk to us, we'll help you, boy," Warmack said. "We won't let that colored boy from down in DeQueen, the one who likes to slice off white women's noses, come in here and spend the night with your little Maxine. If you don't talk to us, boy, your little girlfriend's gonna be a mighty chewed-up little piece of white meat."

Trattner made a snarling sound from deep in his throat, but still he said nothing. Quinn smiled and then drew back his hand. With the back of his left hand, he struck Trattner as hard as he could across the face. His Fairfax High class ring (Class of '25) caught Trattner on the cheek. It opened the flesh in a diagonal line about one inch long. Blood started to ooze out of the cut. Trattner bared his teeth like a cornered hound. Again, he made a growling sound. Again, Quinn struck him with the back of his hand. This time the wound grew larger. Trattner grimaced at the tearing pain of his flesh. Then he resumed an air of icy contempt. Yankee Jews could not break an SS man.

Quinn smiled at him. It was the same smile that Esteban Salazar, Roberto Torres, Luis Echevarria, and many other residents of the East Los Angeles area knew when they were about to be persuaded by John Quinn to tell him what was on their mind. Inside Joachim Trattner, a small spark of fear was ignited. Try as he might, he could not extinguish it. These people were crazy. They left automobiles out to rust in the rain. They dropped thousands of tons of bombs on innocent civilians in the Ruhr. And now this man, this *irischer Mann,* was smiling as he hit Trattner.

Still, Joachim Trattner was an SS man! If he had to die with his secret, he would die. In fact, the thought was soon stiffened by another resolve. Undoubtedly the Reich had other P.O.W.s at large at this very moment working on the same plan. Might it not be better for Trattner to actually die than to even possibly reveal the mission? Trattner weighed the odds of ever achieving his mission against the chance of his talking. Perhaps it would be better if he provoked them into killing him.

Acting on this impulse, Trattner suddenly spoke, just as Quinn was about to hit him again. "You Jew bastards," he said. "Worse than Jews. Jew slaves! You eat Jew shit."

"You think so?" Quinn asked. He smiled again. He looked around at the men in the room. He noticed that the red-headed man was not there any longer. "Hey, you boys think we're Jew slaves?" The trooper and the deputies laughed. Quinn laughed too, then hit Trattner in the face with his fist.

Trattner's head bounced against the wall. "Hey, I thought this boy couldn't talk," Warmack said. "Maybe now he'll give us a little talk. Tell us where he was going so fast he almost ran off the road."

But Trattner was not talking. He was not awake. The most recent blow to his skull had sent him into a welcome respite of unconscious fantasies of rivers and gods and Nordic warriors and missions fulfilled. Quinn studied Trattner's face carefully. Trattner drooled out of the left corner of his lips. Then he formed a word and breathed it more than said it. To Quinn, the word sounded like "Now we'll see." It seemed strange to him that Trattner would talk English in his sleep.

To Warmack, who had learned a few words of German during his stay in Europe after the end of World War I, the words sounded like, *"Nein. Verstedt."* No. Stay. Warmack thought that Trattner must be talking to someone from long before.

To the bald-headed Baptist, Trattner's words sounded like he was talking about a Guernsey cow. Trattner might have said, "No, Guernsey."

Quinn heard Trattner speak again, and this time the words sounded like "Now, she'll see."

But who could "she" be? And perhaps Trattner's unconscious mutterings had far more to do with a fantasy of love long ago than anything connected with escapes from Kriegsgefangenenlager Fort Ord or daring breaks across the country with American girls.

"Let's just hold on," Quinn said. "Let him sleep for a few minutes before we start again. I'll stay with him in case he talks any more in his sleep. I'll call you when he starts to come around again."

"I think I'll stay here, too," Warmack said. "I don't feature this boy taking off again and breaking in your head. I'd be mighty embarrassed."

Quinn and Warmack sat on the cot and waited. Warmack lit a Tareyton cigarette and drew in a deep drag. As he did, he coughed with racking convulsions, then smiled, then drew in another drag and coughed again.

Trattner slumped over onto his side. He drooled more, so that his face now rested in a pool of spittle. He looked almost blue from his bruises.

The deputies and the bald-headed man moseyed back to the front room of the sheriff's castle.

Across the hall from Trattner's cell, the redheaded man had let himself in with his passkey. Maxine had the light out and was asleep on her cot with a thin blanket over her legs. One of the legs stuck out from the cot and from Maxine's dress. The redheaded man leaned forward and began to stroke the inside of Maxine's thigh. She stirred slightly in her sleep, then moaned. The redheaded man was emboldened to run his hand farther up her thighs to her underpants. He stuck his finger under the part between her thighs. Maxine moaned

again, shifted on her cot, then opened her eyes. When she saw
the redheaded man, she gasped aloud.

He put his hand over her mouth so that no one could hear
her. It was already dark so that no one could see into the cell.
"Just take it easy, little lady," the redheaded man said. "I'm
just checking to see if you're all right."

Maxine would have said, "Get your hands off me," if the
hand had not been over her mouth. As it was, she tried to hit
the redheaded man with her fists. He drew back his hand
from her thighs and slapped her across the face. Then he
quickly covered up her mouth again.

"If you can't be a little nicer, you're in for a lot of trouble.
A lot of trouble. Some people don't ever get out of this jail in
one piece."

He sat down on the cot next to her. She did not struggle
any longer. She did not speak. The redheaded man smiled.
"I'm sorry I had to hit you," he said. "I ain't really asking for
anything. Just a little of what you were giving that Kraut."

Maxine smiled at him. She had noticed something that was
too good to be true. The redheaded man had both a gun and
a key on his belt. "You just scared me," she said. "I'm glad
you came in. It was getting cold in here."

The redheaded man did not feel at all cold. In fact, it still
seemed hot to him. But he did not want to complain or quarrel. He did something he would never have done to an Idabel
girl. He ran his hand up to her blouse and unbuttoned one of
the buttons. Maxine still stared at him and smiled. He ran his
rough hand inside her shirt and felt her bosom. Christ. It was
as hard as a rock. The nipple was firm, too. Maxine wriggled
and moaned again.

"Let me get into that little cot with you, sweetheart," he
said. "You won't be cold much longer."

The redheaded man loosened his belt and let down his
trousers. His gun and key ring clanked against the floor. He
gave Maxine a cautionary look, which she ignored. Then he
let down his drawers. Maxine reached over and began to
stroke his thighs, making little kissing sounds as she did. The
redheaded man felt his heart start to flutter. Then, my God,

my God, she got out of bed and started to go down on her hands and knees in front of him. Oh, my Lord, he had seen this kind of thing once in a stag film (*The Bandit of Love—He Steals Their Pussy, Too*), but he never in his life dreamed it would happen to him.

She took him in her hand, and he leaned back against the wall in ecstasy. He knew there was more to life than Pentecostal Church and good old Linda Evelyn. She was really about to put it in her mouth! He closed his eyes in delight.

Maxine felt around on the floor for the gun. With one hand, she unsnapped the holster, pulled out the gun, and brought it down on this fool's head while he had his eyes closed. He groaned and slumped to the cot. In an instant, Maxine had the keys. But which was the right one? If someone in the hall heard her fiddling with the keys, there would be shooting first and questions later. She looked through the bars and down the hall. There was no one in the hall now, but the sound of keys in a lock might bring someone. She would have to be very quiet.

She tried one key after another, keeping one eye on the hallway and another on the redheaded man.

Across the hall, Trattner had reawakened. Quinn held him against the wall by putting his hand against his neck and squeezed. "I just want you to know it was my girlfriend that your friend killed," Quinn said. "I just want you to know that so you'll know I'm not just interested in you because it's my job."

"I don't care about your Jew job or your Jew-loving country," Trattner said. "If you knew how we Germans were trying to save you, you would not be here. You would be on your hands and knees thanking us."

Quinn slapped Trattner again, reopening his wound, making more blood pour out. Alice Burton, who had stayed with Sheriff Warmack in the cell, winced at the sound of the blow.

Trattner spit blood out of his mouth. "You cannot get me to tell you anything. Anyway, I know nothing. I am simply trying to return to my land to fight for my Führer."

Warmack shook his head. So they really did talk like that

after all. Just like in those movies. They really were fanatics after all.

"What's 'Now, she'll see' mean?" Quinn asked.

"I don't know what you're talking about," Trattner said. "I don't care what you're talking about. I demand to be returned to my camp and to have proper medical care."

"What is Siegfried?" Alice Burton asked. "Who is the dwarf?"

Panic raced through Trattner's mind. Had they heard him talking in his sleep? What had he said when he was unconscious?

"I do not want to answer your Jew questions," Trattner said. "I know the Geneva Convention," Trattner said. "There. Now return me to my camp at once or the Red Cross will hear about this." But for the first time, he wore a look of fear.

Alice Burton felt her heart race. Quinn glanced meaningfully toward her. "What's the magic cape?" she asked. "The *Tarnkappe?*"

Now Trattner felt a wave of self-hatred. What weak part of him had spoken in his sleep? How dare they worm these secrets out of an unconscious, beaten man? He really would have been better off dying. What else had he said?

"Those are just fairy stories," Trattner said coolly. "They mean nothing. I demand to go back to my camp."

"Are you supposed to steal something?" Alice Burton asked. "To blow something up? Something magical? Something a magic dwarf owns? You can tell us. We won't tell anyone back at the camp."

Trattner twisted his bruised mouth into a gesture of contempt. "Do you think I would tell Jews like you anything I knew? Anyway, you are wasting my time. I know nothing except that I want to get away from this Jew-loving hell and return to Germany. See if your Jew brain can figure that out." He laughed at Alice Burton until Quinn caught him with yet another blow with the back of his hand. The sound reverberated through the cell.

"Now, you listen to me, you filthy, murdering little Kraut bastard," Quinn spat. "Nobody from the Red Cross knows you're here. Nobody from Germany knows you're here. We can cut you up in little pieces and hang them out for the mosquitoes, and I'd like to do it, to tell you the honest truth. If you don't start talking, I'm going to start cutting," Quinn said. From his back pocket he took a "Black Beauty" switchblade knife. He held it in front of Trattner's face. He pressed the large, chrome hemispherical button on the side. A four-inch blade snapped out with a terrifyingly precise click. It sliced through the air, then stopped, its point only a few millimeters from the bottom of Trattner's bleeding nose.

Trattner's eyes looked wild with hatred and fear. He could face the thought of a bullet in the back of the head. He could face explosions. But knives! It had made him tingle for an hour to kill that counterman back in Nevada. To think of the same thing being done to him electrified his brain with terror. He closed his eyes and thought of the Führer. If he were going to die, he only wished to die quickly so that he did not betray the Führer's confidence in him. He was bathed in sweat, yet he tried to sound defiant.

"I know nothing," Trattner said. "You may not treat me like this. Your men in Germany will suffer if you continue this."

Quinn placed the point of the knife against the tip of Trattner's nose. "No one's going to know," he said. "There's just going to be a body found out in a field somewhere, mostly eaten by coyotes. And that's going to be the end of you," Quinn said, "except that a few people near the jail may hear you screaming for a while."

Alice Burton assumed a genial, friendly tone. "Don't be so hard on him, John," she said. "I think he's ready to tell us everything he knows now. It'll be all right. You want to tell us where you're going, don't you? I know it would be hard on you back at the camp if they found out we'd had this little talk. But we'll put you back in another camp, where nobody'll even know you. Now, just what were you supposed to do?"

Trattner said, "I have told you. I was simply trying to escape. I am allowed to do that. It is my duty. I am not ashamed of anything." He tried, but failed, to regain his icy composure.

252 Benjamin J. Stein

"And the girl, Maxine Lewis?" Alice Burton asked. "Did she just happen to be there? Come on. We know exactly when she was supposed to meet you and Whelchel. We know where she bought your clothes, getting ready to pick you up."

Trattner said nothing. What had Maxine told them? He knew she was not trustworthy. She was, after all, only a worthless whore of a woman. Who knew how many other men she had given herself to before him? Still, he would die like an SS man, as he had urged Thost to do.

Quinn pressed his knife against Trattner's face just under his left eye. "I'm going to start with your eye," he said. "I think I'll do that because Marilyn had such fabulous eyes. I'll never see those eyes again, just because of what you did. So I think I'll just take out those pretty blue eyes of yours."

"You are a fool," Trattner said. "We are fighting your fight. We Germans are bearing the struggle for all of you white people, yet you bomb us and join with the Jews and the Bolsheviks against us. Let me go to fight for you and you will be doing the smart thing."

Quinn looked around the room with a half-smile of amused amazement. "You're an incredible guy, Trattner," he said. "I'm really going to like this."

Quinn pressed the point of the knife slowly into the flesh under Trattner's eye. A spot of bright red blood appeared on the point of the knife. Trattner gritted his teeth.

There was a creaking noise from behind Alice Burton. She turned around slowly, too slowly to keep Maxine Lewis from clapping a hand over her mouth and putting a distinctly cold pistol barrel to her temple.

"All right, let go of him," Maxine Lewis said in an astonishingly clear, authoritative tone of voice. "I'll blow her brains out if you don't let him go right this minute."

The next sound Quinn remembered was Trattner's savage laugh, then the bright gleam in his lupine, ferocious blue eyes. In a flash, Trattner was on his feet, taking Warmack's gun out of his holster, forcing Warmack to unlock his handcuffs, and then picking up Quinn's "Black Beauty" switchblade knife. Trattner grasped the knife firmly and made a circle around Quinn's face, as if he had not quite decided where to stick in the point.

"I do not know," Trattner said finally. "I think I will just let you go to think about what a group of fools you are. We will take your Jew friend with us." Then he laughed cruelly.

"If you make any move to stop us, there'll be her head splattered all over this jail," Maxine Lewis said. "Now let's go."

In a small procession, Warmack, then Quinn, Alice Burton, Trattner, and Maxine walked toward the front of the jail. "Tell them to let us go or you all get killed," Maxine Lewis said.

The bald-headed trooper and two deputies gaped as Warmack appeared before them, hands raised. "They mean business, boys," he said in a relaxed drawl. "Let 'em by."

"Drop your guns on the floor," Trattner said. "I'll kill your precious sheriff in a minute if you don't."

"Go ahead, boys," Sheriff Warmack said. There were beads of perspiration on his forehead. "I don't feel like cashing in right now," he added.

"Now go out very slowly and tell the men outside with the shotguns to stay to the side and let us have one of their cars. One of their own cars. Not a police car," Trattner said.

Warmack did as he was told. With Trattner holding the Highway Patrolman revolver in his back, Warmack moved out the door. His hands were in the air. The deputies looked up at him lazily. Perhaps they thought he was stretching. "Boys," Warmack said to the deputies, "we've had a little setback. That man's got a gun on me and his friend's got a gun on the little girl. Better put down those Winchesters and give this man the keys to your Pontiac, Billy. You'll give it back, won't you?" he asked Trattner with a slight tilt of his head.

Trattner replied by pushing the gun barrel farther into Warmack's back. "We shall see," he said. "Keep walking until we get to the car." He was sweating profusely.

Billy, the deputy, told Warmack that the keys were in the car. He shrugged toward a black Pontiac coupe that stood parked under a huge live oak tree just underneath a street lamp. The sound of crickets chirruping was overwhelming during the few moments when Trattner led the procession toward the car. There was no one on the streets of Idabel to notice what had happened. Only the crickets were awake.

"Now, little bitch," Maxine Lewis said, "whoever you are, you and I will get into the car. You can sit in the back seat with him," she said, thrusting her chin at Trattner. Maxine let go her grasp of Alice Burton for just a moment to open the door of the Pontiac and then push forward the front seat to let Alice Burton in.

In less than a second, the thought flashed through Alice Burton's mind that if she got into that car, all the analysis, clever deductions, and witty observations of all the lawyers of all time would not be enough to save her life. If she did as she was told—as she had all her life—she would soon lie dead in a ditch somewhere in Oklahoma.

So Alice Burton did not get into the car. Instead, she abruptly took one step to the side, wheeled around, and hit Maxine Lewis as hard as she could in the side of the head. Maxine Lewis reeled, fired, and heard the bullet go plumping harmlessly into the upholstery of the car.

At the same instant, Quinn dropped to the ground, rolled away from Trattner's bullet, and pulled out his belly gun, the one he had right there in his belt, the little .32 that had surprised Whelchel back in Santa Cruz. But Trattner was fast. Before Quinn could fire, he was in the car, sitting at the wheel, turning the ignition with one hand and firing at Warmack, the largest target, with the other. With a groan, clutching at his side, Warmack went down. The deputies and the bald-headed trooper ran to him. Blood poured out onto his white shirt.

Quinn was not distracted for more than a few seconds. He fired three shots into the windshield of the Pontiac, shattering it into a hundred thousand pieces. But before he could get off his fourth shot, the Pontiac was moving, with Trattner at the wheel and Maxine clutching the steering wheel as she pulled herself in. The fourth shot hit the trunk of the Pontiac and the fifth shattered the rear window. Maxine Lewis leaned out the window of the Pontiac and fired three times at the deputies and troopers who were by now firing fusillades at the Pontiac.

Her last shot hit the bald-headed man's state trooper car in the gas tank. The friction of the bullet set off sparks. When the sparks met the gasoline vapors, the car burst into flames. The flames spread to the other cars and to the motorcycles. In the dazzling glow of the gasoline fires, Quinn watched the Pontiac speed out of sight along Avenue A, turning off toward Main Street.

In the dust, just outside the ring of fire, Alice Burton still lay in the dirt where she had ducked when Quinn started to fire. She was breathing heavily in the sweltering Oklahoma night air. Despite Trattner's getaway, she felt a powerful surge of elation. She had saved her own life. When a woman had done that twice, anything was possible.

The bald-headed state trooper and one of the deputies chased Trattner with a car they took from the jail's garage. They found the abandoned Pontiac six blocks away in front of 404 Southeast Avenue F. The owners of the house had heard some noises and now that they thought about it, they noticed that their Chevrolet panel truck, a practically new 1938, was gone.

Sheriff Warmack was in surgery for five hours in McCurtain County General Hospital. When he emerged, he was dead of massive thoracic bleeding, which had put him into irreversible shock.

Quinn swore that they would get Trattner for this, among other things. Alice Burton cried. The bald-headed man swore, stamped his foot, and said, "Sonofabitch," even though he was a Baptist. Alice Burton asked if she could use a telephone to call Washington, D.C. Then she wondered what she had to do to get a news blackout on this catastrophe.

WILHELM CANARIS
ABWEHR

May 30, 1943
Memorandum To: Reichsführer, SS,
Heinrich Himmler

My Reichsführer!

Per your requests, the latest documentation on the "Manhattan District" project to develop a fission explosive device is enclosed. As you will read, and as your "scientists" have perhaps told you, the crucial problem at this stage of the project is to determine whether the neutrino is a beta emitter or a beta collector. Frankly, I have no idea of what this means. Apparently, it has something to do with whether the mass of an atom which is torn apart by being struck by another atom is heavy enough to continue the chain reaction required to produce the explosive force which is the aim of the entire project.

The Americans will, of course, solve this problem. However, the usual instant response from Professors Szilard and Einstein has not been forthcoming in this case. The problem may be only one of those that they are considering, with other formulae taking precedence. Or, the problem may be far more difficult than even the "Manhattan District" scientists had anticipated.

In any event, we must at this point question whether even if we obtained the answer to this question we would be substantially closer to a beginning on a fission project. The success of the Siegfried operation is more important than ever, therefore.

The Kursk salient is stalemated at this point. The Division "Grossdeutschland SS" has displayed a firm ability to mount an in-depth defense all around Vyazma. In Kharkov, Manstein and the Eighteenth Panzer Army are (so far) repelling the Soviet counterattacks. As you know, Kharkov is the hub of the entire Donets Basin. If we can keep it, the Russians will be compelled to talk to us about a settlement. I respectfully stress to you, therefore, the urgent necessity of prosecuting the war vigorously in Kharkov as compared with other possible uses of Reich resources.

Enclosed for your eyes only are the transcripts of the most recent meetings in Stockholm. As you will see, the main problems at this point concern the area of the Polish and Czech condominiums. If any sizable area of the Ukraine can be added to joint control, we will have the wherewithal to make concessions on the Czech area. You will notice that the Soviet negotiators have displayed far more flexibility since the inability of the Red Army to dislodge our army from Kharkov. If we could add further weight to the balance scales, we would be in a commanding position to settle the Eastern Front once and for all.

As you are probably informed, our apparatus has made no progress whatsoever in discerning the extent of the Soviet fission project. The penetration of the Soviet scientific establishment has been made almost impossible since the purges of the late 1930s. The climate of fear in the Soviet Union makes any meaningful information-gathering within the Soviet extremely difficult, to put it mildly.

From our Cicero network in Ankara, we have learned that the British "tube alloys" intelligence liaison is rather certain that the Soviets have penetrated the "Manhattan District" to a far greater degree than we thought likely. Moreover, we have reason to believe, again from "tube alloys," that the Soviets are able to act on their information to a far greater extent than we have been. I suspect that the quality of their scientific inquiry is altogether superior to that of our Reich Research Council. The possibility that the Soviets are as much aware of Einstein's and Fermi's contributions to the "Manhattan District" as we are is now a virtual certainty, with still more implications as to the importance of the success of the Siegfried operation. Of course, if the Soviets have thoroughly penetrated the "Manhattan District," they are also aware of the Hechingen ruse, the Americans' interpretation of it, and the concern in Washington. This, combined with Siegfried, is of immense significance to Stockholm.

Finally, as to Siegfried itself: I have enclosed newspaper accounts of the American response to the escape of Oberst Trattner and his travel through America. Since the date of these accounts, there has been a new outburst of violence from Oberst Trattner in a southeast Oklahoma town called Idabel. He killed a sheriff, a local law enforcement officer in American rural areas. This death is the seventh which has been directly connected with Trattner's mission. All have been dramatic and highly visible to the Americans. May I respectfully say that the choice of a man like Trattner for a mission of this sensitivity must now be questioned. His goal was not to kill as many Americans as possible. Nor was it to make his name known in American newspapers. His goal was to be accomplished quietly and effectively. Our project officers in the United States of America now offer only a modest possibility that Oberst Trattner will avoid capture before being able to complete his mission.

If he is captured, I can only offer the hope that he will be executed quickly so that he does not have time to reveal his objective. That will make it at least *possible* that someone else with more discretion could accomplish the same mission.

However, as always, the Intelligence Services of the Reich are at your disposal. As always, we wish you success in this noble endeavor.

Best wishes on your son's birthday and a deeply felt Heil Hitler,

Canaris

R. F. ⚡⚡
Heinrich Himmler
NACHRICHTEN-UEBERMITTLUNG

May 30, 1943
Memorandum To: Admiral Wilhelm Canaris,
                        Abwehr
By telegraph from Rastenburg

Yours of this morning read and received. May I remind you that Intelligence Services within the Reich are directed to provide information for the Führer and his associates to make decisions. Once those decisions have been made, the Intelligence Services, even at the highest level, are bound to aid in effecting those decisions in every possible way.

The Siegfried decision has been made at the highest levels and is not open to question (or to sarcastic comment) at this stage.

The Führer is certain that the Kharkov salient will hold indefinitely and that the implementation of the Final Solution to the Jewish problem requires our greatest effort now.

Best regards and a cordial Heil Hitler,
Himmler, Reichsführer, SS

WILHELM CANARIS
ABWEHR

May 31, 1943
Memorandum To: Heinrich Himmler,
Reichsführer, SS
By telegraph from Berlin. In cipher.

May I assume from your latest communication that
the Führer is fully aware of the "Siegfried" operation? May I also assume that he is aware of the
Stockholm conference in all its implications?
Please reply in cipher.

Canaris

R. F. ⚡⚡
Heinrich Himmler
NACHRICHTEN-UEBERMITTLUNG

May 31, 1943
Urgent Memorandum From: Heinrich Himmler,
Reichsführer, SS
By telegraph from Berlin. In cipher.

I have returned to the Reich Chancery this afternoon. Can you please meet me in my office at 2000
hours this evening? Please bring all documents re-
lated to the Siegfried operation.

Himmler

June 1, 1943,
Washington, D.C.

In Room 115 of the old State Department Building, right smack next to the White House, in a room with white carved friezes along the doorways and in the cornices, two men studied cables from Oklahoma and from Geneva and from Stockholm and finally from Cambria, England. One of the men had a fierce, evangelistic glow in his eyes. He spoke in the accents of a country preacher, adding a nasal "unnh" sound at the end of every word he could possibly attach it to. The other man smoked incessantly, spilling ashes on his gray suit from Lewis and Thomas Saltz. His hands shook uncontrollably as he listened to the interpretation of all that crap from Major Heinrich, who had been brought here on a cruiser just to lay out all that Eighth Air Force had learned when they recovered Powers' and Loughlin's bodies. The major had talked a lot about the Book of Daniel, about statues with heads of gold, chests and arms of silver, legs of bronze, and feet of clay. Then he had started to talk about prophecies.

"I hope you knowunnh," he said, "that this has all been prophesied. The Third Reich is the Kingdom of the East. The Russians, of course, are the bear with two horns, and see, hereunnh, is where the United States of Americauuunnh comes in. . . ." Heinrich had actually started to take a Bible out of his briefcase. It looked extremely well used. What the hell was this guy doing in Psychological Operations?

"Just tell me about the pictures of that Hechingen place," Harry Hopkins said. "Where the hell is it? I never heard of it." He dropped some ash from his Raleigh cigarette into an ashtray of clear glass with the seal of the President of the United States in gold print.

"It's near Strasbourg," Heinrich said. "The crypto machine correlates all photographs with the location of the airplane. Otherwise, we'd never have gotten it. They've built a small village there, right out of nowhere. Crash project. Very hush-hushunnh, as if the prophecy was speaking to them in the clearest of tonguesunnh," Heinrich said. He liked this affectation. He had only picked it up since Powers and Loughlin crashed. If there was a miracle happening right in Eighth Air Force, he wanted to be its Jeremiah.

"And you've been briefed by General Groves?" Hopkins asked.

"Indeed, yesunnh," Heinrich said. "I saw the plans for Oak Ridge. These photos look exactly the same. I'm no expert," he said, "but I'd say that whatever we're making at Oak Ridge, the Germans are probably making at Hechingen. From the air, looks pretty much the same."

"You are no expert," Hopkins said, "and you certainly are in no position to know what's being done at Oak Ridge, are you now?"

"He who hath eyes, let him see," Heinrich said, rocking back into the thick blue carpet on the balls of his booted feet, "and he who hath ears, let him hear." His eyes rolled upward toward the ceiling.

Jesus, Harry Hopkins thought. And they think we can win this war with nuts like Heinrich running around? Aloud, he said, "Thank you very much, Major. I'm sure you'll want to get back to England as soon as you can."

"My duty is wherever I can do some good," Heinrich said piously. He looked demurely down at the carpet.

"I'll make sure you have a fine room at the Statler," Harry

Hopkins said. "And some good food before you go back to England. In the meantime, this is extremely confidential. You understand that?"

"My lips are sealed," Heinrich said.

I wish, Hopkins thought. Then he walked briskly off toward the East Wing of the White House. For once, those fools at the War Department had been right to take his time and the President's for something. This was serious. The President was talking to a group of rice growers from Louisiana, but right afterward, he and Hopkins had to have a talk. There were just too goddamn many coincidences popping up all over the place. And this Trattner business was just another straw about to break the camel's back.

If the devil were to come down among us . . . Hopkins thought. Maybe he already has. Hopkins saluted the Marine guard at West Executive Avenue and hurried into the sunshine and then into the coolness of the White House. Would we recognize him?

June 1, 1943,
Washington, D.C.

"I should have seen it right away," Alice Burton said. "It was so obvious."

"It isn't obvious," Sam Murphy said. "In fact, we're not clear on it at all."

Alice Burton and Sam Murphy strolled down Seventeenth Street, past the palatial headquarters of the Pan-American Union. They paused for a moment to admire the ferns in its soaring, trellised-in-marble courtyard. Tame macaws hooted from the roof, sunlight pouring through their multicolored feathers. By Alice Burton's side, John Quinn stared in amazement at the grandeur of the building. It was like a far more elaborate Union Station, he thought, only with no one inside. Two rows of flags faced each other hanging from the north and south walls of the courtyard. There were flags from every country in Central and South America, in addition to the United States.

Sam Murphy stopped and leaned on one leg against a statue of Simón Bolívar. He wore a light-gray glenurquhart plaid suit from J. Press. His tie was a blue, red, and gray rep from Brooks Brothers. To John Gregory Quinn, Sam Murphy looked like a character from a movie, maybe the rich father of Ann Rutherford in an Andy Hardy movie.

Through Murphy's endless tentacles, Quinn had a new suit and shirt and underwear waiting for him at his hotel room at the Sheraton-Park. It was from Brooks Brothers. It fit better than any suit he had ever owned. Alice Burton must have called in and told Murphy the size. She was an observant kid. Smart, too. She had dropped and rolled back there in Idabel at exactly the right moment. If she had done it a second earlier, Maxine would have shot her through the head. If she had done it a second later, she would have been in the car and unable to break away cleanly.

Now Alice Burton ran a hand through her light-brown hair —which really wasn't mousy at all, when you came to think of it, Quinn thought—and then stared at her white linen two-piece suit as if the fibers held a clue. "I should have guessed that Trattner was saying 'New Jersey'," she said.

"We're not sure that he was," Quinn said. "It sure sounded like 'Now she'll see' to me."

"Really, it must have been a clue about where they were going," Alice Burton said. "Do you remember how upset he got when he realized he'd said something in his sleep? He tried to pass it off right away. He looked worried as hell."

"Our psychologists said that often people dream about for-eign place-names," Murphy said. "Especially if they've had to memorize where they are supposed to go. The place-name stays in their minds. Like maybe when you went to camp and it was an odd name, like Kiamesha or Kieve. I remember that," he said, lighting up a Philip Morris cigarette with his gold Dunhill lighter. "I went to a camp in Maine called Camp Kieve. I would just say the name to myself over and over again before I ever saw it. It was such a mysterious name," Murphy said, transported back to his days as a boy in Har-rison, New York.

"Of course," Alice Burton said. "That has to be it."

"Look," Quinn said, "I don't know much about psychology, but I knew a lot of German kids back at Fairfax High. I didn't go to summer camp," he added meaningfully. "And I can tell you that there are plenty of German words that sound like New Jersey. It is not such a strange name that he would be talking about it in his sleep. It isn't like Kiamesha or Kieve."

Murphy inhaled a great puff of smoke, then slowly let it out through his nostrils. "You're so right," he said with a grin. "He could have been saying, 'Now she'll see.' He might have been dreaming about Maxine Lewis. Or he could have been saying, 'Now we'll see,' referring to settling some old score. Those are both possible."

"The problem is," Alice Burton said, popping a jujube, "that if he *didn't* say 'New Jersey,' we don't have a thing to go on. If he did say 'New Jersey,' at least we've narrowed down the possible places to look. Besides, he was a physicist or a chemist, something like that, in Germany. That could mean something. There are a lot of chemical plants in New Jersey. Du Pont is in Delaware. Right next door."

"So, we might as well assume that he said New Jersey," Murphy said. He stared up at a macaw that was making a particularly sharp cawing sound. "That gives you two something to work on."

"I'm still in?" Quinn asked. "I didn't exactly cover myself with glory in Oklahoma. I thought I'd be sent back to L.A. in a hurry."

"You're now a major in the United States Army, detailed to the Office of Strategic Services," Murphy said, snapping off a crisp salute with the hand holding the cigarette. "Congratulations. It's all been cleared with Captain Parker and with General Marshall."

"You must be joking," Quinn said. "I never even went to Basic Training."

"This is war, son," Murphy said, patting Quinn's shoulder. "We have to make snap judgments. You can thank highly placed friends in the OSS," he said, winking toward Alice Burton. She blushed. "Besides, if you go off and shoot someone besides Trattner, we have to at least *look* like you were doing something official."

Quinn beamed at Alice Burton. He wondered what Rizzuti would make of this. "Nobody asked me," he said.

"You can turn it down," Murphy said in an enormous exhalation of bluish-gray smoke. "No one's making you take it on."

"I think I'll take it," Quinn said. "At least until we find Trattner."

Back out on Seventeenth Street, moseying toward Constitution Hall, Murphy laughed. Just as a D.C. Transit trolley car skidded past, he said, "That could be a long time, Major. I hate to tell you this, but there have been about a hundred escapes from those camps so far. There are five Krauts still missing. We caught a couple of them just as they were getting aboard a Brazilian ship in San Antonio or Galveston, or somewhere in Texas."

"There are still a few missing from the First World War, as far as that goes," Alice Burton said.

"So he might just disappear and we might never hear from him again," Quinn said.

"For all we know, he's already settled down in Peapack, New Jersey, under the name of Hamilton Jones and he's taking the commuter train in to work at the Morgan Bank every day, playing gin rummy in the parlor car," Murphy said. "Stranger things have happened."

"Or, he could be planning to blow up the Navy Yards outside Jersey City," Alice Burton said.

"Or, he could be planning to blow up the Brooklyn Bridge. That's what I'd do if I really wanted to throw a scare into someone," Murphy said. "That would make people think we weren't quite as secure back home in America as we thought."

They all thought about what Joachim Trattner could do in and around New Jersey as they bustled through the mob of lunch-hour pedestrian traffic on Seventeenth Street. At the corner of K Street, they turned and walked across K, then across Connecticut Avenue, and headed for Harvey's. "To have some decent sea bass," as Murphy said, although Quinn had never heard of sea bass. He had heard of bass, but not sea bass.

Over a meticulously served but slightly fishy dish that was indeed sea bass, Murphy laid out his hunches about the possible targets. "There are absolutely crucial railroads going from all over the country to factories and shipyards in New England," Murphy said. "If he could knock out a few of those lines on a regular basis, it would be as good for the Germans as having a fleet of dive bombers off Atlantic City."

In a corner of the dimly lit dining room, paneled with glistening maple, Harold Ickes sat glowering at a Salisbury steak. Sam Murphy waved at him and smiled cheerfully. The famed curmudgeon of the "brains trust" acknowledged Murphy with an even more pronounced frown.

At a table next to Murphy, Quinn, and Burton, a dapper man wearing an old-fashioned pince-nez carefully studied page 3 of the Washington *Daily News*, the city's leading tabloid. The *News* was still giving top billing to the escaped "Nazi thrill-killer" Joachim Trattner and his "gun moll" girlfriend, Maxine Lewis. Under a picture which Scripps-Howard had obtained of Maxine wearing a tight sweater, a headline read "Is Hometown Girl Showing Nazi the Way?"

John Quinn asked if there was any way to get a beer at Harvey's. "Of course," said the waiter. "We have National Bohemian on tap." Murphy shot a look at Quinn.

Quinn had never heard of National Bohemian beer, but he drink it thirstily anyway. It gave him a feeling that he was not completely alone in the restaurant, a working stiff among the swells. The beer was his companion, the beverage of the working man, warming his stomach, telling him that even at Harvey's, there were men and women who were just like him.

"Back in World War I, there was major sabotage at the Tom's River munitions factory," Alice Burton said. "There was some thought that it had been done by escapees from a German prisoner of war camp. That factory's still going great guns. Maybe that's where he's headed." Alice smiled cheerfully at Quinn as if to encourage his beer-drinking.

"Could be, could be," Murphy said. "I just want you two to put yourself in the position of some Nazi bigwig in Berlin. He's got just one shot at doing something really, really big in America. It's got to be something that really rattles a few cages. He could try to assassinate F.D.R.," he added, staring at Quinn's beer.

"God forbid," Alice Burton said hastily.

"Of course," Murphy said. "God forbid."

"God forbid," Quinn added.

"Or he could try to steal some kind of military secret, but he doesn't exactly seem to be the stealthy type, the type who could lie low and get himself into some secret installation," Murphy said.

"That's for sure," Quinn said. "The guy is a gorilla. There's got to be some kind of thing that needs a gorilla to get it done. Now, what kind of job is there in New Jersey that needs a real tough guy to do it? Any little punk who knows about electricity can make a bomb. This has to be a job for a guy who's tough face-to-face. Then again, the guy was a chemist or a physicist or something before the war. Maybe he is making bombs."

"It could be that he's not supposed to do any one thing. Maybe he's just supposed to scare people. Make us all feel less secure on the home front," Alice Burton suggested. She squeezed a lemon slice over her sea bass. "I think he was a physicist, not a chemist," she said. "Maybe he's supposed to do some kind of sabotage that only a physicist could do. Some special kind of damage. Maybe electrical plants."

"Maybe he's just the first one and the Krauts are planning to get a lot of them out and just have them shooting up people," Quinn said. A shiver passed over him, so that even in overheated Harvey's with his new Brooks Brothers suit he felt a chill. It was the chill of the coldest and also the happiest blue eyes he had ever seen, the morning before Marilyn had died on a pavement in Santa Cruz. My God, he had almost forgotten! This was not just a job. This was not even only a patriotic duty. This was a blood oath. He shook his head. Why on earth had he let Trattner get away back in Idabel? Why hadn't he beat him to death right there in the McCurtain County jail cell? Then the sonofabitch would definitely not have been able to do whatever he was supposed to do. Then he could sleep at night when Marilyn's face swam into his mind. He shivered again. He noticed that Murphy and Alice Burton were staring at him.

"Are you all right?" Murphy asked. "You coming down

with something? A cold? I know you've put in some time lately."

"I'm all right," Quinn said. "I just remembered how badly I want that bastard."

Murphy smiled and clapped Quinn on the shoulder. "That's why we have you here," he said. "That's what we're counting on."

Back in Murphy's office, Quinn sat on a red leather couch and looked out at the Washington Monument. There was an endless stream of Capital Transit buses and Yellow Cabs taking people around the enormous plot of ground where the monument stood. Some day, Quinn thought, the traffic would get that bad in Los Angeles. But probably not in Quinn's lifetime. Quinn admired Murphy's office. He admired particularly the autographed photograph of Franklin Delano Roosevelt, which adorned the wall behind Murphy's desk. Joan would have killed for a man with this kind of office.

"You know," Murphy said, "we haven't really paid much attention to that stuff about the magic dwarf and the invisible cape and all that garbage. We really ought to be able to figure out who in New Jersey could be the magic dwarf."

"Let's get a list of the top military and government people in New Jersey," Alice Burton said. "Maybe there's someone who's got a secret the Germans are dying to have."

"Doesn't George Marshall go riding up there sometimes?" Murphy asked. "I think I know someone who used to ride with him." Murphy furrowed his large brow. "Somewhere near Short Hills, maybe."

"Could it be some scientist?" Quinn asked. "Maybe they're planning to steal some secrets for a secret weapon. I keep hearing that Hitler's giving speeches all the time talking about secret weapons. Maybe they're going to break into a laboratory and steal some kind of secret weapon. Maybe that's why they need a chemist."

"Physicist," Alice Burton corrected.

Murphy picked up a Mark Cross pen with one hand. In the other hand he held a Parker 21. He weighed them, as if to see which was the more substantial. He said, "If we had a secret weapon, I don't think we'd be getting our boys killed by the Japs in the jungles of New Guinea. The whole point of Hitler's 'secret weapons' is that there are no such things. It's just men slogging it out in the mud somewhere."

"You can't tell," Quinn said. "There are a helluva lot more airplanes flying around the sky than there were in the last war. They carry a lot more bombs, too."

"Yes," Alice Burton chimed in. "But I wouldn't exactly call them secret."

"Not now," Quinn said. "But at one time, they were secret. You think we were writing press releases about the B-17?"

Murphy lifted his Dunhill lighter and studied it. It was well worn, smooth, shiny. It had Murphy's father's initials engraved on one side. As he had with the pens, Murphy hefted the lighter, first in one hand then in another. Then he flipped a Philip Morris cigarette out of its pack and lit it. "I guess what we want to know really is if there might be something really important going on in New Jersey that we don't know about."

Alice Burton sighed. "Something that Trattner knows about and that we don't know about."

"In New Jersey," Quinn added. "Something that could make a big splash."

Murphy slapped his lighter down on his desk. "I'll look into it," he said. "I don't know anything right now, but I'll look into it."

Quinn watched him. He had an itchy feeling in his head, just like he got when Raymond or Jorge or Alessandro told him that a man had just run down the alley, asked him to hold a woman's purse, then disappeared, and that he didn't have any idea where it came from, man.

Murphy sensed the currents of skepticism coming from the red leather couch. He held his palms upward and smiled. "Really, guys," he said with a toothy grin. "I don't know anything more than I read in the papers."

Alice Burton got up from an armchair. She strolled over to the desk and sat on the edge of it, in her best imitation of Katharine Hepburn baiting Spencer Tracy. "What papers are you talking about, Sam?" she asked. "Those little papers with the red dots stuck on them that say 'eyes only'?"

Quinn said, "If you know about it, you won't do anyone any favors not telling us. If Trattner knows about it already, we have to know."

Murphy said, "I have no idea if Trattner knows. I don't know what goes through his mind. I just know that there is something going on down in Tennessee. It has to do with physics and building some huge thing. I don't know what it's all about. It's incredibly secret stuff. I just heard Wild Bill say once that it was going to make the Germans wish they had never been born."

"In Tennessee?" Quinn asked.

"So I gather," Murphy said.

"A death ray or something?" Alice Burton asked.

"That's what I gather," Murphy said.

"And it's done with physics?" Alice Burton said. "Something like particle physics?"

Murphy laughed irritably. "I don't know," he said. He exhaled sharply. "I don't really think I should have told you as much as I did. At any rate, you now know as much about it as I do."

"Does the project have a name?" Alice Burton asked. "Maybe something about New Jersey? Could Trattner have been saying Tennessee?"

"I know the name," Murphy said. "But I'm not going to tell it to you and it doesn't have anything to do with New Jersey."

"And it's only in Tennessee?" Quinn said eagerly.

"As far as I know. Listen, you two go out, get a rest, take it easy, and just think about what it could be. I'm going to have Miss Pilkerton get you everything that the Library of Congress has in its files about New Jersey, every installation, every bigwig. You two go over that, go out and have dinner, then call me at home tonight and tell me if you have any ideas. Is that all right?"

It was fine with John Quinn, but he still had that strange, itchy feeling, right in the back of his head, as if he were about to go down an alley that was blind and find Raymond waiting there with a straight razor, glistening and finely honed in the sun, or seething with danger under a grimy street lamp.

Four hours later, Quinn sat at a table in the Palladium Room of the Sheraton-Park Hotel. The restaurant was a long, narrow room, made entirely of glass, overlooking Rock Creek Park. By night, Quinn could see an occasional car winding through Beech Drive and the tops of a few oak trees dimly lit by the moon. He could see Alice Burton far more clearly. She was eating her roast lamb chop with extraordinary concentration. Occasionally she picked up a sprig of parsley, twirled it in her hand and said something like "Could it have anything to do with all those oil refineries around Bayonne? If he were to blow those up, it would make a helluva fire."

Then, before Quinn could answer, Alice Burton would say, "No, they're too well guarded. It could be the Holland Tunnel, though. If that were blown up, right in the middle of rush hour, it would be worse than the sinking of the *Lusitania*. Plus, how could we ever get it rebuilt in this day and age?"

Alice then would say, "No, that's dramatic but it doesn't really touch on the war effort. And it has nothing to do with physics." She would return to her lamb chop, eating it carefully so that it did not make any spots on her white silk blouse or her red linen suit. She looked extraordinarily thoughtful, it seemed to Quinn. She had the look of a little girl concentrating deeply on some problem of great importance to her but of little importance to anyone else. In this case, however, there was a great deal of importance to what she was thinking about. Still, the large brown eyes, the furrowed little girl's brow, the pouting lips all said "child." Brave child-woman. Just like Marilyn.

Quinn looked around the room. There were so many generals in immaculately pressed uniforms that he could hardly believe his eyes. At every table there seemed to be two generals, two young WACs—and very few generals' wives. If there were no generals at a table, there were plump men crooking their fingers and talking earnestly to red-faced men. Many of the red-faced men looked as if they might have had a great deal to drink. Other men were clearly chewing tobacco.

They, too, were often accompanied by pretty young women, who did not have the bored, angry, possessive look that was the hallmark of marriage to a man of some importance in this world.

"Lobbyists," Alice Burton had said when Quinn asked her. "Five percenters. This is one of their big hangouts."

Then she went back to thinking about where Trattner could possibly be going. She had to focus every bit of her concentration on that question, because if the truth be told, she was having trouble not thinking about John Quinn.

In his suit, with a good night's sleep and a decent meal, he looked a lot less like a cop and a lot more like a poet. He had sensitive blue eyes and a perpetually concerned look about his mouth, as if he might have been about to burst into a poem by Lord Byron about the joys and sorrows of young love. Once you got over the scars on his hands, they were really extremely sensitive, too. Long fingers and small knuckles. Not at all what she thought of as a cop's hands. He had an intelligent high forehead and a strong, graceful neck, without the intellectual's perpetually bobbing Adam's apple.

Alice Burton ordered a Jell-O mold with pear slices for dessert. Quinn ordered a hot-fudge sundae. "Have you broken the case yet?" he asked her with a friendly smile.

"Not yet," Alice Burton said. She had not broken the case of John Quinn, either. All day long, she had been deeply impressed with the way he stood up to Murphy. Murphy was a man who cowed a lot of people with his smooth ways, his self-assured lockjaw speech, his condescending pats on the shoulders. But John Quinn had not been at all awed. He had simply talked with the man as if Murphy had some details Quinn needed to know. If Quinn was not satisfied with Murphy's answers, Quinn simply kept asking the same questions. That was a cop, but it was also a man who was not afraid.

When Alice Burton thought of all the self-important little creeps at the University of Chicago and all the mumbling, self-promoting little weasels she had met in Washington, keeping their chairs warm while soldiers got their faces shot off in Tunisia, she had to take another look at Quinn. That man, eating his hot-fudge sundae, had been absolutely fearless, unconcerned about his own life twice just in the last few days. At times when he could just as easily have gone to pieces—and no one would have blamed him!

Quinn was the kind of man that the intellectuals in the WPA and the OPA and the OSS, for that matter, dreamed of being. He was physically brave. That was really rare in Alice's experience. The nerve to talk back to a professor was one thing. The selflessness to risk the only thing you have—your life—that was something else again.

And really, Sam Murphy's nerve in handing over that major's commission as if he were a feudal lord giving out something that belonged to *him* when Quinn had earned it by taking a lot more chances than Murphy had ever taken! The Marines were kicking the hell out of the Japs on some little island in the South Pacific called New Georgia, getting their blood drained by leeches in tropical marshes. Sam Murphy was sitting at a desk playing with a Dunhill cigarette lighter. What the hell gave him the right to lord it over John Quinn, who was actually getting shot at?

After dinner, Quinn and Alice Burton danced in the darkened room to a Lester Lanin sound-alike band called "Barney Kaye and his Silky Sounds." The band played cool foxtrots like "Dancing in the Dark," and "Till" and "Old Man River," which Quinn told her was his particular favorite. It sounded right for him. It was a brooding, poetic tune that he could identify with. Deep and cloudy like the Mississippi River. That was John Quinn. She liked the way he held her in his arms. As the band got to "Moonlight in Vermont," she laid her head on his chest. He squeezed her more tightly in his arms, and did not say a word. She could feel warmth coming from him. He could feel warmth coming from her. In her thoughts, Trattner was a long way away. Maybe he was already on a submarine somewhere. It would disappoint Quinn, but it might also save his life. Sweet riddance.

She put her hand on his neck. She could see out into the park, where the moon was sweeping the waters of Rock Creek with bluish, cool rays. It was good, she thought, to know what you wanted.

June 2, 1943,
Mount Vernon, Virginia

Joachim Trattner was impressed. George Washington might have been an American, but the man knew how to live. In addition, the man had *not* freed his slaves upon his death, as so many simpleminded Americans had. George Washington understood quite well that some races were meant to command and other races were meant to obey. He had not suffered under any foolish delusions that everyone was the same.

Trattner strolled down the path past the icehouse, past the tobacco-curing sheds, past the carriage houses, on to the slave quarters. In front of him was a group of about fifty little girls in Catholic school uniforms—blue-and-white checked skirts and white cotton blouses with dark-blue blazers with a crest on the breast pocket. The crest showed a Bible open with a cross glowing out from it. Under the cross were the words "Verbum Dei." The girls walked two by two, mostly gossiping to each other, hardly bothering to look at the cottage where candles were made or the shed where cows were milked.

But Trattner was interested in these things. He observed immediately that the buildings were of unusually solid construction. They had plaster walls—even for the cows—and thick red bricks on the outside. The icehouse, in particular, had thick walls, probably clay, with bricks on both the inside and the outside. Even the candle-making quarters showed great concern for proper construction. The roof was made of wood shingles, which had apparently been fitted together without any adhesive, simply because they were made to mesh so perfectly. Even the slave quarters were made to last. Obviously a George Washington could have taken the easy way and simply built wood-frame slave quarters. But that was not a sign that he expected things to last. He built solid field-stone-and-brick slave quarters so that the slaves would know that there was no thought in Washington's mind that slavery would end anytime soon.

That was solid thinking! That was the kind of thinking that an SS man could appreciate. Why couldn't the Americans understand that if a man as great as George Washington had seen nothing wrong with slavery, then he was simply a prophet for the messiah, Adolf Hitler? Why indeed? Even Abraham Lincoln had said that if he could save the Union by keeping slavery, he would.

Trattner ducked his head into the barrel-making shed. Inside were two soldiers, earnestly discussing which one of them got to go out tonight with "that piece of ass from the telephone company." One of the men was a corporal. The other was a private. When the two men saw Trattner, they looked him up and down, then continued their discussion. The whole point, as far as Trattner could make out, was that the corporal had "gotten laid" the night before by a secretary from the Department of Agriculture and so the private now should have his chance. Really, the Americans were complete animals.

Of course, a man had to take his pleasure. It would have been hypocritical of Trattner to deny that he had taken great joy in Maxine Lewis in the last eight days. But for two soldiers of the fatherland to discuss women in this way where anyone could hear them! It showed a lack of taste, of discretion, which Trattner really could not stomach. Trattner glared icily at the soldiers, who ignored him.

Trattner hurriedly left the barrel-making house and passed the parochial school girls to look into the curing house. In this low, rambling structure, according to the guidebook, the slaves had cooked meat while keeping it well covered with salt, so as to preserve it. The guidebook said that Washington had given orders to his overseers to buy nothing that could be made on the plantation. That was sensible. The Führer had embarked on a similar project in 1934, to make the Reich virtually self-sufficient agriculturally. Why should the *Herrenvolk* risk dependence on envious savages? This George Washington had sound ideas, Trattner decided.

Trattner took a quick look at the dried hams hanging in front of an immense fireplace. Then he walked out onto the path toward the slave quarters. As he emerged into the sunlit afternoon, he looked to his left. He could see the Potomac River flowing peacefully below the lawn, about five hundred meters distant. There was one large tour boat passing in front of his view. Other than that, the waters were slowly rippling against the banks and against each other. Shadows from immense cypress trees fell on the green-gray of the water and made for a study in relaxation and serenity.

In spite of the beauty of the scene, Trattner suddenly felt uneasy. A sense somewhere in the back of his head was warning him, as if mice were running around his brain, treading daintily on his cerebellum to alert him.

He wheeled around slowly. The path was deserted except for two schoolboys walking toward him. They looked pale. They had long, unruly sideburns coming down from their hair. Trattner stared more closely. But of course! Trattner had smelled Jew. The two boys had the effrontery to wear skull caps, those accursed yarmulkes right here, in the home of the father of a Christian people! They were talking to each other about some game. One of them mentioned someone named Rizzuto, and the other kept saying, "Duke Snider could take him any day."

Trattner felt the blood rise in his cheeks. The scar from where that fool in Oklahoma had hit him, that scar began to throb. The two little Jewboys came walking right by Trattner. They were carrying schoolbooks. Probably they were studying something about compound interest or money-lending. Already, even at the age of ten or twelve, Trattner saw, they were developing the crafty, devious look he knew so well. They looked at him sideways as they passed, as if they could tell that he knew exactly who they were. One of them looked fearful as Trattner glared at them.

Really, for these cowardly kikes, America was sending its youth out to do the fighting. How could any people be so stupid as to send the flower of its youth out to war just to protect a lot of scheming Jews? And yet, a grudging admiration came over Trattner. If the Jew was smart enough to exploit a people, to bleed them white, to take their women, and then to persuade them that somehow they were responsible for defending their oppressors, well, that was no small feat.

The Jew was clever and no doubt about that. The Americans could only thank their lucky stars that they had Adolf Hitler to pull their chestnuts out of the fire, to coin his favorite phrase. He was fighting their fight, even if they were too stupid to know it.

Trattner saw that one of the little kikes had dropped his schoolbooks. Trattner strode over to the boys and picked up the book closest to him. "Did you drop this?" he asked with an ironic smile.

"Yes, I did," said the Jewish boy. He looked fearful, as if he, too, had been able to sense that there was a deadly enmity rearing its head in the peaceful countryside of Fairfax County.

"Then you shall have it," Trattner said, not even trying to disguise his German accent. His face became a steel grimace. With one powerful motion, Trattner ripped the book in half along the seam. Then he dropped both halves in front of the small boy.

"Hey, you dropped my friend's book," the taller of the two boys said. "You tore it, too. You have to pay for that."

Trattner grasped the boy's arm and twisted it behind his back. "Pay for it, did you say?" He twisted the arm until he thought it might break. "Pay for it? I don't think so, Jewboy," he said in a hiss through his teeth.

Suddenly, the boy started to scream. Trattner was electrified with the stupidity of what he had done. To allow himself to vent his anger—no matter how well justified the anger—was imbecilic in this situation. To risk everything for a moment of punishment for these Jews was insane. *Mein Gott,* Trattner thought, I must be losing my mind. The whole purpose of the trip to Mount Vernon had been to meet the Army captain, then to linger for a few minutes and leave. If he had thrown it all away for this . . . Abruptly he released the hold on the boy's arm. The corporal from the barrel-making shed ducked his head out and stared. Trattner froze at the corporal's look.

"I'm sorry," he said. "So terribly sorry. I don't know what came over me. I really don't have any idea. Here, how would each of you like a nice twenty-dollar bill if you don't say anything about this?"

In a flash, Trattner drew two twenty-dollar bills from his breast pocket. He handed one to each boy. The taller one was rubbing his arm where Trattner had grabbed him. They were looking at him fearfully. "I just lost control of myself for a minute," he said. "I'm a Jew myself. I was overcome. I . . . I can't explain it. I'm sorry. Please take this money. Buy yourself a new book. Buy yourself anything and just think that Hitler did this to me and to you."

The taller of the two boys smiled at him and put up his right hand. "It's all right. You don't have to give us any money. We understand. I have relatives in Poland."

Then the taller boy took the other boy's hand and walked away. They waved as they walked down the gravel-covered path. The corporal watched the whole scene. Damn, but that man looked familiar. Funny accent, too. Where had he seen that man's picture?

Trattner hurried in the opposite direction from the two boys, then walked up toward the enormous green lawn, overhung by live oak trees, where the tour bus would be waiting to take him back to King Street in Alexandria. He passed by legions of schoolchildren in uniforms and out. They smiled, ate ice cream, held pennants saying "Mount Vernon." They had no idea that there existed in their midst a fool who had almost thrown away the future of the Reich for a momentary grudge. The children, the grass, the blue sky had all been too much for Trattner, who for a moment had forgotten just how serious his mission was. He had been lulled into the sense that he was secure, that things were moving his way, that he was on top of things. Damn it all, it was just plain stupid of him to start feeling so cocky. That was what came of being in America, where everything came so damned easy.

Just look at these children! Except for the Jews, you would never know there was a war going on. You would have no idea that in Europe, tons of bombs were falling on children just like them each and every night. Look how fat the children were! In Germany, even a Krupp could not eat like that today. Their eyes were clear, their voices firm and cheerful, and the whole world except America was ablaze.

Natürlich, in a mental climate like that, one's mind got soft. One got accustomed to thinking that there was never danger. The ease with which Maxine had gotten them out of jail contributed to the whole frame of mind. But that was a cheat. In fact, there was menace everywhere. He had to keep sharp. The captain had promised that the final phase of the Siegfried operation would be anything but easy. It would be more difficult still if Trattner could not control himself and keep from flying off the handle at the sight of a couple of shifty-eyed Jewboys. Really though, the looks those boys had given him! What insolence! He should have smothered them both and thrown them into the river. That would have been a small favor for the Reich, accomplished along the way of a much larger favor. To think he had to apologize to Jews, to pretend to be a Jew!

Still, if the Dwarf would be as tricky a proposition as the captain said, there was no use courting extra trouble.

Trattner got on board a stifling-hot White Motor Company bus. The bus headed out a long driveway toward the George Washington Memorial Parkway. Really, it was intolerable to have to ride in this heat. Sweat started to come out on Trattner's forehead and on his upper lip. He took a white handkerchief from his pocket and mopped his brow. He mocked himself. By Libyan standards, it was cool.

He looked around him at the back of the bus. Two stout old black women, dressed in enormous, shapeless dresses that looked like flour sacks, sat in the last row of seats fanning themselves with stiff half moons of bamboo. Their hair was covered by bandannas. They were laughing at a joke of some kind. They showed perfectly white, even teeth.

Trattner shook his head. The man next to him, a thin fellow with white hair and a pince-nez, shook his head, too. "It's war," the man said. He wore a seersucker suit and a white shirt with a bow tie. "It's war and so we've got to let niggers on the buses to save gasoline. I don't see why they have to be allowed on buses at all, as far as that goes."

Trattner shook his head in acknowledgment, but said nothing.

"When I was a boy, they walked or they didn't get anywhere and it didn't seem to hurt them one bit," the man in seersucker said. "Now they have cars and they ride everywhere, as if they owned the country. I saw it coming," the man said. "I knew how it would be."

"Ummm," Trattner said, trying to sound encouraging but also to sound as if he did not want to be further disturbed.

It did not work. The man kept talking. "Time was when the sheriff would horsewhip a nigger for even looking at a white woman," the man said. "Nowadays they dance with white women in New York City. I have a son in the War Department there. He's seen it."

Trattner tried to ignore the man. For all Trattner knew, the man was leading him on by saying such sensible things. As soon as Trattner opened his mouth, the man might slap handcuffs on him for having a German accent, although he knew his accent could be mistaken for Norwegian. Trattner maintained his glacial silence.

Yet the man continued to talk about some woman who was supposed to sing at Constitution Hall, whatever that was, and who was turned down because she was colored, and more power to the D.A.R. for doing it, whoever the D.A.R. were. Marian something.

Trattner looked at the heavy stands of maple and oak passing by as warm, humid air poured in the window of the tour bus. A guide with a megaphone was saying something about how Abraham Lincoln came out this route to see the "First Battle of Bull Run" in the "War Between the States." Trattner had heard of the Civil War, but never of any "War Between the States." Trattner tried to concentrate only on what he and Maxine had to do when they got back to their hotel in Alexandria. He did not want to hear about how many men were killed at "Bull Run." He wanted to think about how many Aryan lives he would save if he could get the Dwarf firmly in hand.

No more than four hours from Alexandria to the Dwarf's lair in New Jersey. The gasoline coupons and the keys in the Army captain's envelope, now inside Trattner's suit pocket. The map to the Dwarf's house thoroughly memorized and now its ashes in a trash can at Mount Vernon.

He climbed the steps to his third-floor room at the Martha Custis Hotel on Third Street in Alexandria. He turned the key and pushed open the door. Maxine was still out getting her hair dyed. It was just as well, because Trattner did not feel at all up to what she would demand of him. He was ill.

Suddenly, he stepped toward the bed, tripped over her valise, and fell, unconscious, onto the bed. In his stupor, he drooled onto the organdy bedcovers. He was very ill.

June 3, 1943,
Washington, D.C.

Alice Burton looked up. John Quinn's arm was around her shoulders, but he was asleep. At first, she could not remember where she was. The thought that she was in Idabel, with an overpowering din of crickets, came rushing into her mind. She put it out of mind. No, she was in a city. She could hear auto horns and brakes squealing. Then where was she? In Santa Cruz? No, because she could not hear any foghorns nor the sound of waves.

Then she looked at the foot of the bed. It was an ornate, turned-wood affair which looked as if two vases had been placed atop the stern of a rowboat. She realized immediately that she was in a hotel room and then she knew she was in Washington, D.C. Only in Washington were the hotel rooms quite that old-fashioned. Also, only in Washington would she have had the confidence to suggest to John Quinn that they have a drink together in his room before he went to bed.

He had raised his eyebrows and said, "I don't want to force you into anything. You've had a pretty rugged few days."

She had answered in a firm voice, "You're not forcing me into a thing. You've had a rougher few days than I have. Am I forcing you into anything?"

He had brushed her cheek with his hand, right in the Palladium Room, while they were dancing. He said, "It would be swell."

She remembered two shots of rye from a bottle brought up by room service and then a few words of conversation. Then a hug and an embrace in front of a fake Currier & Ives drawing of the Potomac frozen over in winter, with men in top hats skating and children in sleighs playing in the foreground. It must have been much colder in Washington then. Right now, it was warm, almost tropical in Room 602 of the Sheraton-Park Hotel. Of course, it was almost always warm in Washington in the beginning of June. But it was particularly balmy in Washington when Alice Burton was in the arms of John Quinn, a man for this season. Well, what the hell. Why be so cautious? Maybe John Quinn was a man for all seasons. But why think like that? That was the way her mother would think. She might better simply think that she had just had the greatest adventure of her life, culminating in a night of love and closeness, and a feeling of rest that went right into the marrow of her bones.

Imagine, to be able to rest like this with a man you did not even know two weeks ago. That was something to remember. In her whole life, Alice Burton always felt that she was rushing, hurrying to accomplish something, to make herself worthy by doing, to clear up the puzzle of her existence by achieving something that would be noticed, appreciated. Honors in arithmetic. First prize in the spelling bee. Editor of the high school newspaper (*Silver Chips*). Magna cum laude at Northwestern. Editor of the *Law Review* at Chicago. Assistant to Sam Murphy. Always another hill to climb. Catching Joachim Trattner and Maxine Lewis. And now, finding the Dwarf with magical powers somewhere in New Jersey. To be able to rest in a strange room with an Irishman whom she had never known before . . . that was real rest. She could feel the waves of security coming up from Quinn's rising and falling chest. She guessed this was love, just like with Scarlett and Rhett or with Bette Davis and Joseph Cotten.

She ran her finger along John's chest, then she turned her

wrist to look at her watch. Four thirty-five in the morning. She should go back to sleep. They had a lot of thinking to do in the morning.

As she turned over, Quinn stirred. He shivered for a moment and then he looked at her back. She could feel his eyes on her. He hugged her with his arm, cupping one breast with his fingers.

"I'm glad I forced you into this," he said with good-natured sleepiness in his voice.

"You didn't force me into anything," she said. "I tricked you. I'm the smart one, remember. You're the brave one. Or maybe it's the other way around."

She turned to face him. He hugged her face against his chest. She could feel scars there with her lips. He did not have a hairy chest, which was fine with her. She had never equated hairy chests with anything except a lot of hair.

"I think you must have put a spell on me," John Quinn said. "If I ever thought that I could feel this way again, this fast, I don't know what," he said in the slightly confused rambling of half sleep. "You must be a regular genius," he added.

"An Einstein," she said.

Suddenly Quinn's whole body became rigid. He was awake. "Just a second," he said.

Alice Burton sucked in her breath sharply. "Of course," she said. "Of course. And he lives in Princeton, New Jersey. And Trattner is a physicist."

"No," Quinn said. "They wouldn't dare. I mean the man is a legend. Besides, he must be under heavy guard. He's a really important man. He talks to Roosevelt and everything."

"I think it's a damned good shot. I don't want to wake him up now or anything, but when it gets to be a decent hour, I'm going to have Sam call him and get him moved somewhere safe until we find Trattner," Alice Burton said.

"You know," Quinn said. "It's really grasping at straws. Let's not rush into anything until we have a better idea of just what we're trying to do. Why on earth would they want him? He's a genius, but does he know anything about bombs or airplanes? What good would he do the Krauts?"

Alice Burton jumped out of bed. "Sam said the project had something to do with physics," she said. "And he sure knows a lot about physics."

Quinn thought for a minute. "Look," he said, "we don't want to start a panic. Let's just get Sam to get us a car and driver and get us up to Princeton in a hurry this morning and get the professor to a good, safe place."

"We'll just go talk to him," Alice Burton said. "In the meantime, let's call the Princeton police department and tell them to put a few men around his house. Seal it off."

"It wouldn't be a bad idea," Quinn said. "Let's wake up Sam Murphy and get him to do some work for a change."

Alice Burton thought that was pretty funny, so she laughed. They both thought that was pretty funny, so they both laughed. Alice Burton fell into John's arms laughing and he felt strong. To him, she felt warm and yielding. They both decided, without a word, that calling the Princeton police could wait until morning. Einstein had been around a long time. They had only just gotten to know each other.

June 3, 1943,
Princeton, New Jersey

Joachim Trattner turned the rearview mirror around so that he could be certain that his Army hat fitted perfectly. It did. Of course these United States Army uniforms were cheap and tasteless compared with the uniforms of the Reich, but in this case, fashion was hardly the issue. As long as he looked like a major in the United States Army, with the symbol of the Washington Monument inside a triangle that showed he was attached to the Military District of Washington, he was in fine shape. His uniform was spotless and crisply pressed. He was thankful for that.

He looked around on Larkspur Street. It was still before seven in the morning. Maxine was smoking a cigarette. It was a habit she had just picked up. It did not go with her well-tailored WAC uniform, and it certainly did not go with this quiet, well-tended Princeton neighborhood. The frame houses, set well back from the road, were surrounded by immaculate lawns. There were often hedges of juniper, also carefully manicured. The houses had curtains pulled across the upstairs rooms' windows. They also had two cars in the garage.

This was a prosperous neighborhood, probably filled with respectable people who would take it amiss if they saw a woman smoking a cigarette on a corner before seven in the morning. Also, cigarette smoke at that hour of the morning irritated Joachim Trattner. It was a sign of a weak, dependent personality, which he abhorred, as he did all signs of weakness. Additionally, the way he had been feeling all day and especially the day before, he did not need any new upsets.

On the other hand, he knew that Maxine was nervous. If it made her feel better, if it would make her perform better in the next few minutes, he would understand and do what was necessary to tolerate her. He glanced at her with careful, lidded eyes and raised his eyebrows.

"Are you sure the call was made?" Maxine asked. She held a Chesterfield in her hand. Her hands shook terribly. Her eyes were also bloodshot. She looked older this morning than she had looked since Trattner had first met her. She was scared of dying, of course. Trattner recognized the signs. This time, she could see that they were at the last hurdle. They were close to the end, for good or evil, of a long mission. She no longer had the sense of adventure and exhilaration she had had at the beginning. Then she had been a blonde woman with no experience of life. Now she was a redhead with a full knowledge of how death can come without warning, even in the good old U.S.A.

"The call will be made in one minute," Trattner said, glancing at his Hamilton watch. "We arrive within the next ten minutes."

"How far do we have to take him?" Maxine asked.

"It's better that you not know," Trattner said. "The less you know, the safer you are."

"And are you sure they're expecting me in Germany?" Maxine asked, like Florence Chadwick asking if she would be able to get a good meal in Calais.

Trattner stared at her incredulously. "Maxine," he said, "you will be a heroine. You will be the leading woman of the Reich. Adolf Hitler will personally want to discuss the saving of America's forests and mountains with you. Also, the proper ways of loving animals and of eating fine vegetarian meals."

Maxine stretched sitting down, arching her back, making

her bosoms stand out proudly against her twill uniform. "I hope so," she said. Then she yawned. "There's a lot of work to be done. Innocent animals are being slaughtered every day to make people fat."

Trattner took her hand. "The Führer never forgets the sacrifices his friends make, Maxine," Trattner said, looking as sincerely as he could into her blue eyes.

"I can't imagine it," Maxine said, perking up as she blew out a haze of gray smoke. "I, little Maxine Lewis, will be meeting Adolf Hitler. The people back at the real estate office will be pretty amazed." She looked very proud of herself, also slightly dazed.

Trattner realized that Maxine was talking baby talk. She was so scared that she was unable to talk like an adult. She talked of events that would never happen, against a background of grim reality.

A newspaper boy came by on a Schwinn bicycle. He waved at Trattner and Maxine in their Hudson Hornet. Then he expertly tossed rolled-up newspapers onto three lawns on Larkspur Street before he turned down Mercer Street.

Trattner took a deep breath. "Maxine," he said, "you must be confident. The hardest part is over. Who would have ever thought we could get as far as we have?"

Maxine tossed her cigarette out the window. "I thought we would," she said. "Why shouldn't we?" Yet her shoulders shuddered with worry.

"Of course," Trattner said. "And why shouldn't we finish up what we have started? We just follow the steps," he said. "Like assembling a model airplane."

"I'm ready," Maxine said. Trattner's mask of icy confidence descended. Inwardly, he shivered. Still, he patted her knee in encouragement.

She turned the key in the Hornet's ignition. As she did, a woman in rollers and a bathrobe came out the door of the house they were in front of. The woman was middle-aged and looked angry. "This isn't an ashtray," she said. "I don't like getting trash thrown on my front yard. You just pick up that cigarette and take it away with you."

Maxine glanced at Trattner. Her eyebrows lifted in question.

"Get out and pick up the cigarette," Trattner said evenly. "Don't talk to her. Just apologize and then get back in."

Maxine did as she was told. While the woman glared at her and folded her arms in front of her chest, Maxine got out of the car, walked to the still-burning cigarette, picked it up, and carried it back to the car. As she opened the car door she said, "I'm sorry."

The housewife said, "Don't they teach you anything in the Army?"

Maxine did not call her a bitch as she was tempted to do. Instead, she got back into the car and put the cigarette in the ashtray. Then she depressed the clutch, put the car in gear, engaged the clutch, and drove away. As she did, she could see the woman staring after her car, obviously barely appeased.

"Don't think about that," Trattner said. "Just an old woman. Not worth thinking about when we have other things to do."

"I know," Maxine said. "But I wish we could have shot her."

"So do I," Trattner said. He was beginning to feel dizzy. He wished the whole thing were over. Still, he had his duty and his oath. *"Ich schwöre dir, Adolf Hitler . . ."*

The car glided quietly down two blocks of Mercer Street. It passed only a milk truck and the newsboy once again. Then Trattner said, "Look out. It's coming up."

Sure enough, right across the street was a white frame house indistinguishable from its neighbors, except that there were curtains across the living room as well as the upstairs rooms. "Turn around," Trattner said. "Get on the same side of the street as his house."

Maxine made a U-turn in the street and then stopped directly in front of the sidewalk that led to Albert Einstein's front door. Trattner glanced at his watch. Ten minutes after seven. Exactly right.

Off to the east, above the railroad station, the sun broke through some low clouds, flooding Mercer Street with clear, barely filtered sunlight. The light got into Trattner's eyes and he blinked. He felt as if the sunlight were an omen of some kind, expressing to him the highest regards of the Almighty for the project at hand. He felt obliged to grasp Maxine's left hand and lower his head. "We are working the will of the Führer," he said, "and we have his protection."

He opened the car door on the passenger side. Maxine opened the driver's door. They walked up the path to the porch, gray-painted boards leading to a screen door. With exaggerated calm, Trattner rang the front door bell. A pleasant chiming reverberated through the house and out onto the porch. Over its sound, two robins chirruped in the morning heat.

After a moment, there was no response. Trattner rang the bell again. In a moment, the door opened. A severe-looking woman who looked as if she might have stepped out of a confectioner's shop on any street in Rhine-Westphalia appeared at the door in a long cotton dress, a baggy cardigan sweater, with her hair in a bun. She wore silver-rimmed glasses. Her piercing light-brown eyes inquired silently while she asked, "Yes? What is it, please?"

She even had a German accent. And she did not look like a Jew! Perhaps the plants within the United States ran deeper than Trattner had been told. A man in the Manhattan District was one thing, but a housemaid in Einstein's household was another.

If she were a housemaid-Abwehr agent, though, she kept an extremely level head. She simply stared at Trattner while she waited for his answer.

"Miss Dukas?" he asked. Before she could answer, he said, "I am Captain Hunter and this is Lieutenant Dalton. We're here to escort the professor to his meeting with the President. Is it convenient to come in?"

"One moment," Miss Dukas said. "I only got the call a few minutes ago. I am not certain that the professor is dressed."

"May we come in, please?" Maxine Lewis asked, just as she had practiced. "It's been a long drive from Fort Monmouth. If I may, I would like to use your bathroom."

Miss Dukas looked at the woman carefully and then said, "Very well. Captain, will you please wait on the porch? The professor does not like for his routine to be disturbed."

Trattner forced himself to laugh out loud. "I am terribly sorry," he said, "but I wonder if I might use the bathroom, too."

Miss Dukas looked at him curiously. "Are you Norwegian?" she asked. "Or German parents?"

Trattner laughed deprecatingly again. "Yes," he said. "Back in South Dakota. German mother. Doesn't speak English to this day. I guess I still have a trace of it."

The thought flashed through Trattner's mind, Dammit. I warned that fool back at Mount Vernon about this. He assured me they would never know the difference. Out loud, Trattner simply smiled more and said, "But it's everybody's war, now. We all do our part."

"Very well," Miss Dukas said. "I can understand that part. It is our war, too, and we were from Germany originally. Everyone must pitch in, as they say here."

"So true, so true," Trattner said.

"Of course," Miss Dukas said, warming to her visitors as she usually did eventually. "May I offer you some coffee?"

"No, thanks," Trattner said, opening the screen door and walking in. "Is the professor close to being ready? We have a long drive ahead of us."

"I'll go check," Miss Dukas said. "Meanwhile, make yourself at home."

She ushered Trattner into a dark living room that reminded him powerfully of living rooms in Berlin or Munich. It had a huge piano, Russian censers, Oriental rugs, and several moody paintings of bridges and mountains. He sat on a couch of tightly woven material. It was just as uncomfortable as the couches he remembered from Germany! In a moment, he used the bathroom, while Miss Dukas squeezed oranges in the kitchen. Then he sat on a couch with Maxine Lewis. She started to light a cigarette, but he held her hand and shook his head. His eyes looked like burning ice. She marveled once more at his power, his strength.

Within a few minutes, Albert Einstein came walking down the stairs in a pair of baggy chino trousers and a sweat shirt. He looked at Trattner and Maxine Lewis. He seemed to be sniffing the air like a hound. My God, Trattner thought. This man looks like a child. He looks like a totally distracted, completely unaware child. If this is the genuine article, we will have little trouble with him. Trattner was beguiled by the innocence of the man's eyes, his broad untroubled forehead, his wild unkempt hair, his slack childish mouth. His eyes in particular seemed both old and young at the same time, unearthly almost, unlike any eyes that Trattner had ever seen before. The eyes of a saint, or a devil masquerading as a saint, Trattner thought. They made him calm at first, then deeply uneasy. Jews were filled with tricks.

He fought his disquiet and stood to receive the genius Jew. "This is a great honor, Professor," Trattner said. "I hope you may be dressed fairly soon. The President is expecting you for the afternoon on his yacht."

"We will be glad to wait while you dress, Professor," Maxine Lewis said, smiling.

"I am dressed," Einstein said. "My caller told me that this was to be an afternoon of fishing. I am dressed for sports."

Trattner flashed a good-natured smile and said, "As you wish. Are you ready to go?"

Einstein nodded, then snapped his fingers. "I had some documents I wanted to show the President," he said. "One moment, if you please."

The professor ran up the stairs. As he did, he thought, The military man is a fierce-looking specimen. That scar on his cheek. He looks like he just got it. Still, he will be a safe guard for me on this trip to see the President. And if the President wants to see me, it can only mean that they are planning some action on the death camps.

As Einstein pulled a file from his desktop clutter, he heard the telephone ring under a mass of papers. He burrowed for it. That was unusual. He generally let Miss Dukas get the phone. But she might be making coffee for the soldiers. So he burrowed for the telephone.

Downstairs, Miss Dukas started to walk toward the telephone. With a smile on his face, Trattner walked ahead of her and picked it up off the wall where it hung in the kitchen. "I'm sorry," he said. "But this will be our routing. Very secret. If it's for you, you can have it."

While Miss Dukas expostulated, Trattner picked up the telephone. "Hello," he said.

As he spoke, Einstein picked up the telephone upstairs. He heard the voice of Trattner on *his* telephone, which gave him pause immediately. Einstein decided to say nothing for a moment. It was always possible to learn by staying silent.

Then Einstein decided he was being rude. He hung up the phone. It would not do to be snooping on a man who was taking him to meet the President. That was not the act of a high-minded scientist and it was certainly not the act of an Einstein.

Downstairs, Miss Dukas saw Trattner smile and say into the telephone, "I'm sorry. You have the wrong number." Then he hung up the phone. To Miss Dukas he said, "A man asking for the gas company. You have no gas company here, have you?"

Miss Dukas smiled and said, "There are more wrong numbers than ever. The girls at the switchboards are new. All the good ones have gone off to work at Western Electric and make a hundred and fifty a week."

Trattner looked at his watch. "I'm sorry to have to rush such an eminent scientist," he said, "but we are late. Could you tell the professor that it would not do to keep the President waiting? We have to leave at once."

"I'll tell him," Miss Dukas said and scampered upstairs.

At the Princeton Police Station, John Quinn slammed his hand down on the desk. He glared at the police sergeant in front of him, a dumb-looking Italian, just like Rizzuti. "We told you to get some men over there. We called you at five this morning," Quinn said.

"Sorry," the man said. "We didn't get any message. It could be that it got lost in the change of shifts." The man's face was greasy, as if he had been eating sausage or pepperoni for breakfast. He looked as if he could not possibly give a damn about Einstein or about the OSS, or about Franklin D. Roosevelt, for that matter.

"Now you listen to me," Quinn said. "The phones are screwed up. I just got some foreign sonofabitch. So I want you to get me over to that house on Mercer Street right away. Can you do that?"

The Italian desk sergeant looked at his watch. "I don't know," he said. "Two men called in sick. That means they're going up to New York to see the Dodgers. I don't know if I have a car available until around nine."

Alice Burton pricked up her ears. "Wait a minute, John," she said. "Did you say a man with a foreign accent answered the telephone?"

John Quinn stared straight ahead. Albert Einstein had one servant, a woman. The people at the OSS had been very sure of that. "Oh, my God," he said. "I thought he sounded familiar. Oh, good Christ." He turned to the desk sergeant, grabbed the thin man by the front of his blue shirt and said, "If you don't get us over to that house right this second, you're going before a firing squad for high treason or else I'll shoot you myself."

The Italian sergeant gulped. His face turned white.

In thirty seconds, Quinn, Alice Burton, and a reedy corporal of the Princeton Police were racing down Alexander Street, past the Pennsylvania Railroad terminal, in an unmarked Pontiac sedan. "I don't want any sirens," Quinn said. "I just want a lot of backup there right now. If we have any trouble, I want it there so fast that the tires melt."

"I've got you," the emaciated corporal said. "It'll only be about five minutes from here."

"Remember, no sirens," Quinn said. "And when we get nearby, drive real slow."

He turned to Alice Burton. "I'm not sure it was Trattner," he said. "It could have been a bad connection. I just want to be sure."

"It was Trattner," Alice Burton said. "We've been complete idiots all along. When Sam told us about what the Manhattan

Engineering District was working on, we should have guessed it right away. Who the hell else could be a wizard or a dwarf or have magic powers except a guy who's building a death ray or something? And Trattner's a physicist. He knows who Einstein is. He won't pick up the wrong man."

"I'm not sure it was Trattner," Quinn said. "I don't want to spook him if he's got the professor already. I have to play it very carefully," he added.

"Very carefully," Alice Burton echoed. "We have to play it very carefully." She looked wanly out the window. "What if Trattner's already got him?"

"Then we have to do something brilliant," he said. "That's your department. Then we have to figure out how to get back the most valuable piece of goods in America without damaging him."

"I think the first thing we do is to get some roadblocks set up all around this area," Alice Burton said. She turned to the thin corporal. "I want you to call the station and tell them to cordon off this whole area. No cars in or out until we say so. You understand that?"

The corporal nodded. "No cars in or out around Professor Einstein's house, right?"

"Right," Quinn said. "Radio it in now."

The corporal did as he was told. There was a crackling on the radio which was hard to interpret as far as Alice Burton was concerned, although it seemed to be perfectly clear to Quinn.

"And no shooting, either, even if they can't see if Einstein is in the car," Quinn said. "They could have him down on the floor and if he gets shot, the whole thing is ruined."

"Request no shooting," the corporal radioed in on his enormous microphone.

"So how the hell do we stop them? Over," came the reply from the Princeton Police Station.

"You fucking ram them with your cars, you asshole. Over," Quinn shouted into the microphone, grabbing it from the thin corporal.

"Ten-four," came the subdued response from the station.

"Tell them to call KL 5-4444 in Washington, too," Alice Burton said. "Tell them to send up personnel as soon as they can. Tell them we think Trattner's here. With Einstein."

The corporal looked at Alice Burton. "You mean that Nazi who's been killing all those people? You mean he got all the way from California to here? What the hell happened? How did he get this far?"

Alice Burton stared at the corporal. "This isn't 'Quiz Kids,'" she said. "Just call in the message."

Professor Einstein was one mile away in his sweater, just walking out the door, which Trattner was courteously holding for him. "I changed," Einstein said. "I thought a sweat shirt was not sufficiently respectful to the President."

"Yes, it looks very handsome on you, Professor," Maxine Lewis said.

"I hope your work on the unified field is going well," Trattner said.

"Thank you," Einstein said.

As he walked out onto his porch in the warm June morning, he was surpised to see little Dale Graham, his twelve-year-old talking partner on problems of geometry. She was frowning, walking purposefully toward him carrying a brown notebook. When she saw him, she smiled. Her little blue eyes were flooded with tears, though.

"Professor Einstein," she shouted. "I have to ask you something."

The physicist paused and turned toward her as she walked up the stairs to the porch. "Yes, Dale," he said. He was particularly proud of remembering her name. "What can I do?"

"Miss Moore, she's this new teacher and she's really a pill," Dale Graham said. "She doesn't believe that stuff you told me about why *pi* is an infinitely repeating decimal. She says I made it up. She says a famous man would never talk to me, especially a famous man like you."

"I'm sorry," Trattner said in a cross tone. "The professor has an important appointment. He'll talk to you later," Trattner said, trying to look like a severe parent.

Dale Graham searched Trattner's face. "Who are you?" she

asked. "You look mean. Are you kidnapping the professor? My father says somebody's bound to do that some day."

Trattner smiled. "You are a very impolite little girl," he said. "Now we must go."

Einstein felt uneasy. He looked searchingly at Trattner. "I can take a minute to talk to my friend," he said. "I told her I would help her and I always keep my promises."

"No," Trattner said, "we have to leave right now. We have no time for a little child."

"Why?" Dale Graham asked in a whining voice.

Inside Joachim Trattner, something broke. Why should he play this silly game with a twelve-year-old girl and a Jew? He was the man with the gun.

"Why?" he asked in a bone-chilling demand. "Because I said so. Now go," he said, shoving the girl aside and taking Einstein by the arm.

"Stop it," Dale Graham said, with the unerring instinct of a bright twelve-year-old. "You're kidnapping him. I know you. You're that Nazi. I saw your picture in the paper. I know who you are."

Einstein opened his mouth in shock. In one continuous movement, Trattner lifted up his arm and brought it down across the side of Dale Graham's face, knocking her sideways onto the ground in an unconscious heap. With the other hand, he grabbed Einstein's neck and twisted his arm behind his back. "Now we're leaving, Professor," he said. "No more conversation. The President is waiting."

Einstein struggled, but was no match for Trattner's coiled-steel arms and wrists. He was picked up bodily and lifted toward the car. There was a scream from the house. Miss Dukas, who had seen the struggle, ran from the front door.

"Let go of him, you hoodlums," she said. "Let him go."

Maxine Lewis stepped up to Miss Dukas, took out her .38 Colt and brought it down across Miss Dukas' forehead, gashing it wide open and sending Miss Dukas spinning into unconsciousness.

"*Schnell,*" Trattner said, "*ins Auto.*"

But as he looked up the street, he saw a black Pontiac

sedan bearing down on him rapidly. There would clearly be no time to get into the car, start it, and get away. And an escape with a hail of bullets all around would be no escape at all.

"Cover me," Trattner said. "I'm taking this Jew back into the house. We'll have to talk our way out of this. Run ahead of me and have your gun out."

Maxine did as she was told. She scampered up the stairs to the door and ran in, just as Trattner came up behind her, dragging Einstein. Trattner left the door open, held Einstein up for a moment, then hit the professor with a right cross, knocking him against the foyer wall, leaving him gasping for breath and off balance.

Quinn had seen the professor being dragged into the house. As the Pontiac pulled up, he jumped out of the car, with Alice following close behind him. His .38, the Colt Combat Commander automatic Murphy had given to him, was out, its hammer cocked. Alice was right behind him, holding a little .32 Smith & Wesson that she had drawn from the OSS shop. The thin corporal was crouched behind the Pontiac, his .38 out, in firing position.

Quinn's brain raced. He had to get out of that open front yard, get into the house, and save the professor. There was only one way to do it. He would have to ignore the two women, really a girl and an old woman, lying on the grass. They didn't look badly hurt anyway. He would have to go in the way he went after all the Raimundos and Gilbertos and Raymond Carvers and Gilbert Washingtons in L.A. Balls out, right through the front door.

"Follow me and keep low," Quinn said. Then he took a deep breath and vaulted forward across the lawn. By now, Dale Graham's form was behind them. Quinn was up on the porch. Alice was right behind him. He hit the screen door like the Twentieth Century Limited and went right through it into the open hallway. Alice Burton was right behind him.

As they bolted into the house, Quinn expected a shot. He did not expect to be hit on the back of the head with the butt of a .45 automatic. Alice Burton expected gunfire, too. She was used to it. She was not used to being smashed in the face by a gun barrel. She and Quinn slumped to the floor.

"*Schnell*," Trattner said. "Over here." He dragged Quinn over into the living room. Maxine dragged Alice Burton after him. "Now listen," Trattner said after he had deposited Quinn and Alice in a heap. "I want you to go out there to that policeman. You just tell him this. Tell him he passed the exercise perfectly, that he'll get a commendation, and that the two people from Washington will be out in a minute. Can you do that? For me?"

Maxine Lewis could feel the adrenaline racing through her system. This was what it was like to be well and truly alive. This was what it was like to be on the cutting edge of the moment. To think that a few weeks ago she had been selling real estate to factory workers from San Jose and now she was in on the greatest triumph of Aryan bravery. This was the moment she had been living for.

"Of course I can," she said. "No problem at all." She was positively giddy with excitement. As she walked toward the door, she unbuttoned the top two buttons on her tunic. She also unbuttoned the top two buttons on her blouse. As usual, she was not wearing a bra. She would let that cop have a good look before she made a monkey out of him.

Oozing sexuality, with her hips wiggling as if she were a stripper, she walked out the door toward the corporal.

"Hands up!" he shouted.

By now, there was a crowd of neighbors on the street. A woman was bending over little Dale Graham, holding her head in her hands. Another woman, the one who had noticed about the cigarette butt, was staring at Maxine.

"It's all right," Maxine shouted in a confident voice to the cop. "It was just a test. The little girl and the maid got overexcited and fainted. I've called an ambulance."

From the house Trattner watched carefully while keeping a gun on Quinn, Burton, and Einstein. This Maxine woman really was quite wonderful. Maybe he would marry her when they got back to Germany.

Quinn and Alice Burton were still out cold. But the professor was stirring. Trattner had tried to hit him hard enough to put him out, but not to damage that Jew magician brain. Although, God knows, it sometimes took a lot to kill a Jew. They were like water rats, incredibly durable despite their scrawny appearance.

Einstein looked about him but could apparently find no words to speak. Trattner picked him up and put Einstein's arm around his shoulders. Then he drew back his right fist and punched Einstein in the stomach hard enough to knock the wind out of him and keep him quiet for a while longer. As Einstein sagged, Trattner dragged him into the kitchen. He dumped the physicist onto the linoleum floor, then hurriedly went out to the foyer again.

Maxine was in deep conversation with the policeman. She was bending over, showing the man a little, more than a little, of her bosom. "Check with the War Department," Maxine said reassuringly to the thin corporal. "The whole business was an exercise to protect America's top scientific brains. Go ahead. Check on your radio. It was all an exercise and it worked smoothly. You'll get a commendation. Maybe we'll even get you sent over to the European Theater."

"Don't worry," the corporal said. He craned his neck to get a better look at Maxine's bosom. Christ! The broad wasn't wearing a bra at all! He could see the edge of her nipple. It looked mighty good to him. "What's your name, Lieutenant?" he asked. "You gonna be staying in town long?"

"Nancy Dalton," Maxine Lewis said. "I don't know. I have weekend leave coming up. I might want to be here longer. Maybe see some college boys," she added, lifting her eyebrows.

"How'd you like to meet some men?" the corporal asked.

"You know any?" Maxine asked, raising her eyebrows. She smoothed out her skirt, then lifted the hem and straightened the seam on her nylons. She made sure the corporal got a good shot of her thighs. "Listen, I have to go into the professor's house. Make a few calls. You can tell the station that everything's under control. Maybe I'll see you later, huh?"

With that, she walked with a wiggle back into the house. As

she did, she could hear the policeman saying to the crowd, "All right. The party's over. It was just a drill. The little girl got overexcited and the old woman fainted. Let's all go home now. I'll make sure this thing's straightened out."

Dale Graham's mother said, "It looks like someone hit my little girl, Officer."

"No," the corporal said, trying to look official. "She just got a little bump when she fell down." Christ, if he could get a piece of that Nancy Dalton . . .

"This is police business, ma'am," the corporal said. "You take your little girl home and tell her to stay out of the way of the law."

Mrs. Graham glared at the policeman. But she lifted her groggy daughter up and walked home with her. The girl was mumbling about Nazis, but then little Dale always had an overactive imagination. That was why she had been bothering Professor Einstein in the first place, which was the cause of all this trouble.

The corporal called the station house and told them to call off the roadblocks. "It was just an exercise. Over," he said.

"Tell that smartass guy from Washington to fuck himself twice," said the Italian desk sergeant. "He really had me going. Over."

"Wait till you see the dish who's out here guarding Einstein," the corporal said. "I wouldn't mind a piece of her. Over and out."

Then the corporal waited for the ambulance and also waited for Lieutenant Dalton to appear. He could take her to that roadhouse near Trenton. The Tick-Tock Club. They would serve him rye whiskey all night. They knew him.

The crowd began to disperse. Maxine Lewis turned and smiled at the corporal as she walked into the house, closing the door behind her. Then she remembered what was going on. She pointed her pistol at Quinn and Burton and she thought how satisfying it would be to blow a big fat hole in that Jewish dame's head, watch the bitch's brains fall out onto the floor. Then she'd like to shoot that cop right in the nuts. He reminded her a little bit of her first husband, that losing

sonofabitch Charlie Lewis. She'd like to see the look on his
face when he saw the .45 pointed at his pecker. That would
teach him a lesson or two about treating people better. Him
and that bastard Charlie.

Trattner came out of the kitchen, dragging Einstein with
him. He threw the gasping professor onto the floor. He kicked
him in the side. Einstein groaned, and then rolled over onto
his side, to protect it from another kick.

"Yes," Trattner said. "We've got you, you Jew magician.
We have a little surprise for you. Come with me. I want you
to hear it in private." He winked at Maxine. Then he dragged
Einstein to his feet and pulled him into the kitchen. As he
passed out of the living room he said, "You keep an eye on
them. If they move, shoot them."

Trattner shoved Einstein against the counter where Miss
Dukas had been sectioning a grapefruit for him that morning.
The fruit knife was still on the counter. Trattner could not see
it. Einstein could. He put his palm over it and put it under his
sweater. Then he turned to face Trattner. He frowned at him.
"You must be mad to attempt this," Einstein said.

Trattner bared his teeth and drew back his hand. He
slapped Einstein across the face, hard. Blood began to flow
from Einstein's gums.

"*Halt deine Schnauze, Jude Bub,*" Trattner barked. "I'm in
charge now. You are the great physicist. I only went through
two years in the university, working on quadratics. But I have
the gun."

Einstein wiped his hand across his lips. This was an insane
nightmare. This could not possibly be taking place in Princeton, New Jersey, where Einstein could hear the chapel bells
from Prospect Gardens at this very minute.

"You must leave here at once," Einstein said. "This is an
outrage."

Trattner slapped Einstein again across his face. The physicist reeled against the counter. "If it were up to me, I would
just have you cleaning the latrines in Augsburg," Trattner
said. "But you have some Jew magic trick and that's what I
want. In return, I have quite a lot to offer. Normally we don't

make any bargains with Jews. We make them into soap. But I'll make a bargain with you. Jews love bargains."

"I have no idea what you're talking about," Einstein said. He tried to stand as straight as he could. No contingency in his entire life had prepared him for this kind of terror. Except, he thought, for being sent to a Catholic preparatory school in Genoa when he was a small boy. Then the Italian boys would hold him against the wall while another boy spat on him and called him a "Christ-killer." Yes, and that was not even in this century.

"Don't try to be a hero," Trattner said. "It does not suit the Jew to act the British spy. Besides, scientists are not heroes. We know all about the Manhattan Engineering District. We know all about the installations at Oak Ridge and at Hanford. We know all about the whole Jew trick."

Einstein said nothing. He could see that the Nazi was under great strain. He looked like he might be ill. He looked dangerous.

"Now, I am going to take you down to Cape May, Herr Doktor Jew, and I am going to put you on a boat to Sweden and that is going to take you back to your rightful place in Germany. To build that damned bomb for us. I want you to come right now. Quietly. That policeman is still out there," Trattner said. He took out his pistol and pointed it at Einstein's chest. "Let's go."

"I thought you had quite a lot to offer," Einstein said. He was stalling for time. He knew it and Trattner knew it. Both men knew that there was a policeman with a gun outside the house, waiting for an ambulance. Out the kitchen window, Trattner could see the policeman applying a bandage to Miss Dukas' forehead, kneeling by her side. She was still unconscious. But eventually, the policeman had to figure out something. In some time, maybe moments, the OSS people who had been called—undoubtedly—when Trattner answered the telephone would arrive. Time was of the essence.

"I'll tell you about it in the car," Trattner said. "Let's go."

"No," Einstein said. "I'm not going. You can kill me here.

I'm not going. Anyway, I have no idea of what you're talking about."

Trattner snarled and hit Einstein in the face once again. This time the old man did not budge. "You can kill me," Einstein said. "But I'm not going anywhere. And I have no idea what you're talking about. There is no magic weapon. No secret projects. Those are your phrases, not ours."

"Now, listen to me, Jewboy," Trattner said stonily. "We are going to make this quick. We have a lot of your relatives, a lot of Jews, under our control. We have a lot of them in work camps right now. Did you know that?" He leered at Einstein.

"I know that," Einstein said. "It is a crime against humanity. They're not work camps. They're death camps."

"It is the saving of humanity," Trattner said. "The one part of the war that the whole world will thank us for, in time."

"And you think I will help you?" Einstein asked. "You're mad. I would not lift a finger to help you. You are no scientist. You are a murderer. You're all murderers."

Trattner fought the urge to shoot this back-sassing Jew right on the spot. That would have been what he deserved. This back-sassing Jew in a crazy country where people left automobiles outside to rust deserved to die. Trattner was sick of the whole business. He felt dizzy. He wanted to shoot the Jew and get on with his life. But an SS man had his orders.

"Now, listen very carefully to me," Trattner said, "because this will make you happy, and a happy Jew magician will get us that bomb faster. We have a lot of your Jew friends in our camps. Some of them will die of old age, and some of them will die because they aren't used to hard work. And some of them will die because we kill them. You understand?"

Einstein said nothing. Surely he was having a terrible nightmare. This could not possibly be happening in real life. He could see out the window. Children were starting to walk to school. They wore short pants and little caps. A few of them carried baseball bats over their shoulders.

"If you come to work for us, we will let one million of those Jews out of Auschwitz. If you succeed in building that bomb, we will let another million die of old age. They will live in special quarantined areas, of course, but they will die of natural causes. You, just you, can do this. I have the word of the Reichsführer himself on this," Trattner said. "One scientist to another."

"Himmler," Einstein said. "You think I trust his word? What kind of scientist is he?"

"Genetics," Trattner said. "Building a better human being."

Einstein laughed out loud.

Trattner's face turned beet-red. He hit Einstein again in the face. "You dare to question the word of Heinrich Himmler? You dare?" Then he hit Einstein again. Blood started to come from Einstein's nose. It ran onto his gray-white mustache and then stained his sweater. Einstein wiped his nose with his hand. He could feel the knife against his stomach.

Einstein could see that Trattner was losing his grasp on whatever restraints he had. The man could do anything. From what Einstein had read about him in Oklahoma, he was capable of any insane butchery.

"How do I know you'll have the facilities I might need?" Einstein asked. "It can't just be done in a laboratory, you know."

"If the Reichsführer is in support of anything, even in wartime, it happens," Trattner said. He smiled. This was easier than Trattner had thought. Jews were simply masses of jelly, like sea-nettles. They could sting, but they had no backbone, no strength, no spirit. A few blows, some proper calling of things by their right names, and they collapsed and did what they were told. Trattner could sense triumph.

"You may be certain," Trattner added, "that the Reichsführer is just as eager to get this thing done as Roosevelt or anyone else in this Jew country. You will get all the support you need."

"It takes a lot of people and a lot of electricity," Einstein said. "Plus it takes a lot of good scientists. How do I know I'll find them in Germany?"

"We got you, didn't we?" Trattner said.

"Joachim," came Maxine's voice. "I think they're waking up. You'd better come in here."

Trattner grabbed Einstein roughly by the back of his sweater collar and pushed him ahead. "Get moving, Jewboy," Trattner said. "We have to go."

It is all an equation, Einstein thought, and I am a symbol and nothing more. But if I am that valuable a symbol to those beasts, then I would be better off dead than helping them by being in their hands. I will kill myself rather than let them take me to Cape May, he thought.

In the living room, Maxine held a gun on two dazed-looking Americans. One was a florid-faced man with a spreading waistline. He looked like an off-duty cop. The other was an attractive young woman who looked Jewish. She was well dressed in a white cotton hopsack suit.

Trattner leered at them. "Don't you get tired of being such fools?" he demanded. "Are you really this anxious to die?"

Quinn looked at Trattner with as much concentration as he could muster, considering the throbbing cement mixer between his shoulder blades. "You'll never get away. Not a chance," he said.

"You think so?" Trattner asked him. "The truth is that this Jew is leaving with us right now. We have made a bargain with him."

The thought raced through Quinn's mind that now, at the most critical moment of his life, he had failed again. All he had to do was wait outside. Instead, he had run inside and been hit on the head like the dumbest asshole rookie on the Anaheim P.D. Somehow, he was that damned stupid. Marilyn had gone to her grave not knowing that the man she loved was a complete fool. Marilyn would be unavenged, dead, and Quinn would be a failure as a man and a cop for the rest of his life.

"You'll never get away with it," Alice Burton said. "There are roadblocks already."

"Shut up, Jewgirl," Trattner said. "Maxine, if this Jewgirl talks again, kill her anytime you feel like it. With this," he said, as he took a three-inch pocketknife from his tunic pocket. He handed the knife to Maxine. She took it with a cruel grin on her face.

Trattner then reached into his pocket and came up with yet another pocketknife. This one was black and shiny. It had a large round button on its side. Trattner held it up so that highlights from the light in the hall shone on it. Then Trattner pressed the button. A four-inch blade shot out of the handle. Trattner held it up as if it were a prize. "This is for you," Trattner said. "I'm just going to give you a few little scars, just as a reminder of what you did to me. Just tit for tat, as you say." It was Quinn's "Black Beauty" switchblade. Trattner's eyes gleamed as he held the knife.

Einstein saw the same image he had seen a minute before. The boys at the Genoese school, throwing him against a stone wall, spitting on him, calling him "Christ-killer."

"I'm not going with you," Einstein said. He rubbed his hand against his sweater. He could feel the knife.

Trattner whirled around to face him. "Yes, you are, Jew. You'll do what I tell you. I'm not getting into any long arguments with you. You're coming with me. Right now." In one hand Trattner held his pistol. In the other, he had the knife. "If you don't come, I'm going to start cutting up the Jewgirl, right in front of you. Do you hear me? First, I'll cut out her eyes, while she's still alive. You understand?"

"I'm not going with you," Einstein said. "I don't care what you do. I'm not going with you."

"Maxine," Trattner said, "keep the gun on the man. I want to show the professor that we are serious."

He knelt in front of where Alice Burton was sitting. He waved the knife in front of her eyes. Einstein could see the look of terror all across her face. She looked like a fine, sensitive girl, the kind he was trying to protect by building the fission bomb. In a moment, she would be a blind, screaming mass of blood and nerves. Einstein saw Trattner start to press the point of his knife just below the left eye of this innocent girl.

Einstein shouted, "Wait a minute. I'll go. I'll go."

Alice Burton trembled and said, "No, let him cut."

"No," Einstein said. "I'll go. Just stop it and I'll go."

"I knew you would see the light," Trattner said as he

turned toward Einstein. "The Jew has no nerves, even if he can play tricks with physics."

Einstein took a step forward toward Trattner, as if heading for the door. But instead of turning toward the door, Einstein took another step toward Trattner. While the Nazi was folding the knife blade back into its handle, Einstein reached with his left hand into his sweater. Trattner stared at him. Maxine still had her eyes on Quinn. With one quick movement, Einstein whipped his fruit knife out from under his sweater. While Trattner stood mesmerized by the sight of the knife, Einstein lurched forward and plunged the knife into Trattner's chest up to the handle with a terrifying scream.

A look of absolute amazement crossed Trattner's face. It changed to a look of utter pain. Then Trattner gurgled and fell to the floor. Blood poured from his tunic onto the Kirman rug.

Einstein stood staring at him, a look of astonishment on his face. The cry he had just uttered hung in the air. Out the window, through the curtains, Maxine could see the cop running up the sidewalk toward the house.

In a frenzy of rage and fear, she pointed her gun at Einstein. "You killed him," she said. "You sneaking little Jew, you killed him." She pulled the trigger of her revolver. The shot went wild, smashing into a Russian censer above the fireplace. A second shot was never fired.

In one second, Quinn had out his little .32 belly gun, the one that had fooled Whelchel. He did not hesitate at all. In one fluid movement, he cocked the hammer, pointed the barrel at Maxine Lewis' chest, and fired three times. She went down with her mouth twisted into a furious sneer.

The thin corporal burst into the room, took one look at the two bodies oozing blood onto the dark carpets of the living room, and then looked at Professor Einstein.

"Who did it?" he asked.

John Quinn shot a quick look over toward Einstein. The professor looked distracted, unaware.

"I did," John Quinn said. "I did it. I'm a cop."

June 5, 1943,
Stockholm, Sweden

Two men stood on a cobbled street. The street was damp; the sky was overcast and seemingly without depth. One of the men was wearing a long black leather trenchcoat with a civilian suit beneath; he was smoking a cigarette between finger and thumb. The other, shorter, in bow tie and glasses, spoke American English. "A waste," he said.

"You are aware he is not the only one we have," spoke the German.

The American stared across the somber distance, where Lake Mälaren flowed into the Baltic Sea. He shook his head moodily.

"We have many more such to waste," insisted the German in the leather coat.

The American did not reply for a long time. Finally he spoke. "In return, we get?"

The German did not answer directly. Instead, he said, "Let us speak frankly. You and I both know this thing is resolved. In Berlin, they are too close to see the writing on the . . ." His voice drained away and he stood upright abruptly. "We want you to promise you will not use your Jew bomb on us."

The American grimaced. He was not Jewish.

"This thing is settled," the German spoke earnestly, grabbing the American by the forearm. His coat crackled with stiffness. "There is no need for examples over here. If this thing really works as you hope—are you willing to accept the consequences? All we want is your word that, should you decide to give the world an example of your Jew magician physics—"

The American swept an arm out, knocking the hand from his elbow, and spoke gruffly. "Drop the rhetoric, will ya?" He sounded like a detective in a movie.

The German bowed ironically. "Forgive me. I am away from Berlin, but," he tapped the crewcut under his hat, "I am not. What we want is simple. Merely promise to use your weapon, once you have it, over there." He pointed a long finger toward the three o'clock sun. "On the Far East. The yellows." He grinned. His teeth were bad; he had steel fillings.

"And?" the American asked.

"No more Trattners," the German said softly.

The American smiled. As his counterpart said, the issue of Europe was settled. And then they would have to look westward, toward the setting sun.

"Okay," he said. "I think we got ourselves an agreement."

And then two anonymous men shook hands. They were not friends. There was no particular feeling of moment. But a part of the war was over.

And Allen Dulles thought that he had probably come up with a pretty good deal. He also was proud of his Jimmy Cagney imitation, although a goon from the Office of Heinrich Himmler, Reichsführer, SS, was hardly the best judge of American gangster acts. Dulles walked rapidly toward the U.S. Embassy on Kronstadt Place. He had to send a message.

R. F. ⚡⚡
Heinrich Himmler
NACHRICHTEN-UEBERMITTLUNG

Memorandum To: Admiral Wilhelm Canaris,
                          Abwehr
Most Secret and Urgent

Rumors have reached the Führer about an insane
scheme called "Siegfried," which was supposed to in-
volve using Jews to build secret weapons for the
Reich. In particular, this plan was supposed to call
for kidnapping the Jew Einstein and bringing him to
Germany to build a uranium fission explosive.

As you know, the unshakable opinion of the
Führer is that Jewish physics is incompatible with
the defense of an Aryan Reich. Moreover, the Führer
knows that stories about Jewish advances in physics
are tricks and ploys by the British to prolong the
war.

I am certain that you concur with me that any concept of using Jews to advance the vital interests of
the Reich would be counter to the most cherished
ideals of the Reich and would be tantamount to treason. I am further certain that your files will show
that there is no evidence that this "Siegfried" was
anything more than the brainchild of one lone prisoner of war, acting by himself, after having been
maddened by the intrigues of his American jailers. I
further feel confident that your files will reflect that
there was no involvement of anyone at a command
level in this bizarre escapade.

Further, the Führer of course realizes that while it may take time, total victory is the inevitable outcome of this war. The Führer has conclusive proof of this in the stars. Therefore, it would be wasteful and treasonous for any representatives of the Reich to meet with any representatives of the Bolshevik or Western powers. I am certain that you would have never countenanced any such bargaining, as I did not. As to rumors of negotiations in Stockholm, they are only rumors. Your files, as well as mine, clearly reflect that while isolated contacts between Germans and Russians have taken place, they are not part of any overall plan, nor are they authorized by me or anyone in my area of responsibility.

As always, our guidance is taken solely from the Führer and from his vision of the Greater German Reich. Deviation from this first rule of Aryan citizenship will be severely punished.

> Best regards and a sincere
> Heil Hitler,
> Himmler

June 5, 1943,
Washington, D.C.

Sam Murphy toyed with his Dunhill cigarette lighter and looked across the room to John Quinn. Brilliant summer sunlight poured into the room from the windows facing the Washington Monument. The windows were open to allow a breeze to pass through. It was nine in the morning and already eighty degrees. By noon, it would be one hundred. Then there would be a downpour at about five in the afternoon. The rain would turn to steam when it hit the asphalt. The whole city would become one huge sweat bath. But now it was only eighty degrees.

"Look at it this way," Murphy said to Quinn. "If there were never a need to lie, there would be no OSS."

"I never had any problem with it," Quinn said. He sat in the cracked leather armchair facing Murphy. He watched while Murphy lit a Philip Morris, then exhaled a cloud of gray smoke. "I didn't see why a man like Einstein should have to spend one second at an inquest. He can just send in a statement, and that'll be the end of it."

"It won't even begin," Murphy said. He got up from his desk and walked over to the window. He could see the usual crowd of tourists lining up for the hike up the Washington

Monument. "It can't possibly begin. No inquest. No state-
ments to the press. It never happened."

"Why?" Alice Burton asked. "I think John should get some
credit."

"Because we don't want the public to even get a hint of the
Manhattan District. Not even a hint. If they did, they'd say,
'What the hell? Why should we let our sons get shot in Gua-
dalcanal if we've got some bomb that's going to win the war
all by itself?'"

"Good question," John Quinn said.

"We don't even know if the damned thing is going to work.
What happens if we let the Japs and the Krauts kick us all
over the world and then the thing doesn't work? What do we
do then? For all we know, it won't work. My own guess is that
it won't. It just sounds too complicated to ever work," Sam
Murphy said.

"So, that's the end of the whole thing," Quinn said.

"Trattner and Maxine have already been buried. The whole
thing is over. We'll just forget it ever happened," Murphy
said. "Except that you're now in the OSS for the duration if
you want to be."

Alice Burton glared at Murphy, then looked kindly at
Quinn. "It's more than that. You're a hero. We need you. We
don't have many people with your brains and your guts. We
beat not only Himmler, but J. Edgar Hoover. We want to
keep you around."

"Well," Quinn said, "Rizzuti will miss me, but you twisted
my arm."

"Good. By the way," Alice Burton said, smiling, "we picked
up the bad apple in the Manhattan District. Assistant of General Groves. He'll be in jail forever."

"That's where he belongs," Quinn said. "Or else on a slab."

"You can start in a week," Murphy said. "I'd say the two of
you have earned some leave. It's highly irregular, but you can
get yourself ready to report for duty on June 15. You can take
off some time. We may even be able to let you use the official
place down in Caroline County that we got for debriefing

spies. It's supposed to be secluded, quiet, kind of nice. I think you might like it. It's right on the Choptank River."

"Sounds good to me," Quinn said. "I'll have to send for my clothes back in L.A. Maybe get somebody to rent my house."

"You can even go back there and attend to it yourself," Murphy said. "You'll have time."

"That's a long train ride to do by yourself," Quinn said.

"Maybe you won't have to do it by yourself," Alice Burton said. "After all, the nation owes you something."

"I think so, too," Quinn said. Then he winked, a real old-fashioned Irish cop's kind of wink, so that Alice Burton could not possibly mistake it. She winked back and they had a deal.

Epilogue: November 25, 1981, Rancho Mirage, California

Off toward the Santa Susanna Mountains, the sun shot its last pink-orange rays of the day into the light-blue sky. There was a minor brushfire on one of the summits, and its black smoke turned the orange ray into a vivid blood red. The golfers in their go-to-hell red trousers and Cardin windbreakers stared at the mountains, the smoke, and the bloody light and said that this is why you paid three hundred thousand bucks for a little condo at the Mission Hills Country Club. Because of sunsets like that one, which you could see while you were teeing up for the final hole on what was a goddamned fine golf course, considering that it was only twelve years old and didn't really have all the kinks out of it.

In one of the three-hundred-thousand-dollar condos, in a flagstone patio overlooking a pond with real swans, two men and a woman sat in wrought-iron chairs with tightly strung plastic seats and backs. The woman, a mousy-looking type with a kindly, curious face, offered one of the men a sautéed mushroom. She checked carefully to see that she did not get any sauce on her Garfinckel blouse. After all, Garfinckel's had just been taken over by some discount house and probably they would never have merchandise like designer Perry Ellis blouses again. Alice Burton Quinn wanted to keep this one a long time. It was orange, with vertical ruffles, and she thought she looked particularly chic in it. Many of the lawyers who appeared before her during her last term in the D.C. Circuit complimented her on it. She was certain that she was the most well-dressed judge that had ever sat on the circuit, even if more and more of her opinions were being overturned as the Court turned increasingly away from the criminal and corporate decisions of the 1960s. Well, that was life, but still she took a foolish, tiny pride that she dressed so well.

She had been wearing that same blouse the day she ruled that retarded children had a right to federal aid for education. Even if the Supreme Court, going along with Reagan America, had reversed her, she was still proud that a voice had been raised for those with no ability to speak and she was glad it was her voice. Nor was she embarrassed about trying to expand the rights of criminal suspects, even if the mood of the nation had changed.

She and John were always arguing about that. John had the largest security guard and private protection company in Washington. He had experience with some very tough guys. He did not like the way Alice always assumed that a rapist was really a philharmonic pianist gone wrong. They still argued about it, even after John had turned the business over to their son, John Herman, and taken a retired Circuit Court judge and his wife to retirement in California.

"They'd mostly be better off in prison for life, or on Devil's Island," John would say.

"We have a Constitution," Alice would say. "It applies to everyone."

John had grown paunchy and irritable-looking, like a Gaelic fairy whom fate had crossed. But he still had a sense of humor, even after two heart attacks and strict orders to lay off the sauce. He sat in a wrought-iron-and-plastic chair while the smells of barbecuing chicken rose from the gas grill in the patio.

The other man had a clerical collar and a fleshy, florid face. He might have been the same age as John, which was late six-

ties. His face was framed by white hair, like a child's portrait of the hair of God. He had arrived in a rented Caprice and then called John and Alice from the airport and explained that he had some news for them about something that had happened a long time ago.

It was a funny thing, but the first thought that came to John Quinn's mind was that it was about Marilyn, that somehow it was going to turn out that she was not dead. But of course she was dead, buried in a cemetery in La Crescenta, which he sometimes drove to visit. The gravestone, which Quinn had paid for after the war, said "O Youth, O Folly." It was within eyesight of a Pioneer Fried Chicken, at which Quinn was also forbidden to eat. Fried foods. Saturated fat.

"You have to understand that it was all so complicated that we still don't understand it all," Reverend Heinrich said. "The whole village at Hechingen was a phony, of course. We learned that right after the war, but it was classified for a long time. I don't know why. The ways of man are strange."

"But didn't we know that right away?" Quinn asked. He leaned forward in his chair and his cheeks glowed in the evening sunset.

"Not at all," Reverend Heinrich said. "When the pictures from the B-17 photorecon that went down near Hechingen by accident got to Washington, the Pentagon went crazy. The way they had it figured, even if it was a phony, it was so similar to what they had planned for Oak Ridge that the Krauts must have known a helluva lot about Oak Ridge and about the whole Manhattan Districtunnnh." He had a way of adding that last false syllable that reminded Alice of old-time radio preachers, as it was supposed to.

"So the Nazis wanted us to think they were close to developing a bomb?" Alice said. "That much seems fairly clear-cut."

"Oh, but that's where you came in. The whole idea of sending out Trattner to kidnap Einstein was part of it. The original idea had just been—"

"To have him escape and scare people," Alice Burton said, cutting off Heinrich before he could add his "unnhh." "Then *they tied it in with the false factory at Hechingen and got the idea that they would really scare us."*

"Exactly right as far as it goes," Heinrich said. "But then they realized that they had something else a lot bigger going on." He smiled knowingly and took a sip of Chivas Regal Scotch from a Lalique glass.

Off on the golf course, Quinn heard the muffled whoosh of golf cart tires along the asphalt paths of the fairways. When he had been a boy caddying at the Wilshire Country Club, he had carried two bags of clubs for a dime each.

"They had a double plan. The small part was to get the Americans to promise not to use the A-bomb on them. They figured that the Americans wouldn't want all that radiation in Europe anyway, but they weren't positive. So they said they'd trade with us. No more P.O.W. rampages and in return we'd wait and use the bomb only on the Japs," Heinrich said. (He had warmed to his subject sufficiently to stop adding his evangelical suffix.) "That part worked," Heinrich continued. "It was a pretty hollow gesture on our part, since we didn't have the bomb ready until after the Krauts had surrendered anyway, and it was just as hollow on the Krauts' side, because who knows if any more Trattners could have ever gotten out?"

"Probably quite a few, considering how screwed up the camps were. You know some commandants were actually serving the Germans champagne?" Quinn demanded. "That's probably where the idea for the Miranda rule came from." He looked at Alice and winked at her. She stuck out her tongue.

"The Nazis do not come under the Constitution," she said.

"A good thing," Quinn added.

"But the real payoff was supposed to come in Himmler's little diddling with the Russians," Heinrich said. "The Germans had the idea that they just might possibly be able to get the Russians to stop fighting in the East if they pulled the whole thing together rightunnnh," Heinrich said.

"I don't get that one at all," Quinn said. "I'm a slow learner."

To the west, the sky was now a blue-gray with only the faintest flecks of pink. The fires on the mountaintop were

*barely visible. John Quinn could hear the thunk of a golfer
hitting a solid wood shot.*

*"They realized that if the Russians had penetrated the
Manhattan Project, as they call it these days," Heinrich said
slowly, "then the Russians would get not only the news about
Hechingen and about Trattner almost getting Einstein or
maybe even getting him, but also the news about how the
Americans were so upset about it. The Russians might think
Hitler was close to having the bomb. And that would really
scare the Russians to death. Then the Rushganskis might sign
a separate peace. It was Himmler's idea and it might have
worked," Heinrich said. "The Bear of the Two Horns and the
Kingdom of the East might have made peace, and that would
have been just too bad for the Kingdom of Gold and Light,
which is us."*

*Two perfectly white swans waddled out of the pond and up
onto the immaculately groomed rich green lawns abutting the
golf course. They walked over to a palm tree and stood still,
staring at it. The gray light caught their feathers and made
them look sinister, like the bad swan in Swan Lake, Alice Burton thought.*

*"What stopped the plan?" Alice Burton asked. "It should
have worked."*

*"What stopped it was three things, as I believe after study-
ing it for twenty-five years," Heinrich said. "First of all, Canaris was a Soviet agent. He told the Russians that Hechingen
was a phony. But that didn't satisfy the Russians that the
whole German fission effort was a dud, because the Russians
were always afraid that Canaris was a triple agent, feeding
them phony informationunnh."*

*"I see," Alice Burton said, casting a sideways glance at her
husband.*

*"Then the Russians were surprised because the first report
out of Switzerland was that Powers and Loughlin had been
shot down. Even later, the Russkis couldn't believe that that
plane just crashed by itself. Why would the Germans shoot
down a plane taking pictures of something that was supposed
to be photographed in the first place? That made the Rush-*

ganskis really worried that maybe Canaris was tripping them
up. So the tip from Canaris by itself was definitely not
enough," Reverend Heinrich said, reaching for another sautéed mushroom, chewing it, and smiling.

"Maybe it's time for us to take a look at those chicken
breasts on the grill," Alice Quinn said.

"They smell mighty good," Reverend Heinrich said.

"The barbecue marinade is an old Irish recipe," Quinn said
with a wink at Alice.

"Then the second reason is that the Russians had people in
Washington working with Fermi and Szilard who told them
that the Germans couldn't possibly develop a nuclear bomb if
they had ten Einsteins working for them. They just did not
have the equipment or the materials or the understanding.
Nazi physics was back in the nineteenth century when they
lost all the Jews."

From the redwood, steel, and glass clubhouse of the Mission Hills Country Club, three hundred yards from where
Quinn, Alice, and the Reverend Heinrich sat, music and the
sound of laughter flooded the nighttime sky. How long ago it
all seemed to Quinn. Was there ever a time when I dared
great things, when I threw myself through doors to rescue Albert Einstein? "Let's eat," Quinn said. "I suppose the reverend has had a long day. He's probably starving."

"I'll tell Elena to pour the wine," Alice said.

"Wait just a minute," Reverend Heinrich said. "The third
reason. The one that made the Russians refuse to take the
whole escapade with Trattner seriously and made them refuse
to make a separate peace."

"I almost forgot," Quinn said. "What was that?"

"Wellunnnh," Heinrich said. "I got all this from Freedom
of Information Act dossiers on this KGB guy Ostibityanoff,
who was debriefed after he defected in 1963. The third reason
is you twounnnhh."

"Us?" Alice Quinn asked. "Why us? Because we caught
Trattner so fast?"

Reverend Heinrich smiled. "Exactly the opposite. The Russians figured that if the OSS sent a cop and a woman lawyer

after Trattner, how sinister could he be? If Hoover had sent one hundred FBI agents, then Trattner might be real and the whole German fission project might be real. But if two people handled a chase the way you did, let him and that maniac girlfriend get away after you had them in jail, the Russians figured it was all a scheme cooked up by Dulles and the Germans anyway, like the agreement not to use the A-bomb in Europe. Beria himself said that it all sounded as if it was a plot by the OSS and the Gestapo to trick the poor innocent Russians. If it had been a real German escape attempt, the U.S. would have devoted the best they had to finding Trattner instead of you two."

Quinn was red-faced, laughing. "So that's how we saved America, by being so dumb?"

"I thought we were the best America had," Alice Burton Quinn said with a small smile.

Reverend Heinrich ignored their protests. He waved a sautéed mushroom in the warm night air. "If you had been better at your work, the Russians might very well have signed a separate peace and Hitler might still be running Western Europe."

Quinn and Alice looked at each other. Off in the distance, they could see firefighting airplanes dropping water on the brushfire in the Santa Susannas.

Reverend Heinrich sipped at his Scotch. "It all gets back to this," he said. "The Lord works by symbols and by prophecies. He saw the Devil and he sent you, innocent children, to defeat Satan. Who else but children would recognize him? If he came today, would we recognize him? How would we recognize him?"

"We'll be seeing him in person soon enough," Quinn said, "so then we'll let you know."

Reverend Heinrich, lost in a reverie, did not hear Quinn's joke, if it was a joke. He stared into the distance. In the smoky dusk, Quinn thought of Marilyn, dead on a sidewalk in Santa Cruz and of how long ago it all was, and of calculations of state giving no weight to a dead girl with fantastic light-blue eyes. Then he looked over at Alice who looked at the moun-

*tains herself with moist eyes. A lot of years had gone by. A lot
of miracles and a lot of tragedies. Mostly, a lot of just plain
accidents. Quinn squeezed Alice's hand in the warm, dry California night and thought that he was in the palm of God's
hand.*